SAUNTERINGS IN LONDON

BY
MAX SCHLESINGER

TRANSLATED BY
OTTO WENCKSTERN

PREFACE

TO THE ENGLISH EDITION.

PREFACES, generally speaking, are pleadings, in which authors, anticipating public censure, and well knowing how richly they deserve it, adduce sundry reasons why their books are not shorter or longer, and altogether different from the volumes which then and there they bring into the market.

I need not make any such excuses, for I did not write for an English public, nor did I ever pretend to popularity in England. The "Saunterings" were intended for the profit and amusement of my German countrymen; and I must say I was not a little pleased and surprised with the very flattering reception which my book experienced at the hands of the English critics. Their favourable opinion, which they so emphatically and—I am selfish enough to go the whole length of the word—so ably expressed, has probably caused the production of the book in an English dress. The critics, therefore, must bear the responsibility, if the general public should happen to condemn these "Saunterings," as "weary, stale, flat, and unprofitable," and shelve them accordingly.

Max Schlesinger.
London, October, 1853.

THE FIRST PART.
CHAPTER I.

IN WHICH THE READER IS INTRODUCED TO SOME OF THE AUTHOR'S FRIENDS.—THE ENGLISHMAN'S CASTLE.

"ARE you aware, honorable and honored Sir John," said Dr. Keif, as he moved his chair nearer to the fire, "are you aware that I am strongly tempted to hate this country of yours?"

"Indeed!" replied Sir John, with a slight elongation of his good-humoured face. "Really, Sir, you are quick of feeling. You have been exactly two hours in London. Wait, compare, and judge. There are thousands of your countrymen in London, and none of them ever think of going back to Germany."

"And for good reasons too," muttered the Doctor.

"May I ask," said Sir John, after a short pause, "what can have shocked you in England within two hours after your arrival?"

"Look at this cigar, sir! It won't burn, has a bad smell, drops its ashes—and costs four times as much as a decent cigar in my own country. Can you, in the face of this villanous cigar, muster the courage to talk to me of your government and your constitution? This cigar, Sir, proves that your boasted civilisation is sheer barbarity,—that your Cobden is a humbug, and your free-trade a monstrous sham!"

"Does it indeed prove all that? Very well, Sir German," cried Sir John, with a futile attempt to imitate the martial and inquisitorial bearing of an Austrian gendarme. "Come, show me your passport! Did any one here ask for it? Did they send you to the Guildhall for a carte de sureté? Have the police expelled you from London? It's either one thing or the other. It's either sterling liberty and cabbage-leaf cigars, or real Havanas and all the miseries of your police. Take your choice, sir."

"But I cannot take my choice, sir!" cried Dr. Keif. "They have hunted me as you would hunt a fox, across all their fences of boundary lines to the shores of the ocean, and into the very maw of that green-eyed monster, Sea-sickness, which cast me forth vomiting on this barbarous island, where men smoke lettuce and call it tobacco!" saying which, the doctor flung his cigar into the grate, and sung, "Was ist des Deutschen Vaterland?"

But the reader will most naturally ask, Who is this comical doctor, and who is Sir John?

To which I make reply—they are two amiable and honest men who met on the Continent years ago, and who, after a long separation, met again in the heart of London, in Guildford-street, Russell-square.

Dr. Keif is an Austrian and a journalist. There is good in all, but none are all good. Dr. Keif makes no exception to the common rule. He was so far prejudiced as to write a batch of very neat Feuilletons, in which he asserted that the Croats did not altogether conduct themselves with grace at the sacking of Vienna, and that the Bohemian Czechs are not the original race which gave birth to all the nations of the earth. He denied also that German literature and science have ever been fostered by the Servians; he alleged that Göthe had done more for the advancement of science than the twenty-first battalion of the Royal and Imperial Grenadiers, and he was abandoned enough to avow his opinion that a bad government is worse than a good one. On account of these very objectionable prejudices, the Doctor was summoned forthwith to depart from Leipzig in Saxony, where he lived, and proceed to Vienna, there to vindicate his doctrines or submit to a paternal chastisement. But the Doctor objected to the fate of John Huss; perhaps his mind, corrupted with German literature, was unable to appreciate the charms of a military career in the ranks of the Austrian army. Dr. Keif left Leipzig with all possible secresy; nor could he be induced to return, even by the taunts of the official Vienna Zeitung, which justly accused him of cowardice, since he preferred an ignominious flight to a contest with only 600,000 soldiers, twelve fortresses, half a million of police officers, and the "peinliche Halsgerichts Ordnung" of the late Empress Maria Theresa. Whether Dr. Keif lacks courage or not, and all other traits of his character will be sufficiently shown in the course of the Wanderings through London, which we propose to make in his company.

Dr. Keif and the author live in the house of Sir John ———, a full-blown specimen of the old English gentleman, and one worthy to be studied and chronicled as a prototype of his countrymen. This house of ours is the centre of our rambles, the point from which we start and to which we return with the experiences we gathered in our excursions. And since an English fireside and an English home are utter strangers to the most ideal dreams of the German mind, we propose commencing our Wanderings through London with a voyage of discovery through all the rooms and garrets of our own house.

At the first step a German makes in one of the London streets, he must understand that life in England is very different from life in Germany. Not only are the walls of the houses black and smoky, but the houses do not stand on a level with the pavement. A London street is in a manner like a German high-road, which is skirted on either side with a deep ditch. In the streets of London the houses on either side rise out of deep side areas. These dry ditches are generally of the depth of from six to ten feet, and that part of the house, which with us would form the lower story, is here from ten to twelve feet under-ground. This moat is uncovered, but it is railed in, and the communication between the house door and the street is effected by a bridge neatly formed of masonry.

Every English house has its fence, its iron stockade and its doorway bridge. To observe the additional fortifications which every Englishman invents for the greater security of his house is quite amusing. It is exactly as if Louis Napoleon was expected to effect a landing daily between luncheon and dinner, while every individual Englishman is prepared to defend his household gods to the last drop of porter.

You may see iron railings, massive and high, like unto the columns which crushed the Philistines in their fall; each bar has its spear-head, and each spear-head is conscientiously kept in good and sharp condition. The little bridge which leads to the house-door is frequently shut up; a little door with sharp spikes protruding from it is prepared to hook the hand of a bold invader. And it is said, that magazines of powder are placed under the bridge for the purpose of blowing up a too pertinacious assailant. This latter rumour I give for what it is worth. It is the assertion of a Frenchman, whom the cleanliness of London drove to despair, and who, in the malice of his heart, got satirical.

A mature consideration of the London houses shows, that the strength of the fortification is in exact proportion to the elegance and value of the house and its contents. The poor are satisfied with a wooden stockade; the rich are safe behind their iron chevaux de frise, and in front of palaces, club-houses, and other public buildings, the railings are so high and strong as to engender the belief that the thieves of England go about their business of housebreaking with scaling-ladders, pick-axes, guns, and other formidable implements of destruction.

Every Englishman is a bit of a Vauban. Not only does he barricade his house against two-legged animals of his own species, but his mania for fortification extends to precautions against wretched dogs and cats. To prevent these small cattle from making their way through the railings, the Englishman fills the interstices with patent wire-net work, and the very roofs are frequently divided by means, of similar contrivances. Vainly will cats, slaves of the tender passion, make prodigious efforts to squeeze themselves through those cruel, cruel walls, and vainly do they, in accents touching, but not harmonious, pour their grief into the silent ear of night. Vainly, I say, for an Englishman has little sympathy with "love in a garret"; and as for love on the roof, he scorns it utterly.

We now approach the street-door, and put the knocker in motion. Do not fancy that this is an easy process. It is by far easier to learn the language of Englishmen than to learn the language of the knocker; and many strangers protest that a knocker is the most difficult of all musical instruments.

It requires a good ear and a skilful hand to make yourself understood and to escape remarks and ridicule. Every class of society announces itself at the gate of the fortress by means of the rythm of the knocker. The postman gives two loud raps in quick succession; and for the visitor a gentle but peremptory tremolo is de rigueur. The master of the house gives a tremolo crescendo, and the servant who announces his master, turns the knocker into a battering-ram, and plies it with such goodwill that the house shakes to its foundations. Tradesmen, on the other hand, butchers, milkmen, bakers, and green-grocers, are not allowed to touch the knockers—they ring a bell which communicates with the kitchen.

All this is very easy in theory but very difficult in practice. Bold, and otherwise inexperienced, strangers believe that they assert their dignity, if they move the knocker with conscious energy. Vain delusion! They are mistaken for footmen. Modest people, on the contrary, are treated as mendicants. The middle course, in this, as in other respects, is most difficult.

Two different motives are assigned for this custom. Those who dislike England on principle, and according to whom the very fogs are an aristocratic abuse, assert that the various ways of plying the knocker are most intimately connected with the prejudices of caste. Others again say, that the arrangement is conducive to comfort, since the inmates of the house know at once what sort of a visitor is desiring admittance.

As for me, I believe that a great deal may be said on either side; and I acknowledge the existence of the two motives. But I ought to add, that in new and elegant mansions the mediæval knocker yields its place to the modern bell. The same fate is perhaps reserved for the whole of the remainder of English old-fogyism. There are spots of decay in these much vaunted islands; and now and then you hear the worm plainly as it gnaws its way. I wish you the best of appetites, honest weevil!

We cross the threshold of the house.

Sacred silence surrounds us—the silence of peace, of domestic comfort, doubly agreeable after a few hours' walk with the giddy turmoil of street life. And with peace there is cleanliness, that passive virtue, the first the stranger learns to love in the English people, because it is the first which strikes his eye. That the English are capital agriculturists, practical merchants, gallant soldiers, and honest friends, is not written in their faces, any more than the outward aspect of the Germans betrays their straight-forwardness, fitful melancholy, and poetic susceptibility. But cleanliness, as an English national virtue, strikes in modest obstrusiveness the vision even of the most unobservant stranger.

The small space between the street-door and the stairs, hardly sufficient in length and breadth to deserve the pompous name of a "hall," is usually furnished with a couple of mahogany chairs, or, in wealthier houses, with flower-pots, statuettes, and now and then a sixth or seventh-rate picture. The floor is covered with oil-cloth, and this again is covered with a breadth of carpet. A single glance tells us, that after passing the threshold, we have at once entered the temple of domestic life.

Here are no moist, ill-paved floors, where horses and carts dispute with the passenger the right of way; where you stumble about in some dark corner in search of still darker stairs; where, from the porter's lodge, half a dozen curious eyes watch your unguided movements, while your nostrils are invaded with the smell of onions, as is the case in Paris, and also in Prague and Vienna. Nothing of the kind. The English houses are like chimneys turned inside out; on the outside all is soot and dirt, in the inside everything is clean and bright.

From the hall we make our way to the parlour—the refectory of the house. The parlour is the common sitting-room of the family, the centre-point of the domestic state. It is here that many eat their dinners, and some say their prayers; and in this room does the lady of the house arrange her household affairs and issue her commands. In winter the parlour fire burns from early morn till late at night, and it is into the parlour that the visitor is shewn, unless he happens to call on a reception-day, when the drawing-rooms are thrown open to the friends of the family.

Large folding-doors, which occupy nearly the whole breadth of the back wall, separate the front from the back parlour, and when opened, the two form one large room. The number and the circumstances of the family devote this back parlour either to the purposes of a library for the master, the son, or the daughters of the house, or convert it into a boudoir, office, or breakfast-room. Frequently, it serves no purpose in particular, and all in turn.

These two rooms occupy the whole depth of the house. All the other apartments are above, so that there are from two to four rooms in each story. The chief difference in the domestic apartments in England and Germany consists in this division: in Germany, the members of a family occupy a number of apartments on the same floor or "flat"; in England, they live in a cumulative succession of rooms. In Germany, the dwelling-houses are divided horizontally—here the division is vertical.

Hence it happens, that houses with four rooms communicating with one another are very rare in London, with the exception only of the houses in the very aristocratic quarters. Hence, also, each story has its peculiar destination in the family geographical dictionary. In the first floor are the reception-rooms; in the second the bed-rooms, with their large four-posters and marble-topped wash-stands; in the third story are the nurseries and servants' rooms; and in the fourth, if a fourth there be, you find a couple of low garrets, for the occasional accommodation of some bachelor friend of the family.

The doors and windows of these garrets are not exactly air-tight, the wind comes rumbling down the chimney, the stairs are narrow and steep, and the garrets are occasionally invaded by inquisitive cats and a vagrant rat; but what of that? A bachelor in England is worse off than a family cat. According to English ideas, the worst room in the house is too good for a bachelor. They say—"Oh, he'll do very well!" What does a bachelor care for a three-legged chair, a broken window, a ricketty table, and a couple or so of sportive currents? It is exactly as if a man took a special delight in rheumatism, tooth-ache, hard beds, smoking chimneys, and the society of rats, until he has entered the holy state of matrimony. The promise of some tender being to "love, honour, and obey," would seem to change a bachelor's nature, and make him susceptible of the amenities of domestic comfort. The custom is not flattering to the fairer half of humanity. It is exactly as if the comforts of one's sleeping-room were to atone for the sorrows of matrimony, and as if a bachelor, from the mere fact of being unmarried, were so happy and contented a being, that no amount of earthly discomfort could ruffle the blissful tranquillity of his mind!

It was truly comical to see Dr. Keif, when the lady of the house first introduced him to his "own room."

The politics and the police of Germany had given the poor fellow so much trouble, that he had never once thought of taking unto himself a wife. As a natural consequence of this lamentable state of things, his quarters were assigned him in the loftiest garret of the house. Dismal forebodings, which he tried to smile away, seized on his philosophical mind as he mounted stairs after stairs, each set steeper and narrower than the last. At length, on a mere excuse for a landing there is a narrow door, and behind that door a mere corner of a garret. The Doctor had much experience in the topography of the garrets of German college towns; but the English garret in Guildford Street, Russell Square, put all his experience to shame.

"I trust you'll be comfortable here," calls the lady after him, with a malicious smile; for to enter the bachelor's room, would be a gross violation of the rules and regulations of British decency. And before he can make up his mind to reply, she has vanished down the steep stairs.

And the Doctor, with his hands meekly folded, stands in the centre of his "own room." "Oh Bulwer, Dickens, and Thackeray"—such are his thoughts—and thou, "Oh Punch, who describest the garrets of the British bachelor! here, where I cease to understand the much-vaunted English comfort, here do I begin to understand your writings! If I did not happen to be in London, I should certainly like to be in Spandau. My own Germany, with thy romantic fortresses and dungeon-keeps, how cruelly hast thou been calumniated!"

There is a knock at the door. It is Sir John, who has come up for the express purpose of witnessing the Doctor's admiration of his room. He knows that the room will be admired, for to his patriotic view, there is beauty in all and everything that is English. His patriotism revels in old-established abuses, and stands triumphant amidst every species of nuisance. The question, "How do you like your room?" is uttered exactly with that degree of conscious pride which animated the King of Prussia when, looking down from the keep of Stolzenfels Castle, he asked Queen Victoria, "How do you like the Rhine?" And equally eager, though perhaps not quite so sincere, was the Doctor's reply: "Oh very much! I am quite enchanted with it! It is impossible to lose anything in this room, and the losing things and groping about to find them was the plague of my life at home in the large German rooms. A most excellent arrangement this! Everything is handy and within reach. Bookcase, washstand, and wardrobe—I need not even get up to get what I want—and as for this table and these chairs, I presume that the occasional overturning of an inkstand will but serve to heighten the quaint appearance of this venerable furniture!"

"Of course," said Sir John, "certainly! this is liberty-hall, sir. But mind you take care of the lamp, and pray do not sit in the draught between the window and the door."

He does not exactly explain how it is possible to sit anywhere except in the draught, for the limited space of the garret is entirely taken up with draughts. Perhaps it is a sore subject, for, with an uneasy shrug of the shoulders, the worthy Sir John adds:—

"But never mind. Comfortable, isn't it? And what do you say to the view, eh? Beau-ti-ful! right away over all the roofs to Hampstead!"

He might as well have said to the Peak of Teneriffe; for the view is obstructed with countless chimney-pots looming in the distant future through perennial fog. Sir John is struck with this fact, as, measuring the whole length of the apartment in three strides, he approaches the window to enjoy the glorious view of Hampstead hills. He shuts the window, and is evidently disappointed.

"Ah! never mind! very comfortable, air pure and bracing; very much so; very different from the air in the lower rooms. And—I say, mind this is the 'escape,' " says Sir John, opening a very small door at the side of our friend's room. "If—heaven preserve us—there should be a fire in the house, and if you should not be able to get down stairs, you may get up here and make your escape over the roofs. That's what you will find in every English house. Isn't it practical? eh! What do you say to it?"

The Doctor says nothing at all; he calculates his chances of escape along that narrow ledge of wall, and thinks: "Really things are beginning to look awfully comfortable. If there should happen to be a fire while I am in the house, I hope and trust I shall have time to consider which is worst, to be made a male suttee of, or to tumble down from the roof like an apoplectic sparrow."

We leave the Doctor between the horns of this dilemma, and descending a good many more stairs than we ascended, we find our way to the haunts of those who, in England, live under-ground—to the kitchen.

Here, too, everything is different from what we are accustomed to in Germany. In the place of the carpets which cover the floors of the upper rooms, we walk here on strong, solid oilcloths, which, swept and washed, looks like marble, and gives a more comfortable aspect to an English kitchen than any German housewife ever succeeded in imparting to the scene of her culinary exercises. Add to this, bright dish-covers of gigantic dimensions fixed to the wall, plated dishes, and sundry other utensils of queer shapes and silvery aspect, interspersed with copper sauce-pans and pots and china, the windows neatly curtained, with a couple of flower-pots on the sill, and a branch of evergreens growing on the wall round them—such is an English kitchen in its modest glory. A large fire is always kept burning; and its ruddy glow heightens the homeliness and comfort of the scene. There is no killing of animals in these peaceful retreats. All the animals which are destined for consumption, such as fowls, ducks, pigeons, and geese, are sold, killed, and plucked in the London shops. When they are brought to the kitchen, they are in such a condition, that nothing prevents their being put to the fire. And then, in front of that fire, turned by a machine, dangle large sections of sheep, calves, and oxen, of so respectable a size, that the very sight of them would suffice to awe a German housewife.

Several doors in the kitchen open into sundry other subterraneous compartments. There is a back-kitchen, whither the servants of the house retire for the most important part of their daily labours—the talking of scandal apropos of the whole neighbourhood. There is also a small room for the washing-up of plates and dishes, the cleaning of knives and forks, of clothes and shoes. Other compartments are devoted to stores of provisions, of coals, and wine and beer. Need I add, that all these are strictly separate?

All these various rooms and compartments, from the kitchen up to Dr. Keif's garret, are in modern London houses, lighted up with gas—and pipes conducting fresh, filtered, and in many instances, hot water, ascend into all the stories—and there is in all and everything so much of really domestic and unostentatious comfort, that it would be very uncomfortable to give a detailed description of every item of a cause which contributes to the general and agreeable effect. Indeed, such a description is simply impossible. Just let any one try to explain to an Englishman the patriarchal physiognomy of a pot-bellied German stove; or let him try to awake in the Englishman's wife a feeling, remotely akin to sympathy, for the charming atmosphere of a German "Kneipe"; or make an American understand what the German "Bund" is, and what it is good for. To attempt this were a labour of Sysiphus—toil without a result. Nothing short of actual experience will enable a man to understand and value these national mysteries.

CHAP. II.

CHARACTERISTICS OF THE MASSES.—FASHIONABLE QUARTERS.—HOW MR. FALCON SAID GOOD BYE TO HIS CUSTOMERS.—THE CROSSING IN HOLBORN.—MOSES AND SON.—ADVERTISING VANS.—THE PUFFING MANIA, ITS PHASES AND CAUSES.

FROM our house, which is our starting point, we have several large and small streets leading to the south and opening into Holborn, which is one of the great arteries of this gigantic town. Holborn extends to the east to the old prison of Newgate, where it joins the chief streets of the city; in the west it merges into interminable Oxford-street, which leads in a straight line to Hyde Park, and farther on to Kensington Gardens and Bayswater.

"If to this large line of streets," says Dr. Keif, "you add the Friedrichstrasse of Berlin, you get a line of houses which extend from this day, Monday, into next week, and perhaps a good bit farther. But any one who attempts to walk to the farther end of Oxford-street—I say 'who attempts,' for, since the English prefer a constitutional monarchy to an absolute prince, they are surely capable of any act of folly—any one, I say, who performs that insane feat, will find that the Berlin Friedrichstrasse commences at the very last house of Oxford-street."

For once Dr. Keif is wrong. Where Oxford-street ends, there you enter into a charming English landscape—one green and hilly and altogether captivating. But at the end of the Berlin Friedrichstrasse you enter nothing but the sandy deserts of the Mark.

Holborn is a business street. It has a business character; there is no mistaking it. Shops and plate-glass windows side by side on each hand; costermongers and itinerant vendors all along the pavement; the houses covered with signboards and inscriptions; busy crowds on either side; omnibuses rushing to and fro in the centre of the road, and all around that indescribable bewildering noise of human voices, carriage-wheels, and horses' hoofs, which pervades the leading streets of crowded cities.

Not all the London streets have this business character. They are divided into two classes: into streets where the roast-beef of life is earned, and into streets where the said roast-beef is eaten. No other town presents so strong a contrast between its various quarters. But a few hundred yards from the leading thoroughfares, where hunger or ambition hunt men on, extend for many miles the quiet quarters of comfortable citizens, of wealthy fundholders, and of landed proprietors, who come to town for "the season," and who return to their parks and shooting-grounds as soon as her Majesty has been graciously pleased to prorogue Parliament, and with Parliament the season.

These fashionable quarters are as quiet as our own provincial towns. They have no shops; no omnibuses are allowed to pass through them, and few costermongers or sellers of fruit, onions, oysters, and fish find their way into these regions, for the cheapness of their wares has no attractions for the inhabitants of these streets. These streets, too, are macadamized expressly for the horses and carriages of the aristocracy; such roads are more comfortable for all parties concerned, that is to say, for horses, horsemen, and drivers, and the carriages are, moreover, too light to do much harm to the road. In these streets, too, there are neither counting-houses nor public-houses to disturb the neighbourhood by their daily traffic and nightly revelries. Comfort reigns supreme in the streets and in the interior of the houses. The roadway is lined with pavements of large white beautiful flag-stones, which skirt the area railings; it is covered with gravel, and carefully watered, exactly as the broad paths of our public gardens, to keep down the dust and deaden the rumbling of the carriages and the step of the horses. The horses, too, are of a superior kind, and as different from their poorer brethren, the brewer's, coal-merchant's, and omnibus horses, as the part of the town in which they eat is different from the part in which the latter work.

In the vicinity of the Parks, or in the outskirts of the town, or wheresoever else such quarters have space to extend, you must admire their unrivalled magnificence. From the velvety luscious green, which receives a deeper shade from the dense dark foliage of the English beech-tree, there arise buildings, like palaces, with stone terraces and verandahs, more splendid, more beautiful, and more frequent than in any town on the continent.

An Englishman is easily satisfied with the rough comforts of his place of business. The counting-houses of the greatest bankers; the establishments of the largest trading houses in the city have a gloomy, heavy, and poverty-stricken appearance. But far different is the case with respect to those places where an Englishman proposes to live for himself and for his family.

A wealthy merchant who passes his days in a narrow city street, in a dingy office, on a wooden stool, and at a plain desk, would think it very "ungenteel" if he or his family were to live in a street in which there are shops. And, although it may appear incredible, still it is true, that in the better parts of the town there are many streets shut up with iron gates, which gatekeepers open for the carriages and horses of the residents or their visitors. These gates exclude anything like noise and intrusion. Grocers, fishmongers, bakers, butchers, and all other kitchen-tradesmen occupy, in the fashionable quarters, the nearest lanes and side streets, and many of them live in close vicinity to the mews. For no house, not even the largest, has a carriage-gate; and that we, in Germany, shelter under our roofs our horses, grooms, and all the odours of the stable, appears to the English as strange and mysterious, generally speaking, as our mustachios, and our liberalism in matters of religion.

We have endeavoured to draw the line of demarcation between the residential parts of the town and the business quarters. This being done, we return to Holborn.

Dr. Keif does not escape the common lot of every stranger in London streets. His theories of walking on a crowded pavement are of the most confused description, and the consequence is that he is being pushed about in a woful manner; but, at each push, he expresses his immoderate joy at having, for once, got into a crowded street, where a man must labour hard if he would lounge and saunter about. All of a sudden he stops in the middle of the pavement, and, adjusting his shirt-collar (a recent purchase), he takes off his hat and bows to somebody or something in the road. A natural consequence of all this is, that the passengers dig their elbows into the Doctor's ribs, as they hurry along.

"To whom are you bowing with so much heroic devotion?"

"Whom? Why to Mr. Falcon, on the other side of the street."

"So you have found an acquaintance already? That is a rare case. Many a man walks about for weeks without seeing a face he knows; and you have scarcely left the house when—"

"But do you really think I know that Mr. Falcon on the other side of the way?" Saying which the mysterious doctor bows again; and I, taking my glass, find out that there are a dozen Mr. Falcons, hoisted on high poles, parading the opposite pavement. Twelve men, out at elbows, move in solemn procession along the line of road, each carrying a heavy pole with a large table affixed to it, and on the table there is a legend in large scarlet letters, "MR. FALCON REMOVED." It appears that Mr. Falcon, having thought proper to remove from 146 Holborn, begs to inform the nobility, the gentry, and the public generally, that he carries on his business at 6 Argyle-street.

The Doctor, crossing his arms on his chest gravely, while the passengers are pushing him about, says:

"Since Mr. Falcon is kind enough to inform me of his removal, I believe I ought to take off my hat to his advertisement. But only think of those poor fellows groaning under Mr. Falcon's gigantic cards. He is an original, Mr. Falcon is, and I should like to make his acquaintance."

Again the Doctor is wrong in fancying, as he evidently does, that Mr. Falcon sends his card-bearers, with the news of his removal, through the whole of London. Why should he? Perhaps he sold cigars, or buttons, or yarns, in Holborn; and it is there he is known, while no one in other parts of the town cares a straw for Mr. Falcon's celebrated and unrivalled cigars, buttons, or yarns. His object is to inform the inhabitants of his own quarter of his removal, and of his new address.

The twelve men with the poles and boards need not go far. From early dawn till late at night they parade the site of Mr. Falcon's old shop. They walk deliberately and slowly, to enable the passengers to read the inscription at their ease. They walk in Indian file to attract attention, and because in any other manner they would block up the way. But they walk continually, silently, without ever stopping for rest. Thus do they carry their poles, for many days and even weeks, until every child in the neighbourhood knows exactly where Mr. Falcon is henceforward to be found, for the moving column of large scarlet-lettered boards is too striking; and no one can help looking at them and reading the inscription. And this is a characteristic piece of what we Germans call British industry.

There is no other town in the world where people advertise with so much persevering energy—on so grand a scale—at such enormous expense—with such impertinent puffery—and with such distinguished success.

We have just reached a point in Holborn where, a great many streets crossing, leave a small, irregular spot, in the middle. In the centre of this spot, surrounded by a railing, and raised in some masonry, is a gigantic lamp-post, and the whole forms what one might call an island of the streets. Every now and then the protection of this island is sought by groups of women and children who, amidst the noise and the wheels of so many vehicles that dash along in every direction, shrink from a bold rush across the whole breadth of the street. As Noah's dove thought itself lucky in having found an olive branch to alight on amidst the waters of the deluge, so do tender women breathe more quietly, and look around with greater composure, after having reached this street-island, where they are safe from the ever-returning tide of street life.

Leaning against the lamp-post we are at leisure to look around and see the moving beings, things, and objects, which rush past on every side; and for the nonce we will devote a special attention to the various advertising tricks.

The time—Night. One of those clear, fogless, calm summer nights which are so "few and far between" in this large town. The life-blood in the street-veins runs all the fuller, faster, and merrier, for the beauty of the night. Holborn is inundated with gas-light; but the brightest glare bursts forth exactly opposite to us. Who, in the name of all that is prudent, can the people be who make such a shocking waste of gas? They are "Moses and Son," the great tailors and outfitters, who have lighted up the side-fronts of their branch establishment. All round the outer walls of the house, which is filled with coats, vests, and trousers, to the roof, and which exhibits three separate side-fronts towards three separate streets, there are many thousands of gas-flames, forming branches, foliage, and arabesques, and sending forth so dazzling a blaze, that this fiery column of Moses is visible to Jews and Gentiles at the distance of half a mile, lighting up the haze which not even the clearest evening can wholly banish from the London sky.

Among the fiery flowers burns the inevitable royal crown, surmounting the equally unavoidable letters V.R. To the right of these letters we have Moses and Son blessing the Queen in flaming characters of hydro-carbon; to the left they bless the people.[A]

[A] "God save the Queen," and "God bless the people," are the legends of these Mosaic illuminations.

What do they make this illumination for? This is not a royal birthday, nor is it the anniversary of a great national victory. All things considered, this ought to be a day of mourning and fasting for Messrs. Moses and Son, for the Commons of England have this very afternoon decided that Alderman Salomons shall not take his seat in the House.

Motives of loyalty, politics, or religion, have nothing whatever to do with the grand illuminations executed by Messrs. Moses and Son. The air is calm, there is not even a breath of wind; it's a hundred to one that Oxford Street and Holborn will be thronged with passengers; this is our time to attract the idlers. Up, boys, and at them! light the lamps! A heavy expense this, burning all that gas for ever so many hours; but it pays, somehow. Boldness carries the prize, and faint heart never won fair customers. And if it were not for that c——d police and the Insurance Companies, by Jingo! it were the best advertisement to burn the house and shop at least twice a year. That would puff us up, and make people stare, and go the round of all the newspapers. Capital advertisement that, eh!

Being strollers in the streets, we delight in this extempore illumination. It is our object to see and observe; and Messrs. Moses and Son convert night into day for our especial accommodation. A whole legion of lesser planets bask in the region of this great sun. Crowds of subordinate advertising monsters have been attracted to this part of the street, and move about in various shapes, to the right and to the left, walking, rolling on wheels, and riding on horseback.

Behold, rolling down from Oxford Street, three immense wooden pyramids—their outsides are painted all over with hieroglyphics and with monumental letters in the English language. These pyramids display faithful portraits of Isis and Osiris, of cats, storks, and of the apis; and amidst these old-curiosity-shop gods, any Englishman may read an inscription, printed in letters not much longer than a yard, from which it appears that there is now on view a panorama of Egypt—one more beautiful, interesting, and instructive than was ever exhibited in London. For this panorama—we are still following the inscription—shows the flux and reflux of the Nile, with its hippopotamuses and crocodiles, and a section of the Red Sea, as mentioned in Holy Writ, and part of the last overland mail, and also the railway from Cairo to Alexandria, exactly as laid out in Mr. Stephenson's head. And all this for only one shilling! with a full, lucid, and interesting lecture into the bargain.

The pyramids advance within three yards from where we stand, and, for a short time, they take their ease in the very midst of all the lights, courting attention. But the policeman on duty respects not the monuments of the Pharaohs; he moves his hand, and the drivers of the pyramids, though hidden in their colossal structures, see and understand the sign: they move on.

But here is another monstrous shape—a mosque, with its cupola blue and white, surmounted by the crescent. The driver is a light-haired boy, with a white turban and a sooty face. There is no mistaking that fellow for an Arab; and, nevertheless, the turban and the soot make a profound impression.

"We are being invaded by the East!" says Dr. Keif. "They are going to give a panoramic explanation of the Oriental question. If I were Lord Palmerston, I'd put a stop to that sort of thing. It's a high crime and misdemeanour against diplomacy. Pray call for the police!"

But Dr. Keif is wrong again. On the back of the mosque there is an advertisement, which is as much a stranger to the Oriental question as the German diplomates are. That advertisement tells us, that Dr. Doem is proprietor of a most marvellous Arabian medicine, warranted to cure the bite of mad dogs and venomous reptiles generally; even so, that a person so bitten, if he but takes Dr. Doem's medicine, shall feel no more inconvenience than he would feel from a very savage leader in the Morning Herald. The mosque, the blue crescent, the gaudy colours, and the juvenile Arab from the banks of the Thames, have merely been got up to attract attention. There need be no very intimate connexion between the things puffed and the street symbolics which puff them. Heterogeneous ideas are as much an aid to puffing as homogeneous ideas. If ever you should happen to go to Grand Cairo, rely on it, every cupola of a mosque, peeping out from palm-groves and aloe-hedges, will remind you of Dr. Doem and his Arabian medicine, as advertised in Holborn in Europe. Allah is great, and the cunning of English speculators is as deep as the sea where it is deepest.

Hark! a peal of trumpets! Another advertising machine rushes out of the gloom of Museum Street. In this instance the Orient is not put in requisition. The turn-out is thoroughly English.

Two splendid cream-coloured horses, richly harnessed; a dark green chariot of fantastic make, in shape like a half-opened shell, and tastefully ornamented with gilding and pictures; on the box a coachman in red and gold, looking respectable and almost aristocratic, with his long whip on his knee; and behind him the trumpeters, seated in the chariot, and proclaiming its advent. In this manner have the people of London of late months been invited to Vauxhall—to that same Vauxhall, which, under the Regency, attracted all the wealth, beauty, and fashion in England—which, to this very day, still attracts hundreds of thousands; whose good and ill fame has crossed the ocean. Even Vauxhall—the old and famous—makes no exception to the common lot; it is compelled to have its posters, its newspaper advertisements, and its advertising vans.

In no other town would such tricks be necessary conditions of existence; but here, where everything is grand and bulky—in this town of miraculous extent, where generations live and die in the East-end without ever having beheld the wonders of the West-end—among this population, which is reckoned by millions instead of by hundreds of thousands—here, where all press and rush on to make money or to spend it—here, where every one must distinguish himself in some way or other, or be lost and perish in the crowd—where every hour has its novelty—here, in London, even the most solid undertakings must assume the crying colour of charlatanism.

The Panorama of the Nile, the Overland Route, the Colosseum, Madame Tussaud's Exhibition of Wax-works, and other sights, are indeed wonder-works of human industry, skill, and invention; and, in every respect, are they superior to the usual productions of the same kind. But, for all that, they must send their advertising vans into the streets; necessity compels them to strike the gong and blow the trumpet; choice there is none. They must either advertise or perish.

The same may be said of great institutions of a different kind; of fire and life insurance companies; of railways and steamers; and of theatres—from Punch's theatre in the Strand, upwards, to the Royal Italian Opera, which ransacks Europe for musical celebrities, and which, nevertheless, must condescend to magnify its own glory on gigantic many-coloured posters, though it has managed, up to the present day, to do without the vans, trumpets, and sham Nubians.

It is either advertising or being ruined. We have said it before. Many of our readers will think this a bold and unwarranted assertion. It is neither the one nor the other; for it is founded on the experience of many men of business. Of many examples we quote but one.

Mr. Bennett keeps a large shop of clocks and watches in Cheapside. His watches and clocks are among the best in London; they have an old-established reputation, and they deserve it. But their reputation is not owing to their excellency alone; it required many years of advertising, years of continual and expensive advertising, to inculcate this great fact on the obtuse, bewildered, and deluded Londoners. Thanks to Mr. Bennett's perseverance they were at length convinced. And, when a few years ago, the reputation of the firm had spread throughout the length and breadth of the land, it struck Mr. Bennett that now was the time to put a stop to this expensive process of advertising. "In future," said that gentleman, "I mean to take the full interest from my capital instead of paying part of it to the printers." And he set at once about it. In the year in which Mr. Bennett took this bold resolution, the firm spent a few thousand pounds less than usual in advertisements. But the consequences made themselves felt; and as month followed month, they became still more disagreeably perceptible. Mr. Bennett understood that in London virtue is its own reward, provided it keeps a trumpeter; and as Mr. Bennett was not an obstinate theorist, he had again recourse to the printing-press. He advertises to this very day, and to a greater extent, if possible, than formerly. In proof whereof we quote his advertisement in the Catalogue of the Great Exhibition, on which occasion he paid £900 (say nine hundred pounds sterling), for the insertion of his advertisement on the back of the wrapper.

Mr. Bennett's business is as prosperous as ever. Of course, his watches were quite as good during the period he did not advertise; but the public was about to forget him. Advertising is an indispensable item in the expenditure of a London trader.

While we were talking of Mr. Bennett's shop in Cheapside, the little lamp-post Square in Holborn has become more quiet. Two coal-waggons, each with four elephantine, thick-necked, broad-footed horses have suddenly emerged from the darkness of one of the side-streets. The half-circle which these clumsy horses must make in order to obtain a locus standi in the street of Holborn, causes a general stoppage among the vehicles, which up to the present have been proceeding in regular order, at an all but uniform pace. For a few moments we are relieved from the clanking of chains, the rattling of wheels, and the dull rumbling of wooden pyramids and vans. Now is the time for the lesser sprites of the advertising mysteries.

A boy on our right puts printed papers into our hands. On the left, the same process is attempted by an elderly man of respectable appearance, who jerks his arm with what he believes to be a graceful indifference, while everybody else would mistake that same jerk for a convulsive gesture of despondency. Just before us we have a man with a pole and board, recommending some choice blacking, and on the opposite pavement there is a Hindoo dressed in white flannel, with a turban on his head, and with all the sorrow of a ruined nation in his handsome brown face and chiselled features. At his side is a little girl dressed in filthy rags. The Hindoo has a bundle of printed papers in his hand, Sabbatarian, temperance, and other tracts—inestimable treasures—which he offers to the public at the very low price of one penny each. That poor fellow got those tracts from some sacred society as a consideration for allowing them to convert him to Christianity. But his sad face is a sorry recommendation of the treasures of comfort he proposes to dispose of. Better for him to stand in primitive nudity among his native palm-forests, adoring the miracles of nature in the Sun, and in Brahma, than to shiver here on the cold, wet pavement, cursing the torments of want in the image of the sacred Saviour. On the banks of the Ganges that man prayed to God; here, among strangers, he learns to hate mankind. But then he was a pagan on the banks of the Ganges; on the banks of the Thames he has the name of a Christian. Whether or no the Christian is really more religious than the Pagan was, is a question which seems to give little trouble to the pious missionaries. The Bible Society has done its duty.

Our worthy friend, Dr. Keif was, it seems, also struck with the melancholy aspect of the Hindoo. He made a bold rush across the street, put some pence into the tiny brown hand of the little girl, and took in return a tract on "True Devotion," which he did not read, but crushing it into a paper ball, angrily, threw it into the gutter. He had taken the tract out of consideration for the poor man's feelings. "It's begging under the pretence of selling," said the worthy Doctor in a great rage, "but

THE SAUNTER IN HOLBORN.

since the delusion is a comfort to him, I would not for the world offer him money without taking one of his papers!"

It was very naughty in the Doctor to fling that tract away as he did. As a punishment, we were immediately assailed by a set of imps who mistook us for easy victims on the altars of speculation.

Men with cocoa-nuts and dates, and women with oranges surrounded us with their carts. One man recommended his dog-collars of all sizes, which he had formed in a chain round his neck; another person offered to mark our linen; a third produced his magic strops; others held out note-books, cutlery, prints, caricatures, exhibition-medals—all—all—all for one penny. It seemed as if the world were on sale at a penny a bit. And amidst all this turmoil, the men with advertising boards walked to and fro; and the boys distributed advertising bills by the hundred, with smiles of deep bliss, whenever they met a charitable soul who took them.

The coal-waggons are gone, and the street noise is as loud as ever.

Are we to remain here and pursue our studies of the natural history of advertising vans? It is not likely we shall see them all, for their numbers are incalculable. They generate according to abnormal laws. Each day and each event produces another form. The Advertisement is omnipresent. It is in the skies and on the ground; it swells as the flag in the breeze, and it sets its seal on the pavement; it is on the water, on the steam-boat wharf, and under the water in the Thames tunnel; it roosts on the highest chimneys; it sparkles in coloured letters on street lamps; it forms the prologue of all the newspapers, and the epilogue of all the books; it breaks in upon us with the sound of trumpets, and it awes us in the silent sorrow of the Hindoo. There is no escaping from the advertisement, for it travels with you in the omnibuses, in the railway carriages, and on the paddle-boxes of the steamers.

The arches of the great bridges over the Thames were at one time free from advertisements. The masonry was submerged by the periodical returns of the tide, and the bills would not stick. But at length the advertisement invaded even these, the last asylums of non-publicity. Since bills could not be pasted on the walls, the advertisement was painted on them. At this hour there is not an arch in a London bridge but has its advertisements painted on it. But for whom? For the thousands who every day pass under the bridge in steamers. For the Thames, too, is one of the London streets and by no means the least important one.

CHAP. III.

The Squares.—Lincoln's Inn.

A MAN may be familiar with London streets, he may for years have gone his weary way amidst these endless rows of bare, narrow, irregular houses, which are black with fog and smoke, without ever suspecting that gardens sparkling in idyllic beauty are hidden behind those masses of sooty masonry.

This is one of the chief distinctions between London and Paris and other continental capitals. Paris has much outside glitter, much startling show. Its Boulevards, its Place de la Concorde, Place Vendôme, Rue de la Paix, Rue Rivoli, and sundry others of its streets and public places are unrivalled; London cannot vie with them in architectural prodigies. But the brilliant points of Paris, of which Frenchmen are in the habit of boasting, attract our attention only to divert it from the narrow crooked lanes, and the filth of the other parts of their town. Paris sports a clean shirt-front merely to hide the uncleanliness of its general nature. The French are adepts in the art of draping. The English, on the contrary, know nothing whatever of that noble art. The cut of their clothes is inelegant, but the cloth is the best of its kind; their dwelling-houses have the appearance of old chimneys, but the inside is replete with comfort and unpretending wealth; their language is rough, and without melody; but it is energetic, flexible, and expressive. Their metropolis, too, conceals its real beauties. It requires some investigation, some instinct and discernment to discover and enjoy them.

In the broadest part of Holborn, there are on either side certain suspicious-looking lanes, in which pawnbrokers and cobblers "hang out," and where a roaring, though not a very fragrant, trade is driven in greens, meat, and fish. The lanes on the north side communicate with Gray's Inn; on the south, they form an intricate labyrinth, which we enter on our way to Lincoln's Inn Fields.

Travellers proceeding from London to Dover pass through a series of monstrous tunnels, which have been bored through those mountains of chalk, the bulwarks of the British islands. As they emerge from the darkness of the last tunnel, they feel happy and grateful for the fresh sea-breeze which plays around and the vast, boundless view which opens before them. In a like manner, do we breathe more freely as we emerge from the last of these narrow, and by no means sweetly-smelling lanes.

A broad square, filled with trees, flowers, and garden-ground, opens before us. This is one of the many "squares" of which you, O my beloved countrymen, entertain such crude and indistinct notions!

"Squares" are wide, open spots, surrounded by houses, exactly like our own "Plätze." But, instead of the monuments of saints, whom the Anglican Church ignores; instead of the pestilence-columns, which Englishmen object to (though London, like every other respectable old town, had its plagues in olden times); and instead of our beautiful market-fountains, the poesy of which is a sealed book to the English mind, their "Plätze" have been converted into Gardens with broad commodious streets all round the railings. These gardens are not by any means so small as the Germans generally believe. Indeed, in the larger squares, they are of considerable extent. The curiosity of the passers-by is repelled by trees, shrubs, and carefully-trimmed hedges, and the shady walks and the grassplots in the centre are strictly private. Of these squares, Lincoln's Inn Fields is the largest; it covers an area of twelve acres. The joint extent of all the London squares is one thousand two hundred acres. With the exception of Smithfield and Trafalgar-square, all the London squares have gardens, and the trees and shrubs which grow in them improve the air of all the neighbouring streets. Such gardens are found in all quarters of the town, and in many cases they are hidden among the narrowest alleys and gloomiest courts, where the wanderer least expects to find them. They are the most beautiful spots in London, for they present specimens of nature's paradise, blooming in concealment, and all the more lovely are they for that very reason.

Let us return to Lincoln's Inn Fields.

We stand on classic soil. Three sides of this large square are surrounded with buildings, whose open doors shew at once that they are not mere ordinary dwelling-houses. One of them attracts our special attention; it is so black and its columns are so many and so high. It is the Royal College of Surgeons, where the medical students pass their examination in surgery. This house, too, shelters the famous Anatomical Museum which John Hunter bequeathed to the College of Surgeons. All the other buildings are owned by the guild of the lawyers. In the heart of the city, the houses, from the cellars to the garrets, are let out as offices and store-rooms. The houses in Lincoln's Inn Fields, too, are devoted to the special accommodation of lawyers. A walk up and down, and a look at the door-posts, which are black with the names of advocates, suffice to convince us of the lamentable condition of English law.

We have said that this is classic soil. Sir Thomas More, Shaftesbury the statesman, and Lord Mansfield, studied in the precincts of Lincoln's Inn; and Oliver Cromwell passed two years of his eventful life in the same locality. The square has its sad reminiscences too. In the centre of the gardens, where flowers blow and birds sing, there stood at one time a scaffold; and on that scaffold died one of the noblest patriots of England, Lord Russell, an ancestor of Finality John, and son to William, Earl of Bedford.

The crown of England rested in those days on the head of the second Charles. At his side was his brother, the Duke of York, the evil genius of Charles and of England. Charles, and James his brother, listened to the counsels of France and of Rome, for they wanted money, and the Whigs would only consent to vote the people's money in exchange for some crumbs of liberty for the people. Thus it came to pass that England's honour was sold to France, and the "rebellious" Parliament was dissolved, and the press put down; the liberties of the city were curtailed; venal men were placed on the bench, and venal witnesses thronged the courts; the best men of England were put into jail and arraigned on charges of high treason. Among the best and bravest was William Russell.

They accused him of having conspired against the king's life, and sent him to the Tower. Witnesses were bribed to appear against him; they were men of proverbial villany. Among them was Lord Howard, of whom the king himself had said he would not hang the worst cur in his kennel on the evidence of that man. But that man's evidence sufficed to bring the best man in all England to the block. It is the old story—a tail-wagging cur is more considered at court than a thinking man. Lord Russell's head fell in the centre of this very square. Vainly did his wife implore the king's mercy. Lord Russell's head fell in the immediate vicinity of his estates; and the Londoners of those days saw him pass through Holborn on his way to the scaffold. Many wept—many abused him; others jeered at him. The people of that time had even less respect for its heroes and martyrs than the present generation. In our days, even the vilest of the vile are awed into silence when the princes of this earth deliver their political adversaries to the hangman's rope or the "mercy" of a platoon of rifles.

But even in these our own days there is a party in England, there are Englishmen, citizens, writers, and members of Parliament, and most of them truly honourable men, who, while they declare that the British Whigs of those times were patriots and martyrs, do not hesitate rashly to condemn the "rebellious" Parliaments and political parties of the continent. No Englishman, not the most conservative, would dare to deny to Lord Russell one single ray of that glorious crown of martyrdom which the English people and its historians have placed upon his bleeding head.

"It cannot be denied," they say, "that Lord William Russell conspired against an illegal Government; but to conspire against such a Government was his duty; he was justified in so doing."... But if the Russells of those days were justified in vindicating the people's rights against the King, how then can you so smoothly and glibly apply the word "rebels" to the continental Russells of our own days? If armed opposition is treasonable, was it less treasonable in days gone by? Do the rights of mankind dwindle away as century follows century? Or has the great nation of England so small a mind that it cannot distinguish between the merits of a cause and its success?

The Russells of the last centuries shed their blood for this generation. England is free, happy, undisturbed, mighty, strong, tranquil and reasonable; she develops a brighter future from the benefits she at present enjoys. The English know it; and in this knowledge is the secret of their pride. The sanguinary conflicts of the continent, which have hitherto had no results, provoke in Englishmen a smile of mingled pity and derision. "Those people don't know what they are driving at," say some; "if they would be happy they ought to imitate England." And others say, "They want freedom, but they are not practical enough; they do not turn their revolution to advantage as our ancestors did, and as we would do in their place." But I say, it is easy to find fault with others, and a happy man has all the wisdom of Solomon. These English sages do not consider how much easier it was to their ancestors to bring the contest with the power of the crown to a successful issue. The English patriots were not opposed by large standing armies; the contest lay between them and a single family and its faction, and—this is a point which has never been sufficiently dwelt upon—they had no reason to fear a foreign intervention. For England, as the greatest living author[B] says, never fought as France did for the freedom of the world, but for its own freedom. Hence the continental powers paid little attention to the battles of the Puritans, and the contests between Charles and Cromwell. Clarendon indeed considered their non-intervention a great grievance. But this non-intervention of Spain or France was the greatest blessing for royalty in England. If those countries had interfered, the contest for the principles of constitutionalism might have been prolonged to this very day, or perhaps royalty would have been killed outright on the English battle-fields.

[B] Macaulay's Essays, vol. ii.

The history of England—says Macaulay—is a history of progress. Who would gainsay it? At the commencement of the twelfth century, a small and semi-barbarous nation, subject to a handful of foreigners, without a trace of civilisation—large masses enslaved—the Saxons still distinct from the Normans—superstition and brutality everywhere, and the law of the strong hand the supreme law of the land—such was England seven hundred years ago. Then came the bloody civil wars—brain-scorching, land-spoiling, men-consuming, sectarian wars—contests abroad and contests at home—a series of vile, hypocritical, dissolute, and narrow-minded monarchs—and at intervals bright epochs of great times in history and politics, and day was changed into night and night into day, until England attained its present position among the nations of the earth. From one decade to another there may have been periodical retrogressions, but each century gave clear and irrefragable evidence of the progress of England.

If, therefore, in the next years, France should happen again to attain those giddy heights of freedom, which she gained three times already, and which three times have vanished beneath her feet, then let not France, as she is wont to do, wax proud in the scanty shade of her newly planted trees of liberty, and let her not look down contemptuously on the cold, thickblooded, clumsy tree of liberty in England. At the end of the century the two nations may compare their charters; it will then be seen which of them has really and truly had the greatest gains. The blood of France has manured the mental soil of all the world; England should be the last to forget what her liberty has gained by the ideal conquests of France. France, on the other hand, might make the most useful study in considering the consistent carrying out of great political maxims on the British soil.

When two nations express their opinions of one another, and reproach each other with their faults, they are in the habit of paying too little attention to the circumstances which promote or obstruct the advance of freedom. In this respect, the peculiarities of the countries and their geographical position cannot be too highly estimated. Who can tell what would be the condition of Germany, if our country were secure from foreign intervention; and if, as is the case with England, the sea protected it from the violence of its enemies or the insidious advances of its political friends.

CHAP. IV.

Up the Thames.—Vauxhall.

THE RIVER-SIDE.—VIEWS OF THE RIVER.—THE TIDES.—THE BRIDGES.—THE TEMPLE AND SOMERSET HOUSE.—ENTRANCE TO VAUXHALL.—BRITISH DECORATIVE GENIUS.—SOMEBODY RUNS AWAY WITH DR. KEIF.—MAGIC.—NELSON AND WELLINGTON.—THE CIRCUS.—THE BURNING OF MOSCOW.—AN EPISODE AT THE TEA TABLE.

IF you leave King William-street just at the foot of London-bridge and turn to the right, you will find your way into a set of narrow and steep streets, few only of which admit of carriage and horse traffic. The lower stories of the houses are let out as offices, and the upper as warehouse floors; the pavement is narrow and the road as bad as broken stones and long neglect can make it; dirty boys in sailors' jackets play at leap-frog over the street posts; legions of wheel-barrows encumber the broader parts of these thoroughfares;

packing-cases stand at the doors of houses, and cranes and levers peep out from the upper stories. Such are the streets which lead down to the banks of the Thames. It is altogether a dusty, filthy, "uncannie" quarter. A few steps through a black, cornery, nondescript structure of sooty brick and mortar, covered all over with immense shipping advertisements in all colours, and we stand on the bank of the river. An entirely new scene is opened before our eyes.

    Close to our left the mighty grey arches of London-bridge rise up from the river. We look under them downwards where the last ocean ships are crowded together on their moorings, where the distant masts are lost in the haze, and where ocean-life finds its limits, because the bridges prevent those large ships from passing up the river. We look in an opposite direction along the broad expanse of water, with busy little steamers rushing frantically in every conceivable direction; we look up to the parapet of London-bridge, where, high as it is, we see the heads of the passengers, and the crowded roofs of the omnibuses; we look over to the other bank, where a thousand high chimneys vomit forth their smoke and we behold Southwark, that amiable appendix to the metropolis, which at this day has its six hundred thousand inhabitants; and lastly, we look straight down before our feet where half a dozen steamers, closely packed together, dance up and down on the waves; where steam rushes forth noisily from narrow pipes, where hundreds of men, women, and children, run about in inextricable confusion pushing their way to the shore, to one of the boats, or from one boat to another; where the paddles beat the water and the boys start the machinery by shrill screams, while the mooring barges creak as the ropes are drawn tight. We look and behold this is the Thames! This is the great, living, fabulous, watery high-road in the heart of the British metropolis.

    They have abused thee sadly, thou grey Thames, for the filth of thy waters and the fogs which arise from thee. But most unjustly hast thou been abused. At Lechlade where the four rivulets from the Cotswolds join into a river, thy waters are as pure and pellucid as the Alpine streams which spring forth from the glacier. At Lechlade there are no fogs obscuring thy surface; there the air is pure; there art thou romantic and idyllic, innocent alike of the temptations of the world and the vice and filth of the greatest town. For many, many miles further down to Kew and Richmond thou art beautiful to behold, flowing through the emerald green of the meadows and the deep luscious green of the bush, a mirror for the lordly villas and charming cottages which stud thy banks. But most rapidly dost thou rush forward to thy metamorphosis! Most quickly dost thou expand into a broad, grey, elderly man of business. He who saw thee at Richmond will not know thee again at Westminster; and the travelling stranger who only beheld thee between the bridges of the metropolis has not the faintest idea of thy beauties at Richmond. The grey business atmosphere of London has cast its gloom upon thee, as well as on the stones, the houses, and the human beings that inhabit them.

    But, whatever the Thames may lose in romance, it gains in the grandeur and importance of its appearance. Its breadth increases with every step. Navigable to the length of 180 English miles, with a tidal rise to the extent of seventy miles, the Thames takes the largest merchantmen to the immediate vicinity of London-bridge; and as the tide is going out it takes them back, without the help of oars, sails, or steam-tugs. Nature has made the Thames the grandest of all trading rivers; it gave it a larger share of the ocean tides than it ever bestowed on any other river in Europe.

    At the Land's End the tides from the Atlantic are divided into two distinct streams. One rushes up the Channel, and round the North Foreland into the mouth of the Thames; the other beats against the western coasts of England and Scotland, and, taking a southerly direction down the eastern coast, this tide too enters the basin of the Thames.

Hence the tides in the Thames are formed of two different ocean-tides; they are equal by day and by night, and so powerful is the rush of the tide from the North Foreland to the metropolis, that it flows at the rate of five miles an hour.

But here is the boat smoking away right at our feet. There is a rush of persons from the shore, and a rush of persons to the shore. We pay two-pence, scramble down a variety of steps and stairs, and jump on board just as they are casting off. There is no whistling or ringing of a bell, no noise whatever. We are already steaming it up to the far west.

The bank on our left offers no interesting points on which the eye might dwell with pleasure. Manufactories, breweries and gas-works dispute every inch of ground with the ugliest store-houses imaginable. The sight strikes one as that of a large city in ruins. But on our right we see St. Paul's rising from an ocean of roofs. The sun, still visible on the horizon, shines on the roof of the cathedral, and shows the gigantic cupola in the most charming light. St. Paul's ought to be seen from the river by those who would fully understand its grandeur.

We pass through the arches of Blackfriars-bridge and proceed in a line with Fleet-street; before us the stream is spanned by a number of bridges, so that it seems as if their pillars crossed one another, and as if the nearest bridge bore the next following on its arched back. So strange and astonishing is this sight that we are tempted to mistake it for a Fata Morgana and expect to see it dissolve into thin air.

Seven enormous bridges have been built across the river at very short intervals, and unite the more animated parts of the Borough and Lambeth with London proper. Among these bridges is an iron suspension bridge with a bold double arch; another bridge is composed of iron and stone; and the rest are simply built of massive stones. It is true that only three of these seven bridges are freely open to the public, and that the four others exact a toll. But, for how many years past, have the Germans talked of a stone bridge across the Rhine at Cologne, and another stone bridge across the Danube at Vienna! And as yet neither Cologne nor Vienna have mustered the funds for such undertakings! And in London there are seven bridges within a river-length of a few miles. A little higher up, moreover, is Battersea-bridge, and lower down the river there is the Tunnel, and already have they commenced making a new bridge at Chelsea. The English have a right to pride themselves on the grandeur of the British spirit of enterprise. But the German who comes into this country and beholds its marvels, makes comparisons which sorely vex and trouble his spirit.

We pass the Temple, the Chinese Junk, Somerset-house, the new Houses of Parliament, and Westminster Abbey, but we cannot stop to describe them, for we purpose to reserve them for a special visit on another occasion. Besides our attention is engaged by the general aspect of the river and its banks. Darkness has set in. Steamers with red and green eyes of fire rush past us; little boats cross in all directions under the very bows of the steamers; fishing-boats with dark brown sails go with the tide in solemn silence; the lights on the bridges and in the streets are reflected in the water. This is the hour at which matter of fact London dons her poetical night-dress.

We pass Lambeth Palace and its ruin-like watch-tower. The boat stops at Vauxhall-bridge. We get off, and walk through some of the streets of Lambeth; we pass under a railway-bridge, and stand in front of Vauxhall.

"The season is over! every body is gone out of town," etc., write the correspondents of provincial and continental newspapers—"every body"—that is to say, every body with the exception of two millions of men, who make rather a considerable noise in the northern, southern, and eastern towns of London. But of course they are "nobodies"; they are merely merchants, tradesmen, manufacturers, clerks, agents, public functionaries, judges, physicians, barristers, teachers, journalists, publishers, printers, musicians, actors, clergymen, labourers, beggars, thieves, foreigners, and other members of the "vile rabble." Every body else left the metropolis immediately after the Parliament was prorogued by the Queen, and the Royal Italian Opera was prorogued by Signora Grisi. The West-end is now a city of the dead. The deserted streets and the shuttered windows proclaim that all who are not exactly "nobodies," are shooting in Scotland or gaping on the Rhine; that they suffer from the blues in Italy, or that the trout suffer from them in Sweden. But Vauxhall is still open, partly because the weather is so uncommonly mild for the season; partly because there are a good many foreigners in London; but chiefly because Vauxhall has come to be vulgar—and very vulgar too—a haunt of milliners and democrats, "by birth and education."

Vauxhall was born in the Regency, in one of the wicked nights of dissolute Prince George. A wealthy speculator was its father; a prince was its godfather, and all the fashion and beauty of England stood round its cradle. In those days Vauxhall was very exclusive and expensive. At present, it is open to all ranks and classes, and half a guinea will frank a fourth-rate milliner and sweetheart through the whole evening.

A Londoner wants a great deal for his money, or he wants little—take it which way you please. The programme of Vauxhall is an immense carte for the eye and the ear: music, singing, horsemanship, illuminations, dancing, rope-dancing, acting, comic songs, hermits, gipsies, and fireworks, on the most "stunning" scale. It is easier to read the Kölner Zeitung than the play-bill of Vauxhall.

With respect to the quantity of sights, it is most difficult to satisfy an English public. They have "a capacious swallow" for sights, and require them in large masses as they do the meat which graces their tables. As to quality, that is a minor consideration; and to give the English public its due, it is the most grateful of all publics.

The entrance to Vauxhall is dismally dark and prison-like. Dr. Keif objects to the place.

"It's a trap," says he; "the real road to ruin! I am sure the Chevalier Bunsen and that fellow Buol-Schauenstein lie in ambush in some of those dark holes; they will pounce upon me, and seize me, and take me back to Germany, where they have no brown stout, and where I must needs get famous, or die with ennui. Lasciate ogni speranza, voi che entrate!"

Just at that moment a German refugee goes by. He bids us good evening, and is lost in the darkness.

"Ah!" says the Doctor, "that boy has been sentenced to be shot in the Grand Duchy of Baden. I believe they shot him in effigy. He's an imp of fame, and if he dares go in why should'nt I dare it. Let us go in!"

The dismal aspect of the entrance is the result of artistic speculation; it is a piece of theatrical claptrap. For all of a sudden we emerge from the darkness of the passage into a dazzling sea of light, which almost blinds one. All the arbours, avenues, grottos and galleries of the gardens are covered with lamps; the trees are lighted to the very tops; each leaf has its coloured lady-bird of a gas-light. Where the deuce did those people ever get those lamps! And how did they ever get them lighted! It must be confessed that the manager has done his duty. If you can show him a single leaf without its lamp, he will surely jump into the Thames or hang himself on the branch which was thus shamefully neglected.

Dr. Keif, who is disposed to find fault with everything, and who just now protested that the entrance to Vauxhall was a trap expressly constructed for the apprehension of political refugees, asserts that the illumination is enough to spoil the temper of any one.

"Look at those English madcaps!" says he. "In other parts of the town I walk for hours before I find a human being smoking a cigar, and offering an opportunity to light my own weed; and here I stand as the donkey in the midst of three hundred thousand bundles of hay. Which of these lamps shall I select for the lighting of my cigar?"

"This way, sir! Look down there where the Queen is burning in gas," says an Englishman, with a cigar in his mouth, who has overheard the Doctor's lament. And he added—"Light your weed at the flames of Victoria, and implore Her Gracious Majesty that she may be pleased to abolish the duty on tobacco."

From that moment is Dr. Keif lost to the rest of our party. An Englishman, who, spurning all old-established customs and traditions, dares to address a stranger, and to address him too on a subject which has nothing whatever in common with the state of the weather—such an Englishman is a rara avis, and nothing could induce Dr. Keif to forego his acquaintance. Already has he engaged him in conversation, utterly oblivious of the friends who came with him, and of all the world besides. We must try to get on without the Doctor.

The gardens are crowded; dense masses are congregated around a sort of open temple, which at Vauxhall stands in lieu of a music-room. The first part of the performance is just over; and a lady, whose voice is rather the worse for wear, and who defies the cool of the evening with bare shoulders and arms, is in the act of being encored. She is delighted, and so are the audience. Many years ago this spot witnessed the performances of Grisi, Rubini, Lablache, and other first-class musical celebrities.

The crowd promenade these gardens in all directions. In the background is a gloomy avenue of trees, where loving couples walk, and where the night-air is tinged with the hue of romance. Even the bubbling of a fountain may be heard in the distance. We go in search of the sound; but, alas, we witness nothing save the triumph of the insane activity of the illuminator. A tiny rivulet forces its way through the grass; it is not deep enough to drown a herring, yet it is wide enough and babbling enough to impart an idyllic character to the scene. But how has this interesting little water-course fared under the hands of the illuminator? The wretch has studded its banks with rows of long arrow-headed gas-lights. Not satisfied with lighting up the trees, and walls, and dining-saloons, he must needs meddle with this lilliputian piece of water also. That is English taste, which delights in quantities: no Frenchman would ever have done such a thing!

Following the rivulet, we reach the bank of a gas-lit pond, with a gigantic Neptune and eight white sea-horses. To the left of the god opens another gloomy avenue, which leads us straightway to Fate, to the hermit, and the temple of Pythia, who, in the guise of a gipsy, reclining on straw under a straw-roofed shed, with a stable lanthorn at her side, is in the habit of reading the most brilliant Future on the palm of your hand, for the ridiculously low price of sixpence only. This is specially English; no house without its fortifications—no open-air amusements without gipsies. The prophetess of Vauxhall is by no means a person of repulsive appearance. You admire in her a comely brown daughter of Israel, with black hair and dark eyes; it is very agreeable to listen to her expounding your fate. She is good-tempered and agreeable, and has a Californian prophecy for all comers. She predicts faithful wives, length of days, a grave in a free soil to every one, even to the German.

The dwelling of the sage hermit is much less primitive, nor are believers permitted to enter it. They must stand on the threshold, from whence they may admire a weird and awful scenery—mountains, precipices and valleys, and the genius loci, a large cat with fiery eyes, all charmingly worked in canvas and pasteboard, with a strict and satisfactory regard for the laws of perspective. The old man, with his beard so white and his staff so strong, comes up from the mysterious depth of a pasteboard ravine; he asks a few questions and disappears again, and in a few minutes the believer receives his or her Future, carefully copied out on cream-coloured paper, and in verses, too, with his or her name as an anagram. Of course these papers are all ready written and prepared by the dozen, and as one lady of our party had the name of Hedwig—by no means a common name in England—she had to wait a good long while before she was favoured with a sight of her fate. This, of course, strengthened her belief in the hermit and the fidelity of her husband.

We, the Pilgrims of Vauxhall, leave the hermit's cell. Our eyes have become accustomed to the twilight, and as we proceed we behold, in the background, the tower and battlements of a large and fantastically-built tower. Can this be Westminster Abbey, or is it a mere optical delusion? Let us see.

Hark! a gun is fired in the shrubbery. The promenaders, who are familiar with the place, turn round, and all rush in one direction, sweeping us along with them. Before we can collect ourselves, we have been pushed forward to a panoramic stage, on which Nelson, in plaster, is in the act of expiring, while Wellington, in pasteboard, rides over the battle-field of Waterloo. These two figures are the worst of their kind; still the public cheer the two national heroes. No house without its fortifications—no open-air amusements without gipsies—and no play without the old Admiral and the old General.

Wellington has scarcely triumphed over Napoleon, and silenced the French batteries, when the cannonade recommences in the shrubbery: one—two guns! it is the signal for the arena. Unless you purchase a seat in the boxes or the galleries, you have no chance of seeing the exhibition in the circus, for the pit, which is gratis, is crowded to suffocation. Englishmen care more for live horses than they do for pasteboard chargers, fraught though they be with national reminiscences.

The productions of horsemanship at Vauxhall are exactly on a par with similar exhibitions on the other side of the Channel. Britons are more at home on horseback, or on board a ship, than on the strings of the fiddle, or on the ivory keys of the pianoforte. And thus, then, do the men and women dance on unsaddled horses, play with balls and knives, and jump through paper and over boards; half a dozen of old and young clowns distort their joints; a lady dances on a rope, à la marionette; and Miss A., who was idolised at Berlin, and whom seven officers of the Horse Guards presented with a bracelet, on which their seven heroic faces were displayed, condescends to produce her precious bracelet and her precious person in this third-rate circus; and an American Gusikow makes music on wood, straw, and leather; and the horses are neighing, and the whips smacking, and the sand is being thrown up, and the boarding trembles with the tramp of the horses, and there is no end of cheering; and Miss A. re-appears and curtsies, with the seven gentlemen of the Horse Guards on her arm; and another gun is fired, and the public, leaving the circus, rush madly into the gardens. To the fireworks! they are the most brilliant exhibition of the evening. The gardens are bathed in a bluish light, and the many thousand lamps look all pale and ominous. The gigantic and fantastic city, which before loomed through the twilight of the distant future, burns now in Bengal fire. It is Moscow! it is the Kremlin, and they are burning it! Sounds of music, voices of lamentation, issue from the flames, guns are firing, rockets shoot up and burst with an awful noise, the walls give way—they fall, and from the general destruction issues a young girl, with very thin clothing and very little of it, who makes her escape over a rope at a dizzy height. The exhibition is more awful than agreeable; but the public cheer this, as they do any other neck-or-nothing feat. If the girl were to carry a baby on her perilous way, the cheering would be still greater.

It is past midnight. The wind is cold, and fresh guests are crowding in to join the ball, which is kept up to the break of day. But we have not the least inclination to watch the ungraceful movements of English men who dance with English women, or of English women who dance with English men. We hail a cab and hasten home.

At the door we fall in with the Doctor, whom we had lost in the early part of the evening. He is greatly excited, for he has walked the whole way from Vauxhall to Guildford-street. In the parlour we find Sir John and his most faithful wife seated at the round table, with the tea-things before them, waiting tea for us. As we enter, Sir John puts down the Times, in which he has been gloating over a "damaging letter" against the Chancellor of the Exchequer; and the lady of the house welcomes us with a friendly nod and a look of anxious inquiry. That look means, "Have you caught a cold, you or any of you? Or is it a sore throat or a cough! Surely you cannot have been out all night without some slight illness which will justify me in opening my medicine chest?" And she looks at the things to see if they are all in good order, and then the tea is poured out with the utmost precision. A cup of tea is delicious after that long ride from Vauxhall, and there is much comfort and snugness in an English parlour.

The cup, which "cheers but not inebriates," loosens Dr. Keif's tongue. "The tea is very refreshing, Madam," is a remark which the Doctor makes twice every day, in fine and foul weather; and, in making this remark, he always holds out his empty cup that it may be filled again.

"But, most loyal Sir John," continues the Doctor, refreshed by the tea, "it's a mighty difficult task to get through an English evening's pleasure in a single night. To think of all the things I have seen this evening, and for half-a-crown too. Why one-half of them would suffice to entertain the inhabitants of a German capital for a period of six calendar months."

"That is what I always say," interposed Bella, the daughter of the house, with a look of triumph, "London is the cheapest town in the whole world."

"So it is," says Dr. Keif, "awfully cheap. I had some cold beef at Vauxhall, some cheese, and a cruet of wine, and I paid only nine shillings—on my honor nothing but nine shillings. The bread was not included. The waiter gave me a piece after I had asked him long enough. But I had scarcely put it on my plate, and I was lost in its contemplation, when it was carried off by a sparrow. Now that will give you an idea how very large it must have been."

"But what could induce you to drink wine or ask for bread at Vauxhall!" said Bella. "And where have you been all the evening? What did you do with your friend?"

"O I had a delightful conversation with him, and let me tell you he is a clever fellow. Still he is not free from English prejudice, though a great deal of it has been rubbed off on his travels. Of Germany he saw only the south, having been compelled, as he told me, to return to England to look after some property which a whimsical old uncle had left him, under conditions which make residence in this country a matter of necessity. It's a pity! There is a great deal of good in him, and I have no doubt he would be a great genius, if he could but pass a couple of winters at Berlin."

"Indeed! What was his English prejudice?" asked Sir John with great disgust.

"It is not easy to answer that question. National prejudice is like a pig-tail—you can't see it in front. Another cup of tea, if you please, it's only my fourth. And it's scandalous how they teach history in your schools. This new friend of mine is a well-bred man, but he had never heard of Blücher. We looked at the Duke of Wellington riding over the field of Waterloo; and I said: 'Couldn't you find a place for our Blücher?' 'Blutsher,' said he, 'who is Blutsher?' He knew nothing whatever of Blücher and the

Prussian army; and when I told him, that but for the Prussians Wellington would have been made minced-meat of at Waterloo, he actually laughed in my face. Now tell me, most respectable Sir John, how do they teach history in your schools? The French, I know, cook history, and make matters pleasant for 'the young idea.' "

Sir John was silent. The article he had read in the Times had made him magnanimous; and our friend Keif remained uncontradicted.

"I told my companion," continued the Doctor, after a pause, "that the dancing was a disgraceful exhibition; he said, so it was. He had seen the dancing abroad. If he had never been out of England, I am sure, he would have been delighted with the performance of his countrywomen; and, as most Englishmen do in such a case, he would have shrugged his shoulders and set me down as a fool for the unfavourable opinion I pronounced. But he had left part of his prejudice on the other side of the channel, and he himself pointed out to me how ridiculous those people looked, and how the couples clung to one another like woolsacks which cannot stand alone, and how they pushed one another, and marked the time by kicking one another's toes."

"Don't believe," said he, "that there is better dancing in the saloons of our aristocracy. We know nothing of the noble art, and for that very reason do we practise it with so much devotion. Such like unnatural leanings are common with all nations. They are most zealous in what they least understand. The Russians build a fleet, the Austrian affect finances, the Germans make revolutions, the French will have a Republic, and the English dance."

"But surely, Doctor," said Bella, "neither you nor your new friend can deny that better dancing is going on in London than in any other town. This very season we had Taglioni, Rosati, and Feraris, all on the same stage!"

"The old argument," said the Doctor. "Because you have got money, and because you can afford to pay for a good ballet, you pretend that the most graceful dancers are hatched in England. You subsidised the German armies against Napoleon; and now you believe that your red-coats alone vanquished the French. Port and sherry are your English wines; and because you succeed, at an enormous expense, to rear hothouse peaches, grapes, and apples, you will have it that England produces better fruit than any other country. But it's all nonsense. It's money and money, and again money; and with that money you buy up the world, and—— After all, old England for ever! Then another cup of tea for me?"

"Did you see that gas-lit rivulet at Vauxhall?" asked I, for I like to hear the Doctor find fault with England. He does it in such a good-natured, amiable manner, and with a spice of roguishness which is all the more interesting, since in Germany Dr. Keif is generally disliked for his Anglomania. "What," asked I, "do you say to the romantic style of decoration which prevails in England?"

"Of course I saw that rivulet, and had a splendid adventure on its banks."

Dr. Keif is literally overwhelmed with adventures. He cannot go to the next street without a remarkable incident of some sort or other.

"I had lost my companion," said Dr. Keif, leaning back in his chair; "I had lost him in the crowd. I saw a dark avenue in the distance, and I longed for rest. You know, Sir John, we Germans cannot for any length of time go on without peace and tranquillity, although the Times will have it that we are the most restless and disturbance-loving nation in Europe. Well, under the trees, near the rivulet, I espied a loving couple—they walk up and down, and stand still—of course they are happy to be alone and unobserved. But anxious to understand the character of the English, I resolved to overhear their conversation. I passed them several times, but they were silent. Right, thought I, affection makes them mute! Their souls stand entranced on the giddy pinnacle of passion! But they could not be silent all night, especially since it was so dark they could not speak with their eyes. I laid myself in ambush; they approached; my heart beat quick with thrilling anticipation; they were talking—but can you fancy what they were talking about?—Of Morrison's pills, and the mode and manner of their effect in bilious complaints! Of course there was no resisting this; I jumped out of the thicket, leaped across the rivulet, and came home at once."

We all laughed at the Doctor's adventure, and Sir John, too, laughed. Dr. Keif had met with half a dozen adventures on his way home. For instance, he had fallen in with a sailor who told him long stories about Spain. He (not the sailor) had found a drunken woman in a gutter and dragged her out; and Bella declared that that woman must have been Irish. And two vestals had taken hold of his arms, and he had a deal of trouble before he could induce them to leave him alone. In short, there was no end of the Doctor's adventures.

CHAP. V.

The Police.

THE LONDON POLICE.—JOURNEY FROM PARIS TO LONDON.—THE POLITICS OF THE FORCE.—ITS MODE OF ACTION ILLUSTRATED.—DIFFERENCE BETWEEN THE POLICE IN ENGLAND AND ON THE CONTINENT.—DETECTIVES.—ROOKERIES.—THE POLICEMAN AS A CITIZEN.

IN a town such as London is at the present day, where thousands of honest men follow their daily avocations at the side and mixed up with thousands of dishonest men, the Government has but one alternative with respect to the police regulations. It must either resign the idea of organising a surveillance by means of the police, or that surveillance must be carried on according to a highly practical principle.

With the police and other political institutions, it is exactly the same as with our clothes. They would seem to grow with us; but the fact is, as we grow in height and breadth we take care that our coats have greater length and width.

In the same manner, is the police allowed to grow in proportion to the growth of a town; and none but thieves or fools in politics can object to the process, provided always that the police is for the protection and not for the torment of the peaceful citizen.

Scarcely a hundred years ago, no one could dare to walk from Kensington to the city after nightfall. At Hyde Park corner, not far from the place where the Crystal Palace stood, there was a bell which was rung at seven and at nine o'clock; those who had to go to the city assembled at the call and proceeded in a body, by which means they were comparatively safe from the attacks of highwaymen.

Small bodies of men were frequently stopped by the robbers; it happened now and then that the passengers were attacked and sorely molested by a roistering band of wild young fellows, who were fresh from the public-house.

But all this romance came to an end when George II. was stopped and plundered one fine night on his return from hunting. The very next morning a troop of armed horsemen was established to watch over the security of the public streets, and though these were not the rudiments of the London Police (there were already some watchmen and river-guards), yet we consider them as a fraction of the police-embryo which has since grown up to such respectable dimensions.

The Guild of the London police (on the continent they are but too frequently confounded with the older constables) was founded and trained by Sir Robert Peel; they are consequently a product of our own times; and that this product is not a luxury, and that it is more useful than many other creations of our own times is clearly shewn by the great London journals, which daily acknowledge the institution in their police reports. But this institution is very little understood in Germany, and even strangers, who pass a short time in England, are not likely to understand it.

Let us watch the steps of a German, for instance, on his journey across the channel. He leaves Cologne with an express train, and reaches Calais at midnight. Bewildered with sleep, he leaves the carriage; the first object which strikes his view is a large hand painted on the wall. He follows the outstretched index of that hand and finds his way, not to the refreshment rooms whither he wants to go, but to the "Bureau de Police," where he never thought of going. He is cruelly disappointed; but he is an honest man, and not even a political refugee, and he has, therefore, no reason to avoid communication with the French police. They ask for his passport, and if the traveller can produce some document of the kind they are content. The passport may, indeed, be a forgery: its possessor may have stolen it. Napoleon the Great found his way back from Elba without a passport; and Louis Philippe, also without a passport, found his way out of France; but no matter! the French require the production of passports, doubtlessly for some hidden good, for the alcun' bene of Dante.

On his arrival in Folkestone or Dover, many an honest German has, from mere force of habit, put his hand in his pocket and produced his passport ready for inspection. Of course the methodical foreigner was laughed at for his pains. The Emperor of France and his satellites may possibly have an interest in knowing all particulars about those who turn their backs upon them; but constitutional England is not in the habit of asking her guests whence they come, why they come, and whither they go. After a short interview with the Custom-house officers—and these, too, though functionaries, are dressed like all other honest men—the stranger is free of the country; and if his trade be an honest one, he is not interfered with; indeed, he is almost neglected by the public authorities. On his arrival in London, he takes apartments in an hotel, or in a boarding-house, or he takes furnished lodgings, or a house, or a street; no matter, the police do not interfere with him; and to all appearance they pay no attention whatever to his proceedings.

This apparently unguarded liberty is the secret of the real grandeur of the Preventive Service. But that this is possible, is partly owing to the good-will of a liberal government, and partly to the peculiarities of English life and manners. This is a point which we shall, on a future occasion, treat at greater length.

The circumstance that a stranger may walk to and fro between the Isle of Wight and the Orkneys without being questioned, protocolled, and stopped, has caused many a foreigner to doubt the safety of life in England generally. A certain Berlin professor, I am told, got quite angry on the subject. "A man," said he, "goes about in England exactly as if he were disowned by society and removed from within the pale of it. The very dogs of Berlin are more respected! At least they have their numbers taken and are entered into the dog-book (Hundebuch), at the police-office, while in England none but thieves can feel comfortable, since thieves alone are in a manner noticed by the police."

In treating of the functions of the London Police, we ought at once to say, that the police in England is essentially a force of safety, whose functions are limited to the prevention of crime and the apprehension of criminals. All its departments of river, street, and railway police are instituted for the same purpose. There has not hitherto been a political department in Scotland-yard. The police, as at present organised, deals only with the vulgar sins of larceny, robbery, murder, and forgery; it superintends the cleaning of the streets; it prevents the interruption of the street traffic, and it takes care of drunkards and of children that have strayed from their homes. But political opinions, however atrocious, if they have not ripened into criminal action, are altogether without the sphere of the English police.

The policemen, as the free citizens of a free country, are perfectly at liberty to have political opinions of their own; they need not modify or conceal their sentiments when they take the blue coat and the glazed hat. They are required to catch thieves as cats do mice. Some of them are ultra-royalists; others are ultra-radicals. Generally speaking, they are not by any means conservatives. The majority of them belong to the poorer and less educated classes; they take their political opinions from the radical weekly papers. They club together as sailors, cabmen, and labourers do, and take in their weekly paper, which they read and discuss all the week through. They quote their paper whenever they talk politics, and this they do frequently, for your London policeman is as zealous a dabbler in politics as any ale-house keeper in Suabia.

Adam Smith founds his financial theories on the division of labour. The division of labour is also the firm basis of the efficiency of the English police. Since they have not to perform all the functions which weigh on the shoulders of their helmeted and sabred brethren on the continent; since they need not devote their attention to political conversations and movements in the case of individuals or of communities; since they need not keep watch over and give an account of the movements and opinions of strangers and natives; and since they have nothing whatever to do with the secrets of families, the leaders of the daily papers, nor with the unsealing and sealing of post-office letters, they are at liberty to devote all their energy and ingenuity to the efficient discharge of those functions which are properly assigned to them.

It is not a fable, nor a piece of English braggadocio, when it is said, that the thieves are more thoroughly hunted down in this immense city of London, than they are in the smaller German capitals. A foreigner who studies the police-reports of the great London journals, will find there ample matter for admiration and reflection. We quote but one example, to show the manner in which the various parts of the police machine work together. The anecdote may possibly contain some useful hints for the guardians of constitutional towns.

A printer sends one of his men to the stationer to take in stock for the printing-office. It was late on a Saturday afternoon, and the manufacturer promised to have the paper in readiness early on Monday. The man to whom the message was entrusted and who brought back the answer, was, for some reason or other, dismissed in the course of that very evening.

On the Monday, another messenger was sent for the paper. He came back without it. The paper had been taken away a few hours before he arrived at the stationer's. No paper, however, had come to the printing-office. The greatest embarrassment prevailed. A couple of hours pass, and yet the paper does not arrive. Suspicion is at length directed to the man who had been discharged. Inquiries are made at the stationer's, and the description of the person who came for the paper corresponds with the appearance of the suspected person. Upon this, the printer proceeds to the police-station to report the case. What with waiting and sending about, the better part of the day was gone.

Mr. M—then makes his appearance in the inspector's office, and proceeds to state his case. But scarcely has he given his name, when the inspector puts a stop to all further explanations. "You've been robbed, Mr. M—. We know all about it. The thief is in custody, and the goods must by this time have been delivered at your office. One ream of

No. 2 and two reams of No. 5 are wanting; but we know where to find them. They shall be sent to you to-morrow. Good bye, sir."

Mr. M——, who, like every Englishman of the same stamp, is in no wise to be surprised with any thing that may happen between heaven and earth, is nevertheless inclined to think this a strange case—a very strange one indeed. He pushes his hat back, strikes his umbrella on the floor, and turning on his heel, he makes the best of his way home, where he finds "all right," while all the "devils" are frantic with joy that the paper has been recovered, and that Toby, who carried matters with such a high hand, is, after all, nothing but a thief, and sure to be transported.

The state of the case was simply this:—

The man, assisted by a friend, had called for the paper, put it into a cart, and gone off. The worthy pair sold a small quantity in a place where they had, on similar occasions, "done a stroke of business;" and, after this little matter had been settled to their entire satisfaction, they drove off to a public-house at the distance of about five miles from the scene of their crime. This public-house was situated in a very quiet street. The cart and horse were left at the door while the two associates, snugly ensconced in the parlour, commenced enjoying the fruits of their robbery.

They had not been there very long before the policeman on duty became struck with the cart and its freight of paper. He had been on that beat for many months past, and knew that no printer, bookbinder, or stationer, lived in the street. The horse and cart were strangers to him; so were the two men whom he saw in the parlour as he passed the window. The whole thing had an ugly appearance. He meets with one of the detectives, and communicates his suspicions to that sagacious individual. The two fellows, utterly unconscious of the watch set on their movements, produce more money than they could have earned in the course of a week. They are taken into custody and brought up before the magistrate. They cannot account for the possession of the paper, and make a confession in full. The policeman, however, must have been very sure of his case when he arrested them; for in doing so he incurred a heavy responsibility. If his suspicions had turned out to be unfounded, he would have been mulcted in a heavy fine, and possibly he might have lost his place.

Now let us change the venue, and suppose this affair had happened in Paris, Vienna, or Berlin. Not only have the police of those capitals duties of greater importance than the mere catching of a couple of wretched thieves, but it is also altogether absurd to believe that a policeman or "Sicherheitsmann" should pay any attention to the fact of a cart and horse being stationed at the door of a pot-house. Such a thing is utterly impossible. The policemen of Vienna and Berlin change their beats as soldiers do their posts. Possibly they know the street and the outsides of the houses; they may also have some slight knowledge of the most disreputable dens, and of those who habitually frequent them, and, in some instances, they are au courant of the politics of a few honest tradesmen or citizens, who are too harmless to make a secret of such matters.

The London policeman, on the other hand, knows every nook and corner, every house, man, woman, and child on his beat. He knows their occupations, habits, and circumstances. This knowledge he derives from his constantly being employed in the same quarter and the same street, and to—and surely a mind on duty bent may take great liberties with the conventional moralities—that platonic and friendly intercourse which he carries on with the female servants of the establishments which it is his vocation to protect. An English maid-servant is a pleasant girl to chat with, when half shrouded by the mystic fog of the evening and with her smart little cap coquettishly placed on her head, she issues from the sallyport of the kitchen, and advances stealthily to the row of palisades which protect the house. And the handsome policeman, too, with his blue coat and clean white gloves, is held in high regard and esteem by the cooks and housemaids of England. His position on his beat is analogous to that of the porter of a very large house; it is a point of honour with him, that nothing shall escape his observation.

This police-honour constitutes the essential difference between the English and the continental police. Even the most liberal of politicians—not a visionary—must admit, that it is impossible for a large town, and still more impossible for a large state, to exist without a well-organised protective force. It matters little whether the force which insures the citizens against theft and robbery, as other associations insure them against fire and hail-storms, is kept up and directed by the State, or whether it is maintained by private associations—as has been proposed. It is enough to refer to the fact, that philanthropists of the Cobden and Burritt stamp have found reasons as plenty as blackberries against standing armies of soldiers; but that they have never yet dared to deny the necessity of a standing army of policemen.

The police, whenever and wherever it answers its original purpose, is a most beneficent institution. Its unpopularity in all the states of the Continent is chargeable, not to the principles of the institution, but to their perversion. It is the perversion of the protective force into an instrument of oppression and aggression, which the German hates at home; but he has no aversion to the police as such. Even the maddest of the democratic refugees confess to great love and admiration for the police in England. A man may like his cigar without entertaining a preposterous passion for nicotine.

The policeman, no matter whether in a uniform or in plain clothes, is a soldier of peace—a sentinel on a neutral post, and as such he is as much entitled to respect as the soldier who takes the field against a foreign invader. This is the case in England. The policeman is always ready to give his assistance and friendly advice; the citizen is never brought into an embarrassing and disagreeable contact with the police; and the natural consequence of this state of things is, that the most friendly feelings exist between the policeman and the honest part of the population. Whenever the police have to interfere and want assistance, the inhabitants are ready to support them, for they know that the police never act without good reasons.

The detective police, who act in secret, do not stand on such an intimate footing with the public as the preventive part of the force; but whenever they are in want of immediate assistance for the arrest of an offender, the detective has but to proclaim his functions, and no man, not even the greatest man in the land, would refuse to lend him assistance. In Germany and in France no one will associate with an agent of the secret police, a mouchard, or by whatever other name those persons may be called. Every one has an instinctive aversion to coming in contact with this species of animal, for they are traitorous, venomous, and blood-thirsty. And that such is the case, is another proof of the vast superiority of the British institutions over those of the Continent.

That London has not in the fulness of time come to be a vast den of thieves and murderers, is mainly owing to the action of the detective force. Here, where the worst men of the European and American continents congregate, the functions of a detective are not only laborious but also dangerous. The semi-romantic ferocity of an Italian bandit is sheer good nature, if compared to the savage hardness and villany of a London burglar. The bandit plies his lawless trade in the merry green wood and mossy dell; he confesses to his priest, and receives absolution for any peccadilloes in the way of stabbing he may have happened to commit; on moonlit nights his head rests on the knees of the girl that loves him, in spite of his cruel trade. He is not altogether lost to the gentler feelings of humanity, and, in a great measure, he wants the confounding hardening consciousness of having, by his actions, disgraced himself and his species. But the London robber, like a venomous reptile, has his home in dark holes under ground, in hidden back rooms of dirty houses, and on the gloomy banks of the Thames. He breaks into the houses as a wolf into a sheepfold, and kills those who resist him, and, in many instances, even those who offer no resistance. There is no sun or forest-green for him, no priest gives him absolution, the female that herds with him is, in most cases, even more ferocious and abandoned than himself; and if he be father to a child, he casts it at an early age into the muddy whirlpool of the town, there to beg, to steal, and to perish.

The streets which skirt the banks of the Thames are most horrible. There the policeman does not saunter along on his beat with that easy and comfortable air which distinguishes him in the western parts of the town. Indeed, in many instances, they walk by twos and twos, with dirks under their coats, and rattles to call in the aid of their comrades.

Many policemen and detectives, who, hunting on the track of some crime, have ventured into these dens of infamy have disappeared, and no trace has been left of them. They fell as victims to the vengeance of some desperate criminal whom, perhaps, on a former occasion, they had brought to justice. And it would almost appear to be part of the haute politique of the London robbers, that some policeman must be killed from time to time as a warning to his comrades. The guild of assassins, too, have their theory of terrorism.

Another remarkable fact is, that the London policemen, though their duty brings them constantly in contact with the very scum of the earth, contract none of their habits of rudeness, which appear to be an essential portion of the stock-in-trade of the continental police. One should say, that the "force" in England is recruited from a most meritorious class of society, one in which patience, gentleness, and politeness are hereditary.

Look there! A fine strapping fellow crossing the street with a child in his arms! The girl is trembling as an aspen-leaf, for she was just on the point of getting under a wheel. That fine fellow has taken her up; and now you see he crosses again and fetches the little girl's mother, who stands bewildered with the danger, and whom he conducts in safety to the opposite pavement. Who and what is that man? His dress is decent and citizen-like, and yet peculiar; it differs from the dress of ordinary men; coat and trowsers of blue cloth; a number and a letter embroidered on his collar; a striped band and buckle on his arm; a hat with oilskin top, and white gloves—rather a rarity in the dirty atmosphere of London. That man is a policeman, a well got up and improved edition of our own German Polizeidiener, those scarecrows with sticks, sabres, and other military accoutrements, standing at the street-corners of German capitals, and spoiling the temper of honest men as well as of thieves.

It is, however, a mistake to believe, as some persons on the continent actually do, that the London police are altogether unarmed and at the mercy of every drunkard. Not only have they, in many instances and quarters, a dirk hidden under their great-coats, but they have also, at all times, a short club-like staff in their pockets. This staff is produced on solemn occasions, for instance, on the occasion of public processions, when every policeman holds his staff in his hand. The staves have of

THE LOST CHILD.

late years been manufactured of gutta percha, and made from this material they are lighter and more durable than wooden staves. In the name of all that is smashing, what a rich full sound does not such a gutta percha club produce when in quick succession it comes down on a human shoulder. That sound is frequently heard by those who, on Saturday or Monday night, perambulate the poorer or more dissolute quarters of the town, when all respect for the constable's staff has been drowned in a deluge of gin. Matters, on such occasions, proceed frequently to the extremity of a duel. The policeman, like any civilian, fights for his skin; he gets a drubbing and returns it with interest. But since his weapon does not give him so manifest an advantage as a sword would, the public consider the fracas a fair fight. And after all, the combatants must appear before a magistrate; in the police-court they are on equal terms, and witnesses are heard on either side. There is no prejudice in favour of the policeman.

But stop! Look at the crowd in the street. Two policemen are busy with a poor ragged creature of a woman, whom they carry to a doorway. An accident perhaps? Nothing of the kind. The woman is drunk, and fell down in the road. The policemen are taking her to the station, where she may sleep till she is sober. But it was a strange spectacle to see those two men in smart blue coats and white gloves rescuing the ragged woman from the mire of the street.

Let us go on. At Temple Bar there is a Gordian knot of vehicles of every description. Three drays are jammed into one another. One of the horses has slipped and fallen. The traffic is stopped for a few minutes; and this is a matter of importance at Temple Bar. Just look down Fleet-street—the stoppage extends to Ludgate-hill. But half a dozen policemen appear as if by enchantment. One of them ranges the vehicles that proceed to the city in a line on the left side of the road. A second lends a hand in unravelling the knot of horses. A third takes his position in the next street, and stops the carriages and cabs which, if allowed to proceed, would but contribute their quota to the confusion. Two policemen are busy with the horse which lies kicking in the road. They unhook chains and unbuckle straps; get the horse on its legs, and assist the driver in putting him to rights again. They have got dirty all over; and they must, moreover, submit to hear from Mr. Evans, who stands on the pavement dignified, with a broad-brimmed Quaker hat, that they are awkward fellows, and know nothing whatever about the treatment of horses. In another minute, the whole street-traffic is in full force. The crowd vanishes as quickly and silently as it came. The two policemen betake themselves to the next shop, where the apprentice is called upon to brush their clothes.

The continental policeman is the torment of the stranger. The London policeman is the stranger's friend. If you are in search of an acquaintance and only know the street where he lives, apply to the policeman on duty in that street, and he will show you the house, or at least assist you in your search. If you lose your way, turn to the first policeman you meet; he will take charge of you and direct you. If you would ride in an omnibus without being familiar with the goings and comings of those four-wheeled planets, speak to a policeman, and he will keep you by his side until the "bus" you want comes within hailing distance. If you should happen to have an amicable dispute with a cabman—and what stranger can escape that infliction?—you may confidently appeal to the arbitration of a policeman. If, in the course of your peregrinations, you come to a steam-boat wharf or a railway-station, or a theatre or some other public institution, and if you are at a loss how to proceed, pray pour your sorrows into the sympathetic ear of the policeman. He will direct yourself and baggage; in a theatre, he will assist you in the purchase of a ticket, or at least tell you where to apply and how to proceed. The London policeman is almost always kind and serviceable.

At night, indeed, as some say, he is rather more rough-spoken than in the day-time; and when you meet and address him in some solitary street, he is reserved and treats you with something akin to suspicion. Whether or not this remark applies to the force generally, we will not undertake to decide. But it is quite natural that they should not be altogether at their ease in

THE CAB DISPUTE.

solitary or disreputable quarters, and that their temper gets soured thereby. A glass of brandy now and then may also contribute to produce the above effect. But the English climate is damp; the fog makes its home in the folds of the constable's great-coat; the rain runs from the oilskin cape which stands the policeman in the stead of an umbrella; the wind is cold and bleak; and we leave the policeman on his beat with "the stranger's thanks and the stranger's gratitude."

CHAP. VI.

Newgate and its Neighbourhood.

RIVERS UNDER GROUND.—DIVISION OF LABOUR.—EXECUTIONS.—THE PEOPLE'S FESTIVALS.—PREDILECTION FOR CRIMINAL CASES.—STATISTICS OF NEWGATE.—PATERNOSTER-ROW.—SMITHFIELD.—SELF-GOVERNMENT, ITS BRIGHT AND DARK SIDES.

LONDON has, besides the Thames, a great many smaller rivers, the majority of which have, for many years past, been appropriated by the commissioners of sewers and the antiquarians. In the olden days, men went out of the way of rivers. In our own time, the rivers are compelled to give way to mankind. They are vaulted and bridged over, and houses have been built on the vaults, or streets have been constructed over them; and the grocer in the corner shop yonder has not the least suspicion of his house standing on a river, and he never thinks of the lamentable condition of his goods, in case the vault were to give way under him.

One of these rivers was the Fleet river. After it the street is named even at the present day. The site of its bed is still marked by a broad valley street with considerable hills, all built over, on either side. The hills are so steep that heavy drays and omnibuses cannot come down without locking.

This operation, though insignificant, furnishes an opportune illustration of the extent to which the principle of the division of labour has been carried in London.

Just look at that lumbering omnibus, thundering along at a sharp trot. It has reached the brink when the horses are stopped for a second; and at that very moment a fellow makes a rush at the omnibus, bending his body almost under the wheels, and moving forward with the vehicle, which still proceeds, he unhooks the drag, and puts it to one of the hind-wheels. This done, he calls out "All right!" The horses, sagacious creatures, understand the meaning of that sentence as well as the driver; they fall again into a sharp trot down the hill. At the bottom there is another human creature making a neck-or-nothing rush at the wheels, taking the drag off and hooking it on again. "All right!" The horses stamp the pavement to the flying-about of sparks, the driver makes a noise which is half a whistle and half a hiss, and the omnibus rushes up the opposite bank of the quondam Fleet river.

"Time is money!" is an English proverb, and one whose validity is so strongly acknowledged, that in many instances money is freely spent in order to effect a saving of time. Those two men save the omnibuses exactly one minute in each tour down Holborn Hill, for one minute each of them would lose if they were to stop to put on the drag. But one minute's loss to the many thousands who daily pass this way represents a considerable capital of time. If the two men are remunerated at the rate of only one halfpenny per omnibus, their incomes will be found to be larger than the salary of many a public functionary in Germany.

This, then, is another specimen of industry and economy peculiar to London streets. But, let us say, that it is possible only by means of the enormous traffic which crowds the streets of London.

We have, meanwhile, walked down the steep descent. We have crossed the hidden stream, walked up the hill on the other side, and now we stand on a broad plateau, where two large streets cross at right angles. This conformation produces a considerable amount of space between the pavements—a sort of irregular open square, and one which from time to time presents a melancholy spectacle.

One of the street corners is taken up by the old Newgate Prison; and the open place in front serves for the execution of felons who have been sentenced to death at the

Sessions, and who, in the first instance, had been committed to Newgate. It is a shocking custom, though it springs from the humane desire to shorten the agony which the criminal must suffer on his road from the prison to the scaffold.

"Our popular festivals!" said a lady, who had been emancipated by a lengthened residence on the Continent. "You wish to know where the people's merry-makings are held? Go to Newgate on a hanging day, or to Horsemonger Lane, or to any other open space in front of a prison; there you will find shouting, and joking, and junketting, from early dawn until the hangman has made his appearance and performed his office. The windows are let out, stands are erected, eating and drinking booths surround the scaffold; there is an enormous consumption of beer and brandy. They come on foot, on horseback, and in carriages, from a distance of many miles, to see a spectacle which is a disgrace to humanity; and foremost are the women—my countrywomen—not only the females of low degree, but also ladies, 'by birth and education.' It is a shame; but, nevertheless, it is true. And our newspapers are afterwards compelled to chronicle the last death-struggles of the wretched criminal!"

There is no exaggeration in this. A criminal process, robbery and murder, a case of poisoning—these suffice to keep the families of England in breathless suspense for weeks at a time. The daily and weekly papers cannot find space enough for all the details of the inquest, the proceedings of the police, the trial, and the execution; and woe to the paper that dared to curtail these interesting reports! it would at once lose its supporters. Rather let such a paper take no notice of an insurrection in Germany; but neglect a criminal trial, a scene on the scaffold—never!

Let us look into that room. The father of the family, his wife, the old grandmother, with her hands demurely folded, and the daughters and little children, are all crowded round the table. The father reads the newspaper; the family listens to him. The tea is getting cold, the fire is going out, the curtains are still undrawn and the blinds are up; the very passengers in the street—"O tell it not in Gath!"—can see what is going on in the parlour; but the listeners pay no attention to all this, for the paper contains a full report of the trial of Mrs. Manning, or some other popular she-assassin. Did she do the deed? Is she innocent? Did she make a confession? And what about her husband? And how was it done, and when, and where?

It is truly marvellous! These good, gentle people, who would not willingly hurt or pain any living creature, actually warm to the scenes of horror reported in that paper. It is altogether incomprehensible, how and to what extent this passion for the horrible has seized hold of the hearts of English men and women. They languish after strong emotions; they yearn for something which will make their flesh creep. A similar phenomenon may occasionally be observed on the other side of the Channel; but there it forms the exception, while here it is the rule. And on the Continent, too, we find this horror-mongering only in the provinces, where people, wearied with the monotony of their long winter evenings, hunger and thirst after anything like a public scandal or spectacle; but we do not find this sort of thing in large towns, where people have a variety of objects and incidents to attract their attention. But the English on the Continent make long journeys to be present at an execution. Their passion accompanies them even across the Channel. Surely we do not envy their feelings in this respect!

Newgate is a gloomy-looking, ancient building. It is the beau ideal of prison architecture, with hardly any windows, with here and there an empty niche, or some dilapidated carvings; all besides is gloomy, stony, and cold.

Newgate has gone down in the world. In its early years it was devoted to the reception of persons of high rank; it has since submitted to the principle of legal equality, and rich and poor, high and low, pass through its gates to freedom or the scaffold. About three thousand prisoners are annually confined within its walls. The prison can accommodate five hundred at a time, and this number is usually found there immediately before the commencement of the sessions. But the sessions of the Central Criminal Court once over, Newgate is almost empty, for some of its inmates have been discharged from custody, while the majority of them have received their sentence and taken their departure for sundry houses of detention and correction. The prisoners in Newgate are at liberty to communicate with one another; they are not compelled to work.

We pass through Newgate-street and turn to the right into Paternoster-row, a narrow street, from times immemorial the manufactory of learning, where the publishing trade is carried on in dingy houses, and where it runs its anarchical career without the benefit of a censor.

"From times immemorial!" That is a hasty expression. There was a time when Paternoster-row harboured the grocery trade of the city, while the upper stories were taken by Marchandes des Modes and visited by all the beauty and elegance of old London. But gaiety had to give way to religion, and the Marchandes des Modes, taking flight to more modern streets, were followed by the rosary-girls under Henry VIII. Luther's translation of the Bible was publicly burnt in this neighbourhood, and soon after warrants were issued against those who had burnt it. So varied have been the applications of this narrow dusky lane, in which, to this day, the traveller may read an inscription on a stone tablet, announcing that Paternoster-row is the highest point of ancient London.

In our own days this street is to London what Leipzig is to Germany. The departments of the publishing trade are, however, kept more strictly separate. The publishers of Bibles, who send forth the Scriptures in volumes of all sizes, from the smallest to the largest, and who do business in all the civilised and barbarous languages on the face of the earth, exclude all vain and secular literature, such as tales, novels, plays, poems, and works of history. While the publishers of such like works in their turn, generally fight shy of tourists and travellers whose works belong to departments of another class of publishing firms. Juvenile books form a very important department of the publishing trade; and this department, like the infant schools, is entirely devoted to the instruction and amusement of the rising generation. So strenuous are the exertions of those publishers to entice the babes and infants of England into the treacherous corners of the A, B, C, and of the higher sciences, that their solicitude in this respect appears almost touching to those who fancy that all this trouble is taken and all this ingenuity expended, purely and simply for the interest of philanthropy, and of good sound education.

We ought not to stop too long in Paternoster-row. Our presence is required elsewhere. But still we must for the benefit of German mothers and publishers, state the fact, that of late years the publishers of Paternoster-row have hit upon the plan of printing the rudiments of all human science on strong white canvass. English children, in the dawn of their young existence, are as essentially practical as German children. They have an instinctive aversion to all printed matter. The A, B, C, is to them the first fruit from the tree of knowledge, the key to the mysteries and woes of life. Therefore do the children of England detest the primers; they soil them, tear them, roll the leaves, in short treat them with as much scorn and contumely, as though the annihilation of a single copy would lead to the extinction of the whole species.

The practical spirit of English speculation meets this prejudice on its own ground. The primers, or A, B, C, books as they are called in Germany, are printed on canvass, and each leaf is moreover hemmed, for all the world like a respectable domestic pocket-handkerchief. For children are sagacious, and but for the hemming the rudiments of science would, under their hands, be converted into lint. As it is, even the most obstreperous of little boys is powerless in the presence of such a canvass book. And, supposing, he be uncommonly obstinate, and that after great exertion he succeeds in running his finger through one of the leaves; even then he is foiled, for his mother darns it as she would an old stocking; and the monster book appears again as clean and immaculate as a diplomatic note. And the upshot of the affair is that the poor little boy must go without the usual allowance of Sunday pudding.

London is the greatest market for books in the world. Not only does it supply England, but also Asia, Africa, Australia, and those island colonies of the great ocean, in which English daring and English enterprise have established the Anglo-Saxon race, and with it the English language. About 15,000 persons are employed in the printing, binding, and in the sale of books. Their mechanical aids and machinery have been brought to an astounding height of perfection, and an edition of a thousand copies in octavo requires but ten or twelve hours for the binding. But when you consider those bony, broad-shouldered, firm-looking Englishmen, you understand at once that such men could not live on literature alone. Paternoster-row, the centre of the book-trade, carries on its existence in modest retirement amidst a conglomeration of large and small streets, but to the north there is the provoking, broad, impertinent extent of old Smithfield, the notorious cattle-market of London, the greatest cattle-market in the world, the dirtiest of all the dirty spots which disgrace the fair face of the capital of England.

This immense open place, or more properly speaking, this immense conglomeration of a great many small open places, with its broad open street market, is covered all over with wooden compartments and pens, such as are usual on the sheep-farms of the continent.

Each of these pens is large enough to accommodate a moderate sized statue; each of them must, on Mondays and Fridays, accommodate an ox and a certain number of cattle, pigs, or sheep. If by a miracle all these wretched animals were converted into marble or bronze, surely after thousands of years, the nations of the earth would journey to Smithfield to study the character of this our time in that vast field of monuments.

But since such a poetical transformation has not taken place, the appearance of that quarter of the town is curious but not agreeable. Surrounded by dirty streets, lanes, courts, and alleys, the haunts of poverty and crime, Smithfield is infested not only with fierce and savage cattle, but also with the still fiercer and more savage tribes of drivers and butchers. On market-days the passengers are in danger of being run over, trampled down, or tossed up by the drivers or "beasts"; at night, rapine and murder prowl in the lanes and alleys in the vicinity; and the police have more trouble with this part of the town than with the whole of Brompton, Kensington, and Bayswater. The crowding of cattle in the centre of the town is an inexhaustible source of accidents. Men are run down, women are tossed, children are trampled to death. But these men, women, and children, belong to the lower classes. Persons of rank or wealth do not generally come to Smithfield early in the morning, if, indeed, they ever come there at all. The child is buried on the following Sunday, when its parents are free from work; the man is taken to the apothecary's shop close by, where the needful is done to his wound; the woman applies to some female quack for a plaister, and if she is in good luck she gets another plaister in the shape of a glass of gin from the owner of the cattle. The press takes notice of the accidents, people read the paragraph and are shocked; and the whole affair is forgotten even before the next market day.

For years Smithfield has been denounced by the press and in Parliament. The Tories came in and went out; so did the Whigs. But neither of the two great political parties could be induced to set their faces against the nuisance. The autonomy of the city, moreover, deprecated anything like government intervention, for Smithfield is a rich source of revenue; the market dues, the public-house rents, and the traffic generally, represent a heavy sum. In the last year only, the Lords and Commons of England have pronounced the doom of Smithfield. The cattle market is to be abolished. But when? That is the question—for its protectors are sure to come forward with claims of indemnity, and other means of temporisation; and the choice of a fitting locality, on the outskirts of the town, will most likely take some years. For we ought not to forget that in England everything moves slowly, with the exception of machinery and steam.

Smithfield and its history are instances of the many dark sides of self-government. For self-government has its dark sides, commendable though it be as the basis of free institutions. It is to the self-government of every community, of every parish, and of every association, that England is indebted for her justly envied industrial, political, and commercial, greatness. But self-government is the cause of many great and useful undertakings proceeding but slowly; and, in many instances, succumbing to the assaults of hostile and vested interests. The government, indeed, attempts to combat all nuisances by mooting and fostering a variety of agitations. In Germany, it wants but a line from a minister to eradicate small evils, or introduce signal improvements. In England the same matters must be dealt with in a tender and cautious manner; it takes a score or so of years of agitation, until parliament yielding to public opinion, passes its vote for the improvement, or against the nuisance. Great joy there would be in London, if Smithfield, as Sodom of old, were consumed with fire; but the whole of London would have been urged to resistance if the government had presumed, on its own responsibility, to interfere with Smithfield. Is this prejudice or political wisdom? On which side is the greater good—and on which the worse evil? The present happy condition of England has long since answered that question in favour of self-government. If ever there was a question on this point, it has long been settled in the hearts and minds of all continental nations. If they were to act according to their inclinations, I am positive they would "go and do so likewise."

CHAP. VII.

Street Life.—The Post-office.

LONDON AND THE OCEAN.—HOW YOU MAY ATTACK THE REPUTATION OF EITHER.—THE METROPOLIS "EN NEGLIGEE."—THE POST-OFFICE.—THE MODERN LETTER-WRITER.—MONEY ORDERS.—PENNY STAMPS, THEIR USE AND ABUSE.—JOHN BULL AND THE CHANCELLOR OF THE EXCHEQUER.—HOW MR. BULL IMPOSES UPON THAT RESPECTABLE FUNCTIONARY.—WHAT IS A NEWSPAPER?—THE GREAT HALL OF THE POST-OFFICE AT SIX P.M.

"DID you ever see the ocean?" said I, some time ago, to a Vienna friend, as by accident we met in Cheapside. Not far from the spot where from Newgate-street the passenger turns off to the Bank, there is a crossing of some of the most crowded streets. We stood on the pavement waiting for an opportunity, or a stoppage among the vehicles, to make a rush to the opposite side. "Well," said I; "Did you ever see the ocean."

"In a way!" replied my countryman, producing a cigar; and in a moment a match-seller was by his side offering his inflammable wares. "In a manner," repeated my countryman, as he lit his cigar. "Of course I did not come by land from St. Stephen's Place, in Old Vienna. I did cross a piece of salt water as far as I can remember; but that confounded sea-sickness got hold of my stomach, and made me blind to the marvels of the ocean. And—between you and me—I can't say I was much taken with what I could see. I've read a deal about the sea, the wide and open sea, and all its glories. But it's all humbug, that's what it is; or, if you would rather, it's poetic fancy. Water, after all, is but water. And, as for the sharks, you can't see them. There wasn't even such a thing as a storm. The lakes of Ischl are quite as green as the channel, and, perhaps, a shade greener. And last year, when I was on the Platten Lake, on my honour! I could not see to the opposite shore. Water, after all, is but water; and a few miles, more or less, make no difference that I can see. Besides, you only see a certain portion. That's my opinion."

O good and honest Viennese! I stopped my countryman, who was just taking a desperate leap into the road. No doubt he would have reached the opposite pavement in safety; but I stopped him, for I wanted a pretence for shaking hands with him. A Berlin man would never have deigned to declare that the ocean is a humbug, even though he had never gone beyond the bridges of the Spree or Havel river at Potsdam. Humbug has no existence for the real Berlin man, who has been reared in the superlative; and, besides, how can a Berliner, with all his contempt for authority, ever plead guilty to considering an important phenomenon, one which has been established ever since the days of the Great Elector, with less poesy than Henry Heine, and with less interest than Alexander von Humboldt. A Berliner would certainly have held forth on the "absolute idea," or the "relative nothing," or the "subjective view of space"; even though he never felt anything like the meaning of those hard words, and even if, within his secret heart, he had thought exactly as the Viennese did before he got sea-sick. There are things which a Berliner would rather die than say in public.

But my readers are justly entitled to ask what could induce me to connect Cheapside with the first impressions which a continental mind receives of the sea. The association of the two ideas is not by any means so absurd as some very sapient Germans may think. The first impressions which London makes on the stranger's mind are similar to his first impressions of the sea. They are not overwhelming. "A town, after all, is but a town"; that's what my Viennese friend would say. "There are as fine houses in Vienna and Berlin, and some are more imposing. Brewer's drays, foot-passengers, cabs, omnibuses, and policemen—we have them all. A town, after all, is but a town. A few miles, more or less, make no difference. You can't see it all at once!"

But it so happens that my countryman, thanks to the intervention of some friends, gets a place as engineer, at Folkestone. Between ourselves, he is a refugee. But what German, of our days, is not a refugee, or likely to be one? The Germans are a nation of traitors just now; therefore.... No offence.

Now my friend passes his leisure hours on the beach. He looks at the dark waters, and the white spray, and the waves which break at his feet. The waves come and go, and keep coming and going, alternately large and small, fast and slow. At one point they shoot smoothly over the yellow sand; at another they break with a thundering motion against the granite blocks of the jetty, flinging their spray over the stone parapet; and where my friend sits, the waves wash up shells and curious stones, and strange sea-weed, and withered leaves of sub-marine plants and shrubs; and the tides turn, coming in and going out, and the demon of the storm disports itself in the blackened air. The sea is dark and seething, and the fishing-boats, with their masts creaking and groaning, hasten up and down the waves to the gates of the harbour. The water in the very harbour is moved to and fro in violent convulsions; monster clouds, fringed with lightish gray, are driven landwards day and night; are confounded in the gloomy tints of the ocean, which groans and raves, and engulphs its victims, until its strength is exhausted. And the moon breaks through the clouds, preaching peace with her pallid demure face; and the waves are converted by the sentimental saint, and again rush playfully along the sand of the beach; and again they wash shells, and curious stones, and strange sea-weed, and withered leaves of sub-marine plants to the feet of my friend, who, overwhelmed with the spectacle, sits staring on vacancy.

"But you are quite wet, and really you look very sentimental, my dear countryman from the banks of the Danube! Water, after all, is but water! I hope you haven't seen a shark? The lakes of Ischl are just as green as the sea, and perhaps a shade greener. A few miles more or less—what does it matter? A good deal of humbug about it, isn't there?"

"You are malicious, Doctor. On my honour, very malicious! One ought to look at that pool for a year or so to know what it really is."

Pilgrim from the land of passports, when you come to this giant town, in which traffic built its living dykes in every street then do not, in the name of all that is candid, be ashamed to appear, for three days at least, as an unfeeling callous creature. Make no secret of your thoughts. A few houses more or less cannot make an impression on a truly reasonable man!

But, friend stranger, stand for an hour or two leaning against the iron gate of Bow-church, Cheapside, or take up your position on the steps of the Royal Exchange. Do, as my countryman does in lonely Folkstone; let the waves of the great city rush past you, now murmuringly, now thunderingly, now fast, now slow, as crowds press on crowds, and vehicles on vehicles, as the streams of traffic break against every street corner and spread through the arterial system of the lanes and allies; as the knot of men, horses and vehicles get entangled almost at every point where the large streets join and cross, to move and heave and spin round, and get disentangled again, and again entangled. After such a review only can you realise the idea of the greatness of London.

It is said of a stranger, who came to London for the first time and took his quarters in one of the most crowded city streets, that he remained standing at the door the whole of the first day of his London existence, because he waited "until the crowd had gone." A man who would do that ought to rise and go to bed with the owl. It is this which, after a prolonged stay in London so moves our admiration, that there is no stop, no rest, no pause in the street-life throughout the busy day.

In smaller towns, too, there are occasions or times when the streets are crowded in the extreme. The trottoirs of the Paris Boulevards are charming places, and on a beautiful evening they are as crowded, and even more so than the pavements of the London streets. But the crowding on the Paris trottoirs lasts a few hours only during the usual promenade time. London street-life is not bound to time; it is not confined within the narrow limits of a few hours. Indeed there is not a single hour in the four and twenty, in which any one of the principal London streets can be said to be deserted. For when the denizens of the far West retire to rest, at that very hour does the street-life dawn in the business-quarters of the East.

Early in the morning, before the chimneys of the houses and factories, of the railway-engines and steamers, have had time to fill the air with smoke, London presents a peculiar spectacle. It looks clean. The houses have a pleasing appearance; the morning sun gilds the muddy pool of the Thames; the arches and pillars of the bridges look lighter and less awkward than in the daytime, and the public in the street, too, are very different from the passengers that crowd them at a later hour.

Slowly, and with a hollow, rumbling sound do the sweeping-machines travel down the street in files of twos and threes to take off every particle of dust and offal. The market-gardener's carts and waggons come next; they proceed at a brisk trot to arrive in time for the early purchasers. After them, the coal-waggons and brewer's drays, which only at certain hours are permitted to unload in the principal streets of the city. At the same time, the light, two-wheeled carts of the butchers, fishmongers, and hotel-keepers, rattle along at a slapping pace; for their owners—sharp men of business—would be the first in the market to choose the best and purchase at a low price. Here and there a trap is opened in the pavement, and dirty men ascend from the regions below; they are workmen, to whose care is committed the city under-ground, which they build, repair, and keep in good order. Damaged gas and water-pipes, too, are being repaired, and the workmen make all possible haste to replace the paving-stones and leave the road in a passable condition. For the sun mounts in the sky and their time is up. They return to their lairs and go to sleep just as the rest of the town awakens to the labours of the day.

Besides these, there are a great many other classes whose avocations compel them to take to the street by break of day. At a very early hour they appear singly or in small knots, with long, white clay pipes in their mouths; as the day advances, they come in troops, marching to their work in docks and warehouses. Ill-tempered looking, sleepy-faced barmen take down the shutters of the gin-shops; cabs, loaded with portmanteaus and band-boxes, hasten to deposit their occupants at the various railway-stations; horsemen gallop along, eager for an early country-ride; from minute to minute there is an increase of life and activity. At length the shops, the windows and doors of houses are opened; omnibuses come in from the suburbs and land their living freight in the heart of the city; the pavements are crowded with busy people, and the road is literally crowded with vehicles of every description. It is day and the hour is 10 A.M.

Long before this, hundreds of high chimney-towers have belched forth their volumes of thick black smoke, and that smoke obscures the horizon with long streaks of black smut, and mixes and becomes more dense as the millions of chimneys on the house-tops contribute their quota, until a dusky atmosphere is formed, which intercepts the rays of the sun. Such is London by day. That is the enormous city with her deep grey robe of smoke and fog, which she spins afresh every morning, and silently unravels during the hours of the night, that she may, as Penelope of old, keep idlers and courtiers away from her gates.

We are still at the point where Newgate-street opens into Cheapside. It would almost seem as if the whirlpool of human beings that turn about in that locality, had made us giddy, for our thoughts took their wayward flight across the Thames, up to the clouds, and through the gully-holes into the recesses of the city under-ground. We ought now to proceed on terra firma, and with this laudable resolution, we turn to the left, and stop in the front of the post-office at St. Martin's-le-Grand.

The existing arrangements of the English post-office, and the penny-postage, which, in 1840, was introduced by Rowland Hill, have proved so excellent in their results, that the majority of continental states have been induced to approximate their institutions to Mr. Hill's principle. Men of business and post-office clerks are not yet satisfied; they desire a system of cheap international postage, and it is devoutly to be hoped that those pious wishes will, in the end, be gratified. But the majority of the continental governments hesitate before they commit themselves to an experiment, which, in the most favourable case, only promises a future increase of revenue, while in every case it is certain to entail losses on the present. In England, however, the experiment has been made, and the system works well and pays. And the arrangements of the post-office have been brought to a degree of perfection unknown even to the wildest dreams of the boldest political economist of the last century.

With the general penny postage for England, Scotland, Ireland, and the Channel Islands—with a regular, rapid, and frequent transmission of the mails from and to the provinces, there is, moreover, an admirable system adopted for the distribution of letters throughout the metropolis. London is divided into two postal districts: one of them embraces the area within three miles from the Chief Office at St. Martin's-le-Grand; the second district includes those parts of the town which lie beyond the three miles' circle.

The postage, of course, is the same for either district; but the difference lies in the number of deliveries. In the inner circle there are not less than ten deliveries a day.

The construction of the houses contributes much to the efficiency of the system. The postman's functions are here much easier than those of his continental colleagues. He is not required to go up and down stairs, he gives his double knock; and as the majority of letters are inland letters, and as such prepaid, no time is lost with paying and giving change. The frequency of letter-boxes at the house doors tends still more to simplify the proceeding.

At the time of the great Exhibition, these letter-boxes gave occasion to many a comical mistake. Many of our continental friends entrusted their correspondence to the keeping of private boxes, under the erroneous presumption that every door-slit, with "Letters" over it, stood in some mysterious connexion with the General Post Office. But when once properly understood, the practical advantages of these private letter-boxes were so apparent, that they moved all our stranger friends to the most joyful admiration. The system however is nothing without the prepayment of letters, without the English style of buildings, and the English domestic arrangements, according to which each family inhabits its own house. The South-German system of crowding many families into one large house, and dividing even flats into separate lodgings, places insuperable difficulties in the way of any such arrangement, even if the Germans, generally, could be induced to prepay their letters. And the Paris fashion of delivering all the letters at the porter's lodge, is disagreeable, even for those who are not engaged in treasonable correspondence, and who have no reason or desire to elude the vigilance of the police.

After all, Rowland Hill's system of cheap postage is one of the best practical jokes that was ever perpetrated by an Englishman. This famous cheapness is nothing but a snare for the unwary, for the especial gratification of the Postmaster-General and the Chancellor of the Exchequer. In no other country is there so much money expended on postage as in England. A letter is only one penny; and what is a penny? The infinitesimal fraction of that power which men call capital; that miraculous Nothing, out of which the world was made, and out of which some very odd fellows managed to make large fortunes, as it may be well and truly read in juvenile books of first-class morality. But what Londoner can condescend to establish his household arrangements on the decimal system, or on the theory of miracles? Consequently, he writes short letters to his cousins and nieces across the way, and to all his near and dear relations in Yorkshire and the Shetland Islands. It is an incontestable fact, that Englishmen spend more money in postage than the citizens of any other country.

And how cleverly does the Post Office contrive to facilitate the means of correspondence! Besides the large branch offices, there are above five hundred receiving-houses in London, all of them established in small shops, to induce you to enter; and that you may have no trouble in finding them, a small board with a hand, and the words "Post Office," is affixed to the nearest lamp-post, so that you need only look at the lamp-posts to find the place for the reception of your letters. How simple, and how practical!

But there is more behind! Many a man thinks it too great a tax upon his time and patience to put the penny stamp on the envelope; the Postmaster-General steps in and saves him the trouble. He manufactures envelopes with the Queen's head printed on them, and he sells them a penny a piece, so that you have the envelope gratis. They are gummed, too, and do not want sealing. You have nothing to do but to write your letter, put it into the envelope, and post it at the receiving-house over the way or round the corner. These are some of the sly tricks on which the Post Office thrives, so that, with its expenditure exceeding one million sterling, it manages to hand over a large sum of surplus receipts to the Chancellor of the Exchequer.

Nor ought it to be supposed, that, having attained so high a degree of perfection, the English postal administration reclines on its laurels. No! it strains every nerve to effect further improvements; and it has to deal with a public fully competent to understand its merits, and disposed to value them. The greatest praise of a public institution is to be found, not in the eulogies of the press, but in the readiness of the public to avail themselves of the advantages that institution offers, and the improvements and facilities it effects. And the English do this readily and joyfully, whenever their practical common sense becomes alive to the usefulness of an innovation.

In this respect, and in many others, the English Government is in a more favourable position than the continental governments. Its dealings are with a great and generous nation: great ideas find a great public in England. That is the reason why the continental estimates of men and affairs appear so small, compared to the one which the English are in the habit of applying. Particularly with respect to creating facilities to traffic, the Government may venture on almost any experiment. The public support every scheme of the kind, and the public support makes it pay. Take, for instance, the system of money-orders, which was introduced a few years back. Small sums under £5 are to be sent; and in spite of the enormous difficulties and expenses which the scheme had to encounter in its commencement, it is more firmly establishing from day to day; its popularity is on the increase, and above £8,000,000 was, in the year 1851, transmitted in this manner.

Let us now see how the Post Office deals with books, pamphlets, and newspapers. Political papers which publish "news," says the act for that purpose made and provided—"political journals," according to the continental mode of expression—pass from province to province free of postage, with only a small sum for transmission to the Colonies, that is to say, to the Cape and the Antipodes. The penny stamp, which each copy of a political journal is required to have, franks it throughout the whole of Great Britain and Ireland—not once, but several times. A letter stamp is blackened over at the Post Office, to prevent its being used again; but the newspaper stamp has nothing to fear from the postmaster's blacking apparatus. I read my copy of the Times in the morning, and am at liberty to send it to a friend, say to Greenwich. That friend sends the same copy to another friend, say at Glasgow, Edinburgh, or Dublin; and the same copy, after various peregrinations through country post offices, and out-of-the-way villages, finds its way back to London to the shop of a dealer in waste paper. No charge is made by the Post Office for these manifold transmissions; and thus it happens that friends conspire together to defraud the Post Office, and that information finds its way from one end of the kingdom to another without any advantage to the public purse.

I will quote an example of a trick which is still popular with many English families. Suppose a husband and father has reason to expect an addition to his family circle. His friends and relations are desirous to be informed of the event as soon as it shall have come off, but letters, however short, take time to write; and, after all, its a pity to pay so many pence for postage, and children, too, are very expensive creatures. The matter has been arranged beforehand. An old copy of the Times is sent, if the little stranger turns out a boy; if a girl, the father sends a copy of the Herald. The child is born, and the papers are posted. Letters of congratulation follow in due time. Her Majesty has gained another subject, but the Exchequer has lost a few pence. This method has not much political morality to recommend it; but it weighs very lightly on an Englishman's conscience, since the proceeding, after all, is not downright illegal.

"The Chancellor of the Exchequer and I"—says John Bull—"are on the best terms; he cheats me whenever he can; he makes me pay in every conceivable manner; he taxes my wine, my tea, the sunlight, my horse, my land, and my carriage; he is always at it, and he squeezes me as I would an orange. That's his right, and that's why he is Chancellor of the Exchequer. How else could he manage to pay the interest on the national debt, and the army and navy estimates, and all the sundries? We, the nation, are the state, and that's why we ought to pay. But in return, the right honourable gentleman must give us leave to cheat him whenever, as it will happen with the sharpest of financiers, his financial laws want a clause or two, and thus favour the operation. 'Horses above a certain size are taxed to such and such an extent,' says he. Very well! say I. But I move heaven and earth to produce horses under that size, and avoid paying the tax. Carriages with wheels above 21 inches in diameter are taxed. Very well. I get a small carriage made, one which suits the size of my pony. Newspaper advertisements pay a duty of eighteen-pence. Well and good. I advertise the birth of my child by means of an old copy of the Times. That's fair dealing, which none can find fault with. The Chancellor of the Exchequer and I know what we are about. We are a couple of sly ones. John Bull after all pays for everything; but he fights for his money to the best of his abilities. Of course!"

Thus reasons the Englishman, whom the Germans love to consider as an adorer of the law.

The difference between the English adoration and the German contempt of the law, may be found in the fact, that an Englishman takes a delight in outwitting the law, if it can be done in a loyal and honest manner. The German believes he is justified in ignoring the law, since it was imposed upon him without his consent. In other words: the subject of an absolute government does not think the laws—except the laws of nature and morality—to be binding, because such laws were imposed by superior force. The citizen of a free country respects every law, because it presupposes an agreement to which he has either indirectly or directly assented. But let us return to the Post-office.

Though the newspaper-stamp franks the journals throughout England, still it has not been thought advisable to extend the privilege to the postal district within three miles from St. Martin's-le-Grand. All journals posted within that circle must have an additional penny stamp. My copy of the Times goes free to Dublin; but if I address it to a friend in the next street, it pays the postage. But for this salutary regulation, all the news-vendors would post their papers, and the Post-office would want the means of conveyance and delivery for the loads of printed matter which, in such a case, would find their way into the chief office.

The advantages of the newspaper stamp are, however, large enough to induce its being solicited by papers, that are not by law compelled to take it. Punch, for instance, is not considered a political paper. To find out the reason why, is a task I leave to the principal Secretaries of State of her Britannic Majesty. The whole of England is agreed on the point that there is much more sound policy in the old fellow's humped back than can be found in the heads of the Privy Council; and many an agitator in search of an ally would prefer Toby to the Iron Duke.[C] Punch, then, consults his own convenience and takes or refuses the stamp according to circumstances. And as Punch does, so do many other papers, whom the law considers as unpolitical.

[C] The first part of this work left the press early in 1852, when the Duke of Wellington was still alive. It has not been thought convenient to alter this passage, and some others to meet the change of circumstances.—[Ed.]

We turn again to the General Post-office. It is a grand and majestic structure, with colossal columns in the pure Greek style; and with an air of classic antiquity, derived from the London atmosphere of fog and smoke. It is easy to raise antique structures in London, for the rain and the coals assist the architect. Hence those imposing tints! How happy would the Berliners be, if Messrs. Fox and Henderson, instead of constructing waterworks, could undertake to blacken the town, and give it an antique old-established, instead of its parvenu and stuck-up, appearance. They are sadly in want of London smoke and of some other English institutions which I cannot, for the sake of my own safety, venture to specify.

Those who are not awed by the architectural beauties of the London Post-office, should enter and take a stroll down those roomy high walls, where on either side there are numbers of office windows and little tablets. How small are, in the presence of those tablets, all the ideas which Continentals form of a large central Post-office. They are so many sign-posts, and direct you to all the quarters of the world; to the East and West Indies, to Australia, China, the Canary Islands, the Cape, Canada, etc. Every part of the globe has its own letter box; and the stranger who, about six o'clock P. M., enters these halls, or takes up his post of observation near the great City Branch Office, in Lombard-street, would almost deem that all the nations of the world were rushing in through the gates, and as if this were the last day for the reception and transmission of letters.

Breathless come the bankers' clerks, rushing in just before the closing hour; they open their parcels, and drop their letters into the various compartments. There are messengers groaning under the weight of heavy sacks, which they empty into a vast gulf in the flooring; they come from the offices of the great journals, and the papers themselves are sorted by the Post-office clerks. Here and there, among this crowd of business people, you are struck with the half comfortable, half nervous bearing of a citizen. Just now an old gentleman, with steel spectacles, hurries by, casting an anxious look at the clock, lest he be too late. Probably he wishes to post a paternal epistle to his son, who is on a fishing excursion in Switzerland, and the letter is important, for in it the son is adjured not by any means to discontinue wearing a flannel under-jacket. Or an old lady has to post a letter to her grand-daughter at school in the country, about the apple-pudding, for which the grand-daughter sent her the receipt; and what a capital pudding it was, and that the school must be a first-rate school—to be sure! And lo! just as the clock strikes, a fair-haired and chaste English woman, with a thick blue veil, makes her way to one of the compartments and drops a letter. Thank goodness, she is in time! Heaven knows how sorry the poor lad would have been if that letter had not reached him in due course. For an English lover, they say, is often in a hanging mood, especially in November, when the fogs are densest.

Now the wooden doors are closed; the hall is empty as if by magic, and the tall columns throw their lengthened shadows on the stone flooring.

This is the most arduous period of the day for the clerks within. All that heap of letters and newspapers which has accumulated in the course of the day is to be sorted, stamped, and packed in time for the various mail-trains. Clerks, servants, sorters, and messengers, hurry to and fro in the subterraneous passage between the two wings of the building. Clerks suspended by ropes, mount up to the ceiling and take down the parcels which, in the course of the day, were deposited on high shelves. And the large red carts come rattling in receive their load of bags, and rattle off to the various stations; the rooms are getting empty; the clerks have got through their work; the gas is put out, and silence and darkness reign supreme. Here and there only in some little room a clerk may be seen busy with accounts and long lists of places and figures. When he retires to rest, the work of the day has already commenced in the other offices. In this building, business is going on at all hours of the day and the night. The loss of a minute would be felt by thousands, at a distance of thousands of miles.

Hence does it happen that at no time is there a want of complaints about the Post-office clerks and post-masters, while the officials, in their turn, complain of the carelessness and negligence of the public. The public's grievances find their way into the Journals, in a "Letter to the Editor." The sorrows of the Post-office clerks obtain a less amount of publicity; but they may be observed on the walls of the great hall, where, daily, there is a list of misdirected letters, which have cost the post-men a deal of trouble. Directions such as—

"To Mr. Robinson,
"in
America."
Or,—
"To Miss Henrietta Hobson,
"Just by the Church,
"in London."

However rich (some may think), these are not by any means rare; and such small mistakes, I dare say, will happen in other countries besides England, wherever there are simple-minded people who put their trust in Providence and the royal Post-office. In Germany, where every man, woman, and child is registered by the police, the postman may, as a last resource, apply to that omniscient institution; but in England, where the chief commissioner of the police is so abandoned as to be actually ignorant of the whereabouts of honest and decent citizens, the Post-office is deprived even of this last resource. The case would be pitiable in the extreme, but for the comfortable reflection that in England the police do not interfere with the post. The convenience, on the one hand, is by far greater than the inconvenience on the other.

CHAP. VIII.

Sunlight—Moonlight—Gaslight.

THE SUN AND THE LONDONERS.—MYSTERIES OF THE FOG.—HARVEST MOONS.—GAS.—HOW THE CLIMATE WORKS.—FLANNELS.—ENGLISH DINNERS AND FRENCH THEATRICALS.—CURRENT PHRASES.

FASHIONABLE novelists, no matter whether their productions end with marriage or suicide, devote their first chapters to geographical and ethnographical accounts of the country or province in which they lay their plots. Scientific travellers devote the first pages of their heavy and immortal works to the respective telluria and astronomic peculiarities of the country they propose to describe. To my sincere regret, I have not, in my unsystematic wanderings through London, been able to follow so laudable an example; for it requires a long residence and a good deal of careful observation to understand the whims of the London celestial bodies—their goings and comings—and their influence on vegetable and animal life—on the strata of the atmosphere and of mankind.

Since Lot's wife was turned into a pillar of salt, and Lola Montes into a Countess of Landsfeld, there has not, as far as I know, been any female being so much abused as the London sun;[D] but the reasons of such abuse are diametrically opposed. The two first named ladies were found fault with because they saw too much of the world, while the London sun is justly charged with a want of curiosity. It turns its back upon the wealthiest city in Christendom; and, in the presence of the most splendid capital of Europe, it insists on remaining veiled in steam, fog, and smoke.

[D] The sun—die Sonne—is feminine in German.

The London sun, like unto German liberty, exists in the minds of the people, who have faith in either, and believe that either might be bright, dazzling, and glorious, were it not for the intervention of a dark, ugly fog, between the upper and nether regions. It happens, just now, that we have not seen the sun for the last three weeks. But for the aid of astronomy, which tells us that the sun is still in its old place, we might be tempted to believe that it had gone out of town for the long vacation; or that it had been adjourned by some continental constitutional government; or that it was being kept in a German capital, waiting for the birthday of the reigning prince, when it must come out in a blaze; for this, I understand, has been the sun's duty from time immemorial. A three weeks' absence of the sun would make a great stir in any other town. The Catholics would trace its cause to the infidelity of the age; the Protestants would demonstrate that the sun had been scared away by certain late acts of Papal aggression; and the Jews would lament and ask: "How is it possible the sun can shine when the Bank raises its rate of discount?" But the Londoners care as little for a month of chiaro-oscuro as the Laplanders do. They are used to it.

Twice in the course of the last week—for an essayist on astronomical matters ought to be conscientious—twice did the sun appear for a few minutes. It was late in the afternoon, and it looked out from the west, just above Regent's-park, where the largest menagerie in the world may be seen for one shilling, and, on Mondays, for sixpence. All the animals, from the hippopotamus down to the beaver, left their huts, where they were at vespers, and stared at the sun, and wished it good morning. It was a solemn moment! An impertinent monkey alone shaded his eyes with his hands, and asked the sun where it came from, and whether there was not some mistake somewhere? And the sun blushed and hid its face beneath a big cloud. The monkey laughed and jeered, and the tigers roared, and the turtle-doves said such conduct was shocking and altogether ungentlemanly. The owl alone was happy, and said it was; for it had been almost blind during the last five minutes; "and that," as he said, "was a thing it had not been used to in London."

But whatever ill-natured remarks we and others may make on the London sun, they apply only to the winter months. May and September shame us into silence. In those months, the sun in London is as lovely, genial, and—I must go the length of a trope—sunny as anywhere in Germany; with this difference only, that it is not so glowing—not so consistent. In the country, too, it comes out in full, broad, and traditional glory. Its favourite spots are in the South of England—Bristol, Bath, Hastings, and the Isle of Wight. In those favored regions, the mild breeze of summer blows even late in the year; the hedges and trees stand resplendent with the freshness of their foliage; the meadows are green, and lovely to behold; the butterflies hover over the blossoms of the honeysuckle; the cedar from Lebanon grows there and thrives, and myrtles and fuchsias, Hortensias and roses, and passion-flowers, surround the charming villas on the sea-shore. Village churches are covered with ivy up to the very roof; gigantic fern moves in the sea-breeze; the birds sing in the branches of the wild laurel tree; cattle and sheep graze on the downs; and grown-up persons and children bathe in the open sea, while the German rivers are sending down their first shoals of ice, and dense fogs welter in the streets of London.

Here is one of the vulgar errors and popular delusions of the Continent. People confound the climate of London with the climate of England; they talk of the isles of mist in the West of Europe. A very poetical idea that, but as untrue as poetical. Many parts of these islands are as clear and sunny as any of the inland countries of the Continent.

The winter-fogs of London are, indeed, awful. They surpass all imagining; he who never saw them, can form no idea of what they are. He who knows how powerfully they affect the minds and tempers of men, can understand the prevalence of that national disease—the spleen. In a fog, the air is hardly fit for breathing; it is grey-yellow, of a deep orange, and even black; at the same time, it is moist, thick, full of bad smells, and choking. The fog appears, now and then, slowly, like a melodramatic ghost, and sometimes it sweeps over the town as the simoom over the desert. At times, it is spread with equal density over the whole of that ocean of houses on other occasions, it meets with some invisible obstacle, and rolls itself into intensely dense masses, from which the passengers come forth in the manner of the student who came out of the cloud to astonish Dr. Faust. It is hardly necessary to mention, that the fog is worst in those parts of the town which are near the Thames.

When the sun has set in London (the curious in this respect, will do well to consult the Almanack), and when the weather is tolerably clear, the moon appears to govern the night. The moon is a more regular guest in London than the sun; and the example of these celestial bodies is followed by the great journals, the issue of the evening papers being much more regular than that of the morning papers. The London moon is, after all, not very different from the moon in Germany. It is quite as pale and romantic; it is the confidant of lovesick maidens and adventurous pickpockets.

Traveller from the Continent, enjoy the London moon with method and reason! If heaven favored you by sending you into the street on a beautiful, splendid, transparent, moonlit night, in which the shades of Ossian and Mignon sit by the rivers or under the limetrees, while all the poetry you smuggled from your native land awakes in your heart: traveller, if such good fortune is yours, why, then, the best thing you can do, is to go to the Italian opera, for the moonlit nights of this country are as treacherous as its politics. They seem all calm and peaceful; but they are rife with colds and ague. They are most beautiful, but also most dangerous. Every Englishman will tell you as much, and advise you to increase your stock of flannel in proportion to the beauty of the night.

Most regular and reliable is a third medium for the lighting-up of London—the gas. The sun and moon may be behind their time, but the gas is always at its post. And in winter, it happens sometimes that it does service all day long. Its only drawback is, that it cannot be had gratis, like the light from the sun, moon, and stars; but the same inconveniences attend the gas on the Continent, and after all, it is cheaper in England than anywhere else. The Germans are mere tyros in the consumption of gas. The stairs of every decent London house, have generally quite as much light as a German shop, and the London shops are more strongly lighted up than the German theatres. Butchers, and such-like tradesmen, especially in the smaller streets, burn the gas from one-inch tubes, that John Bull, in purchasing his piece of mutton or beef, may see each vein, each sinew, and each lump of fat. The smaller streets and the markets, are literally inundated with gaslight especially on Saturday evenings. No city on the Continent offers such a sight. In the apothecary's shops, the light is placed at the back of gigantic glass bottles, filled with coloured liquid, so that from a distance you see it in the most magnificent colour. The arrangement is convenient for those who are in search of such a shop, and it gives the long and broad streets of London a strange and picturesque appearance.

We have said so much of the climate, that it is high time to add a few words about its results. What then are the effects of the London winters, of the gloomy foggy days, the cold rainy nights, and of the changeable English weather? The Continent knows those results partly from hearsay. They manifest themselves in the character, in the ways, the dress, and the social arrangements of the English.

The British isles rear a strong healthy race of men and women, beyond any other country in Europe. The lower classes have muscles and sinews which enable them to rival their cattle in feats of strength. The women are stately and tall; the children full of rosy health. The middle classes live better, though on an average less luxuriously than the corresponding classes on the continent. Their food is strong and nourishing; it is at once converted into flesh and blood. The British farmers are specimens of human mammoths, however grievously they may complain of their distress since the abolition of the duty on corn. The nobility and gentry pass a considerable part of the year at their country seats. They hunt, fish, and shoot, to the manifest advantage of their health. The very children, mounted on shaggy ponies, take long rides; so do the women, who even now and then follow the hounds. They go out in yachts on the stormy channel and extend their excursions to the coasts of Italy and the West Indian islands. But in despite of this mode of life, which is conducive to health, they pay their tribute to the moist atmosphere of their island, and they all—men, women, and children—submit to pass their lives in flannel wrappers.

"We want," says Sir John, "to be independent of the changes of the weather; and we isolate our bodies by means of suitable articles of dress. We wear flannel, cottons, india-rubber, and gutta percha; we drink cognac, port, stout; we eat strong meats with strong spices. We never pretend that the climate is to suit us; we suit ourselves to the climate. The Continentals act on a different principle, and say they like the result. We like the result of our own principle, and that's the reason why we stick to it."

Flannels in summer and in winter, in Glasgow and in Jamaica; this is one of the ten commandments which few Englishmen care to transgress. But their conservative tendencies which cause them to cling to the habits in which they were reared, lead them into the absurdity of adhering to an English mode of life even when fate or trade have flung them to the furthermost corners of the earth. I understand that English drawing-rooms at Gibraltar are as carefully carpeted as the drawing-rooms of London and Edinburgh. The British drink their port and sherry under the torrid zone; their porter and stout follow them to the foot of the Himalaya. And they do all this, not because they cannot be comfortable without their old habits; but because they protest and devoutly believe, that in all the various climates the English mode of living is most conducive to health.

The proper cultivation of the body is a matter of great importance in England. A French labourer is happy with the most frugal dinner, if, in the evening, he can but afford to take a place and laugh or weep at a vaudeville theatre. The Englishman wants meat, good meat, and plenty of it. The lower classes care little or nothing for "the feast of the soul." John Bull laughs at the starvelings, the French frog-eaters. He has no idea that the French ouvrier is, after all, a more civilised creature than he is, exactly because to the Frenchman his Sunday dinner is not, as is the case with the lower classes of the English, the most important part of the Sunday.

These material tendencies are, of course, fostered by education and society. Originally they result from the climate. The frugality of the Paris ouvrier could not, for any length of time, resist the stomach-inspiriting effect of a fresh sea-breeze.

"A beautiful morning, Sir." "A splendid day, Sir." Such-like phrases are stereotyped formulas for the proper commencement of an acquaintanceship. The English are so accustomed to these meteorological remarks, and these remarks appear so important (because everybody and everything here depends upon the weather), that they rarely, if ever, neglect making them.

"Very pleasant weather, Sir;" or, "Very wet to-day," mutters the cabman as he shuts the door upon you. The same remarks greet you from the lips of the omnibus-driver as you take your seat at his side, or from those of the shopwoman, as a preliminary to that awful "Any other article, Sir?" And the words are always pronounced in that grave, monotonous, business tone which is peculiar to the English even in treating of the most important subjects. It may be sunshine or rain, the tone is always the same. And it has been surmised, that the English residents on the continent are such egregious bores and bears only because the greater constancy of the weather deprives them of those magic formulas, without which they cannot open their minds. How, indeed, is it possible to make the acquaintance of any one unless there is rain, storm, fog, and sunshine at least twice in the course of the four and twenty hours?

CHAP. IX.

The City Capitol.

THE LORD MAYOR'S RETREAT.—THE NINTH OF NOVEMBER.—CITY PROCESSIONS.—"THE TIMES" AND THE CITY.—THE STOCK EXCHANGE.—A PIECE OF SELF-GOVERNMENT.—LLOYD'S.—RETURN TO SIR JOHN, AND SOME OF THE OPINIONS OF THAT WORTHY.

OUR road to-day lies to the east. Seated on the roof of an omnibus, we ride down the Strand, through Temple-bar and Fleet-street, and pass St. Paul's. The road and the pavements are crowded in the extreme; the din is deafening; but the shrill voices of the costermongers in the side-streets are heard even above the thunders of the City.

We stop for one moment at the foot of Ludgate-hill, and look back. We see part of Fleet-street, and as far as our eyes can reach, there is nothing but a dark, confused, quickly-moving mass of men, horses, and vehicles; not a yard of the pavement is to be seen—nothing but heads along the rows of houses, and in the road, too, an ocean of heads, the property of gentlemen on the roofs of omnibuses, which crowd the City more than any other part of the town.

These are the streets whose excess of traffic makes the strongest impression upon the stranger; and this part of London is moreover specially dear to the historian. We, too, propose to take our time with it and to walk through it leisurely. But to-day we are bound farther eastward. We shall leave the omnibus at the further end of Cheapside.

In the heart of the City, less than half a mile from the Thames and London-bridge, various streets meeting form an irregular open place. This irregular place is one of the most remarkable spots in London. For no other place, except that of Westminster, can vie with this in the importance of its buildings and the crowding of its streets, though many may surpass it in extent, beauty, and architectural regularity. It is the Capitoline Forum of British Rome; it holds its temples, the Mansion-house, the Exchange and the Bank. In the centre, the equestrian statue of the saviour of the capitol—the Duke of Wellington. All round are islands of pavements, as in other parts of the town, for the foot-passengers to retire to from the maelstrom of vehicles.

At our right, just as we come out of Cheapside, is a house supported by columns and surrounded with strong massive railings. Two flights of stone steps lead to the upper story; massive stone pillars surrounded by gas-lamps stand in a row in front of it, but neither the gas nor the clearest noonday sun suffices to bring out the allegorical carvings which ornament the roof. This is the Mansion-house; the official residence of the Lord Mayor, who here holds his court, as if his was one of the crowned heads.

Here he lives. Here are the halls in which the most luxurious dinners of modern times are given; here are his offices and courts of justice, according to the ancient rights and privileges of the City of London.

Every year the Lord Mayor elect enters upon the functions of his office on the ninth of November. The City crowns its king with mediæval ceremonies. The shops are shut at an early hour and many do not open at all; for masters and servants must see the "show." For many hours the City is closed against all vehicles; flags and streamers are hung out from the houses; the pavement is covered with gravel; holiday faces everywhere; amiable street-boys at every corner bearing flags; brass bands and confusion and endless cheers! Such is the grave, demure, and busy City on that remarkable day.

While the streets are every moment becoming more crowded and noisy, the new Lord Mayor takes the customary oaths in the presence of the Court of Aldermen, and signs a security to the amount of £4000 for the City plate, which, according to a moderate computation, has a value of at least £20,000.

This done, he is Lord and King of the City, and sets out upon his coronation procession, surrounded by his lieges and accompanied by the ex-Mayor, the Aldermen, Sheriffs, the dignitaries of his guild, the city heralds, trumpeters, men in brass armour, and other thrones, principalities, and powers. The road which the Lord Mayor is to take is not prescribed by law; but according to an old custom, the procession must pass through that particular ward in which the King of the City acted as Alderman. The ward participates in the triumph of the day; and the cheers in that particular locality are, if possible, louder than any where else.

The procession turns next to the banks of the Thames. The Lord Mayor, according to time-honored custom, must take a trip in a gondola from one of the City bridges to Westminster. Fair weather or foul, take the water he must; and the broad river presents a spectacle on such occasions as is never seen in any town of Europe, since the Venetian Doges and their nuptials with the Adriatic have become matter for history.

Splendid gondolas richly gilt, glass-covered, and bedecked with a variety of flags and streamers, bear the Lord Mayor and his suite. Previous to starting, a supply of water is taken on board—thus hath custom willed it. The Lord Mayor's gondola is either rowed by his own bargemen, or it is taken in tow by a steam-tug. And round the gondolas there are boats innumerable with brass bands; and the bridges and the river banks are covered with spectators, and the river is more full of life, gladness, and colour, than on any other day of the year.

The trip to Westminster is short; it is, however, long enough for the company to take a copious dejeuner à la fourchette in the saloon of the City barge. This breakfast is a kind of introduction to the grand world-famed dinner, with which the Lord Mayor inaugurates his advent to power. The dinner is the most important part of the business, as, indeed, the giving and eating of dinners forms one of the chief functions of the City corporations. So, at least, says Punch, and so says the Times.

The Lord Mayor and his suite land at Westminster Bridge. In Westminster he repairs to the Court of Exchequer, where he is introduced to the Judges. He takes another oath; and to clinch that oath, and show that he means to be worthy of his office and of the City of London, he commissions the Recorder to invite the Judges to dinner. This invitation is delivered in quite as solemn a tone as the oath, and the oath is taken in the same business-like manner in which the invitation is given. A foreigner would be at a loss to know which of the two is the most solemn and important.

These ceremonies over, the procession returns the way it came, and lands at Blackfriars Bridge. Thenceforward it increases in splendour and magnificence. The fairer portion of humanity join it in their state coaches—the Lady Mayoress, the Aldermen's and Sheriffs' wives; and after them come Royal Princes, Ministers of State, the Judges of the land, and the Foreign Ambassadors. The procession over, they all sit down to dinner. What they eat, how they eat it, and how much they eat, is on the following morning duly chronicled in the journals. The number and quality of the courses will at once enable an experienced city-man to come to a pretty correct conclusion as to the Lord Mayor's virtues or vices. Meats rich and rare count as so many merits; but a couple of low and vulgar dishes would at once turn public opinion in the City against the City's chosen prince. The Lord Mayor's reputation emanates from the kitchen and the larder, exactly as a great diplomatist's renown may frequently be traced to the desk of some private secretary.

The Lady Mayoress shares all the honours which are showered upon her worthy husband; she is a genuine "lady" for a whole twelvemonth, and perhaps for life, if her husband has the good luck to be honoured with a visit from the Queen, on which occasion it is customary for the Lord Mayor to be made a baronet, while a couple of Aldermen, at least, come in for the honours of knighthood. But if the Queen does not visit the City, the Lord Mayor descends at the end of the year to his former position. For three hundred and sixty-five days he is a "Lord," and his wife is a "Lady"; he goes to Court, and is on terms of good fellowship with royal princes, gartered dukes, and belted earls; and he has the high honour and privilege of feasting the Corporation. His year of office over, he quits the Mansion House, returns to his shop and apron, and is the same quiet and humble citizen he was before.

Of course the shop and apron we have mentioned in jest only. A man who can aspire to the dignity of the mayoralty has long ceased to be a tradesman; he is a merchant prince, a banker, a millionaire. How else could he afford the luxury of that expensive dignity, especially since he cannot but neglect his business whilst he is in office.

The Lord Mayor's pay from the City amounts to £8000, but his expenses are enormous. Woe to him if he be careful of his money, if his dinners are few and far between, or his horses and carriages less splendid than those of his predecessors! Such enormities expose him to the contempt of the grandees of the City. The Common Councilmen shrug their shoulders, and the Aldermen declare that they were mistaken in him. The outraged feelings of the City pursue him even after his return to private life.

He is in duty bound to spend the eight thousand pounds he receives from the City; it is highly meritorious in him if he spends more. Bright is his place in the annals of the City, if he feasts its sons at the expense of double the amount of his official income!

There is much aristocratic pride and civic haughtiness in this city royalty. It rests on a broad historical basis; and it was strongest with regard to royalty at Whitehall, whenever the latter had to apply to the wealthy city corporations for relief in its financial troubles. But it was also a firm bulwark against the encroachments of the kings of England of former days, supported as they were by venal judges and parliaments; and it deserves the respect of the English as an historical relic. Its merits lie in the past; for at present English liberty needs not the protection of a City king.

The prerogatives of the city of London have, of late years, become the subject of a violent agitation. That agitation was commenced by "The Times," on the occasion of the great exhibition. "The Times" holds that it is unreasonable that the city—at the present day a mere function of London—should continue to play the part of the sovereign; that the Lord Mayor speaking in the name of London, should invite the Queen; that, conducting himself as representative of the metropolis, he should be feasted by the Prefect of the Seine, and kissed by Mons. Cartier. What right has the City to such honours, now that London has long since engulphed it? Where are the merits of the City? What does the Lord Mayor? What do the Aldermen? Nothing—unless it be that they eat turtle soup, and patés de foie gras? Is obesity a title to honours?

Thus says "The Times," with great justice, but with very little tenderness. No Englishman who knows anything of the history of his country, will deny that in evil days the City became a champion of liberty against the kings at Whitehall; that the Lord Mayors protected the press, and sheltered the printers from the violence of the government; that on such occasions the City had many a hot contest with the parliaments, and that, to this day, the city members belong to the liberal party. But liberal principles might be adhered to even without the Lord Mayor and his Lucullian dinners. And, as for the City's former services, it ought to be remembered, that there is a vast difference between living institutions and stone monuments. Old towers and castles, which at one time did good service against a foreign enemy, have, so to say, a vested right to the place in which they stand; it were wrong to pull them down merely because they are now useless. But far different is the case with living institutions that jar with the tendencies of the century. To wait for their gradual decay were a suicidal act in a nation.

A great many of the institutions of the City ought to be consigned to mediæval curiosity shops. They were, certainly, very useful in their day, when they had a purpose and a meaning; but so was the old German "Heerbann;" so were the guilds; and so was superstition. It were mere madness to spare them in consideration of past services. They must fall, sooner or later; and the sculptors and historians of England will take good care that the former merits of the City shall not be lost in oblivion.

Up to the present time, the agitation against the arrogance of the city corporations has been confined to the press; to the "Times" belongs the merit of having commenced that agitation. The Londoners have as yet taken no active part in it; and this is another proof of the conservative tendencies which are incarnate in the great mass of the English nation. There is in this conservatism a narrow-mindedness which is the more striking as, in the affairs of practical life, the Anglo-British race can, least of all, be accused of a want of common sense.

In despite of this innate conservatism, the masses are gradually awaking to political consciousness. Formerly it was considered a matter of course, that wealthy persons only were elected to serve in Parliament; or that rich traders only would aspire to the mayoralty, or the dignity of an alderman. Reforms are impending. What will come of them depends partly on the leaders of the movement; on the degree of resistance which the government of the day may oppose to them; and, partly, though the English are loth to admit it, on the course of events on the continent of Europe.

Perhaps we shall resume the question on another occasion. Just now we are in the capitoline market of the city. We leave the Mansion-house, and turn to the other temples which grace the spot.

Opposite to the Mansion-house, is the Royal Exchange; a vast detached building of an imposing aspect. The English are not, generally, famous for their style of architecture; the antique columns, though great favourites, puzzle them sorely. They put them exactly where they are not wanted; and, in many of their public buildings the columns, instead of supporting the structure, are themselves supported by some architectural contrivance. The modern buildings suffer, moreover, from a striking uniformity; they have all the same columned fronts, which we see at the Mansion-house, the Exchange, and several of the theatres. It is always the same pattern, exactly as if those buildings had come out of some Birmingham factory.

This monotony in the style of public buildings would be altogether unbearable, but for the climate. The smoky and foggy atmosphere of London indemnifies us for the want of original ideas in the architects. It gives the London buildings a venerable, antique colouring. The Exchange, for instance, has the appearance of having weathered the storms of a hundred winters, while, in fact, it is quite a new building. Still, it is quite as black and sooty as Westminster Abbey, or Somerset House; and yet it is not even nine years old. The old Exchange was burnt down in 1838; it required six years to complete the new building, which was opened in October, 1844, with much solemnity.

Up to the reign of Elizabeth, the London merchants had no Exchange building; they transacted business in the open air, in Lombard Street, in St. Paul's Church-yard, and sometimes even in St. Paul's; for this cathedral was, at the time we speak of, the great centre of business, fashion, and prostitution. Sir Thomas Gresham, who had frequently acted as the Queen's agent on the Continent, offered to construct an Exchange building, provided the city would grant him the ground to build it on. His proposal was accepted; a piece of ground was bought for £3,737 6d., and the first stone was laid on the 7th June, 1565. At the end of the following year, the building was completed; and to judge from the sketches which still remain, it was designed in imitation of the Antwerp Exchange.

The virgin Queen expressed her high satisfaction with the undertaking most royally, by dining with Sir Thomas Gresham, and bestowing on the building the title of "Royal Exchange." When Sir Thomas, at a later period, was compelled to depart this world, he bequeathed his Exchange to the City, and founded the Gresham College, of which, at the present day, nothing remains but the Gresham Lectures, which are generally, and justly, classed among the city jobs, whose name is Legion.

Gresham's Exchange, with its profuse display of grasshoppers—the founder's crest—fell a sacrifice to the great fire in 1666. So attached had the city merchants become to their new temple of Plutus, that they restored it in preference even to their churches; and, two years after the great fire the New Exchange was completed and solemnly opened by Charles II. Gresham's bust, which had been saved out of the conflagration, was placed in a niche of honor, and a cast brass grasshopper, the last of its numerous family, was raised to the top of the steeple, on which bad eminence it had to stand all weathers, until, relieved by another conflagration in 1838, it has been allowed to find a retreat on the eastern front of the present Exchange building.

Times have altered since the days of Old Gresham, the site of whose Exchange cost less than £4,000, while the present building comes to £150,000, exclusive of the cost of the ground. In his time, grave and sober citizens had mustachios and imperials; and wild young fellows, bent upon mischief and dissipation, repaired to the taverns of the city. In our days everybody is smooth shaved, and there is a chapel in every corner. Formerly the merchants relied on their own understanding and the honesty of their high-born debtors; at present they have no confidence either in the former or the latter: and out of the fulness of their godly despair, they have engraved in front of their Exchange building the motto of the city—Domine dirige nos—Direct us, O Lord, and reveal unto us the time and the hour at which consols and shares should be bought and sold!

The Exchange, as we have said, is a splendid building; but professional architects will shrug their shoulders when they look at it in the detail. Why all those corners on the eastern side, and why those small narrow shops? It is wrong to condemn anybody or anything on mere primâ facie evidence. The architect who designed the Exchange had similar though greater difficulties to contend with, than Paxton in the construction of the Exhibition Building in Hyde Park. Paxton's great antagonist was Colonel Sibthorp, an honourable and gallant member of the House of Commons, who would not consent to sacrifice the trees which adorned the site of the building. "Make what fuss you like about your modern ideas of industry," said the chivalric Don Quixote, "but you shall not touch the trees; they are worth all your industry, and all your foreign nicknacks, and free-trade and nonsense, and, indeed, anything that ever came from Manchester." And what said Paxton? Why, he said, "Let the old trees stand, we will roof them over!" and he built his glass house one hundred feet higher in the middle, and thus made the transept. And there was room for everything and everybody—men and merchandize, stray children and lost petticoats, bad coffee, clever pickpockets from England, France, and Germany—and, sometimes, for the rain, too, when the weather was very bad, and we here sought shelter. But Colonel Sibthorp never crossed the threshold. Mr. Tite, the architect who made the plans for the New Exchange, had to contend with a legion of small conservative Sibthorpes, with a large number of shopkeepers who held places in the Old Exchange, and who insisted on having their shops in the new one. They could not be dispossessed; and in some manner or other it was necessary to sacrifice the beauty of the building to the claims of the vested interests. A great many people cannot understand why there is no covered hall for the accommodation of the merchants on Change, and why they must carry on their business either in the open court or in the arcade which surrounds it. The London climate is certainly not made for open-air amusements or occupations; and an Englishman, though with a threefold encasement of flannel, stands in great awe of draughts and rheumatism.

Nevertheless, the English merchant is condemned, in the fogs of winter and the rains of autumn, to brave the climate in an open yard, and to stake his health and his fortune on the chances of the season and the turn of the market. The reason is, that Englishmen are as much afraid of close rooms as of rheumatism and colds; and the Gresham Committee, which superintended the construction of the New Exchange, decided in favor of unlimited ventilation. Certain branches of business, which in many respects are much more extensive than the speculations in stocks and shares, have for a long time past been carried on in certain saloons. In the Exchange building itself there is a broad staircase, with crowds of busy people ascending and descending, and there is a door with large gold letters, "Lloyd's Coffee House." Let us ascend that staircase, and see what sort of a coffee-house this is. We pass through a large hall, from which doors open to several rooms; at each door stands a porter in scarlet livery. In the hall itself are several marble statues and a large marble tablet, which the merchants of London erected to the Times, out of gratitude for the successful labours of that journal in unmasking a gigantic scheme of imposition and fraud, which threatened ruin to the whole trade of London. In the centre of the hall there is a large black board, on which are written the names and destinations of all the ships carrying mails which will sail from English ports on that and the following day. In the corner to the right there is a door with the inscription, "Captains' Room." No one is allowed to enter this room but the commanders of merchant vessels, or those who have business to transact with them. Next to it is the

"Commercial Room," the meeting place of all the foreign merchants who come to London. We prefer entering a saloon on the other side of the hall, the doors of which are continually opening and shutting; it is crowded with the underwriters, that is to say, with capitalists, who do business in the assurance of vessels and their freights. The telegraphic messages of vessels arrived, sailed, stranded, or lost, are first brought into this room. Whoever enters by this door walks, in the first instance, to a large folio volume which lies on a desk of its own. It is Lloyd's Journal, containing short entries of the latest events in English ports and the sea ports in every other part of the world. It tells the underwriters whether the vessels which they have insured have sailed, whether they have been spoken with, or have reached the port of their destination. Are they over-due?—run a-ground?—wrecked?—lost?

In this room there are always millions at stake. So firmly established is the reputation of this institution, that there is hardly ever a barque sailing from the ports of the Baltic, or the French, Spanish, or Indian seas which is not insured at Lloyd's. Its branch establishments are in all the commercial ports of the world; but its head-office is in Cornhill, and in the rooms of the Exchange. Before we again descend the stairs, let us for one moment enter the reading-room. Perfect silence; tables, chairs, desks; readers here and there; men of all countries and of all nations; all round the walls, high desks with files of newspapers, whose shape and colour indicate that they have not been printed in Europe; they are, indeed, papers from the other side of the ocean—China, Barbary, Brazilian, Australian, Cape, and Honolulu papers—a collection unrivalled in extent, though less orderly than the collections of the Trieste Lloyd's and the Hamburg Börsenhalle. It is here that the stranger from the German continent first receives an adequate idea of the enormous extent of commercial journalism. How far different is this reading-room from anything we see at home? How extensive must be the communications of a nation to which such journals are a necessity! How small does German commerce look in comparison with this! When we were at school, we were told that commerce was a means of communication between the various parts of the world; that merchants are the messengers of progressive civilisation; and that to be a good merchant a man ought to be well read in geography, history, politics, and a great many other sciences. And then we saw our neighbour, the grocer and tallow-chandler, weighing and making up sugar in paper parcels all the year round. He knew nothing whatever of geography, history, or politics; but for all that, he was a wealthy man and a great person in the town, and everybody said he was the pattern of a good merchant. We could not understand this. At a later period, when we lived in a German metropolis, we saw other great merchants, bankers, and manufacturers. They did not make up paper parcels as the grocer and tallow-chandler did; they were dressed with a certain elegance; they read newspapers, and were fond of discussing the events of the day. But many of them had not the least idea of the politics which they discussed, and on which they founded their speculations; they had forgotten whatever they had learnt of geography, commercial topography, and history; and nevertheless they passed as capital men of business and accomplished merchants. Our romantic ideas of the requirements, the influences, and the radiations of the commerce of the world received again a rude shock; but now, suddenly, as accident leads us into Lloyd's reading-room, the old impressions come back again. Thus, after all, the lessons of our school-days were not untrue! These, then, are the messengers of commerce which promote the exchange of civilisation between the continents and islands of the world. Neither sciences nor religions are powerful enough to found those organs. They owe their existence solely to commerce: possibly they may be means to an end; but it is also an undoubted fact that they exert a vast influence on the peaceful progress of civilisation.

Of the 50,000,000 lbs. of tea which are sold in the east of London, a handful has found its way to the West, to Guildford-street. It lies in the bottom of the venerable silver family tea-pot; and this tea-pot stands on the table of the parlour, to which the reader has been introduced on former occasions. The mistress of the house is passing in review her two lines of cups and saucers, headed by the milk-jug and sugar-basin. Mrs. Bella reads Punch, and smiles, not at the jokes, but because she is happy that English liberty admits of such jokes. The two younger daughters of the house occupy one chair between them, where they read "David Copperfield," and two very small grandchildren of Sir John perform a polka in the further corner of the room. Sir John himself, as usual, is reading the Times, and just now he wags his head very impressively, because he has been reading Gladstone's letter about the affairs of Naples. Sir John, though perfectly convinced of Dr. Keif's honesty and good faith, has never at any time given full credit to his statements when that gentleman presumed to hint that the administration of criminal justice in Italy is not altogether so unexceptionable as that at the Old Bailey. But now, since Mr. Gladstone corroborates Dr. Keif's statement in that respect—Mr. Gladstone, who is a native of England, a very respectable man, and a conservative to his nethermost coating of flannel—now indeed Sir John is of opinion that the Neapolitans have, after all, good cause for complaint.

We have returned from our excursion into the city, and reenter the comfortable parlour, shake hands all round, and sit down by the tea-table. Sir John has smuggled the Times under his chair, lest the Doctor should at once have a weapon to attack him with. He asks where we have been; and when we tell him, he leans his head back, purses up his mouth, shuts his eyes, and says "Well?" This "Well" of Sir John's, accompanied by that peculiar movement of the head, means, if translated into common language, "Well, what do you say to London? Mere nothing, isn't it?—A business in Mincing-lane, a mere trifle?—merely a piece of Leipsic or Frankfort—never mind—patience—you'll see what London is. You'll open your eyes by and bye! Only think what enormous sums are turned over at Lloyd's every year!"

Sir John is altogether victorious to-day. We cannot meet him on this ground. In vain does Dr. Keif attempt to demonstrate that there is no reason why Germany should not become as wealthy and mighty as England, if she had only a little more union, a little less government, an idea or so more of a fleet, fewer custom-houses, a little more money and less soldiery. Sir John admits every one of Dr. Keif's propositions; but his 30,000,000 lbs. of coffee, and his 50,000,000 lbs. of tea, and his 20,000,000 lbs. of tobacco, are great facts, and stubborn facts, against which nothing can be said. Germany may be better off a couple of hundred years hence. Of course it may, there is no reason why it should not; but it is very badly off now, and that is a fact, too. And Sir John launches forth into a long and elaborate lecture on insurance companies, premiums, percentages, capital, bonuses, and dividends, intermixed with certain allusions to the impractical and improvident habits of the Germans, and the uselessness generally of all the German professors. The last word, pronounced with a certain emphasis, rouses Dr. Keif from the sleep into which Sir John's statistical and economical expositions had lulled him.

"Long life to all our German professors!" said Dr. Keif, rubbing his eyes. "50,000,000 lbs. of tea in Mincing-lane, and not a drop in my cup. Where's the greatness of England, Sir John?—Good night."

CHAP. X.

Hyde Park.

PILGRIMAGE TO THE FAR WEST.—OXFORD-STREET.—HYDE-PARK IN THE SEASON.—ROTTEN ROW.—THE DUKE AND THE QUEEN.—THE FRONT OF THE CRYSTAL PALACE.—DR. KEIF ENTERS, MAKES A SPEECH ON BRITISH LOYALTY, AND EXIT.—THE IRON SHUTTERS OF APSLEY-HOUSE.—THE BRITISH GENERAL AND THE RIOTERS.

HITHERTO our excursions have been confined to the east; but now we propose leaving Russell and Bedford Squares and the British Museum to the right, and Covent-garden and all its theatres to the left, to direct our pilgrimage through Oxford-street to the West. Oxford-street holds the medium between the city streets and the West-end streets. Its public is mixed; goods, waggons, and private carriages, omnibuses, and men and women on horseback, men of business, fashionable loungers, and curious strangers, are mixed up; shops of all sorts, from the most elegant drapers' shops down to the lowest oyster-stall, may be found in it; and there are, moreover, legions of costermongers, and shoals of advertising vans. Oxford-street is long and broad enough to take in the population of a small town. It changes its character several times, according to the greater or less elegance of the quarter through which it runs. After we have walked a good half-hour in a straight line, and in the present instance we have walked very fast, looking neither to the right nor to the left, we reach a part where the row of houses on the left side terminates, and Hyde Park commences. Here there is a high arch of white marble, which every body admires, and a small stone, which no one notices, because it stands near the pump from which the cabmen fetch water for their horses; an inscription on this stone tells us, that here is the site of the famous Tyburn Turnpike. The arch, a curtailed imitation of the triumphal arch of Constantine, cost George IV. £60,000, and stood in front of Buckingham-palace. A few months ago, it was removed to Hyde Park, where it now stands in all its marble glory. Does it perform the functions of a gate? No! because there is no wall. Is it a triumphal-arch? Perhaps so, to commemorate the bad taste of its founder. At all events, it promotes the interests of unity, for on the opposite side of Hyde Park there has been these many years past a similar gate, which opens a way through nothing, and there is a triumphal arch in the face of it, which trumpets forth the good taste of Punch, whose paternal exhortations could not prevent the Duke of Wellington from being placed on that perilous height.

The English are in many respects like our own good honest peasants. So long as the latter keep to their ploughs, they are most amiable and respectable; but if you find them in town, and induce them to put on fashionable clothes, you may rely on it that thus affected they will give you plenty of kicks. Let an Englishman make a park, and his production will be admirable; but if you wish for an entrance into a park, you had better not apply to him. Fortunately Hyde Park is much larger than its two splendid portals. There is plenty of room to lose them from your sight; and there are a great many agreeable scenes which will banish them from your memory. Passing through the Marble-arch to those regions where the Exhibition building stands, we cross a meadow large enough to induce us to believe that we are far away from London. In the west, the ground rises in gentle hills with picturesque groups of trees on their summits and in the valleys; here and there an old tufted oak, with its gnarled branches boldly stretched out; the grass is fresh and green, though all the passengers walk on it. It is green up to the very trunks of the trees, whose shade is generally injurious to vegetation; it is green throughout the winter and through the summer months, though there is not a drop of rain for many weeks, for the mild and moist atmosphere nourishes it and favours the growth of ivy which clusters round any tree too old to resist its approaches. Thus does Hyde Park extend far to the west and the south, until it finds its limits in bricks and mortar. A slight blue mist hangs on the distant trees; and through the mist down in the south there are church towers looming in the far distance like the battlements of turretted castles in the midst of romantic forests. The trees recede; a small lake comes in view, it is an artificial extension of the Serpentine, which has the honor of seeing the elegance of London riding and driving on its banks. Early in the morning the lake is plebeian. The children of the neighbourhood swim their boats on it; apprentices on their way to work make desperate casts for some half-starved gudgeon; the ducks come forward in dirty morning wrappers. Nursery-maids with babies innumerable take walks by order; and at a very early hour a great many plebeians have the impertinence to bathe in the little lake. But to-day the park and the river are in true aristocratic splendour; here and there, there is indeed some stray nursery-maid walking on the grass, and some little tub of a boat with a ragged sail floating on the lake; there is also a group of anglers demonstrating to one another with great patience that the fish wont bite to-day, but all along the banks of the river far down to the end of the park and up to the majestic shades of Kensington gardens there is an interminable throng of horses and carriages. Those who have seen the Prater of Vienna in the first weeks of May will be rather disappointed with the aspect of the drive in Hyde Park, where the upper classes of London congregate in the evening between five and seven o'clock, partly to take the air, and partly because it is considered fashionable to see now and then in order to be seen. Extravagant turn-outs and liveries, such as the Viennese produce with great ostentation, are not to be found in London. The English aristocracy like to make an impression by the simplicity and solidity of their appearance; and the metropolis is the last of all places where they would wish to excite attention by a dashing and extravagant exterior. They have not the least desire either to dazzle or to awe the tradespeople or to make them envious. They are too sure of their position to be tempted to advertise it: whoever wants this assurance cannot pretend to belong to the aristocracy. By far more interesting, and indeed unrivalled, is Rotten-row, the long broad road for horsemen, where, on fine summer evenings, all the youth, beauty, celebrity, and wealth of London may be seen on horse-back.

  Hundreds of equestrians, ladies and gentlemen, gallop to and fro. How fresh and rosy these English girls are! How firmly they sit! What splendid forms and expressive features! Free, fresh, bold, and natural. The blue veil flutters, and so does the riding-habit; a word to the horse and movement of the bridle, and they gallop on, nodding to friends to the right and left, the happiness of youth expressed in face and form, and no idea, no thought, for the thousand sorrows of this earth. A man of a harmless and merry mind may pass a happy summer's evening in looking at this the most splendid of all female cavalcades; but he who has become conscious of those all-pervading sufferings of humanity which, felt through thousands of years, denied through thousands of years, and asserted only within the last few years by the millions of our earth—he who has pressed this thorny knowledge of the world to his heart, let him avoid this spot of happiness-breathing splendour, lest the thorns wound him more severely still. Then comes an old man, with his horse walking at a slow pace, his low hat pushed back that the white hair on his temples may have the benefit of the breeze. His head bent forward, the bridle dangling in a hand weak with age, the splendour of the eyes half-dimmed, his cheeks sunken, wrinkles round his mouth and on his forehead, his aquiline nose bony and protruding; who does not know him? His horse walks gently on the sand; every one takes off his hat; the young horse-women get out of his way; and the Duke smiles to the right and to the left. Few persons can boast of so happy a youth as this old man's age. He turns round the corner; the long broad row becomes still more crowded; large groups of ten or twenty move up and down; fast riding is quite out of the question, when all of a sudden a couple come forward at a quick pace. There is room for them and their horses in the midst of Rotten-row, however full it may be, for every one is eager to make way for them: it is the Queen and her husband, without martial pomp and splendour, without a single naked sword within sight. The crowd closes in behind her; the young women appear excited; the old men smile with great glee at seeing their Queen in such good health. Dandies in marvellous trowsers, incredible waistcoats, and stunning ties, put up their glasses; the anglers on the lake crowd to one side in order to see the Queen; the nurserymaids, the babies, and the boys with their hoops come up to the railings; the grass plots, where just now large groups of people sat chatting, are left vacant, and the shades of the evening are over the park. The sun is going down behind the trees; its parting rays rest on the Crystal Palace with a purple and golden glare, whose reflection falls on Rotten-row and its horsemen.

In a very short time this spot will be empty.

But all hail to thee, Colossus of glass! thou most moral production of these latter days; iron-ribbed, many-eyed, with thy many-coloured flags, which would make believe that all the nations are united by the bonds of brotherhood; and that peace, universal peace, shall henceforth reign among the sons of men.

The flags flutter gaily through the cool of the evening. There the Prussian colours are all but entwined with those of Austria. Here the Papal States touch upon Sardinia. And down there! O sancta Simplicitas! the Russian eagle stretches his wings, and flutters as if impelled by a desire to fraternise with the stars and stripes of North America!

Our enthusiasm is cooled down by a loud laugh and a shrill voice, which hails us from a distance. It is Dr. Keif who indulges, and not for the first time either, in the questionable amusement of mimicking the mode and manner of speech of a distinguished member of the great Sclavonian family.

"By St. Nicolas!" said the Doctor; "why, you Chop-fallen, look out! Look you at flags, Silly, to find colours your own black, red, gold? Blockheads! Croat is brother likewise; and Czech himself speaks quite good German, ours, when likes, and Emperor permits. Magyar have shall German blows and Italian likewise. Piff! Paff! shot through heart by command German! Is now everything good German, all, Welchland, Poland, and Serbonia likewise, as they would at Frankfort have it! Capital times these!"

"But, my dear Doctor, you are in capital spirits to-night. Some intrigue, eh! Indeed, you look quite smart! Green coat, waistcoat, and cravat, and dirty boots. Why you are dressed after the image of a Russian cavalier. Did you happen to see the Queen, and has that sight made you so very loyal!"

"A truce to all logic!" cried the Doctor; "And don't make any bad jokes about the Queen, if you love me. I respect her; on my soul, I do! But since you will talk of the Queen, I will tell you of the first of May, the day Her Majesty opened this place! You must have read, when it once became known, that the Lady Victoria in her own little person intended to open that great Exhibition, that a rush was made on the season tickets, expensive though they were. The Wicked on the continent smiled at this 'pedantic, antiquated, and unseasonable loyalty of the British people.' These were the very words the miscreants printed in their papers. I trust they won't do so again, and I protest against such language. I am free to confess there is much childish harmlessness and practical calculation in this same loyalty. But if it were innate in the English as some ninnies have had the simplicity to believe—if it were a gift of nature, such as fine eyes, or a humped back, or a free native country—then I say, it would be void of all moral meaning. But it is not the result of thoughtless stupidity; for the Anglo Saxon race is not by any means a race of idiots. And the history of England shews that this British loyalty is not the creature of habit and education; nor is it perpetuated by climatic causes, as Cretinism is in Styria. English loyalty is the expression of conscious respect for the principles of monarchy, when worthily represented. Queen Victoria has neither the energy of Catharine of Russia, nor has she the genius of Maria Theresa. But in her principles of government she has always been just to the voice of the majority. She is a constitutional Queen, such as the Queen of England should be. Let no man tell me that she must be so; that she cannot be otherwise even if she would. She cannot, indeed, send her ministers and the members of the opposition to Botany Bay; nor can she stifle the radical press, or overthrow the constitution as others did in other places. But a Queen, who may select her ministers, dissolve the parliament, and create peers, has a deal of power to do evil. English royalty is not altogether such a farce as the Germans generally believe. That Queen Victoria uses her power for good is her merit; and, because she does so, her's is the most fortunate head of all the heads whom fate has burdened with a golden crown. She is worshipped, adored, and idolised, by millions, who think it the greatest happiness to look at her face. I wish you had been here on that memorable first of May! I wish you had seen this park and the people—and well-dressed people too—thronging Rotten Row to see the Queen go by. The park was literally black with them. You saw nothing but heads to the very tree-tops. They risked their lives for the Queen, for all the world as if they were the most accomplished of courtiers. The whole of the public were mad, excepting myself and her Majesty."

"My dear Doctor, what a splendid opportunity for you to make a revolutionary speech to so large an assembly."

"Yes, indeed!" said the Doctor. "A capital opening for a martyr to the cause. How quickly the populace would have torn me to pieces! But, in sober seriousness, I am not the man I used to be. On this island you doff the revolutionary garment, as snakes do their enamelled skin. When fresh from Germany, I was red and shaggy, as Esau of old; for on the other side of the Channel, affairs were really too lamentable and disgraceful. But, after my first four weeks among these smooth-shaved and really-constitutionally-governed barbarians, I, too, became smooth and mannerly, as Jacob the Patriarch. Another year will make me a constitutional monarchist, and a score of years or so will convert me into an absolutist of Montalembert's stamp. Isn't it disgusting! This impertinently, carefully-observed constitution of the English tears my republican toga into shreds, as day follows day. Only think," continued the Doctor, "of addressing revolutionary observations to these contented Englishmen! It's the most insane idea that I ever heard of! Are revolutions to be stamped out of the soil? Can they thrive without sunlight and rain, without provocation from the higher regions? The mob of our stamp have never yet made a revolution: kings make them. Of course they know not what they do."

There is no stopping the Doctor when he once begins to speak. In his conversations with his German friends, he is eloquent on the merits of England; but at Sir John's tea-table he fights tooth and nail for his beloved Germany. Quite a psychological phenomenon, which may be observed in the majority of the better class of German residents in England.

We walk slowly forward, and leave the park by the gate at Hyde Park Corner. The roads are now empty, for wealth and fashion have gone home to their dinners; and the hackney-coaches and omnibuses are not permitted to enter the sacred precincts. Enormous crowds of these excluded plebeian vehicles are collected at the gate, and move about wildly, to the manifest danger of all those who wish to cross the road. And high above the tumultuous movement and the crowd stands the equestrian statue of the Duke of Wellington, almost opposite to Apsley House, in which the great warrior lived at the time this chapter was penned by the author.

It has rarely been the lot of a man so frequently to witness his own apotheosis as the Duke of Wellington; and yet how gloomy looks Apsley House on the fresh green borders of the park. The windows, shut up from year's end to year's end, and protected by bullet-proof shutters of massive iron—the very railings in front of the house boarded up, to exclude the curiosity of the passers-by—all owing to the riots which preceded the passing of the Reform Bill—riots in which the castles of the Tories were burnt down in the provinces, while in the metropolis the populace threatened the life of the greatest captain of the age.

Of course the Reform Bill would have been passed, even without riots and incendiarism. But it is not fair in Englishmen utterly to forget the bloody scenes which even in late years have been enacting in their own country, while anything like a riot on the Continent induces them to protest, "that those people are not fit for liberty." Nor is it fair in a large party on the Continent, who are always referring to the moderation and good sense of Englishmen, utterly to forget the scenes of blood and destruction which ushered in the Reform Bill.

But what did a British Government do in those days of passion and terror? Did they at once declare that the British people were unfit for liberal institutions, merely because the violence of the catastrophe gave a temporary ascendancy to a couple of thousands of hot-headed mad-caps? Did they proclaim the state of siege? Did they fetter the press? Did they invade and search the houses of the citizens? Were Englishmen tried by courts-martial? Were punishments inflicted for political opinions and thoughts? Did malice go hand in hand with the administration of justice? Nothing of the kind! The incendiaries were arrested wherever they could be caught; but no one on either side of the Channel ever thought of saying, that the British nation was not ripe for freedom!

And what was the Duke of Wellington's conduct when the mob assailed Apsley House? A continental general would have run away, or he would have led an army against the rioters. The Duke barricaded his house to the best of his ability. The old soldier stood up to defend his house and his person. He, the Field Marshal of all European countries, the Warden of the Cinque Ports, the Commander-in-Chief of the British army, he did not issue his orders for the drums to beat, and his soldiers did not fire upon the misguided populace. But when the storm was over, he had bullet-proof shutters made to his windows, and those shutters he kept closed, that the people should never forget their brutal attack upon the old lion. Well done, man of Waterloo! He has since risen in the estimation of the public; but, as I said before, most Englishmen, in judging of the affairs of the Continent, give not one passing thought to the bullet-proof shutters of Apsley House.

CHAP. XI.

The Quarters of Fashion.

THE BEAUTIES OF NATURE.—FASHIONABLE QUARTERS.—LONDON IN 1752.—ST. JAMES'S PALACE.—PAST AND PRESENT.—PALL MALL.—THE LAND OF CLUBS.—MRS. GRUNDY ON THE CLUBS.—ST. JAMES'S PARK.—BUCKINGHAM PALACE.—WATERLOO PLACE.—TRAFALGAR-SQUARE.

THERE is scarcely a nation so fond of green trees and green meadow-land as the English. They adore the splendid trees of their parks as the Druids did their sacred oaks; it is quite a pleasure to see that their conquests of nature, and other successful efforts to train its agencies to the weaving of woollen yarns, and the working of spinning-jennies, have not deprived them of a sense for those beauties of nature which cannot be reduced to capital and interest.

The English people are a gigantic refutation of that current untruth, that over cultivation estranges us from nature. Fire, water, earth, and air, are in England more than in any other part of the world, employed in the service of capital. In England they fatten their fields with manure which has travelled many thousands of miles, and which has been collected from some barren rock on the ocean; in England nature is compelled to produce water-lilies from the tropics, and fruit of various kinds of unnatural size; in England they eat grapes from Oporto—plums from Malta—peaches from Provence—pine-apples from Bermuda—bananas from St. Domingo—and nuts from the Brazils. Whatever cannot be grown on English soil is imported from other parts of the world; but, nevertheless, the English retain their affection for the trees and meadows, forests and shrubs of their own country. This law of nature, which is partly influenced by dietetic considerations, may be observed in any part of the metropolis. The best houses are always near the squares and the parks. That part of Piccadilly which faces the Park is elegant, expensive, and aristocratic; the other portion of that street, which extends deep into the vast ocean of houses, assumes a business aspect, and belongs to trade. But even that portion of Piccadilly which is now inhabited by the aristocracy was a most wretched place about one hundred years ago. There were a great many taverns whose fame was none of the best; and, on review days, the soldiers from the neighbouring barracks sat in front of the houses on wooden benches, whilst their hair was being powdered, and their pig-tails tied up. During this interesting operation, they laughed and joked with the maid-servants who passed that way. As a natural consequence of these proceedings, the quarter was avoided by the respectable classes.

From Piccadilly towards the north, and along the whole breadth of Hyde-park is Park-lane, with its charming houses built in the villa style, and similar to those of Brighton, for they have irregular fantastic balconies, rotundas, and verandahs. In Brighton these contrivances facilitate the view of the sea; here they help to a view of the park. Palace-like in their interiors, and filled with all those comforts which in English houses alone can be found in such beautiful harmony, and yet so unassuming, they do not, by their exterior, overawe the passers-by with the wealth of their inhabitants. Formerly this street was Tyburn-lane. The very name reminds one of hanging and quartering. At the present day, Park-lane, and all the streets around it, are the head-quarters of wealth and aristocracy. Plate-glass windows—powdered footmen—melancholy stillness—heavy carriages waiting at small doors—no shops, omnibuses, or carts—in cold, rainy, winter nights, perhaps here and there a woman and her child half-naked, and more than half-starved, crouching down in some dark corner. Such is the character of this part of the town, where, among old walls and green squares stand the most splendid houses of the aristocracy; and which, with few interruptions only, extends to the regions of Bond-street.

St. James's-street connects Piccadilly with Pall-mall. We are still in the quarters of splendour, and we are approaching the land of clubs and royalty. In the beginning of the 18th century there were a great many theatres in and around St. James's. In the chronicles of those old theatres, there is a deal of matter for the student of the life and character of old London. The managers were speculators; the public were credulous; there was a strong hankering after miracles, and a decided predilection for noise. On the whole, people in those days were much the same as they are now, but there was more coarseness, more massiveness, and less grace. We go down St. James' Street, and reach the point where it joins Pall Mall; there we stand, in front of St. James' Palace, an old, black, and rambling building, with no interest, except what it derives from the past; and even in the past, it was considered as a mere appendage to Whitehall; and only after Whitehall was burned down, did St. James' Palace become the real seat of royalty; and it continued to be so until George IV. took up his residence at Buckingham Palace. At the present day, the old palace is used for court ceremonies only; the Queen holds her levees and drawing-rooms in it. In the three large saloons there are, on such occasions, crowds of people who have the entrée, in full dress, and great splendour, thronging round the throne, which is ornamented with a canopy of red velvet, and a gold star and crown. The walls are decorated with pictures of the battles of Waterloo and Vittoria; in the back-ground are the Queen's apartments, where she receives her ministers. The anti-chambers are filled with yeomen of the guard, and court officials of every description. In the court-yard are the state-carriages of the nobility; and the streets around the park are thronged with crowds of anxious spectators.

These are the moments when that gloomy building is lighted up with the splendour of modern royalty; at all other times, night and day, red grenadiers pace to and fro in front of the dark walls. The court-yards are given up to the gambols of birds, cats, and children; but every morning, a military band of music plays in the colour court.

Pall Mall is one of the most splendid streets in London; its splendour is chiefly owing to the club houses. There are, in this street, the Oxford and Cambridge Club, the Army and Navy Club, the Carlton, the Reform, the Travellers', and the Athenæum. Besides these, there are in London a large number of club-houses, of which it may generally be said, that their chief end and aim is to procure a comfortable home by means of association, in as cheap and perfect a manner as possible.

But the words, "as cheap and perfect as possible," convey quite a different idea to the German to what they do to the Englishman. A short explanation may not, perhaps, be out of place at this point.

A younger son of an old house, with an income of, say from two to four hundred pounds, cannot live, and do as others do, within the limits of that income. He can neither take and furnish a house, nor can he keep a retinue of servants or give dinners to his friends. The club is his home, and stands him in the place of an establishment. At the club, spacious and splendidly furnished saloons are at his disposal; there is a library, a reading-room, baths, and dressing-rooms. At the club he finds all the last new works and periodicals; a crowd of servants attend upon him; and the cooking is irreproachable. The expenses of the establishment are defrayed by the annual contributions and the entrance fees. But, of course, neither the annual contributions nor the entrance-fees, pay for the dinners and suppers, the wines and cigars, of the members. Members do dine at the clubs: indeed, the providing of dinners is among the leading objects of these establishments, and the dinners are good and cheap, compared to the extortionate prices of the London hotels. The club provides everything, and gives it at cost price; a member of a good club pays five shillings for a dinner, which in an hotel would be charged, at least, four times that sum.

The habitués of the London Clubs would be shocked if they were asked to pass their hours and half-hours in our German coffee and reading-rooms; and, on the other hand, persons accustomed to the bee-hive life of Vienna coffee-houses consider the London Clubs as dull though handsome edifices. Lordly halls, splendid carpets, sofas, arm-chairs, strong, soft, and roomy, in which a man might dream away his life; writing and reading-rooms tranquil enough to suit a poet, and yet grand, imposing, aristocratic; doors covered with cloth to prevent the noise of their opening and shutting, and their brass handles resplendent as the purest gold; enormous fire-places surrounded by slabs of the whitest marble; the furniture of mahogany and palisander; the staircases broad and imposing as in the palazzos of Rome; the kitchens chefs d'oeuvre of modern architecture; bath and dressing-rooms got up with all the requirements of modern luxury; in short, the whole house full of comfortable splendour and substantial wealth. All this astonishes but does not dazzle one, because here prevails that grand substantial taste in domestic arrangements and furniture, in which the English surpass all other nations, and which it is most difficult to imitate, because it is most expensive.

The influence which club-life exercises on the character of Englishmen is still an open question among them. The majority of the fairer portion of Her Majesty's subjects hate and detest the clubs most cordially. Mrs. Grundy is loud in her complaints, that all that lounging, gossiping, and smoking deprives those "brutes of men" of the delight they would otherwise take in her intellectual society, and that club dinners make men such epicures, they actually turn up their noses at cold mutton. And even when at home, Mr. Grundy is always dull, and goes about sulking with Mrs. Grundy. To be sure, all he wants is to pick a quarrel, and go and spend his evening in that "horrid club." But there are some women who presume to differ from the views of this admirable type of old English matrons. They are fond of clubs, and hold a man all the more fitted for the fetters of matrimony after yawning away a couple of years in one of these British monasteries. The club-men, say these ladies, make capital husbands; for the regulations of the club-houses admit of no domestic vices, and these regulations are enforced with such severity, that a woman's rule appears gentle ever afterwards.

The windows of almost all the club-houses in Pall Mall have the most charming views on St. James's Park. It is the smallest of all the parks; but it is a perfect jewel amidst the splendid buildings which surround it on all sides. On its glassy lake fine shrubs, and beeches, and ash-trees on the banks throw their trembling shadows; tame water-fowl of every description swim on it or waddle on the green sward near, and eat the crumbs which the children have brought for them. The paths are skirted with flower-beds, with luxurious grass-plots behind them; and on sunny days these grass-plots are crowded with happy children, who prefer this park to all others, for the water-birds are such grateful guests, and look so amiable and stupid, and are so fond of biscuits, and never bite any one. And the sheep, too, are altogether different from all other sheep in the world; they are so tame and fat, and never think of running away when a good child pats their backs, and gives them some bread to eat. And there are green boats, and for one penny they take you over to the other side; and the water, too, is green, much greener than the boat; and there is no danger of horses and carriages, and children may run and jump about without let or hindrance, and there are such numbers of children too. In short, there is no saying how much pleasure the London children take in St. James's Park.

On the Continent, too, there are parks; they are larger, and are taken more care of, and by far more ornamental than the London parks. But all strangers who come to London must find that their imperial and royal palace gardens at home, with all their waterworks, and Chinese pagodas, Greek temples, and artificial romanticisms, do not make anything like that cheerful, refreshing, tranquillising, and yet exciting impression which the parks of England produce. It is certainly not the climate which works this miracle, nor is it a peculiarity of the soil, for fine meadow-land there is in plenty on the banks of the Rhine and the Danube. The English alone know how to handle Nature, so that it remains nature; they alone can here and there take off a tree, and in another place add some shrubs, without, therefore, forcing vegetation into the narrow sphere of arbitrary and artificial laws. Our great gardens at home want wide open grassplots; where such are, the shrubs and plantations encroach upon them; none are allowed to leave the paths and walk over the grass, and the public are confined to, and crowded on, the sand-covered paths, whence they may look at the clumps of trees, and the narrow empty clearances between them. On such spots in England you find the most splendid cattle; children are playing there, and men and women come and go, giving life, movement, and colouring to the landscape; and, since parks are but imitations of nature, life, movement, and colour are absolutely necessary to them.

This life on the green sward in the very heart of the metropolis gives the parks a rural and idyllic aspect; while, on the other hand, it suggested the saying, that all England gives one the idea of a large park.

At the western end of St. James's park is the Queen's palace—a stately building not a grand one; though extensive enough to astonish those strangers who have read in the newspapers that Her Britannic Majesty complains of want of houseroom. And here it ought to be remarked, that, during the present reign alone not less than £150,000 have been voted by parliament for the extension and improvement of Buckingham Palace. Thanks to so large a sum of money, the palace is now both comfortable and splendid, with its façade overlooking the Green park and St. James's park, with the armorial lion and unicorn, which have lately been placed on the gates in so exquisitely ludicrous a manner, that they turn their backs, at one and the same time, upon one another, the palace, and the queen. To the south, the palace commands a view of the ocean of houses yclept Pimlico; to the north it overlooks the shady groves and meadow grounds of Hyde-park; and on its northern side are splendid gardens nearly as large as St. James's park. Thus is Buckingham Palace situated in the midst of green trees, and removed as far as possible from the smoky atmosphere of the metropolis. And yet they say that the site is not so healthy as might be wished; and the royal family pass only a few months in the year in this their official residence. They prefer Windsor, the valleys of Balmoral, and Osborne (the most charming of marine villas) in the Isle of Wight.

We return to Pall Mall, and passing Marlborough House (at one time the residence of King Leopold of Belgium), we enter St. James's square; and passing the famous house at the corner of King-street from the steps of which George IV., on the night of the 20th June, 1818, proclaimed the news of the victorious battle of Waterloo, we proceed in an eastern direction, and, emerging from Pall Mall enter an open place—the end of Regent-street—whence broad stone stairs lead down into St. James's park. This is Waterloo-place, surrounded by columned mansions. On each side of the broad stone stairs are rows of stately palace-like houses. One of them serves as an asylum to the Prussian Embassy, and another is interesting to the continental visitor because it is Lord Palmerston's town-house. In front of the stairs is the Duke of York's column, of which very little can be said, except that it is ninety-four feet high, and some years ago the jumping down from the top and being smashed on the broad stones at its base, was a fashionable mode of committing suicide. It's a pity that none of the poor wretches ever thought of over throwing and jumping down with the statue of the Duke of York, for it stands ridiculously high, and the impression it makes on that bad eminence is by no means agreeable.

We cross Waterloo-place, and passing Her Majesty's theatre and the Haymarket on our left, we hail the equestrian statue of George III. Again the houses recede, and again a gigantic column with a dwarfish man on its top pierces the skies. Then another George—the fourth of the name—on an iron horse, and there are two fountains, and there is also the National Gallery, and St. Martin's Church, and the lion looking down from

Northumberland House upon the street noise and the streams of life and traffic which here cross and recross in all directions. We are at the foot of the Nelson column, in Trafalgar-square, which native enthusiasm and foreign scoffers say is like the Place de la Concorde at Paris. And here we stop for the present. Politeness induces us to say as little as possible of Trafalgar-square. Besides it is high time to introduce our readers to a friend of Dr. Keif's, to whom we propose devoting the next chapter.

CHAP. XII.

Gentlemen and Foreigners.

ONE OF DR. KEIF'S ADVENTURES.—MANNERS AND CUSTOMS OF OLD ENGLAND.—A NEW ACQUAINTANCE.—ENGLISH Flegeljahre.—THE ORDINANCES OF FASHION.—OUR FRIEND'S AUTOBIOGRAPHY.—THE GENTLEMAN'S OCCUPATIONS AND ECCENTRICITIES.—FOREIGNERS.—JOHN BULL ON FOREIGNERS GENERALLY.—STRIFE AND PEACE.

AMONG the thousand-and-one adventures which Dr. Keif had in the very first week of the season, there was one which, as fate willed it, became entitled to a page in the chronicles of our house.[E] One night at the Opera, he met a gentleman whom many years ago he had seen among the ruins of Heidelberg Castle. Dr. Keif was, of course, overjoyed to see his old friend, and, for many days he sang that friend's praises in the most extravagant terms. He told the ladies of the house that the gentleman he had met was a Don Juan, whose very appearance conquered legions of "blue devils," while the glance of his eye was enough to attract and subdue any female heart.

[E] It is of no use concealing the fact, that our house is that of a respectable London citizen. We will, therefore, confess that Sir John is neither a knight nor a baronet, but that we—without the intervention and assistance of Her Gracious Majesty—considering his eminent services on behalf of our readers, knighted him by means of a silver tea-spoon.

"Oh, indeed!" said I; "then he's a dandy?" "Never mind," whispered Dr. Keif, with an air of profound mystery. "He'll be worth his weight in gold as an ally. He isn't even an Englishman, I tell you. That is to say, not a modern Englishman, but a youthful scion of merry old England. Not a trace of orthodoxy is to be found in him, neither in church nor in kitchen matters, neither in criticism nor in politics." And to Sir John the learned doctor said:—

"Sir,—I have found the man who first gave me an idea of the greatness of England; who persuaded me to study 'Johnson's Dictionary'; and to whom I am indirectly indebted for your acquaintance, respect, and friendship."

Of course we were all very desirous to see this remarkable man. And here we ought to remark, that in an English family the introduction of a stranger is not so usual and common-place an event as in Germany and France. Previous to, and after your first visit, the family meet in council. Your good and bad qualities are weighed in the scale of domestic criticism; for every member of the family sees in you, eventually, a bridegroom, brother-in-law, son-in-law, uncle, or master. At all events you are considered as a suitor for the privileges of a friend of the family, for the slight and passing acquaintances of continental life are unknown in these circles. The very servants in such houses are hereditary, and hold their places for life; the nurse is hired for three generations; the coachman's grandfather trained the mare whose great grand-daughter is now the property of the son of the house. The question whether the doors of the sanctuary are to be opened, concerns all the members of the family, and gives rise to lengthy discussions and animated debates. While the parlour votes you a gentleman, low voices of warning are heard from the depths of the kitchen; for the cook says:—

"Sure no one knows what church you go to on a Sunday; and the other day your coat was buttoned up to the chin; for all the world as if you had cause to conceal your linen or the want of it."

Even Miss Lollypop, though but just in her teens, and fresh from the nursery, takes part in the debate, and raises her shrill voice in condemnation.

"I can't bear him, mamma," says she; "and I won't remain in the room when he comes. How can he dare to pinch my cheek as if I were but a child?"

And you, O unsuspecting stranger, have no idea of the sensation which your knock produces throughout the house; and when, on going away, Sir John shakes hands with you, and sees you to the door, asking you to call again, you are, perhaps—continental as you are—cautious enough to consider all this as a mark of cheap and common politeness! You are mistaken. Sir John lays great stress on his religious observance of the ordinances of old English family life, and he quotes, with much emphasis, the following paragraph of that most explicit of all unpublished law books:—

"And in case the stranger, male or female, doth, by a comely form and demure carriage, gain thy British heart, then shalt thou, when he or she departeth, give his or her hand a hearty shake, to signify and prove thereby that he or she shall always be welcome at thy table, at thy fireside, and in the spare bedroom which is on thy premises. But if thou dost not like him or her, then his or her hand shall not be so shaken."

Robert Baxter, Esq., or, simply Mr. Baxter, as we by this time are accustomed to call him, had, thanks to his friend and eulogist, no difficulties whatever to contend with. He marched in with flying colours. He came, saw, and conquered. The "hearty shake of the hand" was resolved upon before he had emptied his first cup of tea at our fireside. By this time, he is the most intimate friend of the family; he comes and goes away at his liking—takes the children out in his gig—and has, in short, made such progress in the space of a very few weeks, that, in direct violation of another paragraph of the family ordinances, he lays hands even on the sacred poker, and actually pokes the fire with it; a privilege which, according to law, should not be conceded, even to a friend, before the expiration of the seventh year of amicable intercourse.

Let no one fancy that these remarks are an introduction to a novellistic plot. To dispel all suspicions on this head, I proceed at once to unmask Dr. Keif's abominable perfidy—one which the ladies of the house vow they will forgive, but which they cannot forget. Only fancy their disappointment! Keif's "Don Juan," his "amiable hero," his "capital fellow," for thus it pleased the doctor to call him—Mr. Baxter, in fact, is a grey-haired old man. Dr. Keif was cunning enough to excuse the incorrectness of his description by pleading short-sightedness. "It never had struck him—indeed it had not—and,—

"After all," said our learned friend; "though not exactly young, Mr. Baxter is youthful. His whiskers, for instance, are brown; and his large, clear eyes, how free and open do they look at all and everything! Has he not an aristocratic hand? Is not his chin round, his forehead white, and his toilet irreproachable? In short, the more I think of it, the more firmly am I persuaded, that Mr. Baxter is quite a Don Juan if compared with your absurd London greenhorns, whose lengthy faces make all the French shop-girls in Regent-street gape."

"True!" said I. "In my opinion, Mr. Baxter's grey hair is his best recommendation, for none but children and old men are truly amiable in England. No creature on earth more excels in charming merriness and bold natural freshness, than your little freeborn, trouserless Briton. But the moment the boy sports the very ghost of a stray hair on his upper lip—the moment he lays in a stock of razors and stiff shirt collars—that very moment does your English boy undergo a most shocking metamorphosis, and one which even Doyle would despair to depict. The 'Flegeljahre'—the period of sowing wild oats—with other nations a mere transition period, scarcely longer than a northern spring, is, in the case of an Englishman, protracted through ten years and more. With the very brightest character it lasts up to six-and-twenty; but it also frequently happens that the modern Englishman, like unto Tully's Roman, remains an 'adolescens' up to forty. There is something altogether indescribable in this English Flegeljahr character. Fancy a cross between an unctuous missionary and a fast under-graduate, duly coated, cravated brushed up and dressed out for the dining-room; and you will have a tolerably approximating idea of the Flegel-youth, who eager to be very respectable and romantic at one and the same time, succeeds in appearing either insufferably tedious or unconstitutionally comical. Is it their hypochondriacal climate? So do the continentals ask every year, when the English exodus arrives on their shores. Or is it Church and State? Is it a fault of education, or a want of digestion, which causes these wealthy, tall islanders, with their red faces and costly coats, to stand forth so queer, and out of the common order of human creatures? They are neat to perfection, and got up regardless of expense in all their details; but take the fellow as a whole, and you find him mighty unsavoury.

"You will find the reason neither in the fog, nor in constitutional liberty. No Act of Parliament forbids a man to cultivate the graces; and the climate enacts flannel only, but by no means the 'Zopf.' It is not a want of education, but a superabundance of it. It is the education of a rigidly puritanical governess, whose name we never pronounce without a feeling of secret awe. That governess is more fervently adored than the Established Church; people fear her more than they did the Spanish Inquisition. As Fate sat enthroned in mysterious majesty above the gods of Greece, so does this cruel mistress lord it over Magna Charta, Habeas Corpus, and all the other glories of Old England. Her name is Gentility! Liberty of the Press and popular agitation avail not against her. The Commons of England have conquered the strongholds of Toryism; Mr. Cobden and his Cotton Lords have trampled Protection under foot, and light is being let even into the gloomy caverns of Chancery. But what agitator dares to league the cunningly separated classes of English society against only one of the one thousand three hundred positive and negative enactments of Gentility, whereby the favoured people of the isles are distinguished from the pagans of the continent—from the immoral, uneducated barbarians—from those 'soap-renouncing' foreigners! Who liberates the freeborn Briton from the fear of 'losing caste' (a genuine British phrase this!), which follows him as his shadow, whithersoever he may direct his steps—which haunts him even in rural retirement—and which, in a town containing near three millions of inhabitants, admits not even of one single circle of free and general sociability! At a political meeting, perhaps, there may exist something like an approximation of the upper and lower classes, and peers and draymen, cheese-mongers and guardsmen, may, on such occasions, breathe the same air, and fill it with their cheers and groans. But I will rather believe that St. Peter's of Rome and St. Paul's of London can come together, than that the cousin of a Right Honourable will knowingly, and with tolerance prepense, eat his dinner at the same table with the keeper of a cheese-shop.

"We, the foreigners, are blind to the graces of the English Flegel-youth. His manners, which we liken to those of a dancing bear, are, in the eyes of the natives, respectable; what we contemn as a mincing chilliness of address, is exalted as the decent reserve of the true Briton. Of course there are exceptions, especially within these latter days. Now and then we meet with daring innovators, who doubt the exclusive decency of English manners. There are bold sceptics, proclaiming in the East and in the West that a man with a coloured neck-tie ought to be able to appear in the pit of the Italian Opera, without thereby obliging all proper-minded females in the five rows of boxes to faint away and be carried out forthwith. Others pretend that at table you may take the fork with your right hand, without by so doing affixing an indelible stigma to your name; and that there is a possibility of pardon, even for the man who eats mustard with his mutton. The very boldest assert that you may take a pea with your knife, and eat the pea too, and yet be a gentleman for all that. These are charming signs of the times; they awaken hopes which another generation will perhaps justify. But, generally speaking, there is no denying it, that the free social spirit of merry Old England is most frequently to be found among the elderly men."

Grey hair, with red cheeks, is pleasing to look at; and doubly pleasing are those colours when they ornament the head of a gentleman, for in such a case they announce the presence of all sorts of manly amiabilities. The word "gentleman" has been shockingly profaned in England. According to Sir John's cynical definition, any man is a gentleman who pays his tailor's bill. The correctness of that definition would appear to be generally allowed, for the name is most liberally bestowed on dandies and blockheads, wealthy tradesmen and sporting men. But in these pages I speak of the "Gentleman" in the truest and noblest sense of the term. He is a joint production of nature, art, and accident; and there are many conditions to the perfection of this beau ideal.

Imprimis, he must not be compelled to eat his roast-beef by the sweat of his brow; for he who has to work for his existence in England cannot, of course, be said to be independent. He must have made the grand tour; for to the English the continent is in a manner a social high school and academy. How miraculously is the innate and indestructible kernel of English character developed in such a man! As he ripens in years, he breaks through that icy covering which in his earlier years surrounded him, and he shakes off the chains of etiquette or bears them with a grace which proves that to him they are not a restraint, but an ornament.

A few years later, he eclipses the flower of the male part of society in Germany and France; his jovial humour is restrained by an exquisite tact; his politeness acquires substance from a free and hearty manner. There is in him so grave and natural a manliness, that to oblige him and to be obliged by him is equally agreeable. It would seem that he becomes younger as he advances in years.

Such a man was Robert Baxter, Esq. The history of his development is short and simple enough: shortly after his introduction into our circle he related it one evening—after dinner, of course. For what does the code of family morals enact and prescribe?

"Thou shalt invite a gentleman to a good and solid dinner, the which consisteth of fish and roast-meat, and pudding and wine. But thou shalt not invite him to the eating of cakes and sugar-plums, and much less shalt thou tempt him to a soirée dansante, where he would have much labour and no sustenance. And at table thou shalt not, as the wicked do, make the said gentleman talk of politics, business, science, and divers other heavy matters, lest peradventure his attention should be diverted from the enjoyment of the various dishes which thou shalt set before him."

Obedient to this law, Sir John gave a grand dinner to all his family to celebrate Mr. Baxter's acquaintance. It was after that dinner that our friend, reclining in an easy chair, gave us the following sketch of his former life:—

" 'Story—God bless you, I have none to tell, sir.' My life has been that of a gentleman—comfortable and monotonous throughout. I was brought up by an uncle—of course, he was rich; most uncles are. He spoilt me and left me his property. I went to Harrow and Oxford, where I learnt that no one ever learns anything in those seats of learning, except fighting, hunting, and the art and mystery of writing Latin verses. And after all, to think of the lots of very clever men we have in spite of those places—truly it is miraculous! Old England,—thank goodness!—can't be ruined; but it wants ventilation. Ventilation in foreign climes is a necessity for the free-born Englishman. That was my idea when I crossed the Channel to Calais. On that occasion I had a curious adventure. Not a duel—no nothing of the kind. I pitched into a Frenchman and knocked him down. The wretch had called me 'un étranger.' I did not understand his mode of speech, but a friend who was with me said the words meant 'a foreigner.' 'A foreigner, you scoundrel!' cried I. 'How dare you say a free-born Briton is a foreigner!' and I knocked him down. He got up and challenged me to fight a duel with him, but the police interfered, and I was arrested. The lieutenant of the police who had to examine me, told me, with a kindness which was altogether undeserved on my part, that the word 'foreigner' was quite harmless, that it had a relative meaning, and that it might even be complimentary. I could not stand that. I had a dim perception of my being wrong, and of having made an egregious fool of myself, but still I could not get over the contemptuous meaning which we connect with the term; and pig-headed as I was, I replied in English:—

" 'Sir, I'd thank you for not addressing such compliments to me. You may call me a non-Frenchman—of course you may; for I am an Englishman and glory in the fact, but I would not be a foreigner—no! not for the world! Rather than submit to such an indignity I'd leave your country at once.'

"He laughed and bowed me out, and that very day I returned to Dover.

"On my second continental tour, I went through Belgium to Germany, and when, after a few years' residence in that country, I came back to England, I was not alone. I was accompanied by a foreigner—a lady who bore my name. She was not strong, and could not bear the climate. She yearned for her country, but concealed her wish to return. When at length I brought her back to the sunnier clime of Southern Germany, it was too late. That sad event happened many years ago, but though she left me, I was not solitary. Heaven be thanked, I have a son, a dear boy, who is now at college at Heidelberg."

"Of course, your son is half a foreigner!" said Miss Lollypop, with a slight toss of her head.

"Nothing of the kind," said Mr. Baxter, with a smile. "He is a Cockney by birth, for he was born within the sound of Bow-bells. But," added our friend, "I wish him to become so much of a foreigner as to enjoy the brighter sides of English life without a superstitious admiration of the darker ones."

A pause of general embarrassment followed the conclusion of this short and fragmentary autobiography. The children looked at Mr. Baxter curiously, enquiringly, for a couple of stories and anecdotes seemed still hovering on his lips. But he sat silent and lost in thought. Probably his thoughts were with his son, the Heidelberg student; perhaps he fancied he accompanied that son in his wanderings through some valley in the Alps or to the ruins of some ancient abbey, rich with curious carvings and relics of the olden time. For Mr. Baxter rides the antiquarian hobby as he does his other hobbies, of which many are as laborious as useless. For it ought to be remarked, that a real gentleman hates absolute idleness; some purpose or object, fantastic though it be, he must have: he defies dangers and courts fatigues. The odd freaks which English gentlemen have, and which they are guilty of, to the signal astonishment and amusement of continental feuilleton-writers and Gothamites, are mere excrescences of that restless desire of activity which is one of the most splendid qualities of the Anglo-Saxon race. Many thousands of

Englishmen, each of whom can afford to make his life one long spell of rest, devote their time and energies to an honourable servitude in the nation's service, and slave for a single word of thanks from posterity, quite as much as the continental bureaucrats do for orders and pensions. If they want the talents or the ambition necessary for such a career, they will devote themselves to farming or support some one of the numerous charitable institutions of the metropolis or their own county—not only with money, for that were no sacrifice—but also by giving it their time, personal attention, and influence. The active charity of the women is quite as great as that of the men; and this explains the reason why, although in England the gulf between wealth and poverty is wider than in every other country, nevertheless up to the present day there are no symptoms of that patient bitterness of hatred among the lower classes—that harbinger of an approaching doom—which has come to other nations with the gloomy evangel of the future on its pale lips.

As a third class, we have the amateurs and patronisers of arts and sciences; the passionate and most persevering observers of nature, who for many months will watch a swallow's nest, or fill their diaries with observations on the signs and marks of instinct in cockroaches and snails; the travellers in every clime, who take their coffee with the Shah of Persia, converse with the Sultan on the superior excellence of English railroads; rhyme on, and in presence of, the cypress trees of Scutari; smoke the pipe of peace with the Camanchees and the Last of the Mohicans; and who now and then watch and register the hangman's tricks of an accomplished despot, in order to recount them to their countrymen, who never believe such shocking stories, unless published under the authority of a gentleman of known respectability, and conservative principles. Those who are altogether unable to employ their leisure hours—that is to say, their lives—usefully, devote themselves to some "sport" with a touching fanaticism, and ride their hobbies with the heroism of world-betterers. Such a man sails in a nut-shell of a yacht to the polar regions, or travels about in Spain to effect the conversion of Jews and gipsies; or he ascends Mont Blanc, and writes a letter to the Times to commemorate his fatigue and folly.

Mr. Baxter, however, had never been up Mont Blanc, and what is more, it is not likely he will ever make the ascent. He is too old, and too clever. On the evening in question, he gave convincing proof of his shrewd good nature and tact for while we were all silent and embarrassed, he leant back, with the most comfortable air in the world, and with a look of innocent slyness at our long-drawn faces. Our embarrassment and silence were caused by a word of which Mr. Baxter had made a liberal use in his autobiography, and which he pronounced with a provoking emphasis. It is a word on which whole chapters and books might be written—the word "Foreigner."

The ancient Greeks spoke of all other nations on the face of the earth as "barbarians"; and for a period, I believe, they were quite right. It is said, whether truly or falsely I will not here investigate; but it is said, that every Englishman thanks God in his morning's prayers, that he has not been created a foreigner. "He is a foreigner, but a very nice man!" "A very gentlemanly foreigner, indeed!" "What a pity he is a foreigner!" Offensive compliments of this sort fall very frequently from British lips. The tone of pity, contempt, and condescension, with which those disagreeable words are pronounced, is applied, not only with respect to the foreigner, but also to the produce of his country. Bad cherries or plums, are at once declared to be foreign; there is no doubt they come from France, Belgium, or Holland. When our cook opens an egg which offends her olfactory nerves, and when she flings it indignantly into the dust-hole, she accompanies it with the sneering hiss of "foreign"! That wretched egg was laid by a Dutch hen. Of course it was; and probably the passage from Holland was very long and stormy. But alas! all Dutch hens come into evil repute; it is at once understood that, "Them nasty furrin hanimals halways lays bad heggs, Sir."

A bold attempt to vindicate the rights and the honor of foreigners was, on one Sunday evening, made in Guildford Street, at dinner time, when the glorious roast beef of Old England graced Sir John's hospitable board.

"This glorious bulwark of your nation," said Dr. Keif, "is of foreign extraction."

Sir John dropped his knife with the shock these words gave him.

"I dont understand you, sir," said he, rather sternly.

"Is not your loin of beef cut from Jütish ox, that was fattened on the Holstein marshes? Go to Smithfield, and ask the sellers where they got that Homeric beef, to which the British owe their strength, humour, and political superiority?"

Sir John was mute with astonishment and vexation. He could not deny the truth of the learned Doctor's sally; yet if he admitted it, what—ay, what was to become of the roast beef of Old England?

"Come!" said Dr. Keif, following up his advantage, and raising his glass, " 'Here's a health to Father Rhine!' What do you say, Sir," added he, turning to Mr. Baxter; "Is there anything equal to the delight of a walking expedition down the Rhine, or up the Ahr or Mosel?"

Mr. Baxter took the hint.

"Charming!" said he. "Even Sir John must confess that we have some reason for our love of continental life; and that travelling Englishmen, after all, know what is good when they stick to the banks of the Rhine, the Danube, or the Neckar."

"Certainly," said Sir John; "to see those countries, and the queer sort of people that live in them, is certainly worth while; but to the English heart there's no place like home. They have not anything extra in those countries, have they?"

"Yes, they have," said Mr. Baxter peremptorily. To whom Sir John replied—

"It's an old proverb, that there's nothing choice or precious in the world, but money will procure it for you in England."

"I beg your pardon," replied Mr. Baxter, with great determination; "there are things rich and rare which could not be had in England—no, not for all the money in the Bank!"

Sir John was extremely shocked. "Sir," said he; "you astonish me: oblige me by proving your assertion. What is it you allude to?"

"Why, of a Volksfest, a people's festival, really and truly a festival in the open air, when all ranks and classes join and mix without any thought or possibility of a mob; where the wine calls forth songs and laughter, but where not a single fist is raised to threaten or strike."

And Mr. Baxter continued, in rather too flattering colours, giving a sketch of the merry German life, and contrasting it with life in England. He expatiated on the general cultivation of the lower classes, on the toleration of German social life—in short, he lost his way in producing so brilliant an apotheosis of German affairs, that he did not, or would not, pay attention to Sir John, who shook his head in an ominous manner.

At first, Dr. Keif rubbed his hands triumphantly, for on Mr. Baxter's free-born British lips each word had the charm of authority. But as our friend went on, the Doctor could not but confess to himself, that Mr. Baxter's victory might possibly lead to that gentleman's utter ruin in the worthy baronet's good opinion.

There was a long and awful pause. At length Sir John rose, and with a smile, by no means a natural one, he walked up to Mr. Baxter, held out his hand, dropped it, and said—

"Sir! It's my opinion you are a respectable man, and I believe you mean what you say; but moderation is good in all matters. You may be just to foreign countries: so am I. But you idolize the Continent, and despise your own country. That—I beg your pardon—but that is not the conduct of an English gentleman!"

Dr. Keif looked very pale and uncomfortable.

"Nonsense, Sir John," said Mr. Baxter good-humouredly. "Let me say a word to you, and then you may judge whether I love my country less than you do. I have never meddled with politics, but I am something of a Tory; for I take the world as it is, and hold that everything which is, is, if not pour le mieux, according to Voltaire's Candide, at least not without good reason. But no one ought to claim all honour and glory for him and his. The people of this beautiful island have the inestimable treasures of liberty, power and honour. England is an impregnable fortress; a charming garden fenced in by the ocean and by rocks; her tranquil safety is cheap at any price! No venomous reptiles creep on her soil; the wolves have been exterminated for centuries past. But in return, the sweets of existence are open only to hard labour and high birth. A consequence of this is, a spirit of caste, a tendency to seclusion, a stubborn and rugged independence. Look at the Continent. What would those poor nations come to, plagued and hunted down as they are, if deprived of the comforting amenities of a kindly sociability? What, they have no unity in their states, no protection abroad, no sacredness of law, no safety at home, and yet you would dispute with them the paltry consolation of having better actors than you have! If their towns, with their eternal state of siege, had our fogs and clouds of smoke, our penitential Sundays and breathless week-days, whoever could resist the temptation of committing suicide? Why, such a state of things were a hell upon earth! And can you believe that Providence could allow such a state of things to exist? But to return to England. This country has the greatest Parliament, the most powerful orators, the most humane police, the freest newspapers, the most untouchable liberty; and with all this you lay claim to a monopoly of good potatoes and manners! You would have all the gifts and perfections of earth! But if this our England could, in addition to her solid political heritage, have the charms of continental leisure hours, why then this same England were a Paradise on earth—literally a Paradise, where no one could ever think of dying."

Sir John was pacified and happy, and said he was. He went about the room singing "God save the Queen," and would not leave off shaking hands with Mr. Baxter.

SAUNTERINGS IN AND ABOUT LONDON.

THE SECOND PART.
CHAPTER I.

Down the Thames.

RIVER SCENE AT LONDON BRIDGE.—COLLIERS FROM NEWCASTLE.—THE CUSTOM HOUSE.—THE POOL.—THE DANGERS OF THE THAMES.—AN ENGLISHMAN AFLOAT.—RE-APPEARANCE OF DR. KEIF AND MR. BAXTER.—BOATING SCENES.—THE THAMES TUNNEL.—PRIVATE DOCKS.—HOW ENGLISHMEN BUILD SHIPS FOR FOREIGNERS.—GREENWICH.—OLD SOLDIERS IN ENGLAND AND GERMANY.—HOTELS AND POT-HOUSES.—GREENWICH PARK.

AGAIN we have reached the foot of London Bridge, the first of those mighty arched and pillared bulwarks, which oppose the onward progress of ocean ships into the heart of the country. The river at this point is nothing but a large settlement of steamers and boats of every description. On our first tour up the river, we saw many groups of small steamers and fishing-boats, with sails of a dusky red; but the masts of the boats were lowered, and the steamers were of a lilliputian kind—undergrown, low-funnelled, small-engined and paddle-wheeled. They were passenger-boats, plying between the bridges. The class of vessels we see here have a more important appearance. You see at once that these are no water penny omnibuses, coasting it between the City and Putney Bridge. Here are broad black hulls, double funnels and capacious ones, high masts, and boats hauled up at the sides; all tell us that these are hardy customers, that can stand a stiff breeze in the Channel and elsewhere. Some of them swing lazily on their moorings; they have just come in from a voyage, and are taking their ease at home. Others blow vast clouds of steam and black smoke; flags are being hoisted on them, hundreds of people cross and recross on the planks which communicate with the wharf or with other vessels. They are just starting—whither? I, for one, know nothing about it. A sailor could tell you all about them; he reads the character of a ship in the cut of its jib; but we continentals, who are scarcely at home in our country, are perfectly lost in this Babel of foreign vessels and seamen. Even for one short trip to Greenwich—we are starting for Greenwich, you know—we had better ask some porter or policeman to direct us to the boat we want, lest by some mistake we might chance to go to Hamburg, Boulogne, or Antwerp. Such things have happened.

Here we are! On a small steamer, next to a black Scotch coaster, crowded to suffocation, and just casting off. The boy at the hatch is waiting for the captain's signal; and the captain, walking his paddle-box, moves his hand; the boy calls out, the engineer makes a corresponding movement, and the steam enters the large cylinders. The machinery is in motion, and the vessel has left the shore. "Dont be in a hurry, miss! You can't leap that distance. You've missed the boat, as a thousand respectable girls do daily, amidst these vast comings and goings of London. There will be another Greenwich steamer in five minutes; so the misfortune, after all, is not very great!"

What an astounding spectacle the Thames presents at this very point below London Bridge! In autumn, when the great merchantmen, heavily laden, coming in from all parts of the world, cast their bales and casks on the shore, from whence a thousand channels of trade convey them to and distribute them over the whole of the earth—in autumn, I say, this part of the river presents a spectacle of a mighty, astounding activity, with which no other river can vie. The vessels are crowded together by fifties and hundreds on either side. Colossal steamers, running between the coast-towns of France, Germany, and Scotland, have here dropped their anchors, waiting until the days of their return for passengers and merchandise. Their little boats dance on the waves, their funnels are cold and smokeless, their furnaces extinct. Sailors walk to and fro on the decks, looking wistfully at the varying panorama of London life. In a semi-circle round those steamers are the black ships of the North. They are black all over; the decks, the bows, the sides, the rigging, and the crew, have all the same dusky hue. These vessels carry the dark diamond of England—they are colliers from Newcastle. The industrial and political greatness of England springs from the depth of those coal-mines. Deprive the British islands of their coal, give them gold, silver, diamonds, instead—fill their mines with all the coins that the kings of this earth ever minted since the creation of the world—no matter! not these, not all the untold treasures of Australia Felix, would supply that living spark which slumbers in the coal. Without their inexhaustible coal-mines, the English nation would still be what they were a thousand years ago, an island people—poor, weak, and neglected, like the Norwegians.

It is so easy to find fault with God and nature instead of our dear selves. Do me the favour to look at this earth of ours! Of all zones, climes, and countries, how few, how very few there are without some unacknowledged treasure, which, if properly appreciated and turned to account would make a nation's fortune. Are the British Nature's favourites? Is their climate more genial; their soil more fertile than those of the countries we and others live in? No! but the difference lies in the use which the English have made of gifts and opportunities common to all. Their soil produces the finest crops in Europe; a grain of British wheat might be picked out of a thousand grains of continental wheat. Out of their coal-mines they have raised the greatest industrial empire that the world ever knew. Of the stormy channel and the ocean, which beat against their rocky coasts, they have made bridges on which their spirit of enterprise careers and domineers over all the world. Water, earth, air, and fire! from these elements sprang the greatness of England. They are common to all; but those who know how to convert them into power, prosperity and comfort, are justly pre-eminent as the most practical nation.

Our boat has just passed the Custom-house. It is a splendid building; it has been burnt down six times, and six times rebuilt on the same site. Radical Free-traders dislike the building where it stands; they would gladly convert it into a hospital, a poorhouse, or a commercial academy. It will take a long time to realise these liberal intentions; for at this present day duties to the amount £12,000,000 are paid in the port of London alone. Nevertheless, the English swear by Free-trade! The vessels which come to London must all appear at the forum of this Custom-house, unless they prefer leaving their cargo in the docks or the bonded warehouses. What crowds of sailing-ships and steamers from all the harbours of the world! What goings and comings; what loadings and unloadings; what a bewildering movement this Custom-house presents! It is actually painful to the eye. And now, thank goodness, we have left all this turmoil behind us.

The further we go down the river, the more closely packed are the vessels on either side. For above two miles the broad Thames is wofully narrow; and the steamers, which run up and down must just pick their way through as best they can. Accidents will happen; and the man at the wheel must keep a sharp look out. Those who never sailed on the Thames, have no idea of the number of black funnelled monsters, yclept steamers, which continually whisk past one another. There is one just now steering right down upon us; within another second our sides must be stove in. Well done! She has turned aside, and rushes past. But scarcely is the danger over, when another monster of the deep comes paddling on; and a large schooner is wedging its way between us and the said monster of the deep; and on our right there is an awkward Dutchman, swinging round on her anchor; and on our left, there is a lubber of a collier, with her gun-wales just sticking out of the water; and there, goodness gracious! there it is—a very nut-shell of a boat, and two women in it, passing close under our bows. I really dont know why we did not upset them, and why the others did not run into us. That nut-shell of a boat had a narrow escape among the steamers, and those women were fully aware of it; and there is no end of accidents, and yet those people will row across the river.

It is a perfect blessing that the English know better than anybody else how to steer a boat under difficulties. Look at that man at the wheel! Immoveable, with his head bent forward, his eyes directed to the ship's course, his hands ready to turn the wheel: that fellow knows what steering on the Thames is! To all appearance, it is not near so difficult as rope-dancing, but I say it's worse than rope-dancing; it requires the most consummate address. And then there's the responsibility! The sailors of all nations stand in great awe of the London Thames. They navigate their vessels to the East Indies; they weather the storms of the Cape, and think nothing of its blowing "big guns;" but none of them would undertake to steer a vessel from Blackwall to London-bridge. "It's too crowded for us," they say; "and the little nutshells of steamers are enough to make an honest sailor giddy; and the river is so narrow. If you fancy you are clear of all difficulties and can go on, there's sure to be some impertinent boat in your way. Turn to the right! Why there's not room for a starved herring to float!"

And the old steersman descends from his high place, and resigns his functions to the Thames pilot. If he is a conceited blockhead, let him try—that's all. But if the vessel comes to harm, the insurance is lost; for the under-writers at Lloyd's will not be responsible for any damage done in the pool, unless the wheel is in the hands of a regular pilot. And they are right, for with all the difficulties and dangers there are few accidents.

Let us then, trusting to the skill of that particular steersman who guides our own destinies and those of our boat, look at the scenery around. A forest of masts looms through the perennial fog; the banks of the river are lined with warehouses; some old and dilapidated, while others are new, solid, and strong. A stray flag fluttering in the evening breeze, a sailor hanging on the spars and chewing tobacco, a monkey of a boy sky-larking on the topmost cross-trees of an Indiaman—these are some of the sights of the lower Thames. Let us now look at the party on board our own vessel; for, after all, we ought to know the people who are in the same boat with us, and who, in case of an accident would share our watery grave.

The boat is full. A first-class ticket to Gravesend costs nine-pence, and the society is of a mixed description—of course. But it is one of the peculiarities of England, that a "mixed society" does not by any means present so striking an appearance as in Germany or France. It is not easy to look into people; and as for their exterior, their walk, manners, dress, and conduct, there is even among the poorer classes, a strong flavour of the "gentleman." The French blouse, or the German "kittel," have no existence in this country; the black silk hat is the only headdress which Englishmen tolerate. A man in a black dress coat, hat, and white cravat, hurrying through London streets early in the morning, is not, as a raw German would fancy, a professor going to his lecture-room, or an attaché on the track of some diplomatic mystery. No; in the pocket of that man, if you were to pick it, you would find a soap-box, strop, and razor—he is a barber. Or, as the case may be, a man-milliner, or waiter, or tailor, or shoe-maker. Many an omnibus driver sits on the box in a white cravat. In Paris, they say, with a black dress-coat and affability, you find your way into the most fashionable drawing-rooms. Men in black dress-coats descend now and then into London sewers, and that, too, without being in the least affable.

The women of England, too, do not betray their social position by their dress. Coloured silks, black velvets, silk or straw bonnets with botanical ornaments, are worn by a lady's maid, as well as by the lady. Possibly, the maid's dress may be less costly; the lady, too, may sweep her flounces with a distinguished air: there may be some difference or other, but who can see all and know all by just looking at people?

See, for instance, that lovely face under a grey bonnet—there! to the left of the cabin-stairs. She has just risen from her seat. What a slender, graceful figure! Pray dont look at her feet. What ease, what decency in her every movement; and how grandly, yet how confidently, does she take the arm of her companion! By Jove, he has got a black dress-coat, and a white tie! A handsome couple! He is well-shaven, has fine thin lips, with that peculiar, lurking smile of superiority, which the most good-natured Englishmen can scarcely divest themselves of; his auburn hair is splendidly got up; his dress is of superfine cloth; his linen is unexceptionable; he has a gold chain dangling on his waistcoat, and dazzling all beholders. That man, for one, is a gentleman!

"He is nothing of the kind," says Dr. Keif; "he does not pay his tailor's bill. He is a journeyman tailor, and the coat I wear is the work of his hands; it is a capital coat, and I will thank him for making it." Saying which, the Doctor made his way to the young couple, and forthwith shook hands with them.

"They are as good as betrothed," said the Doctor, on his return. "Going for a day's pleasure to Greenwich; honest, decent people those. That's what I like in English prudery, that it cares for trifles only. Take it all in all, and you will find that the state of affairs is more satisfactory here than it is in Germany. That girl's father and mother—honest and decent people, I tell you—have no objection to her gadding about for whole days, and half the nights, too, under the protection of her sweetheart. They walk in the park, sit under the trees, talk of love, marriage, household affairs, Morrison's pills, and other interesting subjects; and while they talk, they eat cold beef and hot mustard. And the result is, an honest marriage, without dishonourable antecedents. In Germany, such excursions would be suspicious in the extreme. Where's the prudery, I should like to know." "Well, well," said the Doctor, shaking his head, "it's the nature of the people."

"And of the tie," said Mr. Baxter. "A white tie, and a black dress coat, kill all rakishness and scampishness, even in the most talented individuals. Choke a man with a white tie, squeeze him tight in a black coat, and he must needs be prudent, calculating, and respectable. He can't help it. It's for that very reason I have exacted from my son, at Heidelberg, a vow that he will eschew white ties and black coats, at least, until he is married."

Here we are at the Tower! There is nothing awful in its appearance from the river side, especially since it was repaired and whitewashed, after the great fire. The outer wall is black, and two red sentinels creep to and fro along it. On the bench, just opposite to us, sits an aged quakeress, with three infantine quakers, who have all along fancied they were going to Westminster. They see their mistake, now that the seeing of it can do them no good whatever, and they behave as quakers are wont to do under such circumstances. They evince moral horror, subdued grief, and unctuous comfort, which they apply to one another. A fat gentleman, who sports a linen shirt-front of the dimensions of a moderate sail (the English are fond of displaying large tracts of linen on their ships and bodies), does his best to cheer the stricken family in drab. In the forecastle, there is a group of workmen reading the Weekly Dispatch, which convinces them that Disraeli is the worst man alive. Some German musicians are congregated round the funnel, and a good deal of newspaper reading is going on on the after-deck, while a newsboy calls out the last number of Punch; small children, in charming dresses, are being fed by their mammas; the men sit, or stand about, gaping or chatting; and some stare, with a very respectable horror, at a group of French ladies and gentlemen, who alone make much more noise than all the other people on board. And all the ladies have their parasols up, to attract the sun, I dare say; but it won't do. The sun, O fairer and frailer portion of humanity, will shine when we are out of London, but not till then.

Why should he? What is an excursion on the Thames without the mystic fog of Romanticism? Without the garish light of day, without the depth of perspective, the objects on shore and on the water grow—so to say—out of the colourless mist, presenting fantastic outlines suddenly, mightily, and with a magic grandeur. On our left we fancied we saw hundreds and hundreds of masts rising up behind the houses, from the very midst of dry land. We thought it was an optical delusion; but, as we advanced, the masts and the outline of the rigging came out strong, substantial, and well-defined, against the lurid sky: and just here there is an Indiaman, deeply laden, turning out of the river, and proceeding inland, floating on locks. What we saw were the basins of the various docks which, hidden behind store-houses of fabulous size and number, extend deep into the heart of the country. The river, broad as it is, cannot afford space for the hundreds and hundreds of vessels which lie snugly in those docks.

Our boat, too, turns to the left bank, and stops near an apoplectic grey tower, which reminds us strongly of the donjon-keeps of the city of Linz in Upper Austria. A similar tower rises from the opposite bank. These towers are the gates of the famous Thames Tunnel. We leave the boat to look at this triumph of British science and perseverance. The tower covers the shaft into which you must descend if you would enter the broad pathway under the water, and the sinking this shaft to the depth of eighty feet was the first step in an undertaking which, since its completion, has commanded the admiration of the architects and engineers of all nations. The broad comfortable stairs and the pathway beneath the river, devoid of ornament and lighted with gas, do not indeed present any striking features to the unscientific visitor. Our railway tunnels are a good deal longer; and what mortal, unless he be a practical engineer, has a conception of the difficulties of this particular undertaking? Still those difficulties were enormous. The breadth of the river is above two thousand feet at high water—the weight pressing on the arches is about double the low water weight—among the strata which the workmen had to pierce there was a layer of floating sand—and, in spite of all precautions, the water broke in not less than five times, and several lives were sacrificed. On one occasion, Mr. Brunel, the architect, had a narrow escape. Through a breach of several thousand cubic feet, the water entered the tunnel, which had then advanced to the middle; the masonry and the machinery were destroyed; it took many weeks before the water was pumped out, and the disastrous hole stopped up with sand-bags; the workmen refused to go down again; the contractors had to double their wages; the works had to be carried on by day and by night without cessation, and the strictest watch had to be kept on the river itself, its tides, and its movements. At length, after an enormous outlay of capital and ingenuity, when even the most sceptical part of the public understood that the construction of a tunnel under the Thames was not an impossibility; it was found that the funds advanced by the shareholders were exhausted. The Parliament, however, granted a loan; the whole of England took an interest in the execution of this great undertaking; fresh machinery was invented; fresh workmen were engaged; the second shaft was sunk on the Wapping side of the river; and the English may say—"We carry out whatever we undertake to do. With us great undertakings do not languish for want of public interest and assistance. A crane standing for many years on a half-built tower, as is the case with the tower of the Cologne Cathedral in Germany—no! thank God, such cranes have no locus standi in England. May be, we are an awkward, square-built people; but after all we are a people, and that's what not every nation can say of itself."

Life in the Thames Tunnel is a very strange sort of life. As we descend, stray bits and snatches of music greet our ears. Arrived at the bottom of the shaft, there is the double pathway opening before us, and looking altogether dry, comfortable, and civilised, for there are plenty of gas-lights; and the passages which communicate between the two roadways, are tenanted by a numerous race of small shop-keepers, offering views of the tunnel, and other penny wares for sale. These poor people never see the sun except on Sundays. The strangers in London are their best, and indeed I may almost say, they are their only customers.

As we proceed, the music becomes more clear and distinct, and here it is: a miniature exhibition of English industrial skill. It is an Italian organ, played by a perfect doll of a Lilliputian steam-engine. That engine grinds the organ from morning till night; it gives us various pieces without any compunction or political scruples. The Marseillaise,

German waltzes, the Hungarian Rakowzy march, Rule Britannia, Yankee Doodle, etc., does this marvellous engine grind out of the organ. Those London organs are the most tolerant of musical instruments that I know of; they appeal to all nations and purses. And what is more marvellous still, they are not stopped by the police, as they would be in Vienna or Berlin, even though the cosmopolitan organ-grinder might descend tens of thousands of feet below the bed of the Spre or the Danube. In the present instance, the organ and the engine are mere decoy-birds. You stop, and are invited to look at "the panorama"—at the expense of "only one penny." You see Queen Victoria at that interesting moment in which she vows to "love, honour, and obey" Prince Albert. You also see a Spanish convent, which no panorama can be without; and the Emperor Napoleon in the act of being beaten at Waterloo—the chief scene of every London panorama, exactly as if the great Napoleon had passed all the years of his life in being beaten at Waterloo. The next view shows you M. Kossuth on horseback, on an Hungarian battle-field, which looks for all the world like an English park; and Komorn, of which the impregnability is demonstrated by its being, Venice fashion, immersed in water, with canals for streets, and gondolas for cabs.

Of such like spectacles the tunnel has plenty, but we cannot stop for them. We hasten to the shaft, ascend the stairs, and feel quite refreshed by the free air of heaven.

"There will be a Greenwich steamer in five minutes," says Mr. Baxter, encouragingly.

"What was the expense of that affair under the water?" asked Dr. Keif, while we stood waiting for the boat.

"One penny each."

"I don't ask what we paid. I mean the tunnel, what did it cost?"

"Something like £455,000. The shareholders gave £180,000, and the rest was advanced by the nation. It would take another £200,000 to make the tunnel fit for carriage traffic. Say £650,000."

"A mere trifle! as Sir John would say," remarked Dr. Keif, with a sarcastic smile; "£650,000 make, without agio, six millions five hundred thousand florins in Austrian money. Give Mr. Struve that sum, and he'll liberate the whole of Germany and a large piece of France into the bargain. What, in the name of all that is liberal, can be the use of that tunnel, I should like to know? Is'nt a good honest bridge ten times cheaper and handsomer? You're a practical people, you are; but crotchetty, my dear Sir, crotchetty, that's the word."

"Most amiable of all German philosophers," said Mr. Baxter, "are you, too, among the Philistines? Hundreds of foreigners have said exactly what you say; and none of them seem to understand what practical purpose the originators of this tunnel had in view."

"They wanted, to prove to the barbarous nations of the Continent, that Britons may walk under water without getting wet and without umbrellas."

"And also that there are some things which are not dreamt of in the philosophy of a German Doctor. Why, that alone would be worth the money! But now, let me tell you that this tunnel cost very little more than one-half of what Waterloo-bridge cost. Besides, how can you bridge the river so low down as this? Why you would stop all the vessels, and spoil the London harbour, for you cannot raise a bridge high enough for large sailing vessels to pass under. Well, we've tried another plan; since the vessels cannot pass under the bridge, we make them go over it. We've tried it, and we've done it. There's the tunnel! It is not the architect's fault if it does not pay. Westward the course of empire takes its way in the world generally, and in London especially, and the east suffers accordingly.

Hence it was not worth while to add a carriage-road to the tunnel. The more's the pity! But here's the steamer!"

There's scarcely standing room on the deck. Besides the steamers, there are Greenwich omnibuses, and there is an extra railroad running its trains every quarter of an hour from London to Greenwich—and yet, look at the crowd which surrounds us on all sides! London, too, has its tides, and its high and low water-mark; its thousands and hundreds of thousands rush into the country and back again at regular periods from one twelve hours to another. The majority of London merchants live in the country, and yet they are able to pass their days in the city. Various means and modes of conveyance, and these quick, ready, and cheap, enable them to accomplish that feat.

As we go down the river, the banks recede, and the vessels lie in smaller groups. In their place, we see the very insignificant-looking yards of the London shipbuilders, which extend almost to Woolwich, the seat of the government dockyard. Woolwich is the second depot of the country; Portsmouth is the first.

The English shipbuilders are cosmopolitans, like the organ-grinders. Little do they care for their customers' position, religion, or nation; they build ships for every man who offers his money, and for every country, too, for Denmark, Spain, Austria, Russia, and even for France.

"We have launched many a steamer, which by this time lies in some Russian port in the Black Sea," says Mr. Baxter.

"It's well for you if those steamers remain where they are. But what if Russia were to send your own ships against you? You shall perish by the work of your own hands!"

"Doctor, you are vastly amusing! Some years ago, I believe it was in 1840, I saw a ship launched at this very spot, a brig, and a fine vessel she was, for the Russian fleet. The Russian Ambassador was on the platform, and so was the Consul, and a great many titled and untitled persons. An old friend, my chum at Harrow, had taken me to see the fun. Honest fellow that; a commander in Her Majesty's service, and since dead of apoplexy. We stood by, and saw the vessel glide into the water, and I made the very same remark you made just now. Of course I meant it as a joke. But you ought to have seen how my poor friend, the Captain, laughed at it. He held his sides, and his honest red face turned blue and purple. It was a mercy that he did not then and there die of apoplexy. 'Eh!' cried he at last; 'do you think they can order a fleet as they would a cargo of cheese? Let the Czar send his roubles, and our fellows will build the ships, I warrant you, and good ships too, and without any dockyard jobs. No altering the poop, no taking out boilers, no cutting in halves, eh? But what's a vessel? Nothing whatever, sir. It's of no use without the sailors. He can't order them. Just order me to play the dancing-master, eh? That vessel costs a good deal of money, and our fellows—Heaven bless them!—are very fond of Russian money. They like to build ships for Russia, just because we mean to hoist the Blue Peter against their Eagle. Fear! Apprehensions, eh? Why, sir, I bless that vessel from the bottom of my heart; that is to say, I wish she may go to pieces on her first trip to Cronstadt, or that I may fall in with her with the law against her and a fair chance of some friendly conversation. Dear me! if I should ever live to see that fine Russian fleet burnt off Athens! For a fine fleet it is, sir, and we'll burn it, too, and build the Czar another (for his money, of course), and a fine one; and if that new fleet shews its nose in British waters, why, d—n me—that's all! What fun to see these vessels launched for the Russian service! That's what they all think, except the Ambassador and the Consul, and that's the reason they cheer away with such hearty good will. Just look at that old tar on the other side. He thinks of boarding her one of these fine days, eh! Well turned in the waist, eh?' "

"O well turned English ethics!" said Dr. Keif with a deep sigh, as he stood with folded hands, looking up to heaven. "Do you think, Mr. Baxter, that Germany too will have the good fortune to get vessels from the English dockyards in consideration of certain moneys well and truly paid, and on the strength of similar cosmopolitan principles?"

"Why not? Though for the present we do all we can to prevent the building altogether. That's the strong side of our diplomacy. But take my word for it, if you order the vessels, and pay for them, you shall have them, and they shall be burnt down to the water's edge on the very first occasion. You have a good stock of sailors on your Baltic and Eastern coasts, and with respect to you we had better keep a sharp look-out."

"Thanks for the compliment," replied the Doctor. "I'll report your words to the First Lord of our Admiralty, whenever that high functionary, as yet unborn, shall have come to years of discretion."

Dr. Keif said these words with a bitter smile, and stooping down to pick up a piece of biscuit which a small boy had dropped, he overturned a still smaller girl who was standing by his side, and with the cigar which he held in his hand he burnt the hand of a lady near him, to the intense disgust of that respectable female, who vented her feelings in a piercing, scream. The Doctor, frightened and confused, made a leap backwards, and alighted with wonderful precision on Mr. Baxter's left foot, the very foot in which it is suspected our aged friend has felt some slight twinges of gout, and, to add to the learned philosopher's discomfiture, a gust of wind blew his hat off his head, and lodged it safely on a large newspaper which a fat old gentleman was reading. The biscuit, meanwhile, had been eaten by an Italian greyhound; the small boy screamed, and the small girl screamed; the fat old gentleman expressed his indignation—some people are so awkward! the lady rubbed her hand; and even Mr. Baxter's temper was slightly ruffled. "You see, gentlemen," said that amiable man, "the consequences of a mere mention of the German fleet on board an English vessel."

That inevitable personage who haunts all steamers—the man with the little book who takes the passage-money from those who are without tickets, has at length found us out. His appearance puts a stop to all acrimonious remarks.

Here is Greenwich, and here is the façade and the cupola of the sailor's hospital, with a semicircle of wooded hills in the background. We have left the fog behind us in London, and the evening sun looks out from the clouds as if he would say—"I am alive and in health, for all that the Londoners believe me to be ailing or in articulo mortis." Our boat rushes past the "Dreadnought"—we touch the shore—the engines are stopped—we are at our journey's end.

We stand on the beautiful terrace in front of the Hospital, the house in which Queen Elizabeth loved to dwell, and here at this very spot her courtiers used to take their walks. Their gold embroidered cloaks are gone, and in their stead you see long blue brass-buttoned coats on the mutilated or decrepid bodies of old sailors. A blue coat, a white neckcloth, shoes, white stockings, and a large three-cornered hat with gold lace—that is the uniform of the Invalids, who pass the evening of their lives in this delightful place.

Greenwich Hospital presents the most beautiful architectural group of modern England. Take the most gifted architect of the world, bandage his eyes, put him on the terrace on which we stand, and then show him this splendid building, and he will at once tell you that this is and must be a royal palace. How could he ever suspect that all this splendour of columns and cupolas is destined to shelter a couple of thousand of poor, decrepid sailors! But that it does shelter them is honorable to the founders and to the English nation.

Go to Germany, enquire in the largest and most powerful states what they have done for their disabled soldiers. There is an Hotel of Invalides at Vienna; for Austria, too, has her mutilated living monuments of the Napoleonic wars and the wars against Hungary. But compare that Austrian Invalidenhaus with this asylum for British sailors. A low, unwholesome site, courtyards alike inaccessible to sunlight and air, cloistered corridors, bare, uncomfortable chambers, vast, chilly saloons, and a population of old soldiers stinted even in the common necessaries of life. It is a great piece of good luck for such a pensioner to obtain the post of watchman in one of the Emperor's parks, where, for a few more florins per annum, he has the privilege of waging war against dogs and ragged little boys. Go to Prussia, that military kingdom, look about in that splendid city of Berlin, and do not for mercy's sake refuse your penny to those old men, in shabby uniforms with medals dangling from their button-holes, who hold out their caps with one hand while they grind old rickety organs with the other—if indeed they have two hands left! These are the veterans who made Prussia great and powerful. In return for their services, they have the inestimable privilege of begging pence from travelling Englishmen.

In those days of Corsican tribulations, England too sent her forces to the battle-fields of the continent. England fought, not only with subsidies, but with her armies and her fleets. Thus much is clearly shown, not only by history, not only by the monuments which have been erected in honor of the Duke of Wellington, but still more by the two great hospitals of Greenwich and Chelsea.

Those two hospitals, devoted to the disabled heroes of the navy and army, give incontestable proof of the grateful kindliness of feeling with which the English nation honors its old soldiers. England treats her cripples as a mother would her sick and ailing children. The architectural splendours of Greenwich Hospital are by no means destined to hide poverty and misery within. The gates are open. You may walk through the refectories, the kitchens, the sitting and sleeping rooms. Wait until the "old gentlemen" sit down to their dinner, eat a

THE GREENWICH PENSIONERS.

slice of their meat, smoke a pipe of their tobacco, take a pinch from one of their snuff-boxes, admire the irreproachable whiteness of their cravats, take a seat at their side on the green benches which stand on the smooth lawn from whence they view the Thames, its sails, masts, and flags, the cherished scenes of their early career. Talk to them. They like to fight their battles over again in conversation, and will tell you whether they have to complain of the ingratitude of their country, and which is best (no matter how disgusted our German enthusiasts would be at the mere idea), to be paid so and so much per limb, or to starve on the general dietary of an Austrian Invalidenhaus, or rot in the streets of Berlin on an annual allowance which would hardly suffice to find a Greenwich pensioner in tobacco and snuff.

All round the hospital, and indeed in its immediate vicinity, there are strange scenes of life, such as are not unfrequently met with in England. A few yards lower down the stream stands, in aristocratic exclusiveness, the Trafalgar Hotel, which I beg to recommend to every one who wishes to pay for a dinner twice the amount which would suffice to feed an Irish family for a whole week. If you like to take your dinner with people who hail the sensation of hunger as the harbinger of enjoyment, you had better enter this hotel and remain there for a few hours. The wines of the Trafalgar, like the Lethe of old, wash away the cares of the past; for it is here that, according to an ancient custom, Her gracious Majesty's ministers meet after the parliamentary session. They drink sherry and champagne, and thank their stars that there are no more awkward questions to answer.

As a contrast to this luxuriant hotel, we see, on the other side of the hospital, partly along the shore, partly near the park, and in the interior of sundry lanes and alleys a vast number of pot-houses, tea-gardens, and places of a worse description, where every vice finds a ready welcome. Boys and girls standing at the doors, invite the passing stranger. "Good accommodation. Very good accommodation, sir." We know what that means, and go our way. But that young fellow in the sailor's jacket, with the girl hanging on his arm; they are caught! They enter the house.

Forward to the green, leafy, hilly park! On the large grass-plots whole families are stretched out in picturesque groups, from the grandfather down to the grandsons and grand-daughters, and along with them there are friends, country-cousins, maid-servants, and lap-dogs with a proud and supercilious air, for they know, sagacious little animals, that their owners are continually paying dog-tax for them. This is Monday, the Englishman's Sunday. There they are chatting, laughing, and even getting up and dancing, eating their cold dinners with a good appetite and a thorough enjoyment of sunshine, air, and river-breeze, and they are all cheerful, decent, and happy, as simple-minded men and women are wont to be on a holiday and on the forest-green. And the deer, half-tame, come out of the thicket and ask for their share of the feast, and we go our way up the hill lest we disturb the children and the deer.

From the top of the hill we look down upon one of the most charming landscapes that can be imagined in the vicinity of a large capital. That ocean of houses in the distance, shifting and partly hidden in the mist; the docks with their forests of masts, the Thames itself winding its way to the sea, green, hilly country on our side, with the white steam of a distant train curling up from the deep cuttings; and at our feet, Greenwich with its columns, cupolas, and neat villas peeping out from among shrubberies and orchards.

We share the hill on which we stand with the famous Greenwich observatory. Probably the building has a better appearance than it had at the time when Flamstead, with generous self-denial, established the first sextant on this spot. But even in our days, the exterior of the building is by no means imposing. Here, then, we stand on the first meridian of England. The country's pride has, up to the present time, retained it here, while the French established their meridian at Paris. But the communistic spirit of science undermines the existence of either, and the Greenwich meridian will not, I am sure, resist the spirit of the age. It will sooner or later resign its pretensions in favour of the chosen of all nations.

The road from the observatory to the back-gate of the park leads through an avenue of old chesnut-trees. They are in a flourishing condition, and the chesnuts are quite as good as those of Italy and southern France. Among these trees stands the official residence of the Ranger of Greenwich-park,—a nobleman or gentleman whose duty it is, in consideration of six or eight hundred pounds per annum, to pass a few summer months in this delightful retreat, and to supply Her Majesty's table with a haunch of venison once every twelvemonth. The post is a sinecure, one of those places which every one inveighs against, and which every one would be glad to possess.

We have crossed the park, and are on Blackheath,—a sunny place, which derives its gloomy name from the Gipsies who used to be encamped upon it in the "days of auld lang syne." Neat villas, covered with evergreens, surround this black heath, and a hundred roads and paths invite us to stroll on and on, through garden-land and park-like domains. We resist the temptation. The sun has gone down. We return to the Thames and take a steamer to Blackwall on the opposite coast.

The breeze, the park, and the walk have made us hungry; and thus it happens that, very much against our will, we find ourselves seated at a table which three solemn-looking gentlemen in black dress-coats and white cravats are busily loading with a number of large and small dishes. Each of these dishes—thus English custom willed it—is surmounted by a cover of polished silver, or at least a metallic composition which looks like silver, and each contains some sort of fish. Lovegrove's Hotel has these many years past been famous for its fish dinners, and the fame is well deserved. Nowhere, except perhaps at Antwerp, does a gourmand find so vast a field for the study of this particular department of his favourite science. But more charming than the most delicious eels, mackerel, salmon, soles, and whitebait, is the view from the dining-room.

It is night. We "take the cars," as they say in America, and rattle on, over the houses, canals, and streets, to the City. It took us just fifteen minutes to go all the distance.

CHAP. II.

The Theory of Locomotion.

WHEN DOCTORS DISAGREE, ETC.—CLIMATIC VARIETIES OF LONDON.—LOCOMOTION.—ITS MODES AND DIFFICULTIES.—RULES AND REGULATIONS FOR PEDESTRIANS.—CARRIAGES.—CAB-LAW AND LAWLESSNESS.—CABMEN AND WATERMEN.—NOTES OF AN OMNIBUS PASSENGER.—DRIVERS AND CONDUCTORS.—STAGE-COACHES.—METROPOLITAN RAILWAYS.

"WHAT a dreadful fog there is to-day!"

"Nothing of the kind, Madam. Cloudy and wet, perhaps, and a little misty; but a fog—no Madam, that haze is not a fog. Fogs are yellow and black; in a fog, the carriages and foot-passengers run against one another. It hurts your eyes, and takes away your breath; it keeps one in doors. But this is not what a Londoner would call a fog."

"Is it not indeed, Doctor. Well, then, I must prepare myself for a worse condition than I am now in, low and out of health as I feel."

"Of course," says the Doctor, feeling the fair stranger's pulse. "Have I not told your husband again and again"——

"Are you again harping at the old theme?"

"I am; and I mean to persist until you follow my advice, Madam," replied the Doctor, with great unction. "You ought not to live in this part of the town, the air kills you. You must go and live in Brompton; that's what every London physician will tell you. This part of the town is too bleak and cold for you."

We leave the old Doctor to descant on the vast climatic difference between Regent's Park and Brompton, while we inform the geographers among our German readers of the whereabouts of the latter place. Brompton, then, was at one time a small village in the South-west, between Hyde Park and the Thames. It has, however, these many years lost its separate existence, and been swallowed up by the metropolis, just as many larger places around London have been swallowed up before and since; and Brompton, at the present time, is as much a part of London as Holborn and Islington. The idea of the immense area which is covered by this gigantic town may be approximatively realised from the fact, that many learned physicians discuss the climatic differences of various parts of the town exactly as if they were comparing the climates of Italy and Germany. Expressions, such as "I live in the North," or, "I have taken a house in the West," are common-place and appropriate. This idea of colossal extension ought to be well considered and fully realised by those who wish to understand London life in all its various phases. But, in spite of all divisions into North and South, and East and West, the London of our days is, nevertheless, one single compact town; he who inhabits it must be prepared to go many miles to see a friend or to follow up his business, whatever that business may be. A Londoner loses one-half of his life in locomotion; he would lose more, if his ordinary and extraordinary town travels were not regulated according to some tried and practical theory.

The necessity of expeditious and cheap locomotion in the streets of London has called forth a variety of methods of travelling. The cheapest, simplest, oldest, and most natural of them is walking. In the narrow and crowded streets of the City, where conveyances make but little progress, this method is certainly the safest, and, withal, the most expeditious. Strangers in London are not fond of walking, they are bewildered by the crowd, and frightened at the crossings; they complain of the brutal conduct of the English, who elbow their way along the pavement without considering that people who hurry on, on some important business or other, cannot possibly stop to discuss each kick or push they give or receive. A Londoner jostles you in the street, without ever dreaming of asking your pardon; he will run against you, and make you revolve on your own axis, without so much as looking round to see how you feel after the shock; he will put his foot upon a lady's foot or dress, exactly as if such foot or dress were integral parts of the pavement, which ought to be trodden upon; but if he runs you down, if he breaks your ribs, or knocks out your front teeth, he will show some slight compunction, and as he hurries off, the Londoner has actually been known to turn back and beg your pardon.

Of course all this is very unpleasant to the stranger, and the more delicate among the English themselves do not like it. None but men of business care to walk through the City at business hours; but if, either from choice or necessity, you find your way into those crowded quarters, you had better walk with your eyes wide open. Don't stop on the pavement, move on as fast you can, and do as the others do, that is to say, struggle on as best you may, and push forward without any false modesty. The passengers in London streets are hardened; they give and receive kicks and pushes with equal equanimity.

Much less excusable is the kicking and pushing of the English public at their theatres, museums, railway stations, and other places of public resort. Nothing but an introduction to every individual man and woman in the three kingdoms will save you from being, on such occasions, pushed back by them. You have not been introduced to them; you are a stranger to them, and there is no reason why they should consult your convenience. The fact is, the English are bears in all places, except in their own houses; and only those who make their acquaintance in their dens, know how amiable, kind, and mannerly they really are.

You cannot lounge about in the streets of London. Those who would walk, should go at once to the parks, or parade some square. The loungers you see in Regent Street and its purlieus, are foreigners, chiefly French, as their hirsute appearance clearly shows. An Englishman likes that sort of thing on the Boulevards of Paris, or St. Mark's Place, at Venice; but in his own country he wants the scenery, the climate, the excitement, and the opportunities. A thousand various interests draw him back to his family circle. Though accustomed to the Continent, and its manners and customs, the moment the traveller returns to England, he takes to English customs and English prejudices, and, in the fulness of his British pride, he is very careful lest his appearance and conduct show traces of his residence in foreign countries. The Germans do exactly the contrary.

He who would economise his time and strength, had better keep his carriage—if he can afford it; there are plenty on sale, and of the best of their kind. But the expense of keeping a carriage and horses is by far greater than in any other capital; the wages of the coachman, and the hire of the stabling, etc., are so enormous. And, besides, there is the Chancellor of the Exchequer holding out his hat, for all the world like one of those greedy Irish beggars, asking you to pay duty for the carriage and the horses; for the coachman and his livery; for the servant who stands behind the carriage, and that servant's livery; for the powder he has on his head; for the cane he holds in his hand; for the high box-seat, the hammercloth, and the armorial bearings which are embroidered on it—provided, always, it is your pleasure to indulge in these aristocratic luxuries. Those are the taxes on luxuries, of which there are plenty in this country; and so there ought to be. No duty is paid for tradesmen's carts and vans, if the owner's name and address is plainly written on them; and the tradesmen, who turn everything to advantage, write their names very plainly on their carts and vans, and send them out into the streets to advertise their firms. These tradesmen's carts are the most numerous and conspicuous among the countless vehicles, which pass to and fro in London streets. There is scarcely a shop which has not its cart or van. Of course the grocers have vans, for they send their goods to any distance within ten miles; and so do the bakers, butchers, fishmongers, and greengrocers. They can't help it, for if they were to confine their operations to their immediate neighbourhood, they would soon be crushed by competition. A London tradesman, who deals in articles of daily consumption, had better not try to walk. The very lad who sells odds and ends of meat for the convenience of Metropolitan cats and dogs, has a meat cart, and a clever pony; and on the cart there is a splendid legend, in gold letters "Dog's and Cat's Meat." The retailer of such wretched stuff, would starve in a smaller town; in London he has to keep his horse and cart, and makes a capital living, as they tell me. And on Sunday, when dogs and cats have to live on the stores that were taken in on Saturday, the lad takes his "fancy gal" for a drive into the country, with the legend of "Dog's and Cat's Meat," flaming brightly behind.

The next great branch of the Metropolitan conveyance system, is that of the carriages which ply for hire, with or without a number. The latter, in all their leading features, are similar to the carriages of all the Continental capitals. They are taken by the hour, by the day, week, month, or year. Chief among the former are the London cabs.

"Live and learn," ought to be the motto of the student of London cab-ology. No mortal could ever boast of having mastered the subject. There is no want of police regulations, and of patriots to enforce them; but still the cabmen form a class of British subjects, who, for all they are labelled, booked, and registered, move within a sphere of their own, beyond the pale of the law. The Commissioners of Police have drawn up most elaborate regulations concerning cabs; they have clearly defined what a cab ought to be, but the London cabs are exactly what they ought not to be. The faults of these four-wheeled instruments of torture can never sufficiently be complained of. Not only do they shorten the honest old English mile; but they bear a strong family-likeness to the Berlin droshkies. If the horse is wanted, it is sure to be eating; if the cabby is wanted, he is equally sure to be drinking. If you would put the window down, you cannot move it; if it is down, and you would put it up, you find that the glass is broken. The straw-covered bottom of the cab has many crevices, which let in wind and dust; the seats feel as if they were stuffed with broken stones; the check-string is always broken; the door won't shut; or if shut, it won't open: in short (we make no mention of the horse), to discover the faults of a London cab is easy; to point out its good qualities is, what I for one, have never been able to achieve.

Whenever a stranger is bold enough to hail a cab, not one, but half a dozen come at once, obedient to his call; and the eagerness the drivers display is truly touching. They secure their whips, descend from their high places, and surround the stranger with many a wink and many a chuckle, to learn what he wants, and to "make game of him."

Supposing the stranger speaks the English language fluently enough to make himself understood, of course he will name the place to which he wishes to go, and ask what they will take him for. He may rely on it, that of any conclave of cabmen, each one will demand, at least, double the amount of his legal fare. He demurs to the proposal, whereupon the six cabmen mount their boxes forthwith, return to their stand in the middle of the road, and indulge in jocular remarks on "foreigners," and "Frenchmen" in general. Blessed is that foreigner, if his studies of the English language have been confined to Byron, Thackeray, and Macaulay, for in that case he remains in happy ignorance of all the "good things" that are said at his expense. The retreat, however, was merely a feint; a few skirmishers advance again, and waylay the stranger. Again, and again, do they inquire, "what he will give?" They turn up the whites of their eyes, shrug their shoulders, make offers confidently, and decline propositions scornfully, and go on haggling and demonstrating until one of them comes to terms, and drives off with the victim.

But is there no legal scale of fares? Of course there is, but with the enormous extent of London it was impossible to establish a general fare for each "course" according to the cab regulations of the German, French, and Italian towns. A certain sum, say one shilling for each drive, would have wronged either the passenger or the driver. To get rid of the dilemma the fare was fixed at eight-pence per mile. But who can tell how many miles he has gone in a cab? A stranger of course cannot be expected to possess an intimate knowledge of places and distances. An old Londoner only may venture to engage in a topographic and geometrical disputation with a cabman, for gentlemen of this class are not generally flattering in their expressions or conciliating in their arguments; and the cheapest way of terminating the dispute is to pay and have done with the man. As a matter of principle the cabman is never satisfied with his legal fare; even those who know the town, and all its ways, must at times appeal to the intervention of a policeman or give their address to the driver, not, indeed, for the purpose of fighting a duel with him, but that he may, if he choose, apply to the magistrate for protection. But it is a remarkable fact, that the cabmen of London are by no means eager to adopt the latter expedient.

The Hansom Cabs, which of late years have been exported to Paris and Vienna, are generally in a better condition than the four-wheeled vehicles; but their drivers are to the full as exacting and impertinent as their humbler brethren of the whip. To do them justice, if they are exorbitant in their demands, they at least are satisfactory in their performance. They go at a dashing pace whenever they have an open space before them, and they are most skilful in winding and edging their light vehicles through the most formidable knots of waggons and carriages. The "Hansom" man is more genteel and gifted than the vulgar race of cabmen; he is altogether smarter (in more than one sense) and more dashing, daring, and reckless.

When cabby returns to his stand, he drops the reins, chats with his comrades, recounts his adventures, and "fights his battles o'er again," or he lights his pipe and disappears for a while in the mysterious recesses of a pothouse. His horse and carriage are meanwhile left to the care of an unaccountable being, who on such occasions pops out from some hiding-place, wall-niche, or cellar. This creature appears generally in the shape of a dirty, rickety, toothless, grey-haired man; he is a servus servorum, the slave of the cabmen, commonly described as a "waterman." For it was he who originally supplied the water for the washing of the vehicles. In the course of time, however, his functions have extended, and the waterman is now all in all to the cab-stand. He cleans the cabs, minds the horses, attends to the orders of passengers, opens and shuts the doors, and fetches and carries to the cabstand generally tobacco, pipes, beer, gin, billets-doux, and other articles of common consumption and luxury; in consideration for which services, he is entitled to the gratuity of one penny on account of each "fare"; and he manages to get another penny from the "fare" as a reward for the alacrity and politeness with which he opens the door. But further particulars of this mysterious old man we are unable to give. No one knows where he lives; no one, not even Mr. Mayhew, has as yet been able to ascertain where and at what hours he takes his meals. At two o'clock in the morning he may be seen busy with his pails, and at five or six o'clock you may still observe him at his post, leaning against the area railings of some familiar public-house. But the early career of the man, his deeds and misdeeds, joys and sufferings, before he settled down as waterman to a cab-stand—these matters are a secret of the Guild, and one which is most rigorously preserved. Poor, toothless, old man! The penny we give thee will surely find its way to the gin-shop, but can we be obdurate enough to refuse giving it, since a couple of those coins will procure for thee an hour's oblivion?

We turn to the omnibuses, the principal and most popular means of locomotion in London. And here we beg to inform our German friends, that those classes of English society whose members are never on any account seen at the Italian Opera, and who consume beer in preference to wine, and brandy in preference to beer, affect a sort of pity, not unmixed with contempt, for those who go the full length of saying "Omnibus." The English generally affect abbreviations; and the word "bus" is rapidly working its way into general acceptation, exactly as in the case of the word "cab," which is after all but an abbreviation of "cabriolet."

Among the middle classes of London, the omnibus stands immediately after air, tea, and flannel, in the list of the necessaries of life. A Londoner generally manages to get on without the sun; water he drinks only in case of serious illness, and even then it is qualified with "the ghost of a drop of spirits." Certain other articles of common use and consumption on the Continent, such as passports, vintage-feasts, expulsion by means of the police, cafés, cheap social amusements, are entirely unknown to the citizens of London. But the Omnibus is a necessity; the Londoner cannot get on without it; and the stranger, too, unless he be very rich, has a legitimate interest in the omnibus, whose value he is soon taught to appreciate.

The outward appearance of the London omnibus, as compared to similar vehicles on the Continent, is very prepossessing. Whether it be painted red as the Saints' days in the Almanack, or blue as a Bavarian soldier, or green as the trees in summer, it is always neat and clean. The horses are strong and elegant; the driver is an adept in his art; the conductor is active, quick as thought, and untiring as the perpetuum mobile. But all this cannot, I know, convey an idea of "life in an omnibus." We had better hail one and enter it, and as our road lies to the West, we look out for a "Bayswater."

We are at the Whitechapel toll-gate, a good distance to the East of the Bank. From this point, a great many omnibuses run to the West; and among the number is the particular class of Bayswater omnibuses one of which we have entered. It is almost empty, the only passengers being two women, who have secured the worst seats in the furthermost corners, probably because they are afraid of the draught from the door. The omnibus is standing idly at the door of a public-house, its usual starting-place. The driver and conductor have been bawling and jumping about, especially the latter, and they are now intent upon "refreshing" themselves. The horses look a little the worse for the many journeys they have made since the morning. Never mind! this omnibus will do as well as any other, and we prepare to secure places on the outside.

But before we ascend, let us look at the ark which is to bear us through the deluge of the London streets. It is an oblong square box, painted green, with windows at the sides, and a large window in the door at the back. The word "Bayswater" is painted in large golden letters on the green side panels, signifying that the vehicle will not go beyond "that bourn," and also furnishing a name for the whole species. A great many omnibuses are in this manner named after their chief stations. There are Richmonds, Chelseas, Putneys, and Hammersmiths. Others again luxuriate in names of a more fantastic description, and the most conspicuous among them are the Waterloos, Nelsons, Wellingtons, Taglionis, Atlases, etc. One set of omnibuses is named after the "Times"; others, such as the "Crawford's," are named after their owners.

The generic name of the omnibus shines, as we have said, in large golden letters on the side panels; but this is not by any means the only inscription which illustrates the omnibus. It is covered all over with the names of the streets it touches in its course. Thus has the London omnibus the appearance of a monumental vehicle, one which exists for the sake of its inscriptions. It astonishes and puzzles the stranger in his first week of London life; he gazes at the omnibus in a helpless state of bewilderment. The initiated understand the character of an omnibus at first sight; but the stranger shrugs his shoulders with a sigh, for among this conglomeration of inscriptions, he is at a loss to find the name and place he wants.

But to the comfort of my countrymen be it said, that the study of omnibus-law is not by any means so difficult as the study of cab-law. Practice will soon make them perfect; still we would warn them not to be too confident. Many a German geographer, with all the routes from the Ohio to the Euxine engraven in his memory, has taken his place in an omnibus, and gone miles in the direction of Stratford, while he, poor man, fondly imagined he was going to Kensington. Even the greatest caution cannot prevent a ludicrous mistake now and then; and the stranger who would be safe had better consult a policeman, or inform the conductor of the exact locality to which he desires to go. In the worst case, however, nothing is lost but a couple of hours and pence.

While we have been indulging in these reflections, the number of passengers has increased. There is a woman with a little boy, and that boy will not sit decently, but insists on kneeling on the seat, that he may look out of the window. An old gentleman has taken his seat near the door; he is a prim old man, with a black coat and a white cravat. There is also a young girl, a very neat one too, with a small bundle. Possibly she intends calling on some friends on the other side of the town; she proposes to pass the night there, and has taken her measures accordingly. A short visit certainly is not worth the trouble of a long omnibus journey. Thus there are already six inside passengers, for the little boy, who is not a child in arms, is a "passenger," and his fare must be paid as such. The box-seat, too, has been taken by two young men; one of them smokes, and the other, exactly as if he had been at home, reads the police reports in to-day's "Times."

Stop! another passenger! a man with an opera-hat, a blue, white-spotted cravat, with a corresponding display of very clean shirt-collar, coat of dark green cloth, trousers and waistcoat of no particular colour; his boots are well polished, his chin is cleanly shaved; his whiskers are of respectable and modest dimensions. There is a proud consciousness in the man's face, an easy, familiar carelessness in his movements as he ascends. He takes his seat on the box, and looks to the right and left with a strange mixture of hauteur and condescension, as much as to say: "You may keep your hats on, gentlemen." He produces a pair of stout yellow gloves; he seizes the reins and the whip—by Jove! it's the driver of the omnibus!

Immediately after him there emerges from the depths of the public-house another individual, whose bearing is less proud. He is thin, shabbily dressed, and his hands are without gloves. It is the conductor. He counts the inside passengers, looks in every direction to find an additional "fare," and takes his position on the back-board. "All right!" the driver moves the reins; the horses raise their heads; and the omnibus proceeds on its journey.

The street is broad. There is plenty of room for half a dozen vehicles, and there are not many foot-passengers to engage the conductor's attention. He is at liberty to play some fantastic tricks to vary the monotony of his existence; he jumps down from his board and up again; he runs by the side of the omnibus to rest his legs, for even running is a recreation compared to standing on that board. He makes a descent upon the pavement, lays hands on the maid of all work that is just going home from the butcher's, and invites her to take a seat in the "bus." He spies an elderly lady waiting at the street-corner; he knows at once that she is waiting for an omnibus, but that she cannot muster resolution to hail one. He addresses and secures her. Another unprotected female is caught soon after, then a boy, and after him another woman. Our majestic coachman is meanwhile quite as active as his colleague. He is never silent, and shouts his "Bank! Bank! Charing-cross!" at every individual passenger on the pavement. Any spare moments he may snatch from this occupation are devoted to his horses. He touches them up with the end of his whip, and exhorts them to courage and perseverance by means of that peculiar sound which holds the middle between a hiss and a groan, and which none but the drivers of London omnibuses can produce.

In this manner we have come near the crowded streets of the city. The seat at our back is now occupied by two Irish labourers, smoking clay-pipes, and disputing in the richest of brogues, which is better, Romanism without whiskey, or Protestantism with the desirable addition of that favourite stimulant. There is room for two more passengers inside and for three outside.

Our progress through the city is slow. There are vehicles before us, behind us, and on either side. We are pulling up and turning aside at every step. At the Mansion-house we stop for a second or two, just to breathe the horses and take in passengers. This is the heart of the city, and, therefore, a general station for those who wish to get into or out of an omnibus. These vehicles proceed at a slow pace, and take up passengers, but they are compelled to proceed by the policeman on duty, who has strict instructions to prevent those stoppages which would invariably result from a congregation of omnibuses in this crowded locality.

Our particular omnibus gives the policeman no trouble, for it is full, inside and out, and this important fact having been notified to the driver, the reins are drawn tight, the whip is laid on the horses' backs, and we rush into the middle of crowded Cheapside. Three tons, that is to say, 60 cwt., is the weight of a London omnibus when full, and with these 60 cwts. at their backs, the two horses will run about a dozen English miles without the use of the whip, cheered only now and then by the driver's hiss. And with all that they are smooth and round and in good condition; they are not near so heavy as those heavy horses of Norman build which go their weary pace with the Paris omnibuses, nor are they such wretched catlike creatures as the majority of the horses which serve a similar purpose in Germany. Their harness is clean; on the continent it might pass for elegant. Although fiery when in motion, they never lay aside that gentleness of temper which is peculiar to the English horses. A child might guide them; they obey even the slightest movement of the reins; nay, more, an old omnibus-horse understands the signals and shouts of the conductor. It trots off the moment he gives that stunning blow on the roof of the omnibus, which, in the jargon of London conductors, means: "Go on if you please;" and the word "stop" will arrest it in the sharpest trot.

But for the training and the natural sagacity of those animals, it would be impossible for so many omnibuses to proceed through the crowded city streets at the pace they do, without an extensive smashing of carriages, and a great sacrifice of human life resulting therefrom. We communicated our impressions on this subject to the omnibus driver, and were much pleased to find our opinion corroborated by the authority of that dignitary.

"The city," said he, "is a training-school for carriage-osses and for any gent as would learn to drive. As for a man who is'nt thoroughly up to it, I'd like to see him take the ribbons, that's all! 'specially with a long heavy 'bus behind and two osses as is going like blazes in front. I see many a country fellow in my time as funky as can be, and sweating, cause why? he feeled hisself in a fix. And an oss, too, as has never been in the city afore, gets giddy in his head, and all shaky-like, and weak on his legs. But it's all habit, that's what it is with men and osses."

Well! our man and our "osses" are accustomed to the confusion and the turmoil which surrounds us. With the exception of a few short stoppages, which are unavoidable in these crowded streets, we proceed almost at a giddy pace round St. Paul's, down the steep of Ludgate Hill, and up through Fleet Street and Temple Bar. We are in the "Strand"; and here we are less crowded, and proceed at a still more rapid pace, with twelve inside and nine outside passengers, making the respectable total of one-and-twenty men and women. More than this number it is illegal to cram into an omnibus. That vehicle is among the few places in England where you come into immediate contact with Englishmen without the formality of a previous introduction. Parliament, which has to provide not only for Great Britain, Ireland, and the town of Berwick upon-Tweed, but also for a considerable portion of Africa, America, Asia, and the whole of Australia— whose duty it is to keep a sharp eye on the Germanic Confederation, the French Empire, the Papal See, the Oriental question, and a great many similar nuisances; and which, over and above all these important avocations, has to adjourn for the Easter recess and the Epsom races—though thus overwhelmed with business still the English Parliament has found time to pass some salutary laws for the proper regulation and management of omnibuses, to prevent the over-crowding of those useful vehicles, and to ensure regularity, politeness, and honesty on the part of the drivers and conductors. The laws with respect to omnibuses are few in number; but they work well, and suffice to secure the passengers in those vehicles against insult and imposition. As, however, accidents will happen, so it may now and then come to pass that a stranger, or a genteel and ignorant female is cheated, and induced to pay the sum of threepence over and above the legal fare; but in these cases it will generally be found, that the passenger might have prevented the imposition, if he or she had condescended to enquire of some other passenger as to the exact amount of the fare. Such questions are always readily answered, and every one is eager to give the stranger the information he requires.

On the Continent, it is generally asserted that the English are haughty and shy, that they will not answer if a question is put to them; and that, especially to foreigners, they affect silence, incivility, and even rudeness. There is no truth whatever in such assertions. Any one, whose good or ill fortune it is to make frequent omnibus journeys, will find that the notion of English rudeness, like many other Continental notions, is but a vulgar error. It is true that no fuss or ceremony is made about the stowing away of legs, that an unintentional kick is not generally followed by a request for ten thousand pardons; but, in my opinion, there is a good deal of natural politeness in this neglect of hollow conventional forms, which, after all, may be adopted by the greatest brute in creation. Why should there be a begging of pardon when every one is convinced that the kick was accidental, unintentional, and that no offence was meant? Why should I express my gratitude to the hand that is held out to me in getting in? The action is kind, but natural, and does not, in my opinion, call for a verbose recognition. Those who discover rudeness in the absence of polite phrases, cannot, of course, but think that the English are brutes. But simple and ingenuous characters are soon at their ease in English society.

There were no stoppages in the Strand; but at Northumberland House, in Trafalgar Square, we stop for a minute or two, as at the Mansion House, to take in and let out passengers. Moving forward again, we go up part of Pall Mall and the whole length of Regent Street to the upper Circus. This point is more than half way in the journey from Whitechapel to Bayswater, and that distance—above five English miles—is, after all, only a three-penny fare.

Within the last quarter of an hour we have changed our complement of passengers, and the sky, too, has altered its aspect. Large drops of rain are falling. The driver produces his oilskin cape, a stout leather covering is put over his knees, and over those of the box-seat passengers, whose upper halves are protected by an umbrella. All the outside passengers, too, produce their umbrellas—for few Londoners venture to go out without that necessary protection against the variableness of the climate.

Luckily, however, the shower is over before we have come to Hyde Park Gate, at the western end of Oxford Street. The sun breaks through the clouds, as we turn down that splendid street which runs parallel with the side of the Park. Stately, elegant buildings on our right; Kensington Gardens, green meadows, and shady trees, on our left. Here we leave the omnibus, for we cannot resist the temptation of taking a stroll in these charming gardens. We have made a journey of eight miles. We have seen life on and in an omnibus, in all its varieties; at least, as far as it is possible in a single journey; and we pay for the accommodation the very moderate charge of sixpence.

The London omnibuses, though much abused, are vastly superior to similar vehicles in other Continental capitals; but still greater, as compared to the Continental "Post," or "Schnellwagen," is the superiority of those public vehicles which run in longer or shorter stages across the country. It is a pity these stage-coaches are being driven off the road by the superior speed of the railways. They are going out rapidly. And yet, how glorious it was to ride on the top of one of them! Their decline destroys all the poesy of travelling amidst the leafy hedge-rows on the splendid English roads, which are more similar to our park-roads than to our "Landstrassen." What a wholesome, social, adventurous pleasure it was, to sit on the outside of a stage-coach with about twelve travelling companions, male and female, and drawn by four splendid horses, to skim, as it were, over the smiling garden-like country. No Englishman, of the olden time, was too rich or too aristocratic for this mode of travelling; and the occasional driving of such a stage, and the playing the part of coachman to the public at large, was among the "noble passions" of the sporting aristocrats of the time. Since then, the steam-engine has conquered the length and breadth of the country, and he who would enjoy stage-coach travelling, must go in quest of it to the outlying parts of England; for instance, to the Isle of Wight, where the old coach may still be seen in all its glory. Long may it be so, until, in that island, too, it is compelled to yield to the improvements of the age!

We have already, in another place, given an account of the Thames steamers. But in treating of the chief methods of locomotion in London, we ought not to forget the railroads. They are among the peculiarities and sights of London, for no other town in the world is so large that the communications between its various parts are carried on by means of rails and locomotive engines. Here, where the majority of the termini are, if not in the centre, according to Mr. Pearson's salutary project, at least within the town, the railways which communicate with the interior of the country, and the various seaports, have several stations in the interior of the town, and passengers are conveyed from one town station to another. There are, moreover, railways especially intended for London and the suburbs: among these, are the lines to Greenwich and Blackwall, which communicate with that extraordinary railroad which, forming an enormous semicircle, facilitates the communication between the eastern and the whole of the northern parts of London.

This peripheric line is essentially a London railway; it does not, on any one point, travel beyond the boundaries of that monster town. It is laid out between garden-walls and backyards, between roofs and chimneys; it is bridged over canals and crowded streets, or laid on viaducts for many miles through the poorer quarters, almost touching the houses, and passing hard by the windows of the upper stories. In other places, according to the peculiarities of the ground, the line is carried on through tunnels under the houses, cellars, sewers, and aqueducts. It is a miraculous railway, and one which has been constructed at an enormous outlay of ingenuity and money; but it enables the Londoners to go to the northern suburbs for sixpence, in a first-class carriage too, and in less than twenty minutes. There is no cessation in the traffic of this line; the trains are moving from early morn till late at night; every quarter of an hour a train is despatched from either terminus, and these trains stop at all the intermediate stations.

The journeys being so short, and time, speed, and cheapness the chief objects in view, the railway company have paid little attention to the comfort of the passengers. And here I ought to add, that with the exception of greater speed, which, after all, is the main object, all the English railways are inferior to those of the Continent. In London, and in short journeys, the want of comfortable carriages and convenient waiting-rooms is not a very painful infliction; but woe to the wretch whom fate condemns to go from London to Edinburgh in a second-class carriage at the express speed of fifty miles per hour! It is true it takes him but twelve hours to go that enormous distance; but in those twelve hours he will have ample time and occasion to ponder on the vast difference of second-class accommodation in England and in Germany!

CHAP. III.

The Quarters of Royalty and Government.

WHITEHALL, PAST AND PRESENT.—DOWNING STREET.—PARIS AND LONDON.—ENGLISH AND FRENCH STATESMEN.—THE DIFFERENCE.—THE ADMIRERS OF FRANCE.—ENGLISH RESPECT FOR THE ARISTOCRACY.

FOUR large streets lead from Trafalgar Square to the East, West, North, and South. This square (village and garden-ground in the days of Edward the Confessor) is, in our own days, one of the central points of London life. Trafalgar Square, which drank the blood and witnessed the agonies of Hugh Peters, Scrope, Jones, Harrison, and many others, who were killed in expiation of the execution of Charles I.—where many hundreds were decapitated, stigmatised, and mutilated, to satisfy the vengeance of the Stuarts and their adherents—forms, in 1852, the peaceable, ever-moving, central point, where the roads from the West meet the roads from the East. Down there, where the equestrian statue of Charles I. stands, the street leads to Whitehall, Westminster, the Houses of Parliament, and the Thames. We will walk in that direction; it leads us to places that are among the grandest and most interesting of which London, or any other city on the face of the earth, can boast.

We are here—as Leigh Hunt says—within the atmosphere of English royalty. Each step in this part of the town awakens the strangest recollections, and reminds one of Wolsey, the gifted, the proud, the terrible—of Henry, the coarse and cruel—Elizabeth, the cunning and quarrelsome—James, the pedant and the clown—Charles, the misguided and melancholy—Cromwell, the harsh and unbending—the contemptible, dissolute second Charles—and the doubly contemptible, dissolute Stuart, who succeeded him, and whose Government robbed Whitehall of its glories. The very air is full of reminiscences of the Tudors and the Stuarts—of their splendour and feasting—of their intrigues and vulgarities—of their despotic rule and bloody punishments; and as we walk through the streets, we cannot divest ourselves of the thought, what a strange and quaint sight it would be, if those princes, and their ministers and courtiers, could, for an hour, return to the sunny light of day! What gravity and merriness, madness and thoughtlessness, guilt, misery, and ingratitude! Visible and invisible, singly and grouped, here are the monuments of the history of English royalty, from the downfall of Wolsey to the downfall of James II. That epoch is grand, important, and instructive, and a fit study for the kings and nations of our own days.

Whitehall, such as it is in 1852, bears little resemblance to the Whitehall of 1652.

Wolsey lived in York Palace. He was most vain, fond of splendour, conceit, and tyranny; but for all that, he was the most remarkable man among the prelates of England. His palace was the richest booty which his downfall procured for his master, who at once settled down in it. Here he married Anna Boleyn; here he died; here did all the great men meet, who flattered that crowned tiger until he consigned them to the hands of the executioner, and impaled their heads on London Bridge. Among them were Cavendish, Thomas Cromwell, and Wolsey. Erasmus, also, and Hans Holbein, whose low degree alone saved them from sharing the fate of the king's friends and wives. Among these were the Dukes of Norfolk and Suffolk, the Earl of Surrey, Sir Thomas Wyatt the poet, Catharine of Arragon, Anna Boleyn, Jane Seymour, Catharine Howard, Anne of Cleves, and Catharine Parr, the least unfortunate among these unfortunate women; and the children that were to wear crowns—Edward, Mary, and Elizabeth—these were they that passed in and out of York Palace in the days of Henry VIII.

The spirits of the murdered have probably cast a gloomy shadow on those golden walls, for after Henry's decease his successors avoided Whitehall, and Elizabeth was the first to establish her court there. A change comes over the figures of the past—Cecil and

Burleigh, the two Bacons, Drake and Raleigh, Spenser and Shakespere, Sydney and Lee, Leicester and Essex, stand before us. And after them James I. and his darling "Steenie," and Charles I., Cromwell, and—the executioner.

Charles I. was very active in the improvement of Whitehall. Inigo Jones, the great architect of those days, was employed on it, and Rubens painted the ornaments of the ceiling, for which he received £3000 and the honour of knighthood. It is mere calumny, to say that Cromwell, in puritanic brutality, destroyed the works of art which he found in Whitehall. On the contrary, he made great exertions to save them; we owe it to him that the famous cartoons by Raphael may this day be seen at Hampton Court. But, of course, the Great Protector put a stop to the dissolute and merry life which formerly ruled in the palace. There was no end of praying and preaching in Whitehall; the Barebones Parliament assembled here after the dissolution of the Long Parliament; it was here that Cromwell refused the crown; and here he died, while a dreadful thunderstorm convulsed the heavens. His friends said that nature sympathised with the great man, and his enemies would have it that it was the devil going off to hell with "Old Noll," his brother.

Richard Cromwell, too, passed his short season of power at Whitehall. He was followed by Monk, who kept the place for Charles II. But the merry olden times were gone for ever; they returned not with the dissolute, gloomy-faced prince, although more money was wasted on the Duchess of Portsmouth—not to mention His Majesty's other ladies—than ever had been spent on an English queen.

Evelyn, in his memoirs, thus describes one of the closing scenes of royal dissipation:—"I can never forget the inexpressible luxury and prophanenesse, gaming and all dissoluteness, and, as it were, total forgetfullnesse of God (it being Sunday evening), which this day se'nnight I was witnesse of, the king sitting and toying with his concubines—Portsmouth, Cleveland, and Mazarine, etc.; a French boy singing love songs, in that glorious gallery, whilst about twenty of the greate courtiers, and other dissolute persons, were at Basset round a large table; a bank of at least 2000 in gold before them, upon which two gentlemen, who were with me, made reflectious with astonishment. Six days after was all in the dust!"—Evelyn's Memoirs, vol. i. p. 549.

James II. lived here for a few years, until the mass cost him a crown. His wife fled from the palace on the 6th December, 1688. The king followed eleven days later; and on the 14th February, 1689, the Prince of Orange entered the old palace. It was burnt in 1698.

Let not my readers quarrel with this review of the past. Certain localities are nothing without an occasional glance at the chronicles of olden times; but with those aids to imagination, the very stones become gifted with speech, and proclaim the joys and sorrows, the pageants and horrors which they witnessed in their days.

The remains of Whitehall, like the majority of the buildings which surround them, have been converted into Government offices. Scotland Yard is the central office of the London police, and on the other side of the road is the Admiralty. A little lower down there are two of those splendid Horse Guards, mounted on black chargers, doing duty at the offices of the Ministry of War, and guarding the spot where Elizabeth, in unchaste virginity, and at an advanced and wrinkled age, exacted the homage of her courtiers as Queen of Beauty. We turn the corner of the old Banquet-house and enter a blind alley—it is narrow and deserted. That is Downing Street the famous, where the Colonial and Foreign Offices guide the destinies of the greater part of the globe. It is a curious street, small and dingy, beyond the smallness and dinginess of similar streets at Leipzig, Frankfort, or Prague, and desolate, vacant, deserted—a fit laboratory for political alchemists. At its further end is a small mysterious door, the entrance to the Foreign

Office, in the keeping of a red-coated grenadier, with, I doubt not, a couple of newspaper reporters hidden in his cartridge-box, and intent upon ascertaining the names of those that enter the office. But the notes, which the Foreign Office addresses to the Foreign Courts, do not find their way into the English newspapers—so that even the Times has to copy them from the German and French journals—and this is owing to the circumstance, that those who enter or leave the office keep the notes in their pockets; and that the reporters, though clever, cannot see through the morocco of portfolios and the wadding of coats. They manage these matters better in France: a French journalist takes up his quarters in the reticule of Somebody's lady, or if that cannot be conveniently done, he places himself under the protection of the said lady's maid. Such things are of rare occurrence in England, owing to the immoral prejudice of the islanders respecting the code of morals in matters of politics and matrimony.

What an amount of idolization have not the German authors of the last ten years wasted on Paris! How great their enthusiasm even now, in praise of the men and women of that capital. But if you ask, what the excellent qualities of Paris really and truly are, they will discourse, at great length, on the charms of the Boulevards, the gracefulness of the women, the deep blue of the Paris sky, and the merry, careless, exciting disposition of the Parisians generally. "Now all this is well and good," say I to my Paris friend; "and if I understand you, you set down the Parisians as the A 1. of humanity, because their women are clever, and because those clever women have very small feet; because the Boulevards are capital places to lounge in; because Mabile is merrier than Vauxhall. But as for the blue colour of the sky, allow me, dearest friend, to remind you of Naples, Spain, Paris, and China, where, as they say, the skies are much bluer. All those circumstances make a town very agreeable; but I have yet to learn that they are a fair gauge of the moral worth of its inhabitants." My Paris friend is silent; but after a good long pause, he comes forward with some very general phrases, saying, that there is an unutterable something which embellishes life in Paris, and that there you live in a world of ideas. There is a good deal of truth in this general admission. Life in Paris is charming, more charming than in London and other large towns; but its charms emanate, in many instances, from the darker sides of the Parisian character; and it is absurd to say that the people are entitled to our respect for no other reason, but because we lead a life of pleasure and gaiety in their city.

Why does London produce so much less agreeable an impression than Paris, not only on the passing stranger, but also on those who reside here a considerable length of time? We leave that question for another day. We are now in Downing Street; and, however gloomy the appearance of that street may be—perfidious and egotistical as the Downing Street policy may appear to the Continentals—which, by the bye, proves its popularity here—we can, at least, say in its favor, that it has, within the last twenty years, been less open to corruption by means of money and female politicians, than was the case on the other side of the Channel, in the country of "la gloire," of blue skies and "unutterable somethings." Of course the réunions are less interesting; there is not so wide a margin for intrigue; the ambition of roturiers is kept within the limits of decency; the fair sex, with all its followers and appendages, is confined to a narrow sphere of action; and these are the reasons why—- just as in other matters—English politics have a more sober, business-like, respectable, and tedious appearance than politics in France. It is really miraculous that, in a country which is governed by a Queen, and one who inherited the crown at an early age, there has never been made mention of court and other intrigues, which influenced the conduct of public affairs. Say it is merely by accident; say that such accident is partly owing to the coldness of the blood which runs in the veins of

English women; or, if you please, think of the olden times, when the women of Whitehall made history in as shameless a manner as any women in the Tuilleries or Versailles. No matter! It has been reserved for the 19th century to create a Woman's Court, which excludes all love-intrigues. Such a thing is impossible in France; and if possible, the French would not believe it, nor would they put up with it. A government without female interference, quarrels, and corruption! Monstrous, at least to the French, who, rather than live under such a government, would choose to live in an austere Catonian Republic.

The respect for public decency, which in England is sometimes carried to a ridiculous length, is, nevertheless, of great use for the morality of the Government. Corruption, indeed, is an important item in English electioneering tactics; money and drink are lavished on the voters; but this corruption, however shameless, is confined to the lower classes. Honourable members, who are very pathetic on the neglected education of the people, think very little of treating all the inhabitants of their borough to a preposterous quantity of drink, in order to ensure their re-election. But the corrupters themselves are not so corruptible as the men who for the last ten years—for it is not necessary to go back to an earlier date—held the reins of the government in France. The poor are now and then bought in England; more frequently they are intimidated; but in France—the very French confess it—all are venal, from the highest to the lowest. I am not an admirer of corruption in England; but I like it better than I do corruption in France. If rottenness there must be, it had better be partial and one-sided, than a general corruption of the body politic.

Certainly the small English boroughs, with their electioneering tactics and venality, are disgusting; but still there is some difference between the treating and bribing the peasants and small shop-keepers and that nauseous corruption of all classes of society which is so prevalent in France, more particularly since the reign of Louis Philippe. In England, the polling-days have from times immemorial been days of feasting, drinking, and fighting for the lower classes. The want of political cultivation, ignorance of the important questions at issue, the indifference, and, in many instances, the brutality of the lower classes, make it a matter of small moment to them, whether the barrel of beer from which they drink at an election is the gift of charity, or the devil's retaining fee. No hustings without speechifying—no polling-place without swilling. The witnesses who have been examined by the Election Committees have generally confessed, that the candidate, according "to the old established custom," behaved like a "gentleman"—that he treated the electors to ale and gin, shook hands with them, gave them money, and hired brass bands for their special gratification. A melancholy proof this of the neglected condition in politics and morals of the lower classes in England.

But far more saddening is the spectacle of corruption, which France has exhibited these many years past. It is not the rude and uncultivated mass which sins from ignorance of its own abandoned condition; corruption there extends its sway over the educated, the learned, the wealthy, the refined. It is the despotism of a cynism of venality, such as the world never saw since the days of the Roman emperors. The French aristocracy, the army, the bourgeoisie, the church, and the press, are all in the market. Eloquent morality solicits corruption with the most impudent eagerness, and drives the hardest bargains. In France corruption has become the fashion; it is the law, the essence of politics, and it has almost become a necessity for the attainment of even honest purposes. The poison pervades all the organs of the body politic; and ever since the commencement of the first revolution, the French nation has been convulsed, and caused convulsions among the neighbouring nations. But never at any one time—no, not among all her changes—was there a single period, however short, in which personal liberty obtained that respect which it commands in England. And although this fact is on record, and though it cannot be contradicted, yet there are German admirers of France (the majority of them know nothing of France except the boulevards of Paris), who believe that the French are the chosen people of liberty, the prophets of the nations, and martyrs for their political salvation. True, the history of France is instructive to those who take a warning from it. True the French are a chosen people; indeed, they are chosen to sound the trumpet of war into the ears of the nations. But there never was any fortress save one, which was conquered by the sounding of trumpets—Jericho, in the land and the age of miracles. Singleness of purpose, and honest perseverance, these alone can in our days ensure the victory of great principles. But the sons of France have always been strangers to those two qualities; and the glory which these can give, they have never coveted. They care not for substantial liberty, for it not only gives rights, but it imposes duties also. Freedom is a treasure which requires the most anxious care; he who neglects it, loses it. France obtained it three times, and thrice she lost it; and now the French say again—"Ça ne durera pas." But, it is to be hoped, that the phrase will be flung back again, whenever they shall take it into their heads once more to sound the trumpet of alarm to the countries of Europe.

England, with all her political and social blemishes, has at least come to this, that any danger to the personal liberty of her citizens may almost be considered as an absurd impossibility, while the French are, as yet, so ignorant of the rudiments of national liberty, that they still wish for a strong government; that is to say, one which centralises all the resources, and absorbs all the powers of the State. The various parties are all agreed on this point; they differ only with respect to the person who is to preside over this "strong government." The Legitimists vow that that person must be a Bourbon; the Bonapartists claim the right, as they have established the fact, in favour of a scion of the great Emperor; and the Republicans are eloquent in praise of an elective government; but every one of these partisans reserves to himself a large prospective share of the loaves and fishes, which, as all the world knows, are entirely at the disposal of a "strong government." The ambition of free self-government, which characterises the English, is altogether unknown to the French. Hence they can die for liberty, but they cannot live for it.

In drawing a parallel between the darker sides of English and French politics, I ought not to forget mentioning one important point. In despite of her free press, the partial degradation of her masses, in despite of her civic self-government, England is the most aristocratic country in the world. Whatever modern reformers may strive for or assert, they cannot deny, nor can they root out, the traditional veneration of the middle and lower classes for everything and everybody connected with the nobility. An Englishman, even though he were a chartist, looks at a scion of the nobility with a very different eye, than at his neighbour, by the grace of God, citizen of London, or of Sheffield, or Manchester. A "lord's" presence makes him respectful, even though the said "lord" had taken too much port wine, A "lady's" toilette has a mysterious charm for English women, however bad that "lady's" taste may be. On the continent, too, the aristocracy are looked up to and imitated and quoted, but not by any means to such an extent as in England. The continental nations want that ingenuousness of veneration, that amiable candour which frankly confesses that it "loves a lord." Add to this that the adoration of a noble pedigree does not here, as on the continent, move in the sphere of trifles only, which after all, is, in a manner, excusable. For the wealthy aristocrat is a privileged person from his cradle; he is a landed proprietor, and he is not distracted with struggles for sustenance, favour, place, and fortune. Of course he has leisure to cultivate his taste and form his manners, and to imitate him in those respects would be a merit, even in a root and branch democrat. But the Englishman does not stop there. His desire to imitate the nobility, his craving for titles, make him what is commonly called "a snob." He has greater respect for a cabinet of noblemen than for a cabinet of commoners; he cannot imagine a charitable institution unless it be under the presidency of the Duke of Dumman and the Earl of Tanitary; he judges the character of a Marquis very differently from that of any other man. It requires a very long residence in England and an intimate acquaintance with English society generally to understand and appreciate this weakness in all its bearings. But this weakness is the source of very remarkable monstrosities in the political and social life of England. Their most salient points and corners, indeed, have given way to the progressive tendencies of the age. That progress, though slow, is manifest, and its very slowness is a guarantee against the danger of a relapse.

CHAP. IV.

Westminster.—The Parliament.

THE ABBEY.—THE HALL.—AN M.P.'S LIFE.—THE NEW HOUSES.—THEIR STYLE, CORRIDORS, AND LIBRARIES.—THE SUFFERINGS OF THE PUBLIC.—THE SPEAKER.—SIR JOHN AND DR. KEIF IN THE GALLERY.—LADIES AND REPORTERS.—THE TABLE OF THE HOUSE.—THE SERGEANT-AT-ARMS.—PARLIAMENTARY ETIQUETTE.—THE TWO HOUSES.—DISRAELI.—PALMERSTON.—SIR JOHN PRAISETH THE LATTER.—COLONEL SIBTHORP.—LORD JOHN RUSSELL.—PUBLIC SPEAKING IN ENGLAND.

TWO streets running in parallel lines lead from Whitehall to Westminster and the Houses of Parliament. One of these streets is narrow, dark, and gloomy. In it lived Edmund Spenser and Oliver Cromwell, and through it passed Elizabeth, Charles, and the Protector, whenever their presence was required in either of the two houses. The street was large enough for the royal processions of those days, but it became inconveniently narrow when the traffic of the metropolis extended to this point, and they built Parliament-street, one of the most crowded thoroughfares of western London. After passing through Parliament-street you emerge into a wide irregular place, which may justly be called the most venerable, important, and sacred spot in England—where, on your left, on the bank of the Thames, the new Houses of Parliament tower in their splendour, while before you, amidst broad grave-stones and fresh green plots and delightful trees stands the old Abbey. To the right, you see a perfect wilderness of narrow streets with a large gap broken right through them; it leads to Pimlico, Belgravia, St. James's Park, and Buckingham Palace.

Westminster Abbey is among the grandest and loftiest monuments of ancient architecture; it need fear no comparison, with the vast gothic fanes, finished and unfinished, that stand by the rivers of Germany.

That the structure is completed in all its parts, that while we contemplate it we know that the idea of the architect has been carried out in all its details, that we are not shocked by the ruin-like appearance of an unfinished aisle, or choir, or tower, is the more pleasing to us Germans, since in our own country we have come to believe incompleteness to be inseparable from the idea of a large gothic "Dom." That the reverse is the case in England is creditable to the architects and the nation. Their parliaments have readily granted the sums which were required for the completion of the abbey; and the architect deserves much praise for having, in his original plan, kept within the limits of the probable and possible. With all the liberality of the British nation, who knows whether Westminster

Abbey would not still be unfinished, if the architect, instead of tracing a couple of modest though respectable towers, had indulged his fancy in designing two gigantic structures, mountains of stone and fret-work, like those which hitherto exhausted the resources and foiled the perseverance of the people on the other side of the channel.

It is a characteristic trait in the English nation, that here, where so many public buildings are found, they have all been completed. Parishes, landlords, bishops, and the nation itself, limited their building projects in proportion to their resources. They calculated the expense, and consulted their pockets quite as much as the vanity of the architects, who, after all, are not to be trusted in these things; they make the plan, but they are never called on to pay for it.

Westminster Abbey, the venerable, has been much admired for many centuries past. Thousands have believed, that within its walls the worn-out frame finds sweeter rest after the fitful fever of their earthly career; and to this day there are many whose ambition can only be satisfied by a grave and a monument in Westminster Abbey. The nation has set it apart as the pantheon of their illustrious dead. Many blame them for it; others again doubt whether a fitter or more convenient place could be found or created in these latter days. It is hardly necessary to mediate between these two conflicting opinions. A nation that can offer its great minds a fitting sphere of action, will also find the proper mode and manner of burying its great men, honourable to them and the country which gave them birth. The Huns buried their heroes on the field of battle on which they fell; it is quite natural that the religious sense of the English should prompt them to honour their illustrious dead in the most beautiful church of their island-empire.

Sacred as the Abbey itself, are the domains which surround it. Parliament-street is indeed a crowded thoroughfare; the crowds meet and contend in the crossing which leads to Westminster Bridge; carriages rattle along from morning till late at night; above a million and a half of horses go that way annually into Lambeth; but the Abbey stands at a convenient distance from the public road, amidst green grass-plots, shady trees, and broad grave-stones, and near it you feel as calm and peaceful as in the shadow of a village-church. Narrow foot-paths lead to its walls; fat sheep crop the grass; and iron railings protect the sanctuary from the inroads of horses and carriages.

These railings and the wide open street leading to the south, to Vauxhall Bridge, intervene between the Abbey and the Houses of Parliament. When these are completed in this direction, then will the place which holds them, and the Abbey, and other public and private buildings, assume a different and more satisfactory aspect. At present, the workmen are still occupied with the colossal Victoria tower, whose portal is among the grandest monuments of Gothic architecture. At present the northern tower is still incomplete, raw, and ugly, and the whole space in that direction is boarded up, and covered with loose earth, bricks, and mortar. But when all is completed, then will dust, smoke, and fog lend their assistance, and the new buildings will soon be in keeping with the venerable colouring of the old Abbey.

In front of the new, there is an old stone building, with quaint narrow windows, low doors, and curious turrets. It contains some Government Offices, and Courts of Justice, and the famous Westminster Hall, which is said to be the largest of all covered spaces in the world unsupported by pillars.

Here we find the last remains of the walls of old Westminster Palace, such as it was in the days of King Rufus of traditional and fabulous Norman hospitality. The kings of England resided here for 480 years. The conflagration of 1834 destroyed the last traces of the splendour of olden times, and Westminster Hall alone remained to give us an idea of the grand style of Gothic palaces. But it is only an approximating idea, for with the exception of the northern portal and the window above it, all we now see is a creation of later days. More especially since the Hall has been brought into connexion with the new houses, its character has been changed. On the southern side there are at present broad steps, leading to a sort of balustrade, communicating with the corridors and outer halls of the houses. The quaint old window over the chief portal, with its Gothic ornaments and gigantic dimensions, forms a strong contrast with the new window opposite. And in the evening, when the old house is lighted up with gas, the illumination produces a striking mixture of ancient and modern colouring, which, however, far from impairing the effect of the whole, shows parts of the massive ceiling to the greatest advantage.

While we have been looking at the hall, it has been invaded by about two hundred persons, who form in lines through the whole length of it. It is half-past four, the time at which the Members of Parliament make their appearance, and there are always crowds of idle and curious persons, who, whenever they cannot obtain admission to the gallery, will come and wait in the hall, that they may gaze upon the faces of some of the parliamentary grandees.

We are just in time, for the open place in front of Westminster Hall assumes an animated appearance. Half a dozen policemen come, I know not exactly from which quarter, and take up a position near the gate. Old and young representatives of the people arrive from all parts of the town; some dressed in yellow breeches, and black long-tailed dress coats, come in cabs. They carry ponderous club-like umbrellas. Others arrive in heavy coaches, with a retinue of powdered giants; some come on foot, and others on horseback. Some are dressed down to the laid idéal of quakerish plainness; and others are dressed out with a foppish sort of elegance. The majority drive themselves in two-wheeled vehicles to the temple of their eventual immortality. The latter—and, indeed, those who are on horseback—have their grooms to take care of the horses; and though the masters have the appearance of decent civilians, still the number of servants who assemble in front of the building, impart to the scene a tinge of aristocratic colouring. The difference between the English parliament and our defunct German chambers, is at once apparent, even before we enter the house. In Germany, there were but few servants and carriages. But the English parliament is chiefly composed of wealthy men; for not only do the "necessary expenses" of an election represent a large capital, but the members must also prove a property qualification of £300 per annum in land. This law alone would suffice to exclude men of humble resources, but such are still more effectually excluded by the expenses of that position in society which every member of parliament is compelled to assume. Whatever his profession may be, he must sacrifice it for the time being to his parliamentary duties, and that, too, without any pecuniary indemnification, since the English representatives are not paid, as was the case with their ephemeral colleagues in France and Germany. Life in London is expensive to every one, but the expense becomes serious in the case of temporary residents. Add to this, that every member is, in a manner, in duty bound to be attentive and hospitable to the influential among his constituents. Say, Mr. Jedediah Brown goes up to London for eight days or a fortnight; Mr. Jedediah Brown knows what is proper, and would not, on any account go back to St. Alban's, or Canterbury, Blackburn, Birmingham, or Clitheroe, without calling on the honorable Mr. M. P., the member for the borough, for whom Mr. Jedediah Brown voted at the last election. Mr. Jedediah Brown is an influential person in his own borough; the name of his uncles, aunts, and cousins, is legion; and so is the name of his wife's uncles, aunts, and cousins. The Brown interest is of the utmost importance at election times, and he who would stand well with the borough should, by all means, conciliate the Browns. There is no help for it. Mr. M. P. cannot do less than ask Mr. Jedediah Brown to dinner, drive him out in his carriage, and offer him a box at the opera. Well and good. Mr. Jedediah Brown cannot always remain in London, but he is followed by Mr. Ebenezer Smith, a wealthy man, and one whom the honourable and learned gentleman cannot afford to offend, for the Smith interest, too, is powerful, and the family very large. And after Mr. Ebenezer Smith, comes George Damson, the popular lecturer, and the Rev. Mr. Jones, Mrs. Jones, and the Misses Jones; and Mr. M. P., is compelled to have them all to dinner, and take them down to the house, and get them seats in the speaker's gallery, and platform places at Exeter Hall. All this is very expensive. And, if Mr. M. P. is a married man, of course his wife insists on sharing with him the "gaieties" of the London season; she must go to routs, réunions, balls, and drawing-rooms, and these amusements, though innocent, are vastly expensive. Nor is Mr. M. P. allowed to imitate his Continental colleagues, and take his dinner in a chop-house, or at some cheap table d'hôte; the aristocratic laws of decency preclude him from adopting that course. He must dine at a club, or at a first-rate hotel. He is compelled to have a large house, or, at least, to inhabit one of those "splendid drawing-room floors," which are advertised, as "suitable for members of Parliament and gentlemen of fortune." In short, he must is in duty bound to be a gentleman of fortune. The income of £300, as required by law, is, after all, a mere formality; and Lord John Russell could, without any tendency to radical reform, move for the abolition of the property qualification, since no one, but a man in a perfectly independent position, would ever think of aspiring to the expensive honour of a seat in the House of Commons.

The interior of the Houses of Parliament is grander and more imposing than the exterior. This does not apply to the rooms where the sittings are held, but rather to the entrance hall and corridors. As you enter you come at once into a hall, long enough and high enough to suit any second sized Gothic dome. High Gothic windows, Mosaic floors, palm-tree ceilings, heavy brass candelabras in the old church style, and marble statues on ponderous blocks of stone—such are the chief characteristics of the corridor which leads to the interior of the sanctuary. Doors of solid oak, with massive plate-glass windows, heavy brass handles, and neat ornaments, open from this corridor into a round airy hall, with a number of other corridors opening into all the other parts of the building. This hall is, so to say, the centre of the whole; and the two Houses if we may say so, are on either side of it—the Commons to the north, and the Lords to the south. The other corridors communicate with sundry other parts of the building, with the refreshment-rooms, the library, etc. The Gothic style is adhered to, even in the minutest details, and contrasts strangely with the busy life of the nineteenth century.

The refreshment-rooms, of course, abound in all imaginable creature-comforts. But it is a strange fact, that the Restaurant is even more exorbitant in his charges than the common herd of London hotel-keepers. The legislators of England are shockingly imposed upon in their own house; they are far more effectually fleeced than is the case in the hotels on the Rhine, or in the Apennines. Every drop of sherry and every ounce of mutton is charged as if it were worth its weight in gold. There have been grievous complaints in the House, but the unpatriotic landlord sticks to his prices; he taxes the legislators with as little compunction as those gentlemen show in taxing him and the whole fraternity of licensed victuallers.

The libraries of the House—one for the Lords and one for the Commons—are splendid in all their appointments, and useful, comfortable, and elegant in their arrangements; large fires burning brightly in massive grates, and surmounted by gigantic marble chimneys. Sardanapalian arm-chairs that invite you to read, ponder, and doze; costly carpets; servants in livery waiting upon the Members; large tables covered with portfolios, paper, envelopes, and all imaginable writing materials; splendidly bound books in massive book-cases; and gas-lights most advantageously placed—all combine to make this the most desirable retreat. Two librarians preside over the rooms. Existence is more delightful in these reading-rooms than in the House itself. The debates are sometimes very long, and malicious persons say that now and then they are not very interesting. It is, therefore, but natural that many of the chosen of the people prefer the arm-chairs in their library to their seats on the stuffed benches of the House. Here they may sit and doze or write, even more comfortably than in their clubs; and if a member wishes to indite a letter to his constituents or creditors, he has the accommodation of a special parliamentary post-office within the walls of the building. All this shows that the honourable and learned gentlemen have very correct ideas, and an acute perception of what is truly comfortable.

But even perfection itself is imperfect in this world of ours. A small matter has been neglected in the building of this palace, which has already cost the nation above two millions of pounds. It is the old story. The Houses proper, the saloons in which the sittings are held, are altogether bad in the plan, in their arrangements and appointments, with respect to acoustics, optics, rheumatics, catarrh, and gout.

In the Lords these faults are less obtrusive. The architect's task was easier, and there are in the Lords scarcely ever so many visitors, that the artist, as in the case of the Commons, had to provide for the accommodation of six hundred members, with galleries for ladies, reporters, and the ordinary and extraordinary public, while the room was required to be of moderate dimensions, and comfortable as the old-established domestic English parlour. In the House of Lords the red morocco seats are marvellously comfortable, even for those who cannot boast of a coronet. The high, small, and painted windows admit but of little light; but the men who meet in this room do not care much whether or not they see one another very distinctly. They meet after the sitting in the brilliant saloons of the Earl of Woburn, or the Marquis of Steyne, where they can contemplate one another to their hearts' content. In some parts of the room you cannot very well hear what is said; but even that does not matter: in the first instance, because generally what is said is not worth hearing; in the second, because many noble lords cannot, or will not, speak distinctly; and, in the third, because the reporters help one another whenever they lose the thread of the debate, so that the speeches make quite a figure in the newspapers. Certain very modest lords rely greatly on the talents of the reporters; they mutter, and stutter, and leave out half sentences, and next morning at breakfast it is quite a pleasure to see what a lucid, reasonable, and consistent speech (thanks to the reporters!) they have managed to make in last night's debate.

Twice in the course of the year, a great many persons are anxious to obtain admission to the Lords, and to see and hear everything that is done or said. This is on the occasion of the Queen's opening and proroguing parliament. But on such days, the London sun, loyal throughout, volunteers some extra service, and the Queen speaks more deliberately and distinctly than the majority of the old gentlemen who, on ordinary days, are "but imperfectly heard." And lastly, the Queen's speech is usually printed before it is delivered. The optical and acoustical shortcomings of the room are, for these reasons, by no means striking. The saloon itself, with all its gilt carvings, looks splendid, if not tasteful.

Originally, it was the architect's intention to execute the saloon in which the Commons sit in a very elaborate style; indeed, the ceiling was already covered with paintings and gilt ornaments, when the Commons proved contumacious, and opposed the plan. Speeches were made on that occasion, which would have done honour to an assemblage of Spartans. Indignant remonstrances, which savoured of Puritanism and democratic prudery, were hurled at the head of the unfortunate architect. All this was very natural. Ever since the burning of the old Houses of Parliament, the Commons had sat in some provisional locality. It was a wretched place, with narrow doors, and little windows; the floor was covered with an old carpet; the walls presented a mixture of yellow, grey and black; the stairs were narrow and rickety; the galleries, corridors, and committee-rooms, impressed the beholder with the idea that they formed part of some very poor provincial theatre. In short, everything was exquisitely rough shabby, and dirty. We are all creatures of habit; and in the course of time we become attached, even to nuisances. The members of the old house felt comfortable in their rickety provisional booth; they liked the stairs, the dark corridors, and the narrow cloak-room; they liked the benches—everything suggested reminiscences, and they clave unto the old house. But they had no choice left. It was impossible to promote their provisional abode to the rank of a permanent dwelling. But then, they insisted that the new house should not be much more splendid than the old.

The architect, in his turn, could not conveniently either create dirt, or erect a wooden booth in the centre of the Gothic palace. He adopted a middle course. He removed the more glaring among the ornaments and gildings; the saloon was grained in oak colour; the ceiling was laid in oak-panels; he shut out the light by narrowing and painting the windows; and he made a saloon which is neither old nor new; neither grand nor comfortable; neither modern nor antique; neither simple nor highly ornamental; and neither clean-looking nor dirty; a saloon, in fact, which looks as if it were made of gingerbread.

But the artist, foiled in his attempt at decoration, took his revenge secretly, but terribly. He ventilated the place. Towers were built, which would have served as church steeples, but which, in the present instance, were intended to conduct the atmospheric air upwards, to press it downwards, and finally, to smuggle it into the lungs of honorable members. A steam-engine was erected for the purpose of creating artificial currents of air. He built and pulled down, in order to build and pull down again. All this was very bad. The steam-engine was soon stopped, for the saloon, surrounded as it is by long corridors, has the advantage of such powerful currents of air, that they would serve to create colds, ague, and rheumatism, for all the inhabitants of the United Kingdom. The ceiling had to be brought down, because it interfered with the laws of acoustics. The artificial system of lighting the place had to be reduced to a more simple apparatus, for it endangered the safety of the members, and of the public in the galleries. The currents of air, through the artificial air-holes in the floor, were at once shut out, because they blew up the dust. In this manner, was the much vaunted system of ventilation demolished by bits, until nothing was left except the palpable uncheerfulness of the room itself. But let us enter, and pass the evening within its sacred precincts.

The grand corridor, which leads from Westminster-hall to the Central Hall shelters a great many persons, who sit, walk, or stand about. Many of them look weary and impatient. Who are they? They are the British public. They have orders to the gallery of the House, and wait until their turn comes. Each member is entitled to give an order. There are about six hundred members, and six hundred orders may be issued for every night. But the gallery cannot accommodate more than seventy or eighty persons. Those who come first are first admitted; and when the gallery is full, there is no help for it, the rest must wait. Their turn is, however, sure to come; sometimes much sooner than they had a right to expect. The debates are in many instances so dry and uninteresting that the galleries get emptied almost as soon as they are filled. But on an important night, when the leaders of the house are expected to speak, it may now and then happen that an unfortunate "stranger" waits from three P.M. until past midnight without gaining admission. It is, however, perfectly absurd that, in the construction of the new Houses, no adequate accommodation was made for the public.

As for ourselves, we are in no danger of waiting for admittance, because we had the good fortune to obtain orders for the Speaker's gallery, a place in front of, and a little below, the stranger's gallery. The right of admission to this place is confined to the Speaker; and since that dignitary is not too lavish in his favours, the lucky possessors of orders can be quite certain of ample and convenient accommodation.

It is five o'clock, and we take our seats. At the further end of the room, just opposite to us, we see the Speaker reclining in a comfortable leather-covered arm-chair with a case of solid wood, open in front, and bearing a strong resemblance to an academical pulpit. The Speaker is in his official costume, that is to say, he has a powdered wig and a black silk cloak. But in spite of these venerable attributes, he is by no means staid and majestic, and reclines with the greatest carelessness in his easychair, shutting his eyes as if he were going to sleep and again opening them and looking at papers, or talking to some of the members who have sauntered up to the chair. The whole house follows the Speaker's example; the members stand in groups of twos and threes, talking, or they sit on the broad, stuffed benches, with their legs stretched out and their hats on their heads. They seem intent upon nothing but killing time. The sitting has commenced, but the fact is, that one of the clerks is reading a paper, the contents of which are pretty well known to every one, but which, according to the rules of the House, must be read.

Our friend, Dr. Keif, who, by some malicious contrivance of his own, has managed to get a full mastery over the English language, and who speaks that language with a correctness which is altogether scandalous in a 'foreigner'—our friend Dr. Keif, I say, sits leaning over the gallery, with his hands behind his ears and his mouth wide open, anxious to know what the clerk is reading. But even he gives it up in despair.

"Impossible!" says he. "The men down below talk and laugh and chat as schoolboys do when the schoolmaster is away. What's the good of that wigged fellow reading when no one listens to him? I'd like to throw my gloves down in order to awaken in those members some respect for the galleries. They are not by any means polite. I can't say I like their manners. Am I indeed in an assembly of English gentlemen, most revered and respectable Sir John?"

Sir John is quite an habitué in the house, and as such, he informs the Doctor, that these are mere preliminaries, and that everybody will be quiet enough when the debate has once commenced. Very well. We must have patience. And while waiting, we shall have plenty of time to examine all the parts of the house.

We are, as has been mentioned, in the Speaker's gallery. Behind us is a small and crowded place devoted to the English public, and at its side is the members' gallery. The reporters' gallery is opposite to us, and above it, something like a gilt cage, in the shape of a shut-up verandah, in which a couple of ladies have found a temporary asylum. We cannot see them, but Sir John will have it that one of them is Lady John Russell. A true John Bull is lynx-eyed in matters aristocratic. But what pleasure the ladies can take in being in that gallery, is a mystery to me. They cannot see, they cannot hear, and, what is much worse, they have no chance of being seen.

Dr. Keif cares not for the ladies. All his attention is devoted to the reporters. He is astonished to find them much graver and older-looking, and withal much more ennuyés than the reporters of our extinct German parliaments. There are among them men who have grown old and grey in the profession, and who are likely to belong to it as long as they can hold a pencil.

A few yards from the Speaker's arm-chair there is a table. Who has not heard of that famous article of furniture? It is the table of the House, on which all parliamentary documents are laid. That table has no affinity to the Presidents' bureaux, such as we have seen them in the chambers of Germany and France; it stands on the floor, like any common table, and is covered with green cloth. Seated at this table, their backs turned to the Speaker, are the clerks of the House. They are wigged and powdered, and have heaps of papers and petitions before them, together with some bulky volumes in leather bindings. In short, the table has the appearance of the common domestic writing-table of the study or office. But there is something on the table which at once distinguishes it from all similar articles of furniture, viz., a heavy golden mace or sceptre. So long as this sceptre remains in its place, it is considered that the sitting continues; its removal signifies that the House is adjourned or that it has resolved itself into a committee.

Look there! just by the door is an arm-chair, and seated in it a gentleman in a dark uniform-coat with embroidered collar, knee breeches, black silk stockings, and a small sword. He is the Sergeant-at-Arms, the only armed person in the House; in a manner, the warden and chief door-keeper of the House, whose duty it is to execute the Speaker's warrants against members of Parliament and others who are guilty of a breach of privilege. Such persons are taken into custody by the Sergeant-at-Arms, who confines them in some very snug retreat within the precincts of the Parliamentary palace. While under his protection they are well taken care of, and provided with all the necessaries and luxuries of life, at prices which are by many considered exorbitant.

This man with the sword—whose income, by-the-bye, is about double the "gage" of a German general—has just risen from his comfortable seat. He is moving towards the table. On his arrival in the middle of the room, he stops and bows to the Speaker. He proceeds a few yards, and makes another bow—a few yards more, and bows again; and having thus arrived at the table, he makes a very low bow indeed.

Dr. Keif is quite flushed with excitement and curiosity. "What is that man after?" says he. "He dances and jumps about, as if he were asking the Speaker to join him in a minuet!"

The Sergeant, however, standing in front of the table, mutters a few words, which none but the initiated can understand. He takes the sceptre, removes it from the table, and puts it on something like a stool under it. Next, his face still turned towards the Speaker, he walks backwards, bowing at intervals, gains the door, and introduces two men with wigs on their heads, who, with many low bows, advance into the centre of the room. They are officers of the House of Lords, with some document or message, for which no one cares, because the majority of the members know all about it. Of course we take no interest in the message which has just been delivered to the Commons. The two Houses observe in their intercourse a great many ceremonial laws, the exact details of which are familiar to the older members, while no one else cares for them, but which, nevertheless, are observed by either House with a scrupulous punctilio. The two messengers from the Lords had to be duly announced; they were obliged to bow to the Speaker; they were not allowed to enter while the House was sitting, and for that reason the sitting was adjourned by the removal of the sceptre; they had to walk backwards to the door, looking at and bowing to the Speaker; and after the door had closed upon them, and not before, the Sergeant-at-Arms placed the sceptre again on the table, and the debate was resumed.

All these ceremonies strike a stranger as exquisitely comical; and they are enough to puzzle even an Englishman, who witnesses them for the first time, accustomed though he be to the quaint formalities and observances which are still prevalent in the Law Courts. Certain it is, that most of the continental states would long since have abolished all these traditional ceremonies. The Continentals would have been ashamed of the wigs and silk cloaks; they would have declared, that those old-fashioned attributes of official dignity were an insult to the spirit of the age, and they would have consigned them to the lumber-room; they would never for one moment have stopped to think that dangerous conflicts might possibly result from the condemnation of those insignificant and harmless formalities. Such things have happened in France, and in Germany, too. In the revolutions of either nation, much energy and valuable time has been wasted in an onslaught on mere outward forms and petty abuses, on diplomas of nobility, orders of knighthood, upper chambers, church privileges, and prerogatives of the crown. But there never was a compact majority, which, looking only at the chief points, sought to reconcile the lesser among the conflicting opinions, for the purpose of obtaining those results which every revolution should aim at—personal liberty, and the promotion of the national prosperity. These gained, the rest must follow. When every individual citizen and the nation altogether are interested in the maintenance of the liberties and improvements they have acquired, there can be no idea of a reaction. No person, no class is injured; and peaceful progress, and slow and sure reformatory action, are not only possible, but also necessary and unavoidable.

Even the radicals among the English have an instinctive appreciation of the above truths. The House of Commons has never made war upon the Lords, because the wives of the Lords wear coronets, or because the Queen performs the ceremony of opening and proroguing parliament in the House of Lords. Instead of attacking their harmless privileges, the Commons have driven the iron into the very heart of the Upper House—they have sapped its marrow, and reduced it to a mere shadow of its former self. Nor have the Commons ever attacked certain prerogatives which are essential to the crown, and which insure it its political position, its governmental functions, and its imperial splendour. Just the reverse. Not all the mailed knights and barons of olden times, nor gartered Dukes nor belted Earls, would have defended the dignity of the crown with so much zeal and devotion as the Commons have done for many years past. They are most anxiously scrupulous in their professions and marks of respect for the head of the state. They gave the king his due, freely and fully. But did they ever consent to a curtailment of their own rights? Have they resigned the smallest and least significant of their own prerogatives? Is not their vote the full and firm expression of popular opinion? And did they ever make concessions to the crown at the expense of the people's rights? Never! Those who know the history of modern England, know also how marvellously the Commons have grown in strength, political ability, and power. Indeed, so great is their power, that, magnified by distance, it imposes upon the Continentals, who are led to believe that the head of the British empire is a mere Marionette figure. This opinion is altogether erroneous; for a large amount of power remains still in the hands of the crown. The monarchy of England stands on a firmer basis in 1853 than it did in 1753, when the cry for innovations had not yet been raised on the other side of the channel; it will always remain firm so long as it respects the balance of power among the various estates of the realm. The crown is aware of this, and keeps within its limits even in the face of temptation. And the people in their meetings, and in the press—two engines which are generally terrible to crowned heads—stand by the side of the throne as trusty monitors, but they are not opposed to it. The government avoids anything like a conflict with public opinion; the people do not make opposition for opposition's sake, and the political engine works well from session to session and from year to year.

And, after all, what harm is there in the Speaker's wig, or the Queen's speech addressed to the Lords, and in all the quaint ceremonies and observances? What does it all matter? And why waste even a thought on the reform of such trifles, so long as reform is needed in matters of greater importance?

These arguments, which are strongly redolent of the German constitutionalists of Gotha, are in fact the property of Sir John, who threw them at Dr. Keif's head, when that learned man ridiculed the sergeant-at-arms. They descended to Sir John as an heir-loom from his great grandfather. May they descend from him to his children and the children of his children!

The house has meanwhile got full. A man of elegant appearance has taken his seat to the right of the speaker on the front bench, next the table. He is neither tall nor is he short; he is rather thin than stout; his forehead is high, round, and smooth; he has black eyebrows; brown clear eyes; high cheek-bones; lips firmly set; a pointed chin and black curly hair, with one of the curls drooping right over his forehead. What Englishman but knows that curl which Doyle has so often caricatured in Punch? The possessor of that curl is Disraeli, Benjamin Disraeli, at the time we saw him the Right Honourable Benjamin Disraeli, her Majesty's Chancellor of the Exchequer and Leader of the Commons.

Few portraits of this gifted man have hitherto been published; and Punch may claim the merit of having first introduced his face to the public at large. But Punch's caricature, though clever, is apt to mislead one, and those are very much mistaken who imagine the real Disraeli as a hollow-eyed, round-backed, philosophically shabby-looking, Jewish youth. The real Disraeli has a refined and aristocratic appearance. His neckcloth may now and then be tied in a startling knot—the curl on his forehead, is somewhat romantic—but in all other respects Disraeli answers to the beau ideal of a well-dressed English gentleman. And there he sits, throwing his right leg over his left and now his left over his right, talking to his next neighbour, the Right Honourable Sir John Pakington, her Majesty's Secretary of State for the Colonies, or turning to some member of the party behind him. There he sits, taking papers from his pockets or from the table, but generally busily engaged in trimming the nails of his white hands. Such as he sits, with his hat pulled over his face and to all appearance lost in deep thought; or, starting up, taking off his hat and answering a question in a smiling, cutting, sarcastic manner; or leaning over listening to a speech and taking notes:—such as he sits on the ministerial bench, this Right Honourable Benjamin Disraeli, of plebeian Jewish descent, but at present Minister, Chancellor of the Exchequer, and Leader of the House of Commons, must be an object of interest to every one, no matter whether he be a gifted sage or a gifted humbug.

His talents shine with transcendent brightness in opposition; and it is not too much to say, that he is the only capable man of whom his party can boast. He has compelled them to acknowledge him as their leader; he has left them no choice: they must either take him or perish. He is the great Protector of the Conservatives; and the Liberal party are free to confess, that they have suffered much from his antagonism. When Disraeli, rising from his seat, doffs his hat, and prepares to speak, the House is all silence and attention. The very reporters, who have just sat out their turn, hasten back to the gallery to hear him, for they all, even those attached to the liberal journals, feel a special interest in Disraeli, the author—the member of their guild. He is not an agreeable speaker. His voice is harsh and jarring; his manner is rather repulsive than winning; but his sneers, his sarcasms, his malicious attacks, are sure to tell, for he never aims at generalities, but hurls his scorn directly at certain men and sets of men in the House. At such moments, he looks in every direction but the one in which he has launched his arrow. Disraeli's sarcasms have raised him a host of enemies, and justly too, as every one must confess, who reads his Parliamentary speeches since his first Arabian razzia upon Sir Robert Peel.

To be witty is not, after all, so very difficult for those who care not to what extent they wound the feelings of their adversaries. But look at the man on the Speaker's left hand—there! on the further end of the first bench—he that holds a handkerchief in his hand. That man does these things with greater finesse. He is quite as witty as Disraeli, and he, too, has a telling answer to every question; but, withal, he does not get personal and offensive. That man is a general favourite, and every one is silent when he rises. That is Lord Palmerston, the notorious Lord Firebrand; he who, according to the opinion of the continental politicians, thinks of nothing but the most convenient means of overthrowing all the thrones in Christendom.

"This, then," whispers Dr. Keif, imitating his great enemy Kappelbaumer, the spy of the imperial and royal police at Vienna—"this is that my Lord von Palmerston, the evil genius of all reasonable European Cabinets! That's the man, with his white, innocent-looking little whiskers, his delicate features, the striped neckcloth, and the brown trousers, which, I dare say, were presented to him by Mazzini. But do tell me the truth, is it really that tall old gentleman, lying on the bench rather than sitting, and talking to his neighbours, exactly as if he were in the ale-house? Well, by Metternich! this Herr von Palmerston has such a pleasing appearance, that I could never have believed in his atrocious wickedness, if I had not been a reader of the German newspapers these many years past. What astonishes me most is, that those people down there have not the decency to avoid talking to him, for, after all, he is a convicted rebellion-monger, whom no well-disposed citizen of Vienna or Berlin would like to be seen with in the street. But no, as I said before, there's nothing in the appearance of the man to frighten one. Really, there's nothing exciting, or rebellious, or conspiratory, that I can see! And only think, what a mass of very uncivil notes he has written!"

"That's because he is a great diplomatist!" rejoins Sir John, with marvellous unction. "For the very reason that you hate him we like him. He is exactly what a Foreign Secretary ought to be, popular at home and unpopular abroad. Eh, sir! catch that man standing up to advocate the cause of a continental despot, or conduct himself in a manner which would justify his enemies in calling him the minister of such and such a king or emperor at the court of St. James's. Why, sir, what's a chief of the Foreign Office good for, if he does'nt do the bull-dog's duty—barking and showing his teeth, to frighten the housebreakers and such like wretches! And was'nt Lord Palmerston a capital bull-dog? Did'nt he bark with a loud voice, to the terror of the whole neighbourhood? And was there any one bitten by him? Certainly not, he merely offered to bite—showed his teeth—and the Continentals knew what it meant. But, of course, they don't like him any the better for it."

"I do wish he'd make us a speech," said Dr. Keif. "How does he speak?"

"Just as I like it!" responded Sir John. "His is a frank and open address—no pathos, no excitement—reasonably, intelligibly, mannerly, as an English gentleman should speak. It's his nature; he could'nt be rude, even if he were to try, excepting, always, when he sits down to correspond with the foreign powers. In the House, he never on any account is guilty of a personal attack; but he is so clever, that he can with the greatest ease provoke a laugh at the expense of those who ask idle and impertinent questions."

Sir John, thus singing the praises of Lord Palmerston, is interrupted by shouts of laughter proceeding from the body of the House. What is the matter? Colonel Sibthorp has come in, and, after bestowing a look of sublime contempt on Mr. Roebuck, who entered at the same moment, the gallant colonel, though scarcely above a minute in the House, has taken part in the debate, and uttered one of those profound and gentle remarks, the fame of which will be for ever connected with his name. Colonel Sibthorp's portrait in "Punch" is true to the life; in his short speeches, there is a good deal of common sense and natural shrewdness; but there is a comicality in his diction which makes them rather amusing than impressive. His remarks on this particular occasion are for the benefit of Lord John Russell, who is just speaking of the Militia. Colonel Sibthorp intimates to the noble Lord, that certain persons know nothing whatever of certain matters; but the ex-premier is not to be put out of countenance by such like soft impeachments, accustomed as he is to hear them from the lips of the gallant colonel. The House, too, after laughing at the sally, gives its undivided attention to the great orator. For Lord John is generally allowed to be a good speaker; his friends assert it, and his enemies do not deny it. In Paris he would make fiasco; in England he commands admiration. His mode of speaking is simple, pointed, and reasonable. He talks as a man of business to men of business; his exposition is practical; he enters largely into details, and provokes contradiction. He is a little broad-shouldered man, with clever eyes, wrinkled cheeks and forehead; he has a short neck and high shirt-collars, thin lips, and a sallow complexion; little boots, tight checked trousers, and holds his preposterously large hat in his hand. So he stands before us, with one of his hands stuck into his trousers' pockets.

His speech will be found in the parliamentary intelligence of the morning papers. It is one o'clock, A.M., and no one seems yet to think of adjourning the debate. Sir John would have no objection to see the debate close; but Dr. Keif reminds him of the family who are waiting at home. "We shall have no chance of a cup of hot tea," says he, "unless we go at once." Thus exhorted, we return home, take our tea by the parlour fire, and talk at great length of English speeches and orators, and of the parliamentary system generally.

There is a good deal of peculiarity about public speaking in this country. A certain monotony, and an utter absence of passionate emotion, are among the chief qualities of a good parliamentary orator. Such a speaker appears cold and dry in the eyes of a foreigner; but whenever he does not succeed in remaining unimpassioned, whenever he gets violent, the impression he produces is decidedly disagreeable. The same may be said of the action of the hands. Every Englishman who takes the platform at a meeting, every member who rises from his seat in Parliament to address the House, shows at once that he is firmly resolved to make no movements with his hands and arms. He secures his hands to keep them out of harm's way; and the positions he takes for that purpose are not by any means æsthetic or pathetic. One man puts his hands in his trousers' pockets; another hooks his thumbs in the arm-holes of his waistcoat; some put their hands behind their backs; and others cross their arms over their chests à la Napoléon. In this manner do they begin their speeches; but since the speeches are long, it stands to reason that the speaker cannot always remain in the same position. Besides, as he proceeds with his subject, he warms to it, and then commences the most astonishing action of the arms and the body generally. One man moves his hand up and down as if he were the leader of a band presiding over the performance of a gallopade; another stands with his hands clenched, and makes a rowing motion; and the third moves his right hand in circles, each circle ending with a sort of push at the audience. Others—for instance, Lord Dudley Stuart—beat time on the table; and others—for instance, Lord Palmerston—swing their bodies to and fro in imitation of a pendulum.

All these attitudes are not by any means elegant; but it is customary in England for public speakers to conduct themselves with all possible nonchalance, and to address their hearers as merchants do in a conversation on mercantile affairs. Besides, there is no tribune in the House of Commons, and it is, therefore, quite natural that the members are at a loss what to do with their hands. Public speaking, in fact, is by no means an easy matter; and to be an efficient Member of Parliament requires the whole of a man's time and energies. Committees in the morning, debates from four o'clock in the afternoon until after midnight, the speaking and the listening to speeches, surely these fatigues are enough to shake a man's health. Who would find fault with the most conscientious Member of Parliament for his desire to escape from town in August, and recruit his strength in the Highlands? And then think of the Ministers, who, besides attending the sittings, have to superintend their offices and departments. Dr. Keif is right when he says, "I'd rather be impelled into Germany than be a minister in England. Sir John! Vivat Germania! Germany for ever!"

CHAP. V.

The Periodical Press—Its Mechanism and Distribution.

THE ENGLISH PRESS GENERALLY.—THE "TIMES" AND THE OTHER JOURNALS.—THE EVENING PAPERS.—THE PUBLICATION OF THE MORNING PAPERS.—ANTICIPATION OF NEWS.—SPECIAL TRAINS.—PUBLICATION OF WEEKLY PAPERS.—THE READING PUBLIC.—ADVANTAGES OF WEEKLY PAPERS.—THE PROVINCIAL PRESS.—WHY IT CANNOT FLOURISH.—TRANSMISSION OF NEWSPAPERS.—THE NEWSVENDERS.—A SCENE IN THE "GLOBE" OFFICE.—YOUNG HOPEFUL, THE NEWSBOY.—MR. SMIRKINS, THE PARTY-MAN.—THE NEWSVENDER'S EXCHANGE.

THE Germans have, at all times, professed great respect for the English press; and justly, too, considering the excellence of its political articles, its miraculous versatility, the conscientiousness of its reports, the general usefulness of its contents, the enormous geographical sphere into which it finds its way, the grave and manly tone of its language, and especially its thoroughly independent position, and with it, its stupendous moral power. The English press is more concentrated in its means than the German; it is more sober, versatile, and honorable than the French; and it can be more relied upon, and is more decent in its tone, than the American press. It surpasses all three by the grand solidity of its deportment. It may well be said, that no nation on earth, old or new, could ever boast of such a political press as that of which the English nation can boast.

In one point only, the English political press is over-estimated. Its issues and its profits are generally considered to be much larger than they really are. It is not difficult to discover the grounds of this erroneous view. People think mostly of the Times, because it is best known and most frequently quoted. The condition of the English journalistic press is estimated after this, its most important representative. The premises are false, and so is the conclusion. We do not here propose to open the ledgers of the English newspaper offices, and to take down the number of copies sold. A great deal of falsehood, and a great deal of truth, has been published in Germany on this subject. We will here only say, that the Times prints daily from 40,000 to 50,000 copies, and that the other journals together have an issue of the same amount. This is enough to show, that no conclusions can be drawn from the statistics of the Times to the statistics of the other great morning papers. These numbers prove also, that English journalism has fewer readers than journals in Germany or France, though certainly its geographical diffusion is by far greater. But it were equally wrong to draw conclusions from the number of copies sold to the number of readers. The position of the periodical press to the public is so peculiar in this country, that a detailed account is necessary for its proper understanding. We propose to give that account in the following pages, and begin by stating the well-known fact, that the English political papers are divided into morning, evening, and weekly papers, into monthlies and quarterlies, and into metropolitan and provincial journals. The essential difference between the morning and evening papers, is to be found in the time of publication. The first edition of the latter is published at four, or half-past four, in the afternoon; a second edition is published at six o'clock; and, on important occasions, a third edition, containing the parliamentary intelligence of the evening, badly reported, and in execrable style, is published at seven o'clock. Some of the evening papers, too, are cheaper than the morning papers, and they are all half a sheet in size; but they have the advantage of giving the contents of the day-mails, and the accounts of the money-market. The evening papers generally contain much less matter than the morning papers. Their sale too is small, and with the exception of the Globe and the Sun, they are none of them independent, but form part of the property of certain morning papers. The Standard, for instance, is but a later edition of the Morning Herald; the same is the case with the Express, which belongs to the Daily News; with the Evening Mail, which belongs to the Times; and the Evening Journal, which is a satellite of the Morning Chronicle. The sale of these papers is limited, and their expense is not generally thought to be very large.

The morning papers are published in time for the early railway trains. The first few thousands of the copies printed, are at once despatched into the provinces, and the copies which are destined for metropolitan circulation, reach the readers generally about nine o'clock, when a great many Londoners are at breakfast. The Morning Post alone is in the habit, as it appears, of receiving very important intelligence, such as "Elopements in High Life," or "the last odds against Black Doctor," between the hours of six and eight in the morning, for this fashionable journal appears frequently at the break of day, with the exciting heading, "Second Edition!" The first edition, it seems, was sold in the course of the night; perhaps between one and three, A.M. The less important papers publish their second edition at twelve o'clock, and in it their foreign correspondence, which has arrived with the morning mails. In the case of any extraordinary event, they publish a third edition at three o'clock.

It is impossible to speak too highly of the despatch and correctness of the printing in the English newspaper offices. Where so much praise is due, there has, as a matter of course, been some exaggeration likewise; and the newspaper offices are the subjects of many a popular myth, which it is worth while to reduce to simple truth. Both Englishmen, and the foreigners that are within their gates, will now and then, at eight o'clock in the morning, read "our own correspondent's" letter in the Times, and be struck with some remarkable piece of intelligence it contains. An hour or so afterwards, perhaps, the postman brings them a letter from some continental friend, and lo! that letter contains the very news which they have read, printed in large type, in the morning paper. Now, however expeditious compositors, printers, and newsmen may be, the setting up of matter, the striking it off, and distributing it through the various channels of trade, to the farthest ends of the town, require a certain amount of time. How, then, is it possible, since my private letter and the Times correspondence came by the same mail—how, in the name of all that is strange, does it happen, that the paper prints the news so much sooner than I receive it through the Post Office? Why it looks "nae cannie," as a Scotchman would say!

Still the result is brought about by the most natural and simple means. The morning papers have their continental correspondence sent by mail, but the letters are not directed to London, but to an agent in Dover. That agent, who is generally connected with the railroad or the Post Office, receives his parcels immediately after the arrival of the steamers from Calais and Ostend. He directs them to his principals in London, and sends them off with the express train. Of course the mail letter-bags reach London by the same train; but the mail-bags have to go to the Post Office, where the letters are taken out and sorted, and distributed among the various district offices, which, in their turn, distribute them among the letter-carriers. The letters cannot, therefore, reach their various destinations before eight o'clock, though it frequently happens that they come at a much later hour. But the parcels sent direct from Dover are emancipated from the necessary delays of the Post Office. A messenger receives them as the train dashes into London Bridge Station; they are at once hurried away to the printing offices, set up, printed, and despatched to all the news-shops of London. And while this is going on in the printing office, the Post Office clerks are opening the mail-bags, and sorting and stamping the letters for the regular delivery. A certain portion of time, say a few hours, are necessarily lost at the Post Office; and this loss of time to the public, and the advantage to which the newspapers turn it, has puzzled many persons, particularly strangers. All the popular tales of special trains and steamers are mere fables. The Times, with all its power of capital, cannot have faster vessels than the mail steamers that run between Calais and Dover; and if at Dover it were to engage a special train, that train could not go faster than the express. But even if greater speed were attainable, the experiment would be too costly for daily use.

On important occasions, indeed, in the case of unexpected arrivals of interesting continental news, or when large and important meetings are being held in the provinces, and the intelligence to be conveyed to town is too heavy for the telegraph, the great London journals do not shrink from the expense of special trains, which convey to them the reports of the proceedings, as taken down by their correspondents. But in the transmission of mere news—of those "facts," to which Mr. Cobden would confine the newspapers—the telegraph is at once cheaper and more expeditious.

A few years ago, when there were no railroads, and when the steamers were neither frequent in their passages nor punctual in their arrivals, the Times had organised its own system of couriers, and for a long time it competed with the Morning Herald as to the greatest expedition in the conveyance of the Overland Mail from Marseilles to London. At one time the Times had the best of it; on another occasion the couriers of the Times were beaten by the couriers of the Herald; the agents of the papers sowed their money broad-cast on the route between Marseilles and Calais; they outwitted one another in retaining all the post-horses, until these expensive manœuvres were finally rendered unnecessary by the railway service and the submarine telegraph. In this respect, too, the most fabulous stories have long been current in Germany, where, it is generally believed, that the Times has its score or so of special trains steaming away on all the railroads of England from year's-end to year's-end. The English newspaper service is by this time established on a firm, expeditious, and economical basis; and extraordinary means are resorted to only on extraordinary occasions.

The weekly political papers are published on Saturday, and some of them on Sunday morning, while a few publish a second edition on Monday morning. They live on the news of the daily papers; the better class among them have a single correspondence, a weekly Paris letter, but they have not the telegraphic despatches, nor do they maintain a staff of correspondents and reporters. They simply condense the news as given by the morning journals, while some of them spice the abstract with an original remark or two for the convenience of a peculiar class of readers. Besides these they have a few leading articles, and "Letters to the Editor." These letters are, in many instances, more interesting than any other part of the paper, and under an able editor their moral effect is greater even than that of the leading articles. This department has been utterly neglected by

German journalism, though there can be no doubt of its being eminently suited to the capabilities and necessities of the German public.

We have no intention of discussing the literary and political merits of the various "Weeklies." Their importance and popularity, too, is not a theme for us. These things are, moreover, well known in Germany. But in our opinion, it is worth while to inquire into the circumstances to which the weekly press in England owes its circulation and popularity, while it never prospered either in France or in Germany. A combination of causes produces this result. The morning papers are too expensive and too voluminous for the middle classes, especially in the country. Their price is a high one, not only according to the German, but also to the English mode of reckoning. But in the present state of the law, it is impossible to produce a daily paper which can compete with the other journals at a lower price. It has been proved to the satisfaction of Parliamentary Committees, that what with the paper, stamp, and advertisement duty, a great journal can only pay if it has an immense circulation. Still more strikingly has this been shown in the struggles and sufferings of the Daily News. That paper was set up in opposition to the Times. The Manchester men advanced a large capital, à fonds perdu, and the competition commenced with an attempt at underselling. The "Daily News" was sold at threepence per number; and the consequence was, that the funds of the party were really and truly "perdu." The price was raised to fourpence; still the concern was a losing speculation. Finally the Daily News condescended to take fivepence, as the other journals do, and it is now more prosperous.

But fivepence is a high price for a paper, even according to English ideas. It is very silly to say, that in England a sovereign is to the Englishman what a florin or a thaler is considered to be to the German. The remark may hold good in the case of the favoured few—the dukes, cotton-lords, and nabobs; but among the middle classes, the relative value of a sovereign and a thaler assumes a very different aspect. The middle class forms the bulk of newspaper readers; it is not so easy for that class to pay six pounds per annum for the "Times" or "Daily News," as the payment of six thalers (the average price of a Zeitung) is to the middle classes in Germany.

Besides being too dear, the morning journals are too large for the majority of the public. Many persons cannot spare the time to read all the parliamentary intelligence, and the police and law reports, and the railway and mining articles; others are too lazy, while the majority of provincial readers combine the two objections with a third. They are too busy, lazy, and generally too indifferent. They would take a comfortable view of the events. They are not over curious, and will not be compelled to swallow a daily dose of news. They are not so hot-blooded as a French portier, who cannot think of going to sleep without a look at least at the evening papers; and in politics they enjoy a greater degree of phlegm than all the continental nations together. They say, and are justified in so saying, "We live in a quiet country, where everything and everybody has his place. Nothing whatever can happen that we are any the worse off for knowing a few days later. A dissolution perhaps? Why let them dissolve the parliament, there will be a general election—that's all. Resignation of ministers? There are as good fish in the sea as ever came out of it. A foreign war? Very well, we'll pay for it, but they wont invade us, thanks to the sea and the wooden walls of England. All of which proves that a man need not be in a confounded hurry to know the last news!"

And as for the working classes they want money, time, and, indeed, they want the mind, for the daily press. Weeklies are cheaper and more palatable. Their news is more condensed; it is more popular; they contain a deal of demonstration and furnish useful reading all the week through.

It is therefore not at all astonishing that the weekly press should have experienced an enormous increase within the last few years, while the few daily papers that were started in that period, proved utter failures; while the majority of even the old established papers were far from being prosperous. Hence, too, the enormous sale of the weeklies, whose prices range from three-pence to nine-pence. First and foremost in prosperity is the Illustrated London News, whose sale is said to amount to 100,000 copies. The Weekly Dispatch, selling from 60,000 to 80,000 copies, comes next. It is a radical paper, though I doubt whether any German reader would ever discover its radicalism. The Weekly Dispatch is the favourite of the lower classes. The Examiner and the Spectator, though superior in point of style and political ability, are less read than the Germans generally believe; but Punch (for Punch too is essentially a political paper), is prosperous, easy, comfortable, and influential, as indeed it fully deserves to be.

The non-political papers, the monthlies and quarterlies, the clerical journals whose name is legion, the critical papers, the penny weekly papers which fatten on stolen property, the military and naval gazettes, the papers devoted to banking, architecture, gas-lighting, agriculture, mining, railways, colonial affairs, and all imaginable professions and branches of industry, these we mention only to say that we must leave them to scientific and professional travellers. But we add a few words on the provincial press of England.

It is insignificant. Any interest it may possess springs from local causes, as is the case with the Glasgow, Manchester, and Liverpool papers. This applies also to the Irish journals, whose tone, generally speaking, bears traces of more genius and less conscience than the tone of the English press.

The English provincial press in particular can advance no claims to Irish genius. It wants originality, unless it be original deliberately and with speculation aforethought to say the thing which is not true; to bring news of ministerial changes, which is news indeed to the officials of Downing-street, and to perpetuate the fiction of a highly distinguished omnipresent and omniscient "London Correspondent," who is a member of all the clubs; who passes every one of his evenings in all the theatres and at all the fashionable parties, and who is on terms of the most bewildering intimacy with all the great men of the day. A great many of these papers drag out a weary and unprofitable existence, while others make much money. The expenditure of most of them is confined to the cost of the paper and printing; the taxes due to the state and the outlay of a modest capital on scissors and paste.

There is no possibility of improvement in this respect, since in England a political paper cannot thrive unless it be established in London. The owners of the provincial newspapers cannot help it; they have no control over the political and geographical circumstances which determine the fortune of the English press.

Not only does it stand to reason that a metropolitan journal is in a more favourable position than a provincial journal, since the national life and action radiates and is concentrated in the mighty heart of the country; but London, with its population of two millions and a half, is not merely the capital of a vast empire, it is also an imperium in imperio, a kingdom in itself. Many kingdoms have a less population than London has, and many countries furnish not half the amount of matter for journalism which London supplies. And though they had the matter it would be divided over a vast area, and its instant collection and publication would be impossible. Concentration has incalculable advantages for the daily press, as is plainly shown by the great journals of Paris and London.

In another respect, too, the London papers are favoured by circumstances. The geographical extent of England is so small compared to its political power, the country is so completely covered with a network of railroads and telegraphs, that space is lessened in a marvellous degree. Thus is the London press enabled to collect intelligence in all parts of the country in less than no time, as the English say, to gather it by centripetal attraction and send it forth by centrifugal radiation. Sitting on the banks of the Thames, a short railway journey from the narrowest portion of the channel and thus, of all the large towns, most near to the Continent, London is the most efficient mediatrix and exchanger of news between the Continent and England and the Continent and America. As capital of England, of a country which has always carried the mails of all the nations and parts of the world to all the nations and parts of the world, London is the great political, mercantile, and scientific storehouse of the world. No other periodical press can boast of such favourable circumstances; and the London press is safe from the competition of the periodical journals of the seaport-towns, because distance in England is of very little moment in the communication of intelligence, and, because favoured as it is, it can afford to pay, and occasionally to pay largely too for extra means of speed and priority of information.

Let us now turn to the mechanical means and contrivances by which the London papers are distributed among the public.

The transmission of newspapers in Germany is a government monopoly: it belongs to the post. The post-offices in Germany accept subscriptions to the various newspapers and forward them to the subscribers. The English post-office has nothing whatever to do with newspaper subscriptions. It forwards newspapers exactly as it forwards other parcels, whenever they are posted, but it does not undertake to obtain them from the publishing-office. The newspaper-offices, too, know nothing of the continental system of abonnement; they sell their papers over the counter, and for cash, exactly as all other wholesale dealers do. Under these circumstances, the public want retail shops, and such retailers are to be found in the newsvenders.

Generally speaking, the newsvenders occupy small shops in or near some of the principal streets, where they frequently carry on the business of stationers as well. They supply their London customers with papers; they send papers to their customers in the provinces, and they lend papers by the hour or day. For success in the various branches of his business, the newsvender wants a good connexion and a small capital. His connexion once established, he can make a guess at the numbers of each paper he is likely to want, and for these he sends to the various publishing-offices. The news-boys are the chief "helps" and props of his trade.

In the dawn of morning, even before the publication of the great journals has commenced, the newsvender, represented by his boy, is at his post in the outer room of the publishing-office. These plenipotentiaries of the various newsvending firms sit and gape and rub their eyes, or warm their hands by the fire, until the first batch of papers is hurried into the room. A thin, sleepy man, who has hitherto been hid in a kind of cage, gets up from his office chair and takes charge of the bulky parcel. The boys at once make a rush towards the cage, and the taller ones elbow their way up to it, while the small boys must be content to wait until their turn comes. "Fifty copies!" "One hundred copies!" "Two hundred copies!" Each bawls out the number he wants, puts down his money, and runs off through the moist, cold, morning air to another newspaper-office, or back to the shop, where the various numbers are put into wrappers as fast as it is possible for human hands to perform that operation, and despatched by rail to the various country customers. All this is done at express speed; and the newsvender's boy, though gifted with a leaning to politics, can hardly find the time to stop by a street lamp and read the last "Submarine from Paris."

He is hard at work all the morning. When the parcels have been despatched into the provinces, he is at once compelled to devote himself to the other important section of his daily duties, and provide for his master's town customers, of whom there are two classes, purchasers and hirers of newspapers. The former receive their papers about nine o'clock through the medium of the news-boy. The latter receive their papers at various times according to the terms of the contract. Some keep a paper two hours, some keep it three or four, and the terms are, for the short period, 6d., and for the longer, 1s. per week. It is the newsboy's business to know all the various customers of this kind, and to call with the paper, and for it, at the exact time desired by each individual reader.

He is less occupied between the hours of eleven and three. If not compelled to "mind the shop," the newsboy, if gifted with a correct estimation of his political position, will devote these leisure hours to the perusal of the various journals within his reach. If not of an intellectual turn, he indulges in a comfortable fight with some sympathetic printer's devils, in some quiet square or court. Duty calls him again at three o'clock. He has to call for the newspapers which are "out," and he has to secure the supply of evening papers at the moment of their publication—all for that evening's country mail. The publishing-offices of almost all the London papers are to be found in the line of road and the parts that thereunto adjacent lie, from the Strand to St. Paul's, where journals of diametrically opposite tendencies reside in dangerous proximity to one another. In this quarter of the town they are near to the Exchange, the post-office, and the chief railway-stations; and the chief newsvenders, too, live generally in the narrow lanes and alleys which run out of the principal streets.

Those who wish to study the natural history of the news-boy, should take their stand in the publishing office of an evening paper, at half-past three or four o'clock in the afternoon. A small apartment, divided into two smaller apartments by means of a wooden partition, and the outer half dusty and dirty to the last degree, and crowded with boys, who there wait for the paper, which is just going to press. It happens, now and then, that the publication is delayed for half an hour, or so; on such occasions, the youths in attendance display a remarkable amount of ingenuity in their praiseworthy efforts to kill the time. The innate street-boyism of these small creatures is tinged with a literary colouring. The little "devils" are evidently inspired with the devilries of the newspapers which they sell. Some are free-traders, others are protectionists; not from conviction, but from the urgent desire of their nature to have a good and sufficient reason for wrangling and fighting. We watched their proceedings on one occasion, at the time when Lord Derby and Mr. Disraeli were "in," as a very ragged boy said, in so sententious a manner, that it would have done honour to a very old member of the House of Commons.

"Eh, Jim!" cried a diminutive boy, with black eyes, red cheeks, and fuzzy brown hair. "Eh, Jim! sold no end of

THE NEWSPAPER BOYS.

Heralds, I dare say. You're in, you know; clodhoppers that you are!" "Herald's a ministerial paper; beats the Times hollow, don't it? Kick's it into the middle of next week, eh? Well, I hope it'll do your master some good, but it don't do you no good, Jim, my boy; you're as lean as a bone, you are!"

To which, Jim, a light-haired, spare-made, freckled youth, replies:

"You're the parties as gets fat, so you are. Them as is 'onest people, never gets fat! How's the Globe? eh! Don't you think one publication a week is more than enough? You've got no news, noways, now that we are in."

Saying which, he takes off his cap—the beak of it went a long time ago, on the battle-field of Holywell-street—and flings the dirty missile into Tom's face; and Tom, who would parry it, puts his fist into Dan's face; whereupon, Dan, starting back, kick's Jack's shins; and Jack gives it to Dan, and Dan to Tom, and Tom to Jim, and there is a general melée. The quarrel is finally settled by the armed intervention of four tall boys, who for some length of time watched the chances of the fight from a bench in the furthest corner of the room. A few blows and kicks, the combatants are separated, and the publishing office is tranquil. At this juncture, the inner door is opened, and a man with spectacles, and a large parcel of wet Globes makes his appearance. The four tall youths rush up to the wooden partition, to the exclusion, the manifest disgust of the smaller fry of boys. All their movements betray the consciousness of their Flegeljahr dignity. Mr. Smirkins, the publishing clerk, who has just entered, treats them with marked distinction. He greets them with a smile; tells them it is "rather wet to-day;" and goes the length of inquiring after the state of their health. One of them, a genteel youth, with very stiff shirt collar, and a very new hat, is quite a favorite with Mr. Smirkins. That gentleman has, for the last years, devoted his time and talents to the Globe office, and has come to consider himself, not only as an integral part of that Whig paper, but also as an important link in the heavy chain of the Whig party. He mentions the Whigs, as "our party;" and in speaking of the Globe, he says, "we." The advent of the Derbyites to power, has been a severe trial to Mr. Smirkins' feelings; he is less fat and jovial now, than he was under Lord John Russell. He looks care-worn. A faithful servant of his party, he grieves to see the Globe neglected by those high in office.

"How many copies?" says he to the youth with the shirt-collars. "Ten? Here they are. I dare say you take a good many Standards since we———"

No! the truth is too harsh for Mr. Smirkins. He cannot conclude the sentence, so tries another mode of expression.

"The Standard's looking up, I dare say?"

But the youthful newsvender has all the discretion of a London man of business. He replies to Mr. Smirkins' question with a few "Hem's and Hah's"; and Mr. Smirkins, foiled in his attempts to obtain intelligence of the prosperity of the other party, goes on distributing his papers among the boys; and the boys, rushing out to distribute them all over the town, make great haste, that they may be in time at the newsvenders Exchange.

These boys, strange though it may appear, have their own exchange where they meet at five o'clock. Not indeed in colonnade and marble halls, not even in a tavern parlour, but in the open air, at the corner of Catherine-street, Strand. There they meet, shouting, squabbling and fighting in hot haste, for they have not much time to lose. All the papers must be posted by six o'clock. Here spare copies of the Herald are exchanged for spare copies of the Daily News, the Times is bartered against the Post, according to the superfluities and necessities of the various traders. The exchanges, of course, are made on the spot, the papers are posted, and the newsvender's business is over for the day. On Saturdays, however, many of their shops are kept open till long after midnight, for the accommodation of the working classes and the sale of the Sunday papers. Tom and Jim and Dan and Jack have received their week's wages, and take a stroll in Clare Market or join their friends, the baker's and fishmonger's boys, in some bold expedition to distant Whitechapel.

CHAP. VI.

The Bank.

APPEARANCE OF THE BANK.—WANT OF RESPECT IN THE PRESENCE OF PUBLIC FUNCTIONARIES.—THE PUBLIC AT THE BANK.—MYSTERIOUS COMFORTS.—ENGLISH TASTE.—THE WONDERS OF MACHINERY.—A STRANGE LIBRARY.—PRINTING THE NOTES.—HIDDEN PALACES.—THE TREASURY.—BAD SOVEREIGNS.—DR. KEIF; AND WHY THE ENGLISH KNOW NOTHING WHATEVER OF THE AFFAIRS OF GERMANY.

WE have already, on a former occasion, looked at two of the city temples—the Mansion-house and the Exchange. We now return to the Capitoline mart of the city, to inspect the third of its temples—the Bank of England.

Its outward appearance is mysterious. Half wall and half house, it is neither the one nor the other; and yet either at one and the same time. For a wall there are too many niches, blind windows, columns, and finery; for a building it wants presence; it is too low, and has not even window openings. But it appears from the architect's plan that this strange façade is meant for a wall, and, having the artist's word for it, we believe, though see we do not, and sit down satisfied.

Standing free on all sides as the Exchange, the Bank is divided from the latter by a thoroughfare called Threadneedle-street. Its western limit is Princes-street; in the north intervenes Lothbury, and in the south Bartholomew-lane, between the Bank and the neighbouring houses. It forms a square; and yet people say it demonstrates the squaring of the circle, the grand problem of modern philosophy.

We enter. The gate does not strike one as solemn and imposing as might be expected in a gate leading to the laboratory of a great wizard. No Druid's foot on the threshold; no spectral bats such as abound in nursery tales of treasure-seeking. No! not even a couple of grenadiers, who, in our dear fatherland are a necessary appendage to every public building; really everything looks worldly, business-like, and civil. A red-coated porter answers our questions, and tells us which way to go. He is an elderly man, and certainly not strong enough to arrest a mere lad of a communist, if such a one would attempt to divide the property of the British nation. A shocking idea, that!

We cross a small court-yard, and mount a few steps (why should'nt we?) and, all of a sudden, we are in a large saloon. This saloon is an office—it matters very little what particular office it is—but it makes not a disagreeable impression as our German offices do where everything is official and officious, oppressive, and calculated to put people down. On the contrary, there's a vast deal of good society in this office: at least a hundred officials and members of the public. The officials have no official appearance whatever; they are simple mortals, and do their business and serve their customers as if they were mere shopboys in a grocery shop. There is in them not a trace of dignity! not an atom of bureaucratic pride! It is exactly as if to serve the public were the sole business of their lives. And the public too! Was such a thing ever heard of in a public office? Men, women, and boys, with their hats on! walking arm in arm as if they were in the park. They change money, or bring it or fetch it, as if they had looked into a neighbour's shop for the purpose. Some of them have no business at all to transact. They actually talk to one another—stand by the fire in the centre of the room, and warm their backs! The impertinent fellows! Why, they have no respect whatever! They forget that they are in a public office. How dare you stand there you dolt? How dare you scratch your head, and hold your pipe in your hand? I should'nt wonder if it was lighted—it would be like your impertinence! Get out as fast as you can; if you dont the police will make you! Really not a trace of respect! It's no wonder they say we are near doomsday.[F]

[F] The readers of passages like the above will not be astonished to learn that Dr. Schlesinger's book has the honour of being prohibited in some of the best-governed states of Germany, but more especially in Austria.—[Ed].

Ranged in long rows along the walls, the Bank clerks sit writing, casting-up accounts, weighing gold, and paying it away over the counter. In front of each is a bar of dark mahogany, a little table, a pair of scales, and a small fraction of the public; each waiting for his fare. The business is well-conducted, and none of them are kept waiting for any length of time.

The saloon just by is more crowded. We are in the middle of the year, and the interest on the three per cents. is being paid. What crowding and sweeping to and fro. At least fifty clerks are sitting in a circle in a high vaulted saloon, well provided with a cupola and lanterns. They do nothing whatever but pay and weigh, and weigh and pay. On all sides, the rattling of gold, as they push it with little brass shovels across the tables. People elbowing and pushing in order to get a locus standi near the clerks; the doors are continually opening and shutting. What crowds of people there must be in this country who have their money in the three per cent. Consols!

Strange figures may be seen in this place. An old man with a wooden-leg sits in a corner waiting, and Heaven knows how long he has been waiting already. Of course, a wooden leg is rather an encumbrance than otherwise in a crowd. The old man seems to be fully aware of the fact. He looks at his large silver watch—it is just twelve—puts his hand to the pocket of his coat, and pulls out a large parcel, something wrapped up in a stale copy of the Herald. What can the parcel contain? Sandwiches! He spreads them out, and begins to eat. He likes them too. He takes his ease, and makes himself perfectly at home. I dare say it is not the first time he has waited for his dividends.

That young lady on our left is getting impatient. She has made several attempts to fight her way to one of the clerks; she tried to push in first on the right, and then on the left, but all in vain. John Bull is by no means gallant in business, or at the theatre, or in the streets: he pushes, and kicks, and elbows in all directions. Poor pretty young lady, you'll have a long time to wait! It's no use standing on your toes, and looking over people's shoulders. You'd better come again to-morrow.

The little boy down there gets much better on. A pretty fair-haired fellow that, with a little basket in his hand. Perhaps he is the son of a widow, who cannot come herself to get her small allowance. The boy looks as if about to cry, for he is on all sides surrounded by tall men. But one of them seizes him, lifts him up, and presents him to one of the clerks. "Pray pay this little creditor of the public; he'll be pressed to death in the crowd!" And they all laugh, and everybody makes room for the boy; for it ought to be said to John Bull's credit, he is kind and gentle with children at all times. "Well done, my little fellow! Now be careful that they dont rob you of your money on the way. How can they ever think of sending such a baby for their dividends!"

In this wing of the house, office follows after office; they are all on the ground-floor, and receive their light through the ceiling; they are all constructed in a grand style, and many of them are fit for a king's banqueting-room. In them money is exchanged for notes, and notes for money; the interest on the public debt is paid; the names of the creditors are booked and transferred. It is here that the banking business is carried on in its relations with the bulk of the public.

These offices are, consequently open to every one; they are the central hall of the English money market, the great exchange office of London. Every Englishman is here sentinel and constable, for every Englishman has, or at least he wishes to have, some share in the Bank. But those who would enter the more secret recesses of the sanctuary, must have an order from one of the Bank Directors. We are fortunate enough to have such an order, which we show to one of the servants. He takes us, shows us into a little room, and asks us to wait a few moments.

The room in which we are is a waiting-room. There are many such in the house. A round table, a couple of chairs, and—and nothing else! that's all the furniture. Really nothing else! And yet the room is so snug and comfortable. It is altogether mysterious, how the English manage to give their rooms an air of comfort, which with us is too frequently wanting, even in the houses of wealthy persons, who furnish, as the phrase goes, "regardless of expense." Every German who comes to England must be struck with the fact. Whether the apartments he hires be splendid or humble—no matter, he is at once alive to the influence of this charmed something, and he will sadly miss it when he returns to Germany. Yes! it must be—the charm must be in the carpets and the fire-place. Surely witchery does not enter into the household arrangements of sober and orthodox Englishmen!

It's a pity they did not make us wait a little longer, the room was so comfortable. Another servant has brought our order back, and told us that he is to be our guide. Passing through open yards and covered passages, we come to a clean and well-paved hall, in which the steam-engine of the house lives. Large cylinders, powerful wheels, rods shining as silver, the balls of the whirling governor heavy as four-and-twenty pounders, and the space under the boiler a hell en miniature. Everything powerful and gigantic, and yet clean, harmonious, and tasteful.

Yes! tasteful is the word. The English are frequently, and in many instances justly, taunted with their want of taste. They have an awkward manner of wearing their clothes; they are bad hands at designing and manufacturing those charming nippes, for which the French are so famous; their grand dinners and festivals, their fancy patterns and articles of luxury, their fashions and social habits, are frequently at war with the laws of refined taste.

But there are also matters in which, in point of taste, they are superior to all other nations. Such, for instance, in the cultivation of the soil, the manufacture of iron and leather, etc., etc.

Give a French, German, Spanish, or Belgian artisan a piece of iron, and ask him to make a screw for a steam-engine. Give just such a piece of iron to an Englishman, with the same request. The odds are a thousand to one that the Englishman's screw will be more neat, useful and handsome, than the screw produced by the artisans of the other nations. The Englishman gives his iron and steel goods a sort of characteristic expression, a sort of solid beauty, which cannot fail at once to strike every beholder. The Germans saw thus much in the Great Exhibition; and they may see it in every English house, if they will but take the trouble of examining the commonest kitchen utensils, or the tongs, shovel, and poker in the most ordinary English parlour. They are all massive, solid, weighty, and tasteful.

It's a splendid sight, this steam-engine at the Bank! It is complete, and in keeping in all its details. It is the mind which moves all the wheels and machines in the house. Its power is exerted in the furthest parts of the establishment; it moves a thousand wheels, and rollers, and rods; it stands all lonely in its case, working on and on, without control or assistance from man. With us, too, the steam-engines have emancipated themselves, and do not want the support of their masters; but the furnace is still a mere infant, and wants stokers to put its food into its mouth. But here the furnace, too, is independent: it procures its victuals, and feeds itself according to its wants. The large round grate is moveable; it turns in a circle on its horizontal plane, and pushes each point of its circumference at regular intervals, under an opening from which the coals fall down upon it. The keeper of the engine has nothing whatever to do but to fill the coal-box and light the fire in the morning. Steam is generated, it enters the cylinders, moves the pistons and the wheels, and the grate commences its rotary movement. From that moment forward, the engine works on without assistance.

As we proceed we shall be able to judge of the multiplied usefulness of this remarkable engine. We have followed our guide up a narrow flight of stone steps, and are now in rooms which form a striking contrast to the saloons which we examined in the first instance. They are dark and dusky workshops, in which the materials for the use of the Bank are being prepared. Here, for instance, is a man in a small room preparing the steel-plates on which the notes are to be engraved. His is a difficult task, even though the engine moves the sharp hard wedge which scrapes and polishes the plates. It produces a shrill screaming noise, one which it is by no means agreeable to listen to for any length of time; and besides the labour is most wearisome and monotonous. But it is one of the dark sides of this age of machinery, perhaps it is the darkest, that the sameness of his mechanical labour tends to stupify the workman; that he ceases being an artizan or artist, and comes to be a mere help to his machine, which requires no talents or abilities in its servant, but merely exactitude and promptness. All he has to do is to put the plate or the spindle on the exact spot, where the machine can seize, handle it, and finish it.

Another room is devoted to the preparation of printer's ink, for the printing of the notes. A quantity of black matter is being ground. A simple operation this; even dogs might be trained to perform it, and give satisfaction. But here, too, the machine does the work, and does it, too, with astonishing accuracy. All the workman has to do, is to put the black mixture between the rollers; they take it, crush it, grind it, and drop it ready for use. If a single grain of sand be found in the mixture, the machine has neglected its duty—that's all. But you wont find a grain of sand even if you were to search for it in many tons of the ink.

The workman explains the process.

"The ink," says he, "must pass between these two large rollers to be ground. The rollers are of strong steel; they are very hard and heavy. But small particles of sand or stone would soon take away their polish. That's what this side-cutting is for. Look here. I hold the point of my knife exactly at the point where the rollers touch one another. Did you see how at the slightest touch they separated? This happens whenever any hard body, however small, finds its way between them. They dont take it, but drop it, and in this manner they keep their polish."

It is marvellous! This machine is most simple, and yet we could stand for hours to see it work. What is a sensitive plant to these heavy steel rollers, which are so sensitive that they recede at the touch even of a grain of sand! And it is all done by means of the cutting and the weight. It is no use attempting to describe these things without a diagram. And even that is unsatisfactory to those who never saw the machine in motion. But we revoke the pert remark we made just now. A dog cannot be trained to do this work; even the labour of man could not supply the labour of this machine. Enough for man that he made it.

Through the various work-rooms, each of them devoted to some part of the manufactory of notes, we come to the large work-shops of the printers and binders. In either of them steam is at work, and so are human beings. The Bank of England, which in the first year of its existence wanted only one ledger, requires now at least three hundred ledgers to register its accounts; they are all lined, paged, and bound in the house. It is one of the most interesting features of the Bank, that all its requirements, with the sole exception of the paper, are manufactured on the premises.

Exactly as in the stone-paved hall of the lower story, where we watched the great central steam-engine feeding itself, so we find in other rooms large machine monsters moving up and down, and to and fro, rattling, hissing, and thumping, and frequently not doing anything that we can see, although our guide tells us, that the results of their labours will become apparent to us in other parts of the building. And they stand, moreover, alone, completely left to themselves; in the rooms in which they work, in the corridors leading to those rooms, not a human creature is to be seen, not a human step to be heard, nor is there a trace of human influence that we are aware of. And then this measured rotation of the large wheels; the busy movement of the straps; the never tiring restlessness of the pistons, which seem to move faster the longer we look at them. There is something grand in these rooms, void of the presence of man, where the mind of man invisibly hovers over the world of machines, as the Spirit of God over the face of the waters in the hour of creation. It is grand, but it is also awful.

We feel quite relieved when we get down into the paved court-yard, where a living two-legged labourer walks by; and yet neither the place nor the man is very agreeable to look at. The yard has a neglected appearance, and the iron shutters which cover the place where the windows are supposed to be make it still more gloomy.

"That is the library of the Bank," remarks our guide.

We are not likely to be astonished by anything. We just saw workshops without men; why should there not be a library without books? Let us have patience and wait. Perhaps some very clever machine will open the iron shutter from the inside, thrust forth its arm, and hand us a catalogue. No? Well, for a wonder, our guide, who is very polite, though by no means over-communicative, opens a small door, and motions us to enter.

A low, narrow, vaulted passage, which reminds us of the casemates or bomb-proof galleries of fortresses; a few rays of light straggling in through some grating somewhere; at the end of the passage a heavy iron door which opens into a small windowless room lighted up by the most consumptive-looking gas-jet imaginable. Our eyes are quite unused to the light; but, gradually as we get accustomed to it, we can see the objects around us. We stand in front of a railing, and behind it stands a little man in a black dress coat, and with a white cravat.

"This gentleman is the librarian of the Bank;" says our guide. Still no trace of books.

The man in the black dress-coat opens a door in the railing, bids us enter, and shows us an enormous number of parcels and bundles of notes, ranged along the walls up to the very ceiling. They call this the library of the Bank; but, in truth, it is its lumber room. It is an asylum for the notes which have been paid in at the Bank. They are valueless; for the Bank never issues the same note twice. They are kept and locked up in the library, I forget how many years, in order to be produced in the case of a theft or forgery, or any other matter of the kind. Afterwards they are burnt.

Every now and then clerks come in with fresh bundles. A few minutes ago these small papers were worth—Heaven knows how much money. "They are now mere waste paper. They have had their day. Many a note leads a long and honourable life; goes to the Continent, to India, or Port Adelaide; and returns to the Bank much the worse for wear after all its journeys. Other notes have scarcely a day's roving license in the world; to-day they are issued, and to-morrow they are paid in. It's accident, or fate, or Providence." Saying which the librarian makes his bow, turns round, and returns to his desk.

We leave the library. The way is frequently very short from the old bookshop where good books and bad books are alike given up to dust and moths, to the printing-office, from whence they are launched forth into the world. Thus it is in the Bank. We have scarcely left the library, and we are already in the department where they print the notes.

The printing from the plates is simple enough. The wonders of the machinery consist chiefly in the spontaneous advance of the numbers (each note has its own number, and a double set too), and in the control which the machine exercises over the workmen. There is no inspector to watch the printer. The machine, which he compels to print, compels him to be honest. The machine registers the exact numbers that are being printed, and registers them too in a distant part of the establishment. That the machine can do this with astonishing accuracy; that it masters the intricacies of our system of numbers; and that it produces the numbers at the same moment in different places; is a triumph of human invention which almost startles us. It is also the result of the various systems of wheels which we saw working all alone in other parts of the building.

A great deal more might be said of the astonishing results of this most perfect system of machinery. But, since description is out of the question, we should only reproduce our own impression. Still we must tell the fairer portion of our readers that at the Bank even the washing is done by machinery, and that the establishment manages to get on without female labour.

The dirty linen of the Bank—that is to say the cloths which are used in the printing process—are sent to the washhouse, where they are compelled to perform a pilgrimage through a number of large pails full of hot and cold water. They are then washed by wheels; then dragged into hot water and next into cold water, wrung out and hung up in a drying room. And all by steam—all by machinery! No busy housewife—no able-tongued laundresses—no disturbance of the house—and no washing-days! There is no saying how shocking a want of respect of the whole female sex is implied by this process! But then the poor mechanics are quite as badly treated. You must put up with it, Madame. The Bank can and will do without you.

Our guide leads the way to other regions. We enter the reception and meeting-rooms of the Governor and the Directors.

Charming open places, with lawns and shrubberies, and here and there a shady tree—clean, well-sanded paths—it is quite evident that we have left the manufacturing districts, and are in the midst of the parks and homesteads of Old England. And these buildings, rising up from the lawns, are palaces, with columns, large stone steps, and carved ornaments. Their interior excels in splendour the wildest anticipations we might have formed. Saloons, high and lofty as cathedrals, splendid cupolas everywhere, and an overwhelming profusion of panelling, architectural ornaments, rich carpets and furniture, fit for a king's palace. We would gladly remain here and see nothing else; but our guide is determined on our admiring all the sights of the house.

We follow him to the guard-room, where a detachment of soldiers from the Tower enter every evening and pass the night, to protect the Bank "in case of an emergency." We follow him to the Bullion Office, a subterranean vault, where they keep the gold and silver bars from Australia, California, Russia, Peru, and Mexico; where they weigh them, sell them, and from whence they send them to the Mint. These vaults are very interesting to the admirers of precious metals.

But is this all? No! nothing of the kind. Our guide—a real guide—has reserved the most interesting part of the exhibition to the last. He has taken us through several yards and passages. He knocks at a large door, which is opened from the inside. Two gentlemen, in black dress coats and white cravats, stand in a large room, which receives its light through a lantern in the top. In the centre of the room is a heavy bureau. The walls are covered with iron lock-ups and safes. This is the Treasury of the Bank, where they keep the new notes and coins.

One of the gentlemen looks at our order, and, with that unpretending dignity which characterises the English, he turns round and opens some of the iron safes. They are filled with bags, containing 500 or 1000 sovereigns each. He takes some of them and puts them into our hands, to convince us, as though we ever doubted of the fact, of the bags being filled with good sterling money.

The other gentleman—they are both dressed as if they were going to a levée—takes a bunch of keys, and opens a large closet filled with notes. The most valuable and smallest bundle is again put into our hands. "You have there," says he, "two thousand notes of one thousand pounds each." Two million pounds sterling! Surely an enormous sum to hold in one's hand. An army in paper, containing the power of much evil and much good, especially since the paper is not mere paper and since, at a few yards' distance, you may change it into "red, red gold," as the poets say. But as we are not in a position to perform that alchymistic process, we return the notes to their keeper. "Good bye, Sir." "Good morning, gentlemen." We have left the Treasury, without being either wiser or richer men. Of course, because we were not allowed to carry off its contents.

We enter another large room, with the neatest, prettiest steam-engine in it, and with a variety of other small machines, whose complicated wheels are kept in motion by the said engine. The bulkiest object in the room is a large table, literally covered with mountains of sovereigns. A few officials, with shovels in their hands, are stirring the immense glittering mass.

"It is here that they weigh the sovereigns," whispers our guide. We stand and watch the process. Ignorant as we are of the exact principles of the machines, we are altogether startled by their fabulous activity.

Besides the mysterious system of wheels within wheels, each of these marvels displays an open square box, and in this box, slanting in an angle of 30°, two segments of cylinders, with the open part turned upwards. A roll of sovereigns, placed into one of these tubes, passes slowly down, and one gold piece after the other drops into a large box on the floor.

All the clerks have to do is to fill the tubes. The sovereigns slide down, but just at the lower end of the tube the miracle is accomplished. Whenever a sovereign of less than full weight touches that ticklish point, a small brass plate jumps up from some hidden corner, and pushes the defaulter into the left-hand compartment of the box, while all the good pieces go to the right. This little brass plate, hiding where it does, and popping out at intervals to note a bad sovereign, is an impertinent, ironical, malicious thing. There is an air of republicanism about it. As to the sharpness of its criticism, we actually do not believe that any republican would attempt to compete with it. For who would estimate the virtues of his fellow-men by grains, especially in the law of crowned heads!

We cannot see enough of these active machines. The small plates of brass show themselves pretty often as old and worn out sovereigns glide down. Not one of them is allowed to pass; and withal these small plates act with so much quiet promptitude and calm energy, and altogether without noise or pretension.

One of the clerks is kind enough to explain the purpose of this process.

"The Bank selects the full weighted sovereigns from the light ones, because all the money we pay out must have its full weight."

"And what do you do with the light ones?"

"We send them to the Mint after we have taken the liberty of marking them. Shall I show you how we do it?"

He takes a handful of the condemned ones, and puts them into a box, which has the appearance of a small barrel-organ. He turns a screw, or touches a spring—it is clearly impossible to note each movement of the man's hand—and there is a sounding and rushing noise in the interior of the box, and all the sovereigns fall out from a slit at the bottom. But mercy on us! how dreadfully disfigured they are! Cut through in the middle. The Victorias, and Williams, and Georges, all cut through their necks; in fact, beheaded! And that's what the English call "marking a bad sovereign." It makes us shudder. We are positively afraid. We cant stay one minute longer. "Good morning, sir." "Good morning, gentlemen."

What with our confusion and distress, we quite forgot to thank our kind guide. We are again in the street: to our left is the Exchange, to our right the Mansion-house, and before us the Iron Duke on horseback, and all around the furious, rattling, ceaseless crowd of vehicles; the moving and pushing of the foot-passengers; women hunted over the crossings; walking advertisements; street-sellers; red Post-office carts; the dusky streets, and the heavy leaden sky—the City in its working dress!

At home, while we are sitting at tea, Dr. Keif wastes much valuable eloquence in trying to convince Sir John, that the English can never get a proper understanding of German affairs: 1st, because it is hardly possible even for a German properly to understand them; 2nd, because the English newspapers have none but English correspondents in Germany, who know just as little of that mysterious country as he (Dr. Keif) knows of banking; 3rd, because the English consider all other countries with exclusive reference to their own country; and, 4th, because they fancy that reform can be brought about by peaceable public meetings, even in countries where those who attend such meetings are at once arrested, and locked up in fortresses or houses of correction; 5th, because social life in England is vastly different from social life in Germany; 6th, because Britons are too ignorant of the geography of Germany; and, 7th, because there are many who might understand German affairs, and who have very good reasons for not wishing to understand them. As we cannot follow the learned Doctor through the whole length of his argument we leave him to fight his own battle with Sir John, and merely remark, that an armistice was concluded at two o'clock in the morning, after which the belligerent parties went into night-quarters. And with this satisfactory intelligence we close the chapter.

CHAP. VII.

Four-and-twenty Hours at the Times' Office.

CROSSING THE ROAD.—THE OWNERS OF THE "TIMES."—ITS SOUL; ITS EDITORS.—DIFFERENCE BETWEEN THE "TIMES'" EDITORS AND THE "REDACTEURS" OF GERMAN NEWSPAPERS.—THE POLITICS OF THE "TIMES."—HOW THEY WRITE THE "LEADERS."—SECRETS.—LETTERS TO THE EDITOR.—THE MANAGER'S DEPARTMENT.—WHAT THE EDITORS DO.—THE PARLIAMENTARY CORPS.—THE REPORTER'S GALLERY AND REFECTORY.—DIVISION, DISCIPLINE, AND OCCUPATION OF THE REPORTERS.—MR. DOD.—THE SUMMARY-MAN.—THE STAFF.—THE PENNY-A-LINERS.—SOCIAL POSITION OF ENGLISH JOURNALISM.

ELEVEN A.M. One of the wheelers of a four-horse omnibus slipped on the pavement and fell down at the foot of the Holborn-side obelisk, between Fleet-street and Ludgate-hill. There's a stoppage. The horse makes vain endeavours to get up; there is no help for it, they must undo reins, buckles and straps to free him. But a stoppage of five minutes in Fleet-street creates a stoppage in every direction to the distance of perhaps half a mile or a mile. Leaning as we do against the railings of the obelisk, we look forwards towards St. Paul's, and back to Chancery-lane, up to Holborn on our left, and down on our right to Blackfriar's-bridge; and this vast space presents the curious spectacle of scores of omnibuses, cabs, gigs, horses, carts, brewer's drays, coal waggons, all standing still, and jammed into an inextricable fix. Some madcap of a boy attempts the perilous passage from one side of the street to the other; he jumps over carts, creeps under the bellies of horses, and, in spite of the manifold dangers which beset him, he gains the opposite pavement. But those who can spare the time or who set some store by their lives, had better wait. Besides it is pleasant to look at all this turmoil and confusion. And how, in the name of all that is charitable, are the London pickpockets to live if people will never stand still on any account?

The difficulty is soon got over. Two policemen, a posse of idle cabmen and sporting amateurs, and a couple of ragged urchins, to whom the being allowed to touch a horse is happiness indeed, have come to the rescue, loosening chains and traces, getting the horse up and putting him to again. It's all right. The fall of a horse gives exciting occupation to a score of persons, and even those who cannot assist with their hands, have at least a piece of excellent advice to give to those who can, exactly as if this sort of thing happened only once in every century in the crowded streets of London.

We may now go on. Halfway up Ludgate-hill, where the shops are largest and their silks and Indian shawls most precious and tempting to female eyes, is a small gateway, through which we pass on our road to the Times office. It leads us into a labyrinth of the narrowest, the most wretched, ill-paved, and unsavoury streets of London. We stumble over a couple of surly curs, that would gladly bask in the sun if sun there were to bask in, and over a troop of dirty boys that are trundling their hoops, and twice we stumble over orange-peel, lying on the pavement conspicuously as if this were Naples. At length we turn to the left, into a narrow street, and reach a small square of the exact dimensions and appearance of a German back-yard. There are two trees quite lonely behind an iron railing, and a door with the words "The Times" on it.

A porter takes our cards; a messenger leads the way into the interior of the building. Glad as we are to see the kind old gentleman who does the honours of the house, and acts as cicerone on such occasions, we can do without him. We propose trying the trick of the diable boiteux, and for the term of a day and a night to watch the proceedings of the editorial department of the Times for the benefit of foreign journalists generally, whose introductions procure them admission to the printing-office only.

It is ten minutes past eleven o'clock. Mr. M. M.—the manager, the factotum, the soul, and, at the same time, the sovereign of the Times—has been in his office these ten minutes. We were detained by that wretched wheeler.

The soul, then, of the Times has taken his place in the editorial body. Who is this "manager," and what are his functions?

Mr. Walter founded the Times; he reared it, fostered and organised it, and gave it the stamina by means of which it has reached its height of power. It was he who first attempted the use of machinery; he invented a new system of composing the type; he was a writer on the paper, and, in extreme cases, he has been known to act as compositor. His was a universal genius, and one of no mean order. He died in 1847, and bequeathed the Times to his family.

The present Mr. Walter, the chief proprietor of the Times, is a member of Parliament, and, as such, his time and energies are devoted to public business. The care and the responsibility of conducting the business of the Times has devolved on a manager, Mr. M. M. This gentleman is neither what we in Germany call a redacteur, nor is he what we would call an expeditor or accountant. He is just all in all, being the sovereign lord and master within the precincts of Printing-house Square.

A heap of papers lies on his desk. At his side sits the editor du jour. What his functions are will be seen in the following lines:—

The editorial functions of the Times are in the hands of several individuals, exactly as in the case of the great German journals. But, in Germany, each editor has his own separate department, for instance, home politics and foreign politics, or the literary and critical departments. They come to an understanding on the most important points, and then act altogether independently of one another. Besides, they meet frequently, and have plenty of opportunities to exchange their views and defend their opinions. Hence they very often quarrel, and their quarrels lead to frequent editorial crises. Far different is the case with the Times, where, besides the manager, there are two editors—Mr. John D———and Mr. George D———, with a third gentleman as sub-editor. The two editors take the service by turns, but they do not confine themselves to separate departments. Each of them has, at the time he conducts the paper, to see that it has that tone which has been decided upon in council. However, we will not anticipate. Having here hinted at the many merits of the editorial department, we continue to act as invisible spectators in the Times office.

We mentioned before, that a large heap of papers was lying on the desk of Mr. M. M., and that the editor du jour was sitting by his side. What are these two gentlemen doing? They read the most important journals of the day, take notes of their leading features, they talk over the topics of the leading articles for the next day's paper; but this is not enough. The material for the leaders having been selected, they are discussed in detail; notes are taken of some of the more leading features of the subject, and, if need be, the tendency is marked out. In many cases there is no need of this, but on some occasions the last measure is indispensable. The extraordinary and quick transitions of the Times are sufficiently known in Germany. The politics of the Times are an inscrutable mystery to most men, even to the majority of Englishmen; but the simple solution of the mystery is, that the Times either follows the lead of public opinion, or that it contradicts public opinion only when—more far-sighted than its contemporaries—it foresees a change; that under all circumstances, and at all times, it aims at a special critical interest; and with an iron consistency, and in an astonishing sobriety, it advocates this critical interest unsparingly, to the sacrifice of every other interest. That is the whole enigma of its seemingly changeable politics. It seizes with an unerring grasp that which is profitable for England, no matter how pernicious it may be for the outside barbarians. It is humane, constitutional, liberal, and even sentimental in its views of foreign countries, if England finds her advantage thereby; but it is also capable of imagining an eternal spring in the icy plains of Siberia, if an alliance with Russia should happen to advance English interests. It would even defend the slave trade, if it could be convinced that the cessation of that traffic would ruin the Lancashire cotton manufacturers.

The Times has often been reproached with its sudden and unaccountable changes of policy, and these reproaches have been made in England and out of England; but surely there is a rigid political consistency, one which sometimes becomes demoniacal, in this Times' policy. It may here be said, that the Times has now and then advocated views which certainly were not very advantageous to the interests of Great Britain. Such cases there may have been; but then we have never said that the Times is infallible. With all its prescience and circumspection, the Times has sometimes been wrong in its views; but we ought to remember that the very best editors are not omniscient, and that the strongest of us are occasionally influenced by human sympathies and antipathies, which stand in the way of an impartial decision. What we have said is of general application, namely, that the leading idea of the Times policy, which is carried out with an iron consistency, is the promotion of British interests; that for the sake of this consistency, it is not afraid of committing the most flagrant apparent inconsistencies, and that this is the simple explanation of its mysterious character. At no one time has the Times been the organ of the Government or of the opposition: it was always independent. On certain questions it supported the ministers of the day, on others it opposed them; but it never made opposition for the sake of opposition, and was unbending only in those questions which really affected the existence of the nation, for instance, in the contest between Free Trade and Protection. It may well be said of the Times, that it adheres to no one principle, merely on account of the excellence of its theory. Tried practical usefulness is the faith to which it adheres under all circumstances.

In England, the Times is the champion of gradual and reasonable progress; while, in its foreign policy, it clings to old allies and time-honoured systems of government; and the very Times which the English justly consider as a moderately liberal paper, is abused among the liberals of the Continent as a moderately reactionary organ. While Protectionist papers have, for years past, accused the Times of having given itself up to the evil genius of democracy and the demons of Manchester: the Radicals of all countries, are fully persuaded that the same Times is in the pay of Austria, Russia, and of all the devils generally. But the fact is, that the Times is as little democratic as it is Russian; it is as little paid by Willich as by Rothschild; and, under all circumstances, and for very good reasons, it will always be found to be rather Russian than Austrian; and rather Austrian than French; and always, above all things, it will be found to the English, egotistical; that is to say, political. To ask the Times, or any other reasonable political paper, to take a general purely humanistic standing point, and to ground its verdicts on the politics of the day, on the eternal laws of the history of civilization, and of moral philosophy; to ask it, in short, to write morals instead of politics, is absurd; and he who can make such a demand, knows nothing whatever of the position or the duties of a political journal. As well might he desire that diplomatists should always scrupulously adhere to the truth, or that a political paper, renouncing the interests of its own country, should devote itself to moral philosophy; in which case, we would advise it to establish its office in the most lonely island of all the lonely islands in the Pacific. But to what regions have our thoughts taken flight! We ask the reader's pardon for this monstrous digression; the temptation was too great, and we naturally thought of the tendencies of the Times while the manager and editor consulted about to-morrow morning's leaders.

The consultation is over. A few short notes have been taken of its results, and a sort of programme been made for every leader. Documents, letters from correspondents, and other papers are added to each programme, which is put into an envelope, and sent by messenger to a certain leading article writer, who, a few hours afterwards, sends in his article ready written. These leading article writers of the Times are altogether in an exceptional position. At the German newspapers, the leader-writing is generally done by the editor; now at the Times, the principle is generally acted upon, that the editor should rather edit the paper, than write it. The arrangement is thoroughly reasonable in theory, as well as in practice. Every one is naturally partial to his own productions. Who would quarrel with an editor if he prefers his own article to other essays, when he has the selection among various papers on the same subject. To save the editors from this temptation, and to give them full leisure to edit attentively and impartially, they have been mostly relieved from writing. There are, however, exceptions to this salutary rule; and we understand that the witty and humouristic leaders on local affairs, which, vie with the best of the French feuilletons, are from the pen of Mr. M. M.

The leading article writers have the programme of their articles sent to their respective domiciles. None but the editors know who these gentlemen are, and what their position in life is. They never, except on extraordinary occasions, come to the Times office. They have pledged their words to lay no claim to the authorship of their own articles, or to reveal their connection with the Times. They have renounced all hopes of literary fame; whatever credit is due to their productions belongs to the Times, which monopolises all the honor, and bears all the responsibility. Such an author has nothing but his pay; he has sold his work to the journal; and with it, he has sold the right to change it, to alter expressions, to remodel parts of it, or to condemn the article altogether. The article is a piece of merchandize with which the purchaser may do what he likes. If the writer ceases to agree with the tendencies of the Times, he is always at liberty to break off the connection; but so long as that connection continues, he is compelled to submit the form of his articles to the critical verdict of the editors.

The editorial department of the Times really edits the paper, while our German editors only write and select. The former method is evidently for the benefit of the journal, while the latter is more agreeable and profitable to the writers. The system of the Times requires what it would be impossible to find in Germany—the power of enormous capital, a gigantic city such as London is, and English characters, that is to say, men, authors of first-rate talent, who will sacrifice praise and notoriety, and take money in their stead. Is this self-denial created by the mere desire of making money? Do the leading-article writers of the Times rather care for the effect which is produced by their anonymity? Do they rather care for the cause which they advocate than for their own celebrity? Are they perhaps more disinterested, and our German literary men more selfish? Is the greater moral excellence to be found here or on the other side of the channel? These are delicate questions, which we will not here discuss. It will be seen, from what we have said, that the rule of the Times' office is more despotic the than journalistic government in Germany. We shall return to the subject on another occasion; but for the present we turn again to the desk at which the manager is sitting.

Besides the newspapers, he has a large heap of manuscript before him, letters to the Editor, a selection of which always appears in the Times. Their number is legion. The editors have received these letters and opened them. They have condemned those which are clearly unfit for the use of the paper, but the more important letters, some of which may affect the policy of the journal, have been reserved, and are now submitted to the manager's consideration. Old Mr. Walter was not indeed the man who first introduced these letters into the English press, but he certainly did much to favour this participation of the public in the labours of journalism. In Germany, too, the idea has been adopted, but, as is usually the case with excellent English customs, it has been spoiled in the adoption. In England these letters form the most important polemical part of the journal; in Germany they are on the level with the advertisements. Their insertion is paid for in Germany; in England a journal acknowledges its obligations to its correspondents. The public take a peculiar interest in the press to which they contribute, and a man whose letter is inserted in the Times considers himself in a certain degree as connected with the establishment; he becomes its champion, and reads it with great assiduity and interest. The authors of rejected letters, on the other hand, are offended; they get angry with the Times, they abuse it, and from sheer hatred and spite, they read it all the more eagerly. A journal can exist only by means of half a world of friends and a whole world of enemies, if indeed such an unalgebraic expression is admissible. It can survive anything but indifference.

But, besides the material interest which public letters have for the English newspapers, there is also a higher and more general interest. Public affairs are more effectually discussed in this manner; public opinion, uttered by private persons or corporations, finds a ready expression; abuses are exposed; matters of minor importance to the community, but of paramount importance to every individual citizen, are brought forward examined and canvassed; and events which happen in outlying parts of the country, in small towns on the coast and villages on the mountains, where no paid correspondent ever lived, and whither the foot of a regular reporter has never strayed, are expeditiously forwarded to the great organs of public opinion. So long as the insertion of such communications must be paid for, it is impossible that they can be of any mentionable advantage either to the journal or to the public. Of course, the introduction of this English system requires the gigantic size of the English papers, but even in smaller papers the editors may always make a suitable selection.

We believe that a favourable result would soon become apparent; for local affairs, the events of the province, or city, in which the paper is published, will always be most interesting to the public, because they affect it most. Call it John Bullish, if you please; abuse it as a grovelling matter-of-fact feeling, but you cannot deny that the greater number of readers care much more for a letter on hackney coaches, than for the most excellent article on the international relations between Russia and Persia. But, for charity's sake, we trust our readers will not misunderstand us! Heaven preserve us from the misfortune that our German journals should become unmindful of Russia, while they discuss their local affairs! But surely a way might be found of doing the one without neglecting the other. Even its worst enemies cannot accuse the Times of a want of attention to European interests, and of "haute politique"; but the Times is, nevertheless, the most conscientious and indefatigable local journal of London. Nor is it ashamed to follow up an article on the French empire, with another article, and one which displays as much genius, on the overgrown bulk of the Aldermen, or the sewers of Houndsditch.

This letter, then, and this, and this, and those two, will go in to-morrow; the rest find a temporary asylum on the floor. A few are reserved for further consideration. The manager casts a glance at the foreign letters, which have come by the morning mails. This done, the editor leaves him, and devotes himself to the details of his particular department. The consultation, and the perusal of so many papers, have taken a couple of hours. The editor may, by this time, leave the office, but the manager has a great many things to do before his day's work is over. To him belongs the correspondence with the foreign agents and correspondents of the journal, and with the leader-writers, whose accounts he settles. He has to see the sub-editor, who superintends the technical department of the management, and he has to listen to that gentleman's report. He sees the printer, who gives a general account of the sale of the Times on that particular day. The cashier makes his appearance, with the totals of yesterday's accounts, and the sums realised from the sale of the paper, the insertion of advertisements, and the exact amount of the duty on stamps and advertisements, which has been paid to the state. The manager has to take notes of the net results of all these accounts. By this time, it is five o'clock, and another editor makes his appearance. There is always some topic to be discussed; some event on which it is necessary to come to an understanding; some motion before the House, and some debate coming off in the course of the evening, on which it is necessary to say a few words. The manager's labours are ended with this consultation; he leaves the office. From five to nine o'clock, the current business is discharged by one of the editors. He reads the leaders and reports which have been sent in; he transmits them to the printing-office, and receives all letters, parcels, and messages that arrive. There is always plenty of work to be got through—quite enough, and sometimes too much for one man. The editor who transacted the current business of the morning arrives at nine o'clock to share the labours of his colleague, and remains a longer or shorter period, according to the heaviness of the night. But one of the two gentlemen never leaves the office until the journal is ready for press, when he gives it the Imprimatur. Besides, he issues instructions as to the number of copies to be struck off. There is no fixed number, and the impression varies according to the greater or less interest of the contents of such day's Times.

But what business—so will German readers ask—can detain an editor until late at night? The German redacteurs work scarcely ever up to midnight; the French redacteurs get through their labours by eight or nine o'clock in the evening. Why should English editors be at their post until three or four o'clock in the morning?

Besides the arrival of telegraphic despatches at almost any hour in the course of the night, the English editors are detained by parliamentary business. The reports from the House of Commons come in in batches sometimes as late as two or three o'clock in the morning. The parcels from the provinces and from Ireland arrive with the last trains by ten or eleven o'clock. The provincial reports are usually shortened; this duty devolves upon some decrepit reporter, the results of whose labours are submitted to the approval of the editors. They have moreover to receive persons who call on urgent business, members of Parliament, who wish to correct the proofs of their speeches, or who desire still further to expound their views to the editor to prevent the possibility of misunderstanding; schemers who rush in with some patent invention which will remove all the evils that flesh is heir to, and a host of strange customers of every country and of every degree. In short, an editor of the Times is not tempted to imitate Lord Byron, and to publish "Hours of Idleness." It is very often four o'clock before the last of them hails a cab and hurries off to his house in the far west.

We cannot allow our readers to follow his example. We detain them in the Times' office, and propose taking them to Westminster, on a tour of enquiry into the manners and customs of the English reporters.

And here it may be as well to remark, that an English reporter has an important position in literary circles, as well as in the estimation of his own journal; that the name of reporter applies strictly to the gentlemen who report the Parliamentary debates; and that, for the proper discharge of these functions, it requires journalistic abilities of no common order, great versatility, and an intimate knowledge of public affairs and public men.

Let us make an excursion to Westminster; a Hansom cab will take us in a quarter of an hour. We get out at a provisional boarded gate, which leads to the reporters' gallery, walk through a court-yard, which is full of bricks and mortar, enter a gothic door to the left, mount a couple of flights of stairs, open a glass door, and enter a small room, in which there is a very large fire. This room, and the stairs and corridors, are lighted with gas, even at mid-day; for it is one among the practical beauties of Westminster Palace, that the working-rooms of the reporters have scarcely any daylight. The architect, however, has done all in his power to indemnify them for the faults of his design. Their rooms are as comfortable as can be; and nowhere, either in Germany or France, is so much careful attention bestowed on the convenience of the press. There is a good reason why there is so large a fire in the little room we have entered. It is the ante-chamber, and also the refectory of the reporters. It contains a table, on which are sundry dishes of meat and pastry—not at all a Lucullian supper, but quite enough for a frugal journalist, who has no ambition to dine at the table of the Parliamentary Restaurant. Some pots and kettles are on the hob by the fire, in which the water simmers and seethes most comfortably, inviting all hearers to a cup of tea or coffee. On a wooden bench by the door sit two very sleepy boys, half roasted by the fire, and waiting for manuscript. Two gentlemen, with their hats on, are seated at the table; they converse in a low voice, and drink tea from very large cups; they are reporters, just off their turn. Other reporters come in and go out; the little glass door is continually opening and shutting; and the servant, too, who presides over these localities, and makes politics and coffee, is never idle, for he has many masters. In spite of all this going and coming, the little room is comfortable, and it is very pleasant to sit and chat in it. These English reporters are altogether stately and serious men; in many instances, their whiskers are grey with age and their heads bald. No green-horns are they; no young fellows, who practise writing in the gallery. Such an Englishman, with his long legs and his smooth-shaved face, has always a solid appearance, no matter whether he be a journalist or a drayman. I believe that kind of thing is the result of race of blood, and of education.

A narrow corridor leads from the ante-chamber to a set of two rooms, which communicate with the gallery of the House by means of another corridor. All these rooms and corridors are covered with thick carpets; green morocco-covered sofas are drawn up against the oak-panelled walls; writing-tables are placed in the window niches; large fires burn in marble chimneys; an air of substantial comfort pervades the whole. In the panelled walls there are, moreover, closets, for the reporters to put their great coats and papers in; and a small apartment at the side of the large rooms is devoted to a washing apparatus—large marble basins, with a plentiful supply of hot and cold water. The English love to have numbers of these in their public and private buildings; on the Continent they are painfully struck with the absence of these helps to cleanliness; and they mention the carelessness or indifference of our countrymen in this respect in terms of the most unqualified reprobation.

There is not much to be said of the reporters' gallery. It fills the narrow side of the house, and is just below the ladies' gallery and above the Speaker's chair. It has two rows of seats, scarcely more than four-and-twenty, and attached to each seat is a comfortable desk.

None but the reporters of the great London papers are admitted to this gallery. Not only the public generally but also the reporters of provincial journals are excluded, solely from the want of space to accommodate them. The admission of Foreign journalists is therefore quite out of the question. Demands to this effect when made have been met with a determined, though polite, refusal. If it be considered that there are four-and-twenty seats in this gallery, that each of the great London journals has, on an average, about twelve reporters, and that the aggregate number of reporters amounts to above eighty, it will be admitted that the complaints about want of space are well founded. The functions of the staff of reporters, the division of their labours, and the manner in which they discharge their duties, may best be learned from an inquiry into the organisation of the Times staff of reporters; for the Parliamentary corps of the other papers are fashioned after its model.

The Times keeps a staff of from twelve to sixteen reporters to record the proceedings of the two houses. Some of them are engaged for the Parliamentary session only. The majority of them are young barristers, whom the connexion with the great journal enables to follow up their legal career, and who have, moreover, the advantage of that thorough training which young lawyers obtain in the gallery. Others have annual engagements, they are the "Old Guard" of the Times, on whose efficiency it can rely as on the working of its printing machines. After the session the corps is scattered to all the four corners of the globe; the barristers repair to their chambers in the Inns of Court and live upon the gains of their summer's labours. A few of the old guard remain in London at the disposal of the journal, which requires their services to attend large meetings, or the progress of the Queen through Scotland. The rest take their ease in the provinces, the public libraries, in their families, or on the continents of Europe, Africa, Asia, or America. A true John Bull, say all the English, has always some reasonable object in view, however mad his proceedings may appear to the outside barbarians.

An elderly, grey-haired gentleman—the summary man—forms an important addition to the Parliamentary staff. It is his duty to prepare those condensed reports of the sitting, which may be found in every English journal. He ought to attend in his place from first to last, that the summary may come into the printer's hands immediately after the house is up. His relative position to the other reporters is that of a corporal to the privates. And since we have alluded to military grades and dignities, we propose at once to introduce our readers to the captain of the corps, Mr. Charles Dod, editor of the famous Parliamentary Companion, who commands the Parliamentary corps of the Times, and whose authority is acknowledged by all the reporters of the London journals generally.

Mr. Dod must excuse the curiosity of foreigners, and permit us to inspect him and the corps under his command. Mr. Dod then is an amiable gentleman, who has the whole of the Parliamentary history of Great Britain at his fingers' ends, and whom many honourable members, young and old, might consult with the greatest advantage.

To the Times, Mr. Dod is in the house what the manager is in the office; he manages every thing connected with Parliamentary matters; he publishes to his corps the day and hour of the next sitting. At one time he may be seen in the gallery, helping and instructing the less experienced among his corps; on other occasions, he finds his way into the House to procure some document or statistical return from the members or the clerks. Anon he hurries to the Times' office to read, shorten, and edit the copy sent in by the reporters, in short, on a heavy Parliamentary night, Mr. Charles Dod is everywhere and nowhere, that is to say, he is always rushing from Westminster to the Times' office and back again.

He generally divides his corps into two detachments. The young reporters take the upper house, the old guard do duty in the House of Commons, whose sittings are longer, while its motions and speeches are of greater importance, and its debates more intricate. In either house it is a rule that reporters relieve one another by turns, from half-hour to half-hour. Mr. H., for instance, takes his seat at the commencement of the sitting with Mr. C. who comes next by his side. The first thirty minutes over, Mr. H. retires; Mr. C. takes his seat, and Mr. R. takes the place which has just been vacated by Mr. C. The summary-man takes a position in the rear. To-morrow evening the turn commences where it left off this night, so that each reporter has an equal share of the work.

But how does Mr. H. employ his time after his half-hour's turn in the gallery? He has about two hours until his next turn, but a few minutes only of these two hours can he devote to relaxation. A cab stands ready for the use of the reporters. He proceeds to the city and his desk in the reporter's room of the Times' office, where he converts his "notes" into "copy." This process takes about an hour or an hour and a quarter for every turn of half-an-hour. If his report be a verbatim report—and such must be made should an important man speak on an important question—the writing it out takes more time. Every thing depends on the character of the sitting, but if the labour threatens to become overwhelming Mr. Dod interferes, and sends for reinforcements from the gallery of the House of Lords.

The "copy" having been prepared by the reporter, and put in type in the printing-rooms, proofs, struck off on long, narrow slips of paper, are sent into the editorial sanctum, where the matter, already condensed by the reporters, is frequently subjected to further condensation; and Mr. Dod, who makes his appearance from time to time, assists in this process. The proofs thus edited are corrected, struck off again and submitted to the writer of Parliamentary leaders, who, on all important occasions, attends in the House itself, and who in the dawn of morning commences his article on the debate which has just been closed. A few hours later that article is in the hands of the London public, while express trains hurry it to the most distant parts of the empire.

If the house sits until two o'clock in the morning, the labours of the last reporter, of the Parliamentary leader-writer, and of one of the editors, are protracted until three and sometimes four o'clock. This is hard work, harder than continental journalists ever dream of. But it is the same in all professions! An Englishman, no matter whether he be a tradesman, or a merchant, or a journalist, never thinks of doing things by halves, because in this country things cannot and must not be done by halves. No country in the world offers so wide a sphere for a man's talents and activity as England does, provided he has energy, perseverance, and resignation. An English reporter in his holidays, stretching his long legs on the banks of the lake of Zürich, is an enviable personage in the eyes of a German journalist. Of course, no one can tell how hard he has been at work these nine months.

It is four o'clock, A.M. We have passed fourteen hours at the Times' office. The labour is now left to the printers; and the two large machines which finish 10,000 copies per hour. But weary though our readers may be, we cannot allow them to depart, for there are many matters which require mentioning.

Hitherto we have spoken of the Parliamentary corps only. But there are other reporters in the service of the Times and of other great journals, to whom we must devote a couple of pages.

Among these are the standing reporters in London, who are occasionally employed as "outsiders," but who generally work in the office. They make extracts from English and Foreign journals, and write reports on colonial affairs. There are also reporters on music and the drama, while the reviewing of books claims the services of a third critic. There are few special reporters for the proceedings of the law courts. These reports are generally sent in by barristers who practise in these courts.

The police-reports, too, are not furnished by special reporters; but the Times and the other London journals take them from a man who keeps his own police-court corps, and who, in his relations with the papers which employ him, is personally responsible for the correctness of the reports.

The records of local events and accidents are furnished by the so-called penny-a-liners, those vagrant journalists, who are up by day and by night, and who are present at all the police-stations, who always come in time to witness the perpetration of some "Horrible Murder," and who hasten along with the fire-engines to the scene of every "Extensive Conflagration," taking notes, which they make as long and as interesting as they possibly can, and selling them to the various journals. They are strange persons, active, acute, and seasoned. They flourish during the recess; for at that time the London journals are not too choice in their selection of matter; and at that time they make large sums of money from the sale of their "Atrocious Murders," "Extensive Conflagrations," and "Extraordinary Friendships" between "dogs, rabbits, and water-rats," or from their chance reports of the proceedings and public addresses of some successful French philanthropist. If the editors did not most ruthlessly cut down their lengthy contributions, the business of the penny-a-liners would certainly be most lucrative. As it is, many of them manage to live, and to live well.

The last-named three classes of English journalists serve several or all the papers at the same time. Their honesty is guaranteed by their own interest; for they would soon lose their customers if they dared to send in incorrect reports. In this conviction lies their organisation. It is based, as every other profession or trade is in England, on the two-fold system of material advantage and unlimited competition.

As to the organisation of the staff of reporters and collaborators, especially at the Times, a great deal might be said that would appear altogether fabulous to our German journalists. We allude to the strict subordination in matters of the daily duties of the paper. We cannot, however, enter into details which might possibly lead us away from the subject-matter. Suffice it to say, that every Times reporter should at all times be fully prepared to undertake a mission to any part of England or of the continent, and that he should not leave his home for any length of time without leaving directions where he may be found, in case his presence were unexpectedly required at the office.

We mention these matters only to show how strict is the business-character which pervades even journalism in England. Besides the business connection, there is but little of social intercourse between the various employés on a journal. The very reporters of the Times hardly see one another except in the office or in the House. Their intercourse with the editors is strictly limited to the service of the journal. They have to send in their "copy." What the editors may please to do with that "copy" concerns them as little as the shoemaker who sends in a pair of boots and is duly paid for them. He, too, has no control over the use which his customer may make of them. The reporters on an English journal sacrifice their individuality to the "Office" in order to remain in that position to an advanced age, or, if they are men of real talent, to create for themselves a free and independent position in literature. They all, from the leader-writer to the foreign correspondent, and from the foreign correspondent down to the penny-a-liner, submit unconditionally to the authority of the editorial body. They write in their various departments what they have undertaken to write, and they send it in. Whether or not it be printed, whether it be shortened, altered, or put aside as waste paper, is no affair of theirs. What German journalist, even the greenest among the green, would submit to such a "desecration of his talents," as our poor dear Germans would call it.

And now farewell, O Times' office, with all thy leader-writers, editors, parliamentary reporters, collaborators, compositors, and printers! Thy colossal machines move with a stunning noise until six o'clock, when the press is stopped for a few moments for the insertion of some late continental despatch. The steam is then put on again; the hundreds and hundreds of curiously-shaped wheels turn faster and faster, with bewildering regularity, and large broad sheets of printed paper are heaped upon the board. The printing and publishing is scarcely over when the editors make their appearance. With the sole exception of Saturday nights, the door of the Times' Office is never closed.

CHAP. VIII.

A Frenchman's Notions.

DR. KEIF AT DINNER WITH A FRENCHMAN.—MONS. GUERONNAY.—GRAND INTER-NATIONAL CONTEST.—AN ARMISTICE.—SIR JOHN SERMONISES.—THE GLORY OF FRANCE AND THE DOWNFALL OF ENGLAND.—SUNDRY REMARKS ON THE OPERA AND THE BRITISH FEMALE; ON ENGLISH MUSIC AND FRENCH POLITICS.—SIR JOHN A TRUE JOHN BULL.—A CONTROVERSY ON THE STAIRS.

"DR. KEIF has got nothing to eat," said Sir John. "I say, Dr. Keif has nothing whatever to eat. Bella, how inattentive you are to your neighbour."

"But, Sir John," said his wife, "Dr. Keif is no infant. He will speak if he wants anything."

"Nonsense, he forgets it. Dr. Keif, your plate, if you please."

But the learned Doctor is deaf to Sir John's warning voice. He is engaged in an interesting conversation with his neighbour, M. Gueronnay, from Paris.

M. Gueronnay is an elderly gentleman, with a youthful head of hair, red cheeks, and preposterously black whiskers. He is grave of aspect; but there is in his small black eyes an inexhaustible fund of good nature and conceit. For the last twenty years he has every season paid a visit of a week or two to Sir John, and each time he finds London gloomier and more unbearable. In fact, nothing but his affection for his old friends could induce him to leave the paradise of Paris for a week's punishment in the fog and smoke of the Thames. But, however great his disgust may be, he is amiable enough to conquer it; he eats and drinks as an Englishman, laughs and jokes with the ladies all day long, and sheds a few tears at leave-taking. To complete the picture, we ought to add, that M. Gueronnay makes a vow every year to return as a married man, and to bring his wife with him.

Heaven knows what can have happened between him and Dr. Keif, while the rest of the family were eating their roast beef; but everybody is struck with the fact that they talk violently, and both at the same time, too.

"Dr. Keif, your plate!" says Sir John.

"He does not hear you," responded Bella. "I dare say he is again talking politics."

"Order!" cries Sir John, now for the third time. "Dr. Keif, M. Gueronnay, another piece of pudding."

But the two arch-foreigners murmur an excuse, and turn again to one another.

"Yes, surely," says Dr. Keif, "the sun rises in the West."

"You allude to the sun of the mind?"

"Certainly! and the West is Paris."

"A la bonne heure. Thus do we understand one another."

"Just so, M. Gueronnay; an opinion after your own heart, isn't it? What I cant understand is, that the world does not settle down to sleep quietly, since Paris thinks and acts for it. What more can be required for the general regeneration of humanity than the Journal des Débats, that is to say, the diffusion of useful knowledge—Madame Rachel, that is to say, the art-education of mankind—and a few Chasseurs d'Afrique, that is to say, liberty?"

"Not bad; you have French esprit. Well, you flatter us."

"Indeed," says Dr. Keif, very gravely. "Even the Paris Cancan, immoral though it may appear, has, after all, decency and grace enough to civilise half the world. Am I not right? And if la France has been put into the stocks, it is merely because she has been dancing all night for the benefit of distressed humanity; her present misfortune is, after all, nothing but a fresh proof of creative genius, which conceals the profoundest of all modern ideas of emancipation; for, if you please, whatever la France will do that she can do. She takes the resolution, in the face of all Europe, and in plain daylight, to lie in the dirtiest gutter that can be found, and lo! she performs the feat. Alas, for the blindness of the other nations, who do not also lie down in the same gutter, and who will not understand that there must be salvation in the pool in which it pleases la France to wallow!"

"Stop! stop!" replies M. Gueronnay. "What does all this mean?"

"It means simply that the French are the most conceited, insane people on the face of the earth."

"Mais, Monsieur, I am a Frenchman!"

"Of course you are," continues the Doctor, with a low impressive voice. "You cannot deny that the French go on sinning on the strength of their constitution! Pray let me go on. That they are a nation of spirited fools, genial ragamuffins, overgrown gamins, and revolutionary lacqueys, who can neither govern themselves, nor will they allow any despot 'by the grace of God' to govern them for any length of time."

"Now pray let me have my say."

"And that, after their fourth revolution, and their third republic, they will surely fall down at the feet of some Orleanist or Legitimist prince; and after that, by means of universal suffrage, they will sell themselves to some romantic hairdresser, dancing-master, or cook. I, for one, vote for Soyer. He at least has learned something at the Reform Club."

The most outrageous blasphemy, uttered in the presence of the grandmother of an Anglican bishop, cannot have that dreadful effect which Dr. Keif's words produced on the nerves of his neighbour. He is first paralysed, then astonished, and in the next instance, angry. He would speak, but he cannot utter a word, for Dr. Keif has seized the wretched man by the topmost button of his coat, and in this position he pours broadside after broadside into his ears, saying continually—"Pray let me go on!" "Now do hear me," "I know exactly what you wish to say." Poor M. Gueronnay! All his endeavours to escape are vain, for the Doctor knows no pity for a Frenchman. His hand holds the button with an iron grasp, until, at length, he concludes with the following coup de grace:—"Pray understand me. All I wish to say is, that the French—surely I have not the least intention of offending you—the French are on their last legs, because the last particle of marrow has oozed out of their bones by dint of lying; but that does not prevent their being even in a state of profound degradation, exactly like the Spaniards, Italians, and Irish—spiritual, amusing, and rather an interesting nation."

"In-fi-ni-ment obligé," cries M. Gueronnay, jumping up and making low bows. "How did you say a-mu-sing? Infiniment obligé, Doctor, your German modesty is extremely complimentary."

"No compliment whatever, M. Gueronnay," replies Dr. Keif, rather embarrassed; "nothing whatever but my candid opinion."

The Frenchman casts an epigrammatical glance at the Doctor, buttons his coat, as if preparing for some grand resolution, and says with a loud voice—"Sir, you are"—a long pause. Everybody rises from the table. "Monsieur," continues the Frenchman, "you have never been in Paris."

"Certainly not," says Dr. Keif.

"That is enough. That is all I desire to know. Enfin!" and M. Gueronnay, shrugging his shoulders in a crushing manner, turns his back upon the Doctor.

This scene created a general confusion at the dining-table. Everybody was silent. The lady of the house, whose profound knowledge of the "Dictionnaire de l'Academie" commands M. Gueronnay's special respect, has taken him to the window, and tries to soothe his feelings, by assuring him that Dr. Keif is certainly wrong-headed in the true Germanic style; but that he is, after all, a good-natured eccentric person, and nobody's enemy but his own. Dr. Keif, meanwhile, with a forced smile on his lips, and green and yellow with rage, promenades the room. He is evidently not satisfied with himself. Sir John alone has kept this seat at the table; and, enforcing his views by several thumps of his dessert-knife, makes a very instructive speech on that Parliamentary order which is observed at all public dinners in England. Who could even think, while dinner is on the table, of conversing on any other subject but the domestic virtues of the turtle, the sole, and the salmon, the tenderness of roast lamb and venison, the bees-wing of port wine, and all the other good things which are especially fit to establish a delightful harmony between Whigs and Tories, High Churchmen and Dissenters, Cotton Lords and old aristocrats? There's the rub. That's what the foreigners will never learn; they cannot do a thing at the right time, and poison their very meat with politics!

I dare say Sir John is right; but his speech is interrupted by the coffee, which has greater effect upon the company than his practical philosophy. Dr. Keif and Sir John take their coffee by the fire.

"Are you aware," says the latter, "that your remarks have been very offensive to our French friend? We Englishmen can never approve of a wholesale condemnation of any nation. If you had said those words in the House of Commons, you would have been called to order; and I really think there is an Act of Parliament—"

"Well never mind your Act of Parliament! the less you say about it the better. There are examples of examples. You are always preaching manners to people, and—. Never mind, just provoke me, if you please. I'm exactly in a temper."

"But my dear Doctor, I really can't understand what is the matter with you."

"Well, I'll tell you. People believe that a German's skin ought to be as thick as that of a rhinoceros. I was not in the least angry, but merely gave that fellow change for his five-franc piece. Just as we sat down to dinner he said a few words which I don't care to repeat. In short, he said that we Germans were not very likely to set the Thames on fire."

"Very wrong indeed," replies Sir John, turning to M. Gueronnay. "I'll tell him so; he must make an apology."

"For God's sake be quiet! An apology, ridiculous! I'm ashamed of my childishness, that his vapid phrase could ruffle my temper; but that is what a man comes to. In

Germany I used to laugh at our patriots; and here I'm covered with patriotism as with a cutaneous eruption, and irritated by the slightest touch."

"Nonsense, sir! Consider it is only the word of a Frenchman!" said Sir John, almost instinctively attacking the weakest side of the sapient and wrathful Doctor. "And I say a Frenchman is no one. But now be reasonable, and shake hands with Mons. Gueronnay. I say—Mons. Gueronnay! You, Sir! Confound the Frenchman!" muttered Sir John, with earnest devotion, "Confound him, he won't hear!"

The attempts at mediation between the two foreign powers are here interrupted by George, the tiger, bringing in a letter.

"Dr. Keif, if you please, a letter from Mr. Bonypart."

A flagrant absurdity flung into the midst of a quarrel is, after all, the readiest means to restore good will and smooth the ruffled tempers. George's blunder makes everybody laugh. Dr. Keif is at once assailed with many questions as to the "Emperor's" intentions. "Is it an invitation to Paris? Is it a challenge? or the offer of a pension?"

"Yes, it's in his own hand," said the Doctor, and pocketed the mysterious document.

"Is it, indeed!" cried the Frenchman, in a state of delightful amazement. "Is it a letter from Louis Napoleon—pardon! I would say, from his Majesty the Emperor himself?"

"Suppose it is, I can see nothing in it to justify your opening your eyes to that extent!" said Mrs. Bella, with the prettiest imaginable little sneer. "I'm sure Dr. Keif is by far more respectable than one half of his majesty's old friends and companions. But perhaps you will say Dr. Keif holds very strange opinions on the subject of the French nation. Just so, Mons. Gueronnay. Your emperor, I'm sure, thinks even worse of your countrymen than Dr. Keif does, and that's why he is your Emperor!"

"Order!" shouts Sir John, "I'll fine you a shilling if you say another word about politics."

"Hear! hear!" said the Doctor. "But I will explain the matter to Mons. Gueronnay before I go. My friend Baxter has come to town and promises me no end of adventures, if I—"

"Mr. Baxter!" quoth the lady of the house, looking up from the supplement of the Times, which for the last few minutes had engaged her attention. "Mr. Baxter! Really George is getting duller every day; he mispronounces even English names. The fact is, Mons. Gueronnay, that boy George cannot on any account repeat or remember a foreign name. Whenever any German comes to the house and sends up his name, George will make the most shocking mistakes. He will not learn, and gives to every foreigner the very first name he happens to think of."

"He takes them from the newspapers," said Mrs. Bella. "The Doctor is continually teaching him politics. It's true, Doctor, you spoil all our servants. That boy George is too fond of reading, and reading is almost a vice in a young—"

"Aristocrat," adds Dr. Keif. "But I beg your pardon: lackey is the proper word."

"In short," continues the lady of the house, "there is no getting on with him. He turns Schulze into Shelly, and converts Fritze into Sir Fitzroy. The honest name of Müller becomes in his mouth Macaulay, and a Prussian gentleman of the name of Lehman is always announced as Lord Palmerston. He is so fond of great names."

"Delicious!" cried Mons. Gueronnay. "What a subject for Scribe!"

"Ladies and gentlemen, I cannot wait for the tea-hour; for at nine o'clock, I am expected at the cigar-divan in the Strand;" saying which, Dr. Keif prepared to leave the room.

"Stop!" said Sir John, consulting his watch. "You've plenty of time; exactly sixty-one minutes."

"How exact you English people are—punctilious!" We need scarcely inform our readers that the speaker is Mons. Gueronnay. "Sixty minutes and one! What Frenchman would say sixty minutes and one! Tell us, Mons. le Docteur, are your adventures so very important that they depend on the minute?"

"By no means! Nothing but an appointment of many weeks standing with Mr. Baxter. We propose making an expedition into the theatrical quarters, and I dare say we shall drop in here and there at half-price."

But the Frenchman cannot understand how any one can go to the theatre at this unseasonable time of the year. He has always understood that in London there are but two entertainments worthy of the notice of un homme comme il faut: the Italian opera and the French theatre at St. James's. But they are closed now that the season is over. It is true that the Queen does now and then pay a visit to some of the obscure English theatres; but surely she does that for no other reason but to humour the national prejudices of the English.

The ladies cry out against these shocking opinions; but all their protests cannot shake the smiling and gallant and withal obstinate Frenchman.

"Enfin mes dames!" cried he, "you have not an idea of all you must forego in London. You are very fortunate that you have never been at Paris. Par Dieu! Paris! It is there, mesdames, where the common life is a delicious farce; every salon is a stage; every apartment has its coulisses, and every one, from the duke down to the portier, knows his part. Your honest Englishmen can neither act, nor can they judge the action of the stage. An English actor is an unnatural creature, exactly like a Paris Quaker. Where can you find more passion for art than with us! Paris has not half so many inhabitants as London; but it has more theatres, and they are always more crowded than your churches. The poorest ouvrier cannot live without basking in the splendour of the stage; he drinks milk and eats bread for toute la semaine, that he may have some sous to go to the Variétés or the Funambules on Sunday night. Show me the Englishman who would sacrifice a beefsteak for the sake of a theatrical representation. Allez! allez! You weave, and you spin, you steam and you hammer, you eat and you drink, at the rate of so many horse-power, but to enjoy your life, that is what you do not understand. Am I right, madam?" The girls look at one another, and do not exactly know what to say.

Sir John, in his easy chair, shakes his head and mutters, "There are good reasons for the difference."

"Ah ça," continues the Frenchman triumphantly, "there are reasons; but, let me tell you, the reasons are atrocious! First, a theatrical piece would desecrate the Sunday evening, and the Sabbath must end in the same wearisome manner in which it commenced. If you mention this to an Englishman, he will make a long face, and say something about the morals of the lower classes. Ah, surely the lower classes in England are extremely moral! You can see that on Monday morning, when the drunkards of the night before are accused before the fat Lord Mayor. One has bitten off the constable's nose; another has knocked down his wife, and kicked her when she was on the ground; and a third has been knocked down by his wife through the instrumentality of a poker. It is nothing but morals and gin; but, Dieu merci, they have not been at the theatre. Do not tell me, because you have more churches and chapels than there are days in the year, that your lower classes go to church. For the poor there are no benches in your churches; your religion is only for respectable people, and while they pray they rattle the money in their pockets. And then there are thousands of Quakers, and Methodists, and Latter-day Saints, who even on week days shun the theatre as a place of abomination. How is it possible for a theatre to prosper? And lastly, you are so fond of your fire-places and parlours, that it is almost impossible to induce you to go out; and you have such a strange passion for green grass, that you live far away in the suburbs, and want a carriage to come back from the theatre in the dawn of the morning. These dreadful distances are ruinous to the purse, and prevent all civilisation. Let me tell you, Monsieur le Docteur, that your admirable Englishmen do not monopolise all the wisdom of the world; but let them go. I do not pity them; but I am sorry for the poor daughters of Albion. Parole d'honneur, Mesdames, you would not regret it if the beautiful dream of Napoleon were accomplished. Ha, what a merry life! Fancy our great army landing on your shores one fine morning. Before the sun is risen our gallant soldiers are in the city; they say, 'Bon jour,' they conquer, and are conquered by the charms of the fair-haired Anglo-Saxon ladies. Our soldiers demand nothing but a due recognition of their transcendant merits. You may keep your Bank, your religion, and your Lord Mayor. France covets nothing but the glory of killing the dragon of English ennui. Hand in hand with the fair sex, our invincible army will perform the work of restoration. On the first night there is a grand ball of fraternisation at Vauxhall. On the following morning the liberators publish a manifesto, which decrees that there shall be at least one French vaudeville theatre in every parish."

The girls on the sofa listen with awe-struck curiosity, and the Frenchman continues his harangue.

"And after a few years, when these new institutions shall have taken root in the hearts of Englishmen, the heroic army returns to sunny France, saying, 'Now we understand one another, and now there will be eternal peace between us.' The regeneration of merry England, by means of Norman blood, will outlive many centuries. But if you relapse again into your puritanical spleen, then we shall come again. And the daughters of Albion stand on the chalky cliffs wailing, and stretch their white arms after their liberators. How do you like the sketch? Is it not chivalrous? Is it not full of the most touching disinterestedness? How do you like it, Sir John? Do not be frightened, it is merely une idée."

But Sir John is far too angry to reply, and M. Gueronnay turns again to the Doctor.

"Parole d'honneur," says he, "it is a perfect disgrace, the education of the women in England! N'est ce pas, even your German philosophers must admit, that the Grand Opera is the cynosure, the academy, the flower of high life—of elegance, enfin, of civilisation. Eh bien! go to the opera, take a good glass, and you will despair. Beautiful women, you will find in plenty in the boxes, in the stalls, and in the gallery. But please to take your glass, and you will see they are all mere raw material. A splendid breed, certainly—a little heavy in the bones—large feet, but that makes no difference—but a complexion—hair—flesh—tell me, am I impartial, or am I not? Mais, mon cher, they are all rough diamonds. It makes one's heart bleed, to think how this race of women might be brought out, and what a treasure these brutal Englishmen are neglecting! I will say nothing whatever of the toilet. Take a Paris grisette, give her three-quarters of a yard of tulle and two yards and a half of ribbon, and she conquers the world; but an English woman—say Lady A.—with her California of shawls and diamonds on her person, has the appearance of a clothes' stand. But, as I said before, I will not go the length of asking for a genius for toilet. I will suppose that the light-haired marchioness, with those superb curls, has the good sense to get her fashions from Paris, and that, as a constitutional lady, she is governed by the advice of her responsible French maid. She does not insist on having a scarlet shawl and a light green dress with orange flounces, and a cavalry hat with ostrich feathers. No; she is bonne enfante—she listens to reason."

"Bon."

"But my dear Doctor, all this is of very little use. Listen to me, and let us confine our remarks to the light-haired marchioness. She leaves her box. Her carriage stops the way. She enters it. Now tell me, what is her behaviour? Throws she backwards one of those dilating, radiating, dangerous glances, which one might justly expect of her—without which, public life, even in the largest town, lacks all public interest; which the fair sex actually owe to those around them; for after all, what were women created for but to beautify the earth? But our light-haired marchioness walks straight on, as if she had blinkers to her eyes; she walks in a business-like manner—in the way of a student who enters his college, or a clergyman on his way to church; and though she makes but a few steps, I should know her as an English woman among the thousands of the women of all nations. Not a trace of hovering, of gliding, of jumping, or a little coquetry; nothing of the kind. If you meet her, she looks you straight in the face, exactly as if you were a statue or her husband. Be on your guard, she kicks! In sober seriousness, she raises her foot in such a manner as makes me wish that I could box her dancing-master's ears. Yes, yes, my friend, Lady A. commands my fullest respect, so long as she sits in her box and conducts herself as a statue. Her bust—classic! Her white hand, with long taper fingers—noble—very noble—though a little too thin; her face, full of hauteur! à la bonne heure! in her large blue eyes there is even the shadow of a shade of romance; and round her lips plays something like a smile, which has caught a cold and is afraid of coming out in the open air. But her forehead is a little too severe for me; behind it there is a good deal of scripture reading and history, and details of the money-market, perhaps even Latin and Greek. Her long taper fingers write a firm hand; I am quite sure they can, without the least musical scruples, hammer on the substantial keys of a Broadwood. Of course they can; but do you know what these carefully-trimmed fingers cannot do? They cannot move a fan! Do you know what this beauty, with all the slenderness of her waist, and all the fulness of her shoulders, can never attain? Deportment! She has two left arms and two left hands. A French waist can languish, love, hate, smile, and weep; but this beautiful English woman, during the performance, looks at the libretto as if it were a book of common prayer. Now and then she raises her fan like a screen; and perhaps in one of the entre-actes she condescends to a little coquetry. Such things happen now and then. You see how impartial I am. Mon Dieu! how awkward she is! Enfin, she wants the je ne sais quoi. And, au bout du compte, one fine morning you read in the Post, that such and such an accomplished and very chaste lady, who happens to be the youngest daughter of a half-ruined house, has eloped, that is to say, she has run away, with some red-cheeked chaplain or groom. Don't tell me what the English are!" says M. Gueronnay, drawing a deep breath, and wiping the perspiration off his forehead with a triumphant look, as if he had captured the British fleet and brought it to Cherbourg. "There is your Italian Opera!"

"But you cannot pay such singers in Paris," interrupted Sir John, mustering up all his courage. "And as for decency and good manners, I do not think they can be found in your Tuilleries. None but gentlemen are admitted in Her Majesty's Theatre."

"Gentlemen—that is to say, black dress coat and black pantaloons; 'tis a pity that wigs and hair-powder are not also de rigueur. If we are to believe what the Morning Post says, the ladies in the first row of boxes fainted away, because a foreigner with a blue neck-tie had by some means or other gained admittance to the pit. Mind he had paid for his place, as well as everybody else. My dear Sir John, good manners are not innate in you; and because you cannot rely on your instincts, you draw up an orthodox code of decency, and observe it strictly to the letter, as if it were the law of the land. A black dress coat is de rigueur, black pantaloons ditto; but the dress coat and the pantaloons may be old, dirty, and shabby. Only think, you pay your money and submit to be schooled by a theatrical lackey. I would not submit to it, that's all; none but the English, who adore the aristocracy, would ever put up with such impertinence. But the foreigners are justly treated. Why should they go to your Italian Opera House? Can they not go to Paris; and do not Grisi, Mario, and Lablache also sing in Paris? We do not, indeed, crowd all the talents of Italy into a single opera, because our ears are not made of cast-iron."

Dr. Keif thinks it high time to mediate between the vainglorious Frenchman and the incensed Sir John. "You go a little too far," says he. "All English ladies are not like your light-haired marchioness, and there are exquisite connoisseurs in music in London; but I am quite free to confess, the powers of digestion of the public amaze me. John Bull listens to two sympathies by Beethoven, an overture by Weber, two fugues by Bach, ten songs by Mendelssohn, and half a dozen arias and variations at one sitting, and then he goes home and falls asleep in peace. At the theatre, a tragedy by Shakespeare, a three-act melodrama from the French, a ballet, and a broad London farce, do him no harm, so great is the strength of his stomach."

"A capital remark! I am sure we shall understand one another," whispers M. Gueronnay. "The cry here is always for large quantities. The Englishman throws down his sovereign and wants a hundred-weight of music in return. Mon cher Docteur, you should come to Paris. Do not smile, and do not allow our friend here to make you too partial to the English. Sir John is the best fellow in the world, but entre nous, he is very queer. But you, my dear doctor, you have esprit, you are not without a certain talent for observation. Why should you rest in this town? I am sure your eyes will be opened after your first quarter of a year in Paris. Par Dieu, Paris! Does not the whole of the civilised world wear the cast-off clothes of Paris? It is quite ridiculous your shaking your head at our having got rid of our constitution; but in return Europe trembles at our nod, and enfin ça ne durera pas. We may change and change again. Constitutions of original Paris-make we have in plenty. We have had more of them than England, Germany, and Italy—in fact, what is there that Paris has not? Do you want religion? there is Lacordaire and Lamennais; and there is the Univers—religions of all shades. Are you fond of philosophy and religion? Go to Prudhon. To tell you the truth, I myself do not care for philosophy and religion; they are either of them mauvais genre. I am for civilisation and property; and I should not mind seeing M. Prudhon hanged, but that does not prevent me, as a Frenchman, being very fond of him. In one word, the world is but a bad imitation of Paris. In Paris you find heaven and hell, order and liberty, the romance of orgies, and the solitude of the cloister, in the most charming harmony and in the grandest and most elegant form. But above all," said M. Gueronnay, very impressively, "do not believe that you will ever learn to speak the French language unless you go to Paris. Impossible; you will never catch the accent. And England is the worst climate for French pronunciation that can be found. Look at me! I, a Parisian, still feel the pestilential influence of this English jargon, which they are presumptuous enough to call a language, and whenever I go back from London I am ashamed of myself, and dare not speak to the family of my porter."

"Monsieur Enfin," said Sir John, as he accompanied the Doctor to the door, "has been bothering you, but, dear me; what can you expect of a Frenchman? a harmless fellow, but queer, very queer! You might make a good deal of money if you shewed him in Piccadilly. At one time I took some trouble with him, and tried to give him an idea of what England is, but it was of no use. You cannot argue a dog's hind-leg straight. You will never catch me quarrelling with him, that's all."

"It is the story of the pot and the kettle," said Dr. Keif, when he was in the street. "Each one says of the other that he is a queer fellow." Saying which, the Doctor smiles, without the least suspicion that he is quite as queer as the rest.

It is past midnight when the Doctor returns from his nocturnal expedition, the adventures of which shall be duly recorded in another chapter. George opens the door to him. "The family have gone to bed," says he, "but the two gentlemen have not yet adjourned." Indeed their voices are plainly audible in the hall, and Dr. Keif looking up, beholds Sir John and Mons. Enfin on the landing, each holding a flat candle-stick with the candle burnt down to an awful degree of lowness, in his hand. The case is as clear as daylight. False to his principles, Sir John is engaged in a desperate attempt to "reason the dog's hind-leg straight."

Dr. Keif came just in time to enjoy the climax of the controversy.

"Enfin—the less you say about literature the better. What English author ever made a revolution?"

"I assure you, sir, Shakespeare—"

"And I assure you, sir, that, in my opinion, Shakespeare is entirely deficient in power. No power whatever, parole d'honneur! Coarse! Ah yes! he is indeed coarse. But power? Ah, my dear sir, where will you find it?"

"And I tell you, sir, that your grisettes and lorettes and actresses want grace, that's what they do. And why do they want it? To be graceful, a woman should be decent, sir, and respectable, sir; and your grisettes are not a whit better than they ought to be!"

"Good night, gentlemen," whispers Dr. Keif, as he passes them on the landing. "Don't settle the question now; I should like to say a few words about it to-morrow morning."

They stare at him in a bewildered manner, and the very next moment they dispute as fierce as ever.

"Mons. Gueronnay thinks Shakespeare lacks power; and Sir John is disgusted with the French women, because they want grace! Why it's as good as a play!" mutters Dr. Keif as he gains his own room.

CHAP. IX.

The Theatrical Quarters.

THE THEATRES.—THE POOR MAN'S SUNDAY.—GROUPS FOR HOGARTH.—DR. KEIF AND MR. BAXTER AT THE OLYMPIC.—TRAGEDY AND COMEDY IN ENGLAND.—MR. AND MRS. KEELEY.—MR. WIGAN.—MR. KEAN AND THE BRIMLEYS.—METHODISM.—A PENNY THEATRE.—THE PANTOMIMES.—THE BALLET.—THE STAGE IN ENGLAND AND GERMANY.—MATERIALISM.—DRURY-LANE AT 11·45 P.M.—MERRY OLD ENGLAND.—DRURY-LANE AT 1 A.M.

THE space between Oxford-street and the Strand, the chief thoroughfares of Eastern and Western London, is occupied by a quarter of the town which, in many of its parts, we would not recommend for the residence of strangers who desire respect and consideration from their London acquaintances. On the other hand, nothing can be more interesting to a curious traveller than a careful examination of this quarter. We say a careful examination; for the mere walking through it on the occasion of a visit to the theatres is not enough to exhaust this mine of strange and curious sights. Of course, every stranger walks through this quarter, for in it are the most ancient and renowned among the theatres of London, namely, Covent-garden and Drury-lane.

Old and venerable houses are they, with blackened columns and sooty walls, and surrounded with the questionable traffic of an equivocal neighbourhood. A theatre in prudish London has not much good fame to lose; these two have never at any time stood amidst the fragrance of gardens or parks, or the splendours of a court. The flight to the west has not been caused by them. But, strange to say, the modern smaller theatres, too, are to be found in the outskirts of this half-genteel region. The Lyceum, the Strand theatre, and the Adelphi, are in the Strand. Most dingy and dirty-looking are the streets which surround the Olympic. The Princess' theatre, elated with the occasional visits of royalty, has sought an asylum in Oxford-street; and the half-classic Sadler's Wells has gone far out to the north, into staid methodistical, and humble Islington. But Her Majesty's Theatre, the favourite of the greatest in the land, raises its colonnade in the immediate vicinity of Leicester-square, the modern Alsatia of young France! Are we not, in the vicinity of the Haymarket, before and after midnight, exposed to the blandishments of those fair, frail creatures, that have nothing in common with the Muses, Graces, and Fays, but their state of celibacy? In short, is not the Venus vulgaris notorious for its predilection for a half-fashionable neighbourhood! When, therefore, you date your letters from Long-acre, and when, on receiving such a letter, the face of John Thingumbob, Esq., experiences a perceptible elongation, and his manner of speaking to you afterwards suggests to you the idea that he has been iced, then believe, O stranger, that our respectable friend, John Thingumbob, Esq., doubts not the safety of your own virtue, but the stability of your finances.

In Drury-lane itself, the painted cheek is less frequently met with than in the Haymarket; the deadly sins which revel in this classic neighbourhood do not use paint, and scorn to employ the blandishments of seduction. Their names are Poverty, Drink, and Dirt.

In the Strand, just opposite to majestic Somerset-House, and half-hidden by the railings of the church-yard, which encroaches upon the natural dimensions of the street, there is a narrow passage, which turns up into Drury-lane. That lane, though of unequal breadth, is always narrow, and numberless are the blind alleys, courts, and passages on either side. The first and second floors of the high and narrow houses, shelter evidently a class of small tradesmen and mechanics, who in other countries would pass as "respectable," while here they work for the merest necessaries of life, and, like their customers, live from hand to mouth. A few of them are usurers, preying

THE GIN PALACE.

upon poverty, coining gold from its vices and morbid longings. As for the garrets of those houses, we would not for the world answer for the comfort of their inhabitants. All the lower floors are let out as shops, in which are displayed dingy dresses and articles of female ornament, coarse eatables, cheap and nasty literature, shockingly illustrated; thick-soled shoes, old clothes, awful cigars—all at very low prices. But the gin-palaces are the lions of Drury-lane; they stand in conspicuous positions, at the corners and crossings of the various intersecting streets. They may be seen from afar, and are lighthouses which guide the thirsty "sweater" on the road to ruin. For they are resplendent with plate glass and gilt cornices, and a variety of many-coloured inscriptions. One of the windows displays the portrait of the "Norfolk Giant," who acts as barman to this particular house; the walls of another establishment inform you, in green letters, that here they sell "THE ONLY REAL BRANDY IN LONDON," and a set of scarlet letters announces to the world, that in this house they sell "THE FAMOUS CORDIAL MEDICATED GIN, WHICH IS SO STRONGLY RECOMMENDED BY THE FACULTY." Cream Gin, Honey Gin, Sparkling Ale, Genuine Porter, and other words calculated utterly to confound a tee-totaller, are painted up in conspicious characters, even so that they cover the door-posts. It is a remarkable fact, that the houses which are most splendid from without, appear most dismal and comfortless from within. The landlord is locked up behind his "bar," a snug place enough, with painted casks and a fire and an arm-chair; but the guests stand in front of the bar in a narrow dirty place, exposed to the draught of the door, which is continually opening and shutting. Now and then an old barrel, flung in a corner, serves as a seat. But nevertheless the "palace" is always crowded with guests, who, standing, staggering, crouching, or lying down, groaning, and cursing, drink and forget.

On sober working-days, and in tolerable weather, there is nothing to strike the uninitiated in Drury-lane. Many a capital of a small German country is worse paved and lighted. Nor is misery so conspicuous and staring in this quarter as in Spitalfields, St. Giles', Saffron-hill, and other "back-slums" of London. But at certain bestial periods, misery oozes out of all its pores like Mississipi mud. Saturday and Monday nights, and Sunday after Church-time, those are the times in which Drury-lane appears in full characteristic glory. A Sunday-afternoon in Drury-lane is enough to make the cheerfullest splenetic. For to the poor labourer the Lord's day is a day of penance or dissipation. The cotton-frock and fustian-jacket are scared away from the churches and the parks by their respectful awe of rich toilettes and splendid liveries. For the poor man of England is ashamed of his rags; he has no idea of arranging them into a graceful draperie in the manner of the Spanish or Italian Lazarone, who devoutly believes that begging is an honest trade. Even the lowest among the low in England are proud enough to avoid the society of a higher caste, though that superiority consist but in half a degree. They consort with persons of their own stamp, among whom they may walk with their heads erect. Church and park have moreover no charm for the blunted senses of the overworked and under-fed artizan. He is too weak and fatigued to think of an excursion into the country. Steamers, omnibuses, or the rail, are too expensive. His church, his park, his club, his theatre, his place of refuge from the smell of the sewers that infect his dwelling—his sole place of relaxation—is the gin-palace.

To provide against the Sunday, he takes a supply of fire-water on Saturday evening when he has received his week's wages, for with the stroke of twelve the sabbath shuts the door of all public-houses, and on Sunday-morning the beer or brandy paradise must not open before one o'clock in the afternoon, to be closed again from three to five. Hence that unsacred stillness which weighs down upon Drury-lane on Sunday-mornings. The majority of the inhabitants sleep away their intoxication or ennui. Old time-worn maudlinness reigns supreme in the few faces which peer from the half-opened street-doors; maudlinness pervades the half-sleepy groups which surround the public-house at noon to be ready for its opening; chronic maudlinness pervades the atmosphere. And if a stray ray of light break through the clouds, it falls upon the frowsy loungers and the dim window-panes in a strange manner, as though it had no business there.

It is Saturday-night, and the orgies of Drury-lane have commenced. "That's the way thou shouldst look," says Dr. Keif, hurrying forward to the divan in the Strand; "that's the way thou shouldst look, thou Citta Dolente, to awe us with thy charms. Oh for a Dutch painter of the old school to turn this scene into a Höllenbreughel."

A dense fog, with a deep red colouring, from the reflection of numberless gas-jets, and the pavement flooded with mud; a fitful illumination according to the strength of the gas, which flares forth in long jets from the butchers' shops, while the less illumined parts are lost in gloomy twilight. If your nerves are delicate, you had better not pass too close by the gin-shops, for as the door opens—and those doors are always opening—you are overwhelmed with the pestilential fumes of gin. The pavements are crowded. Slatternly servants with baskets hurry to the butchers and grocers, and the haunters of the coffee-houses of Drury-lane elbow their way through the very midst of the population—the sweepings of humanity. A wicked word this, but the only one fit for these forms of woe and livid faces, in which hunger contends with thirst, and vice with disease.

What subjects for Hogarth on the narrow space of a couple of flag-stones! How ravenous the craving which flashes from the eyes of that grey-haired woman, as she drags a slight, yellow-haired girl—perhaps her own child—to the gin-shop! The little girl follows in a dumb wooden way; but her small slight hand is shut with an anxious grasp, as though she feared to lose her weekly earnings—the wages, perhaps, of hard work, or still harder beggary. She stumbles at the threshold, and almost falls over a couple of children that are crouching on the ground, shivering with cold, and waiting for their father within. The father comes, staggering and kicking the air, with manifest danger to his equilibrium, and cursing awfully. The kick was meant for his wife, a thin woman, with hollow yellow cheeks, whose long serpent-like curls are covered with an old silk bonnet, while her stockingless feet are contained in large slippers. She counts five copper pence in her bony hand, looks at her drunken husband, and at the fatal door, and at the costermonger's cart in the middle of the street; and she counts her pence, and recounts them, and cannot come to the end of them, though they are but five. The large oysters in the dirty cart, too, excite her appetite. Which is it to be? the public-house or a lot of oysters? "Penny a lot, oysters!" shouts the man, as he moves his cart forward. A dozen greedy eyes watch his movements.

Similar groups are met with at every step. At the door of almost every gin-shop you see drunken women, many of them with children in their arms; and wherever you go, amidst the confused noise and murmur of many voices, you hear distinctly the most awful oaths. It is not at all necessary to quote those oaths. Let it suffice, that one of them, beginning with a B, startled Dr. Keif's ears a hundred times at least in his walk through Drury-lane.

"Adventure number one!" said Mr. Baxter, to whom our friend communicated the result of his observations.

The fact is, Dr. Keif and Mr. Baxter are seated in the pit of the Olympic Theatre, which is small enough to enable even a short-sighted person to make the public in the boxes and the galleries the subject of a physiognomical study. The "Caucasian population" of Mr. Disraeli's novels may be seen in large numbers enjoying their sabbath. The pit and the upper gallery are filled with sentimental cooks and housemaids, intermixed with a sprinkling of females, to whom we do but justice if we describe them as lorettes in a small way. They enjoy the patronage of a select assembly of beardless shopmen and attorneys' clerks, who treat them to ginger-beer, soda-water, lemonade, and oranges. The curtain has just fallen.

"How do you like it?" asks Mr. Baxter.

"Why I think we have seen enough."

"Wait one moment, I want to look at some one I know. Am I to understand that you didn't like the piece?" said Mr. Baxter.

"On the contrary; I like it very much. There's nothing like a piece of tragical clap-trap in your English theatres."

"Ay!—well!—just so! But then the piece was 'done' from the French."

"The natural source of the modern British drama. But never mind the piece; it's the acting which amuses me. Mrs. Lackaday telling young Ronsay of her boding dream, and Ronsay pitching into her with a declaration of love—you must confess that the scene would have done credit to the most wooden marionettes."

"Yes, indeed! That scene was capital!"

"Was'nt it! The fellow stood there, like a big gun, until his turn came, and then he went off! He turned his eyes upwards, that you might have seen the whites at the distance of a mile; and he sparred with his hands, as if preparing for a set-to with the moon; and all of a sudden he stood stock still again, exactly like a gun, and the audience was fairly enraptured! And did it not strike you, that the two people had the same modulation and declamation, as a married couple of forty years' standing, whose features have acquired the same expression, and whose limbs have fallen into the same mode of movement? At times I am inclined to believe, that the tragic actors, male and female, have been ground their trade to the tune of one and the same patent barrel-organ. Their pathos is set to music. They all delight in the same pause between the article, the adjective, and the substantive; they all make endless stops, and utter the word which follows with a kind of explosion. I presume these poor fellows try to imitate Macready."

"That is to say," remarked Mr. Baxter, "they caricature him."

"But do you know whom Macready caricatures or imitates? I have read a good deal about Garrick, Kemble, and Mrs. Siddons, and I ought to swear by them, as you all do; but still I cannot help suspecting that, even in the golden period of English tragedy, 'all was not gold that glittered.' There is no originality. There is too much respect for antiquated traditions among the craft."

"Certainly there is a good deal of tradition about it. But our actors are not at liberty to depart from those ancient ways; and the slightest deviation would raise a storm against the unfortunate innovator. The taste of the public demands—"

"Indeed! and how does it happen that the period of the Garricks, Kembles, and Siddons did not create and lead you to a better taste? Has England gone back in education and refinement? Why it is just the reverse. The art of tragic acting must formerly have been subject to the same vices as in our days. What you say about the taste of the public is a very lame excuse. I am of opinion that your English public might be trained to a better taste; they are not fond of criticising; their feelings are not used up, and they are eminently grateful. Their taste is unrefined, but they are inclined to respect grace and dignity. Look at Madame Celeste. She carries everything before her by the grace of her untraditional movements."

"But then she is a pretty French woman," said Mr. Baxter, laughing, "and pretty women, you know, will carry every thing before them. But now come before the curtain is up, for Mr. Ronsay will certainly deafen us this time."

"Good evening, Mr. Brimley," whispered Mr. Baxter, as we went out, touching the shoulders of a young man who sat in the darkest corner of the pit with his hat slouched over his face, his great-coat buttoned up to his chin, and a large shawl tied round his neck, as though he were occupying the box-seat of an omnibus instead of a pit-seat in a hot and crowded theatre. The young man jumped up, blushed over and over, seized Mr. Baxter's hands, and talked to him very earnestly, and, as it appeared, imploringly.

"Adventure No. 2," said Mr. Baxter, when the two friends had gained the street. "That tall young fellow with the red whiskers is a Mr. Brimley; he is twenty-five years of age; he manages his father's business in the city; he is likely to have £200,000 or £300,000 of his own, and he trembles like a school-boy lest his papa should hear of his secret escapades."

"What escapades are those? if it is a fair question."

"Perfectly fair. His great crime is, that this evening, for the first time in his life, he has gone to the theatre."

"Impossible!"

"But fact. I know Peter Brimley, Esq., and Mrs. Brimley, and the whole family. A set of more honest, respectable people does not exist between the Thames and the Clyde; but if they were to understand that Mr. Ebenezer Brimley, their son, had crossed the threshold of frivolity, and placed himself on a seat of ungodly vanity, there would be more lamenting and howling among the uncles and aunts of Brimley House than there would be over a bankruptcy of the firm of Brimley and Co. These people are Methodists, and yet Ebenezer the Bold has taken the first step. Since stolen water is more sweet and intoxicating than brandy honestly purchased, I am afraid Ebenezer will drink the poisonous cup to the dregs. Some of these fine days we shall hear of his having gone off with Mrs. Lackaday. Poor fellow! he has not the least idea that she is on the wrong side of forty, and he is evidently much taken with her painted beauties. Never mind, I will be silent as to the past, because I have promised him. He wont sleep this night, I tell you, that little boy of twenty-five, for fear lest some incautious word of mine might betray the secret."

"Then it would appear that M. Enfin is not, after all, so very wrong," said Dr. Keif.

"Nor is he; but your Frenchman cannot see farther than the tip of his nose. The Puritans and low church people form a powerful faction in England; but the round-heads, though great nuisances, are wanted so long as there are cavaliers. And now let us enter this temple of art."

We pass through a low door, and enter a kind of ante-chamber, where we pay a penny each. A buffet with soda-water, lemonade, apples, and cakes, is surrounded by a crowd of thinly-clad factory girls, and a youthful cavalier with a paper cap is shooting at a target with a cross-bow, and after each shot he throws a farthing on the buffet. Passing through the ante-chamber and a narrow corridor, we enter the pit of the penny-theatre, a place capable of holding fifty persons. There are also galleries—a dozen of wooden benches rise in amphitheatrical fashion up to the ceiling; and, strange to say, the gentlemen sit on one side and the ladies on the other. This separation of the sexes is owing to a great refinement of feeling. The gentlemen, chiefly labourers and apprentices, luxuriate during the representation in the aroma of their "pickwicks," a weed of which we can assure the reader that it is not to be found in the Havanna; but they are gallant enough to keep the only window in the house wide open.

Just as we enter we see the director, a small curly-headed man, with a red punch face, ascending the stage by means of a ladder. He makes two low bows, one for the ladies and one for the gentlemen, and delivers himself of a grand oration, to excuse some small deficiences in his institution. At every third word he is interrupted by the cheers and remarks of the audience.

"Ladies and gentlemen," says he. "I am sorry I cannot produce a prima donna to-night. Jenny Lind has sent me a message by my own submarine telegraph, asking for an extension of her leave. You would not surely shorten the honeymoon of the nightingale. Why, to do that would be as bad as cruelty to animals. Madame Sontag tells me, quite in confidence, that she is falling off, and that, although her voice is good enough for Yankee ears, she wants the courage to make her appearance before the refined public of No. 17, Broad-street, London. Mdlle. Wagner was at my service, cheap as any stale mackerel; but could I insult you by producing her? Would not every note have reminded you of the fact, that she values nothing in England but its copper pence. Besides, the terms of friendship which subsist between myself and Mr. Lumley—there are considerations—I hope you'll understand me, ladies and gentlemen!"

"Question! question!"

"Maybe you are astonished that these boards are uncarpeted, and that no painted curtain displays its glories to your eyes!"

A voice from the gallery:—"At your uncle's, eh?"

Another voice:—"Nonsense! His wife has turned the stuff into a petticoat."

"How little you understand me, ladies and gentlemen. In the first place, it is but decent that our stage should lament the death of the Iron Duke"—

Interruption:—"No first place! Don't you try to be funny, old feller!"—Blasphemy—groans.

"Ladies and gentlemen, pray listen to me. Let all be serene between us. I have nothing to conceal. Ladies and gentlemen, the overture is about to commence!"

The speaker vanishes through a trap-door, through which two fellows presently ascend. One is dressed up to represent an Irishman; the other wears the characteristic habiliments of a Scotch Highlander. They play some national airs, and while thus engaged strip themselves of every particle of their outer clothing, and appear as American planters. Some one from below, hands up a couple of straw hats, which they clap on their heads, and the metamorphosis is complete. They then go to the back of the stage and return with an unfortunate "African." The part is acted by no less distinguished a person than the director himself. His face is blackened, he has a woolly wig on his head, and heavy chains on his wrists and ancles; and to prevent all misunderstandings, there is pinned to his waistcoat an enormous placard, with the magic words of "Uncle Tom."

The planters produce meanwhile a couple of stout whips, which instruments of torture they use in a very unceremonious manner, in belabouring the back of the sable protegé of the Duchess of Sutherland and the women of England generally, when all of a sudden, that illustrious negro, exclaiming, "Li-ber-r-r-ty! Liber-r-r-ty!" breaks his fetters, and turning round with great deliberation, descends into the pit. Exeunt the two planters, each with a somerset.

Transformation:—Three forms issue from the back door; a colossal female, with a trident and a diadem of gilt paper, bearing the legend of "Britannia"; after her, a pot-bellied old gentleman, with a red nose and a spoon in his right hand, while his left holds an enormous soup-plate, with a turtle painted on the back of it.

Britannia, heaving a deep sigh, sits down on a stool, adjusts a telescope, which is very long and very dirty, and looks out upon the ocean. The gentleman with the red nose, who, of course, represents the Lord Mayor of the good City of London, kneels down at her feet, and indulges in a fit of very significant howlings and gnashings of teeth. The third person is a sailor-boy complete, with a south-wester, blue jacket, and wide trousers, who dances a hornpipe while Britannia sighs and the Lord Mayor howls.

Now comes the great scene of the evening! Somebody or something, diving up from the very midst of the pit, makes a rush against the stage. It is the Uncle Tom of the last scene; but surely even Her Grace of Sutherland would not know him again. His face is as black and his hair as woolly as ever; but a cocked hat, a pair of red trousers and top boots, and an enormous sword, brings it home even to the dullest understanding, that this is a very dangerous person! Besides, on his back there is a placard, with the inscription: "Solouque—Napoleon—Emperor"!!

The monster bawls out "Invasion!" while, to the great delight of the ladies and gentlemen, he bumps his head several times against the chalky cliffs of Britain, which, on the present emergency, are represented by the wooden planks of the stage. The very sailor-boy, still dancing his hornpipe, shows his contempt for so much ferocity and dulness. He greets the invader with a scornful—"Parli-vow Frenchi?"

At this juncture, the conqueror becomes aware of the presence of the short ladder, and mounts it forthwith. The boy vents his feelings of horror and disgust in an expressive pantomime, the Lord Mayor howls louder than ever, and the gnashing of his teeth is awful to behold; but just as the invader has gained the edge of the stage, he is attacked by the sailor, who, applying his foot to a part of the Frenchman's body which shall be nameless, kicks that warrior back into the pit. The public cheer, Britannia and the Lord Mayor dance a polka, and the sailor sings "God save the Queen!"

"If the French ambassador could but know of this!" said Mr. Baxter, as the two friends were pushing their way out through a crowd of new comers. "That one kick would give rise to half a dozen diplomatic notes. Alas, for the liberties of Old England! Now I am sure the Lord Chamberlain's deputy would never have permitted this scene in a Drury-lane pantomime."

"I'm glad of it," said Dr. Keif, testily, "since it seems to hurt you, who are a moderate Tory. But why did we go away?"

"It was so hot. But what do you say to this sort of thing? Here you have the low and the uneducated in raptures with a histrionic representation. Are you still of opinion, that the people of England are without dramatic affinities and theatrical instincts?"

"I never expressed such an opinion. Just now we were talking of tragic acting; but as for your comic actors, they are exquisite. No one can equal Matthews at the Lyceum or Mrs. Keeley. There you have natural freshness, energy, lightness, and refinement. Our German comic plays and actors are nothing to it. You see I can be impartial, and I will plainly tell you what my impressions are. When I saw 'Romeo and Juliet' at Sadler's-wells, I had to bite my lips to keep myself from laughing. Juliet, instead of proceeding from an Italian nunnery, appeared fresh from a finishing school at Brompton; the orthopedical stays and the back-board were not to be mistaken. And as for Romeo, so great was my confidence in him, that I would, without the least hesitation, have handed an express-train over to his care; he was so cool, sharp, and collected. It was just the same with Mercutio, Tybalt, and Friar Lawrence. Not that they were deficient in mimic and vocal power—no such thing! but because they conducted themselves in a frantic manner, and because they got up and down the scale of human sounds from a whisper to a roar. For the very reason that they did all this, I came to the conclusion that there is no tragic passion in these gentlemen. I saw them afterwards in comedies, and they delighted me. The broader the comedy, the nearer it approaches to the farce, the more natural does the acting appear to me. Dont laugh at me; but I never enjoyed anything so much as I did the last year's Christmas pantomime at Drury-lane. There you have plastic jokes, madness with method, edifying nonsense—a kaleidoscope for aged children."

"How you go on!" said Mr. Baxter. "Don't you know that those pantomimes, for the most part, are nothing but a tissue of stale jokes taken at random from the last volume of Punch?"

"No matter! The jokes, however stale, strike one as new by dint of a clever arrangement and a judicious intermixture of all the follies of the season. It is not an easy matter, let me tell you, to translate a printed witticism into an intelligible and striking tableau. Quick and dreamlike as the scenic changes are, not a single allusion can escape the audience: they are all executed in a lapidary style. Life in London garrets and streets, shops and cellars, shown up in a sort of carnival procession—surely there is a good deal of art in that! Hogarth might have sketched this sort of thing with a drop or so more of gall; but I doubt whether he could have surpassed it in striking truthfulness. Besides I prefer seeing such scenes acted to seeing them engraved. These are the plays to bring out the mechanical excellence of your countrymen. Your young gentleman appears stiff and awkward enough in the drawing-room. But your clown on the stage is the beau ideal of mercurial agility. The fellow has patent steel springs in every one of his joints. Our own misnamed 'English riders' are mere lay-figures if compared to the clowns which overleap one another in your Christmas pantomimes. There is but one dark spot in their representations, namely, the ballet. To see twenty or thirty female Englishmen of full regulation-size dancing a ballet, is an overpowering luxury. To this day I protest that nothing was farther from the thoughts of those worthy virgins than the performance of a dance, but that their elongated legs were so many geometrical instruments moving about with a view to the practical demonstration of the various problems in Euclid. English ladies, as all the world knows, are madly fond of the higher branches of abstract science."

"You are a rabid critic, and a rabid critic you will remain to the end of your days," said Mr. Baxter. "You Germans cannot get on without classifications and generalisations. For instance, you think proper to imagine a profound philosophy in the Christmas pantomimes, which, after all, are acted for the special delight of the infant population. And you dare to doubt the genius of Garrick, Kemble, Kean, and Siddons, merely because you know that a few bad actors are now and then in the habit of murdering Shakespeare. However, it is impossible to exhaust the subject of the difference between English and German taste. Our tragedy is as strongly pronounced as our comedy, and what you blame in the former, you like in the latter. I am free to confess that our actors overdo their parts; but they do not overdo them to such an extent as you fancy, accustomed as you are to the contemplative, monological pathos of the German tragedians. Possibly our heroes would be all the better for a gentler roar, but certainly it cannot be said of them, that their acting is soporific. But let us leave this wordy theme! There is no denying it, that the best days of the stage are over, here and in Germany: with you from the want of substance, air, and elbow-room; with us, from an excess of overwhelming practical activity. Besides there are many other causes which it is impossible to enumerate. There is but one point to which I would call your attention; and I would have you mind it whenever you make comparisons. With us, dramatic art has never been idolised as in Germany; we have never considered it as an institution for national education and an academy of ethics. Within the last few years only this view has been adopted and enforced by some writers. I can understand what your stage has been to you since the days of Lessing, and the losses and wants for which in Germany it was an indemnification. But you began at the wrong end. The drama is the flower of national life; you sought to convert it into its seed and root. On some occasions you have even gone the length of considering it the fruit and the object of national life. You cared more for the ideal reflection than for the real action which was to be reflected. It has often made me smile to hear your æsthetical patriots clamour for a German fleet or a German emperor, for no other reason but because these two 'properties' would do an immense deal of good to the drama; and I have also smiled when listening to their lamentations that Germany can never be great and powerful, since her national stage is sustained by the leavings of the French theatres. Our managers import loads of French farces and vaudevilles, and the papers show them up for it now and then; but no one believes our nationality in danger. As well might we fear the most serious consequences to the power of England, from the importation of French milliners, stays, and Culs de Paris."

Mr. Baxter made a short pause, and, since Dr. Keif would not speak, he continued his oration pro domo.

"Let me tell you, that there are thousands of Englishmen in town and country, who quote Shakespere as they do the Bible, but they know nothing whatever of the stage; and there are patrons of the stage, to whom you may demonstrate the decline of that institution, without eliciting one word of reproval against the Foreign Office. In Germany, the stage is petted and subsidised by a score or so of royal and princely personages. English theatres are speculations, as all other commercial undertakings; they have nothing to rely on but the support of the public. The Queen takes a box at the Princess's, or at Covent Garden; no one will ever expect her to do more for the 'national drama,' or the Italian opera. The very boards which yesterday witnessed the death struggles of Desdemona and the jealousy of the Moor, are this evening given up to Franconi or a band of Indian jugglers. If any one here were to lament this 'desecration of the Temple of the Muses,' he would simply make himself ridiculous. The dog of Aubrey, which excited Göthe's and Schiller's indignation, will be a welcome guest on any London stage, so it pays. But for all that, the public know how to distinguish between poesy and clap-trap. Our actors take their position in society as gentlemen, though they have not, as your actors, the 'position of public functionaries.' Our dramatic authors do not indulge in oracular preface, because they do not think it absolutely necessary that they should be prophets, while they do think it absolutely necessary to be entertaining. A poetical entertainment ennobles; poesy which is not entertaining falls short of its mark, and remains without effect. I am free to confess, that Sheridan and Otway remain unsurpassed in their respective lines. Shelley's Beatrice, though unfit for the stage, has indication of dramatic genius of a high order; but one swallow does not make a summer. Our critics regret this; but they do not lament it as a national misfortune—they do not demonstrate from this fact the spiritual and moral decline of the nation. They are aware that dramatic productiveness is not to be had to order, that guano and artificial tendencies cannot raise a crop; they have been content with the works of Cumberland, Knowles, Bulwer, D. Jerrold, and Tom Taylor, without measuring their productions by the standard of the most renowned precedents, or abusing each individual author because he is not a Shakespeare. And for all that, Old England flourishes in power and glory. But stop, we have lost our way, and got into Seven Dials, which is, after all, but a worse edition of Drury-lane. Let us go back. The 'Witches' Sabbath' must by this time be at its height, and we may as well look at what is going on."

They picked their way through a very narrow and dark lane.

Dr. Keif heaved a deep sigh and said—"I see you have stored up a lecture for my benefit. Your sallies and innuendoes go right against the rotten side of our German hot-house life; but—but surely you must admit, that the stage is an indication of the spirit and taste of society; and certainly you are the last man whom I could have expected to deliver this matter-of-fact sermon, to which I have just had—politeness compels me to call it—the pleasure of listening. My Germanic opposition has driven you into the ranks of the Manchester men. But surely you cannot possibly have the face to tell me, that the one-sided, utilitarian tendencies of England are beautiful."

"Beautiful," replied Mr. Baxter, with a sigh. "Did I call them beautiful? Surely not; but necessity, my dear Doctor, is a mighty goddess. We, too, who are dilettanti, would be better off for ourselves and others, if we had learnt something of agriculture, political economy, or some substantial profession or trade. This remark applies to nations also. What's the use of going in pursuit of 'the Beautiful' and 'the Great,' when you are at a loss how to clothe Beauty and shelter Greatness. Pray be candid for this once. Was it not the case of the German Titans, when a mere chance, an earthquake, flung the keys of the house within their reach? Were they not, most of them, wilful dreamers, dabblers in politics and poetry—men who judged the progress of events after its picturesque or dramatic effect; and who, though brimful with schemes for the improvement of the 'people,' and overflowing with sympathy for the sufferings of the same 'people,' had not the least idea how to set about gaining an army, improving the finances, establishing the good cause on a basis of material interests, saving time, and making the most of the favour of the moment? These matter-of-fact virtues and abilities were everywhere wanting. And now what has been the result for the Beautiful and the Great?"

"But Sir," said Dr. Keif, "I protest your words make me giddy. Are you my old friend Baxter? You speak in the spirit of the Quaker Bright, and Cobden of plausible reputation. Do you really believe that the German revolution made fiasco, because the Germans read Schiller and Göthe; and that England is great and powerful, only because a sense for art and good taste is confined to the favoured few, while the life of your middle classes is spread over the dead level of the flattest materialism imaginable?"

"You are mistaken. One-sidedness is a sad thing under any circumstances; but if the choice be left me, I would prefer British one-sidedness to the German. And as for our materialism, it has been wofully exaggerated on the continent. England has a large family, many mouths to feed, sir, and appearances to be kept up, too, namely, the traditional pomp and splendour of an old aristocracy and of the crown. The nation has doubled its numbers within the last two hundred years, but our island has not increased in size, though certainly a large extent of waste land has been reclaimed. Britannia must rule the waves if she would keep her own. Rob us of our wealth, and we are utterly lost. But no one can rob us of our wealth, because that wealth is founded on what you call our prosaical materialistic character, and what we describe as the indomitable energy and calm deliberation of the people. The Englishman understands the necessity of an untiring, practical industry and devotion to that industry has in him become a second nature. Labour, my dear Sir, civilizes the masses and ennobles the few. Consider your own words, and just think how childish it is to hold forth against the 'flat materialism' of a nation which is in a fair way of fully conquering the elements and withdrawing the veil from the secrets of nature! That at the present day utilitarian tendencies are predominant, even in literature, who can deny? But the brains that labour in the service of 'the useful,' labour also, and knowingly, too, for the benefit of humanity. Our middle classes, though not such great theatrical critics as the Germans, are attracted, and surely they are improved by a great many other sights. Just join the crowd of holyday makers that have come to see the launch of a gigantic steamer in Southampton, Liverpool, Glasgow, or Blackwall, and from a thousand sparkling eyes proud thoughts will flash at you—not mere nabob-thoughts and gold-freight speculations, as you Germans fancy; but anticipations of a better and nobler future, hopes of peaceful intercourse among and the progress of all nations; dreams of civilization in Dahomey and other barbarous countries—in short, thoughts of which no art-philosopher need be ashamed. Go to the Polytechnic———."

The fog has vanished in Drury-lane; for about midnight the London sky is usually clear; the moon looks out from behind the steeple of St. Mary's church in the Strand, and at each street-corner stands a policeman, he being on the look-out. The progress of the two friends is stopped by a dense crowd, surrounding a couple of Irish women, who are settling a little "difficulty" of their own. Ragged little boys stand in dangerous proximity, urging them on, and making very laudable exertions to procure for the street the gratification of a "real fight," for hitherto the two Amazons have used their tongues rather than their fists, and indulged in an interchange of epithets beginning with b and ending with y, and repeated with extreme volubility an incredible number of times.

"You've got no pluck! you daughter of a dog's daughter, that's what you hasn't!" shouts a little imp of a fellow, jumping right between them, and splashing all the bystanders. With bursts of laughter and many curses, the crowd disperses down the street and follows a stretcher, carried by two policemen, who have just issued from a dark gateway. On the stretcher, her head and legs hanging down, is a tall, consumptive-looking girl, with her hair loosened and sweeping down like a black veil.

"They're taking her to the station-house," says a woman with a pipe and a strong Irish accent—"taking her to the station-house, for the blessed dthrop is such a stranger in her throat—poor Poll! believe me, gintlemin, it's only hunger has made her drunk—only hunger!"

Through all the various sounds of yells, groans, and curses, we hear at a distance the unharmonious concert of two barrel-organs, one of which is grinding out a woful caricature of the Marseillaise, while the other, addressing itself to the human family generally, informs them, with an awful screech, that "There's a good time coming, boys," which cheering intelligence is, in the end, qualified by the growl of "Wait a little longer." A few yards on, a beggar-boy with naked feet, and with an almost naked back, has taken up his post where the mud is deepest in the road, and sings, with a thin, small voice, "Ye banks and braes of bonnie Doon." Nobody cares for him, for the public are attracted by two artists who are performing in the next street. They are brothers, by their looks, and work together. The younger, a tiny boy with an aged face, taxes the ingenuity of the public by conundrums, whose chief characteristic is, that they are almost always political and smutty. "Why is her most gracious Majesty like a notorious pick-pocket?" shouts he, in a tone which would do honour to a trained school-master. While the public are trying to find the answer, the elder brother imitates the songs of birds and the voices of beasts. They all give it up. "Because she is often confined," says the little boy, with a most indecent wink at some females. And the songs of birds and voices of beasts are again imitated, and conundrums of a still grosser description propounded and explained; and the hat goes round and comes back with a few pence and half-pence in it.

"And this is classic soil," said Mr. Baxter. "The whole of this ought to be sacred to the antiquarian, to the adorer of the so-called merry old England. When I shut my eyes—and mind, if I can manage to shut my ears and nose too—I see Nell Gwynn, the merry friend of Charles II., with very thin dress, and not much of it, and with her pet lamb under her arm, walking out of the great portal; she vanishes through the green gate in Lord Craven's garden. The rays of the setting sun gild the curiously-carved gables of the villas in the Strand, but the cavaliers are already on their way back from the play; and Kynaston, dressed in the costume which he wore on the stage for the part of Juliet, takes a drive with some discreet ladies of fashion, rank, and pleasure."

"A merry life, indeed!" said Dr. Keif. "Keep your eyes, ears, and nose shut, and go on."

"Not now, dear Doctor. If you are curious on the subject, I will send you some of the old books and chronicles of the time. You will find that theatrical doings in those days, however interesting, are rather instructive than taking. I dare say, you fancy the age was without prudery, and there you are right; but the natural healthy cheerfulness which we find in Shakspeare had long since evaporated. The period of the restoration was insolent but not merry. That the cavaliers were rude and brutal means nothing; the upper classes generally were rude and brutal in all countries at that time; but ours added to a barbarous brutality, a more than French dissoluteness of morals. Strange enough were the doings of the last Stuarts. Fancy yourself in Great Russell Street, following the troops of cavaliers and ladies, with long curly locks à la Vallière, on their road to the theatre. As they leave their chairs or carriages, or dismount from their horses, they draw their masks over faces heated and bloated with drink. Almost everybody is masked. The custom comes from the times of the Puritans, when people went secretly to the theatre. The dissolute second Charles, with his gloomy gypsy face, comes just in time to stop a brawl between the Duke of Buckingham and Killigrew the actor. Killigrew has disarmed the duke, and laid his scabbard about his grace's ears. Buckingham will send a couple of bravos by and bye, and half kill the actor—a fate which even poor Dryden could not escape. The play begins amidst the interruptions and howling of drunken noblemen who occupy the foreground of the stage, trip up the heroine, and kick the hero into the orchestra. His Majesty, meanwhile, in the presence of his lieges, ogles one of his numerous mistresses, or makes smutty speeches to an orange-girl, with a voice so loud that it is plainly heard on the stage. That is a scene from merry Old England!"

All of a sudden the lights are put out in the gin-palaces, the barrel-organs are silent, the howling and cursing shrinks into a hoarse murmur; and the multitude disperse gradually, like muddy water which runs through the gutters and is lost under ground. The street is all silent and lonely; only one tall figure comes with rapid and noiseless steps out of one of the alleys. It looks round in every direction; but there is no policeman in sight. It steps up to our two friends, and looks at them in silence with staring glassy eyes. It is not the spirit of midnight, nor is it a ghost; but neither is it a form of flesh and blood, for it is all skin and bones. And the clear light of the harvest-moon displays a half-starved woman with an infant on her arm, to whom her bony hand is a hard death-bed. For some minutes she stares at the strangers. They put some silver into her hand, and she, without any remark or thanks, turns round and walks slowly away.

"The holy sabbath has commenced," said Dr. Keif, "the puritanical sabbath, on which misery feels three times more miserable."

"My dear friend," said Mr. Baxter, "twenty-five years ago you might have found the whole of Oxford Street crowded with figures similar to the one which has just left us. If you would see them in our days, you must seek for them in some dark corner of Drury Lane. And Puritanism in 1853 is mild and gentle compared to the Puritanism of the Round-heads; it is nothing but a natural reaction against the dissolute Cavalier spirit which has come down even to the commencement of this century. In the English character one extreme must be balanced by the other. Either merry and mad, or sober and prude; we are either drunkards or teetotallers, brawlers or peace-twaddlers. Of course, if harmonic and measured dignity, if the instinct for beauty of form, were innate in us, then, indeed, this nation would not be the persevering, hard-working, powerful John Bull which it is; or if it were, we should shame your German proverb, that the trees nowhere grow into the heavens. Good night, Doctor; and 'au revoir.'"

APPENDIX.

CORRESPONDENCE.

Letter I.

Sir John to Dr. Keif.
Hyde Cottage, November 15.
My dear Doctor,

Herewith I return the proof-sheets of Part II. of the "Saunterings in and about London;" and I beg to thank you for them; although I know you sent them less for my amusement than because you wished to procure for me a sort of private view of myself and my prejudices as you call them. Never mind! an English gentleman can afford to hear the truth spoken anywhere and anyhow; and, if you promise to resign some of your Teutonic crotchets, I gladly pledge my word in return, that I will never again try to reason a Frenchman's hind-leg straight; for, after all, that unfortunate dispute was the worst our friend could lay to my charge.

Now, as for our friend's book, which you tell me is to be published at Berlin—the most intelligent and erudite of all the German capitals—really, Doctor, I do not half like the idea! How are these two little volumes ever to give the Germans a proper idea of what London really is? A good many capital descriptions there are—but, dear me! how much there is that is wanting. I tell you the very things are wanting which would most improve the German mind, if your friend had but condescended to notice them. Not a word does he say of our picture galleries, incomparable though they undoubtedly are. The Bridgewater, Vernon, and Hampton Court collections are not mentioned; nor is the British Museum—nor St. Paul's—nor the Colosseum—nor Madame Tussaud's—nor are Barclay and Perkins! He does not even mention our most magnificent streets and quarters. Regent-street, Bond-street, Belgravia, and Westbourne-terrace are most wickedly neglected by our flighty friend. He has not a word for the monster concerts of Exeter-hall, and he absolutely forgets that there are such places as Covent-garden, Billingsgate, and Hungerford markets. The Zoological-gardens, the Botanical-gardens, Kew, Richmond, Windsor, arts, literature, charities—all are passed over in contemptuous silence.

My dear Doctor, I put it to you; if those places and matters are not mentioned at all, how are the foreigners ever to understand what London is? The people of Berlin are actually led to believe that we have no picture-galleries and hospitals! Your friend might write ten volumes without exhausting the subject. Don't you agree with me? We must have a word or two on the subject when you come to see us.

The country is charming just now. Where, out of England, can you find such beautiful green meadows, and so mild an air, in November? I walk about without a great coat, thinking of the mountains of snow in Germany, and of the wolves that make their way over the mountains and into the very sanctuary of the Cologne Cathedral. It's a little damp now and then—especially after sunset—but it doesn't matter; for in the evening I have my fire and my newspaper. The fact is, there's no comfort except in England, and in the country! Come and look at our cottage. The children expect you; so do I.

Yours, etc.

P.S.—At this season of the year you had better take a glass of Cognac in the morning. You'll find some bottles in the cellar. Before going to bed take one of my pills. You'll find a box on my table. Don't be obstinate. You can have no idea of the dangers of an English November.

Letter II.

Dr. Keif to Sir John.
Guildford Street, November 16.
My dear Sir,

I think of coming on Sunday. In the meanwhile I must give you some sort of explanation respecting the incompleteness of our friend's "Saunterings."

He might indeed, in his book, have mentioned all the remarkable places and sights of your metropolis; but he could only have mentioned them. He preferred taking up a few strong features and phases, and expatiating on them. Of course a great deal was passed over in silence; you, as an Englishman, have the greatest right to complain of such neglect. But, most respectable Sir John, pray do not forget that in this manner mention has not been made of many things which are by no means agreeable to British ears when commented upon by foreigners. A good many capital descriptions there are; but, dear me, how much is wanting! I tell you the very things are wanting which we Germans, I trust, shall never think of imitating.

Not a word of your dog and rat fights. Not a word of the manifest incompetency of the majority of your sculptors and painters. Not a syllable of your unequalled musical barbarism. Not a word of the stupendous prostitution—of the dirt—the dissoluteness—the bestiality—in the lower Thames quarters and the Borough. No detailed descriptions of your gin palaces and sailors' saloons—your learned professions—the intricacies of the law—medicine swamped in charlatanism—your High Church—your Low Church, and sectarian fanaticism—your bigotted Universities, Oxford and Cambridge—the narrow-mindedness of your aristocracy, and the snobbism of your middle classes: all these matters are altogether left out.

My dear Sir John, you are quite right. It would take ten volumes to exhaust the subject. Between ourselves, perhaps you would not half like it if our friend were to continue his "Saunterings."

London is awful just now. Where in all the world can such fogs and such a pestilential atmosphere be found, except in London? The wolves in the Cologne Cathedral are mere creations of your free-born British fancy; and, as for the present absence of your great coat—do I not know that Englishmen brave even the rigours of a German winter in check trousers and dress coats? But they are cunning enough to don those respectable habiliments over sundry layers of flannel. Have you left off your vests, etc.? Of course you are comfortable in your country cottage, and I shall come to admire you in all your glory.

Yours, etc.

P.S.—Your medical advice is valuable; I mean, in part, to conform to it. I found the Cognac, and shall take it as directed. But your pills I shall not take. I'm reading the French papers, and they do quite as well.

THE END.

Printed in Great Britain
by Amazon